LORD WRATH

Beastly Lords Book Six

SYDNEY JANE BAILY

cat whisker press
Massachusetts

Copyright © 2020 Sydney Jane Baily

ISBN: 978-1-938732-40-9
Published by cat whisker press
Imprint of JAMES-YORK PRESS

Cover: cat whisker studio
In conjunction with Philip Ré
Book Design: cat whisker studio

DEDICATION

To the readers who've persisted and read their way
through this entire series of fallible, lovable men
and the smart, passionate women
who fell head-over-heels for them

I thank you with all my heart!

OTHER WORKS
by
SYDNEY JANE BAILY

THE RARE CONFECTIONERY
Series

The Duchess of Chocolate
The Toffee Heiress
My Lady Marzipan

THE DEFIANT HEARTS
Series

An Improper Situation
An Irresistible Temptation
An Inescapable Attraction
An Inconceivable Deception
An Intriguing Proposition
An Impassioned Redemption

THE BEASTLY LORDS
Series

Lord Despair
Lord Anguish
Lord Vile
Lord Darkness
Lord Misery
Lord Wrath
Eleanor

PRESENTING LADY GUS

A Georgian-Era Novella

ACKNOWLEDGMENTS

As always, thanks to my mom, Beryl Jean Baily.

PROLOGUE

1852, Whitechapel Road
East End of London

"You came," said her tormenter, his tone laced with delight.

As if she'd had a choice! He'd become more insistent and threatening over the past two weeks.

"What do you want from me?" Sophia demanded, wishing she hadn't acted so impetuously this time. She hadn't hesitated to leave her driver outside the Burlington Arcade and hail a hackney so no one would know of her destination.

The address she hadn't recognized turned out to be a frighteningly squalid place. A crooked sign proclaimed it The Pig and Whistle. As the cabbie sped away, leaving her there, she had no choice but to go inside.

The interior was worse than the exterior, if possible. The room with a bar along its left-hand length and a handful of sticky tables made up the paltry tavern. The few patrons were dressed in rags, and every one of them glanced at her when she let in the light from the street, then continued to stare slack-jawed at the fine young lady in their midst.

As she turned to flee, *he* had stepped out of the shadows and beckoned her to follow him upstairs. When she hesitated, he promised a hackney would take her swiftly home after they'd spoken. If he hadn't caught her in a compromising situation in France, she would not have spared him an instant of her time.

How could she have been so careless?

While living with friends of her mother, she'd stayed in their luxurious, albeit small, townhouse in Paris, which afforded none of them much privacy. Foolishly, she'd been caught *in flagrante delicto*.

After returning from her year abroad, a little wiser and more cynical, with polish and a superb accent, she'd hoped to leave certain indiscretions behind.

Back in London, however, the tyrant had approached her, claiming to want merely her silence regarding his own private matters. To her, these amounted to nothing more than boastful words to his French cousin, which she'd overhead while not understanding their meaning. She knew only how the men had laughed and toasted to an impending *coup* with fine Bordeaux. It all seemed a lifetime ago.

Along with her own reckless imprudence in Paris.

Recently, off-hand remarks her persecutor made had needled her with fear. He vowed to ruthlessly disclose her wild behavior to her parents—unless she did him a favor. She could not imagine what she could do for him, but apparently, the time had come to find out.

Preceding her blackmailer into the seedy upstairs room, Sophia turned to face him and gasped.

CHAPTER ONE

1852, Mayfair, London

Lord Owen Burnley paced the floor of his study. When he reached his desk for the third time, he sent every item from the surface crashing to the floor with a sweep of his arm. It had been one day since they'd found his sister's lifeless body, he and his friend Whitely, after a frantic search. Only twenty-four hours since she had been strangled.

He stood and stared at nothing.

Two days earlier, he could still have spoken to Sophia, asked her a question, touched her pretty hair, and smiled at her. Never again. Someone had choked the life out of his sister and even left the rope around her pale neck. Her eyes had remained open, too.

"*Aahh,*" Owen howled. His gut twisted with imagining her fear and pain in those final moments, until he, too, could barely breathe. And his parents! *Dear God, his devastated parents!*

His mother had fainted at the news and taken to her bed, her physician dosing her with laudanum every time she nearly came to the full awareness of her only daughter's death. And their father had looked . . . broken. The earl aged a decade in the span of minutes. He'd doted on his little girl, sent her to France when she'd asked to spend a year there, and, when she'd returned to London, he'd set her up for her first Season with new gowns and the greatest of expectations.

All dashed. Snuffed out with Sophia's last breath.

Squeezing his hands into fists, Owen closed his eyes, summoning her pretty face before him.

"I vow to get you justice."

He would bring his sister's murderer to light.

And then kill him with his own bare hands.

LADY ADELIA SMYTHE ENTERED her family's townhouse on Hyde Park Street, shut the door softly, and leaned against it. Closing her eyes with relief at being once more in her own home, she stood there for a few seconds and breathed in the familiar scent of lemon furniture oil. Some things never changed. And she liked that. Too many things did change, quickly and not for the better. Her brother was the primary constant in her world. And the lemon polish.

Footsteps heralded another constant. She felt the floor shake and heard the staccato steps, opening her eyes to the butler's hasty appearance. She knew Mr. Lockley wished he'd been there to open the door for her, but, alas, she thwarted him regularly. When she did go out, which was as infrequently as possible, she returned when least expected—usually before a social event was even halfway over.

If she was lucky.

Today, it had been a croquet match at Lady Turbity's estate a mile outside Town. The older lady continued to invite Adelia in kind memory of her mother, who had been friends with Lady Turbity when they were young. The countess also hoped to do a little matchmaking by putting Adelia in a group with two bachelors, Lords Roleston and Whitely.

The fourth member, Miss Darrow, was a few years younger than Adelia, infinitely more social, and she entirely mesmerized Lord Roleston. Lord Whitely, like Adelia, was only there as a kindness to the hostess, filling in for his good friend Lord Burnley, whom they all knew had recently suffered a death in his family. And Adelia had made it an even number.

Because of his friend's bereavement, Lord Whitely was distracted and quiet, thankfully not interested in flirting. All Adelia had to do was keep her head down and hope no one spoke to her. As it turned out, she played a very good game of croquet. *After all, shouldn't that be the point?*

When it was over and the others all headed indoors to eat, drink, and do more of the dreaded socializing, Adelia had made her escape. She'd done her part by making sure no one went without a partner, and she could force herself to do no more.

"Tea, Mr. Lockley, would be most appreciated in the drawing room," she told her butler. "Is my brother at home?"

"No, miss. Not expected until dinner."

Unlike herself, if Thomas wasn't expected, he would rarely return early and throw the household into disarray. *Poor Mr. Lockley!* He'd probably had his feet propped up in his private basement sitting room whilst enjoying his own cup of tea.

"If you send in Meg with the tray, I won't need anything further from you until dinner," she assured the butler, who nodded, took her gloves, bonnet, and mantle, which she held out to him, and then disappeared.

The event was over! Adelia wanted to whistle a happy tune, except she couldn't whistle to save her life. Still, she had a skip in her step as she crossed the tiled foyer and entered the drawing room in its calm green and cream colors. In a few minutes, Betsy brought in tea, but she also had mail on the tray. And it looked like . . . invitations! *Drats!*

A shiver of dread ran down Adelia's spine, and she ignored the thick envelopes, some lightly tinted, some scented, all with their wax circles stamped by an aristocrat's imposing seal.

As soon as Thomas returned, they must have a chat about how she could start to graciously decline these.

Yes, she was an earl's daughter. Yes, she had social responsibilities.

Nevertheless, it seemed to Adelia, since both her parents were now deceased, she ought to be given leave to beg off pointless evenings after enduring four years of them. She would ask her brother to let her retire and become his permanent lodger. If she were capable, she would offer herself as his hostess until such time as he married. As the most awkward, inept female to ever grace London's *ton,* however, that position was anathema to her. Thus, while Thomas had continued to urge her to make a marriage arrangement, as her father had done before dying a year and a half prior, her brother had never forced her to host an event at their home. He was too kind for that.

Two years younger than she, Thomas had taken up the Smythe earldom and, as he'd been trained to the position, was more than adequately managing the family business from what she could tell. They had a shipping manager who guaranteed coal reached the storage facilities at the great docks for steamships and at the train stations for the steam locomotives. Additionally, they employed a labor overseer who kept the miners happy, and their father's accountant, Mr. Arnold, managed the ledgers as he always had.

Thomas also had good friends in their mining company, chief among them Victor Beaumont. The man had been particularly useful when the son took over from the father, as Mr. Beaumont was also their company's chief engineer.

All Thomas had to do was keep his sweet nature intact and, eventually, find a wife.

Adelia wanted her brother to be happy. Nonetheless, she hoped he would wait until his early thirties before marrying the woman who would be the new Countess of Dunford, mistress of their townhouse and country estate.

The very notion sent Adelia into a tailspin of doubt and anxiety. *Would a new wife want an old sister hanging about? Unlikely.*

She withdrew a leather folder from a drawer in the sideboard as well as a nearly empty tablet of paper. From under the sofa, she slid out her rosewood, portable writing desk. Sitting on a winged chair, she set the desk upon her lap and lifted open its cover to create a tidy, compact workspace—the tool for creating her only hope for a future, her writing.

She had two novels already completed, and the current story about the villagers from their country estate in High Wycombe was three-quarters finished. As a youngster, after closeting herself in her room, away from the loud shouting of her father, Adelia had read voraciously whatever books she could gain access to. She still did, although with much more freedom as to what she could consume. When she found she had a knack for storytelling, she began to spend her allowance on books, tablets of paper, and the best Perry & Co. steel pens.

Keeping her own counsel, she'd shared her scribblings with no one, not even Thomas. And whenever she could escape from a ballroom or a dinner party, or a croquet tournament as she had today, she immediately returned to it. Only her personal maid, Penny, knew about her mistress's secret passion and kindly gathered the pages together in a tidy bundle if Adelia ever fell asleep writing.

Thus, while she waited for Thomas, she wrote. It came easily. She had many stories, mostly of human drama, gleaned from her years as the perfectly invisible wallflower. People stood close by and told the most appallingly personal tales of romance and deception. As long as Adelia remained quiet, her head inclined so her good ear was positioned outward, she could catch almost all of what was said.

And while only she had read her stories, she hoped they were suitably entertaining, in the rustic vein of George Sand, who was widely known to be the French woman, Dudevant. Adelia had read every one of her novels from the past twenty years and hoped she was honoring the genre with her own attempts.

Tapping her page with her pen, she reread the last few paragraphs and began to write.

Hours later, her forgotten tea long since grown cold, she heard Thomas return. Adelia's stomach grumbled as she shuffled her pages into order and slid them between their leather cover.

She would need another tablet soon, she thought, tucking everything away slowly and casually under the chair while her brother strode into the drawing room. Strange how he never asked what she was working on, probably assuming she was writing vapid letters to flighty female friends she didn't actually have.

He crossed the room as she stood, and they embraced. She could smell a little brandy on his breath. She sighed.

"Why the sigh, Dilly-girl?"

"You were out drinking," she said, yet relieved it wasn't whiskey or gin.

He smiled and shook his head. "I was at White's talking business with Victor. Naturally, we had brandy."

"I hope it was a good meeting," she said, but before he could answer, she added, "I am famished. Are you ready to dine?"

Glancing at the invitations, Adelia scooped them up and preceded Thomas into the dining room with its pretty blue-and-silver striped wallpaper. It still seemed odd sometimes that it was only the two of them. In earliest childhood, there'd been a third Smythe sibling, Frances, who'd passed from a wasting illness. It had begun as a small cough that ultimately took the life of the skeletal three-year-old. Not long after, the next birth had resulted in the death of both Adelia's mother and the baby.

Her father had changed for the worse. Lord Richard Smythe had always been loud, brusque, and often heavy-handed when he wasn't obeyed quickly. Without her mother's tempering nature to soothe him, he had grown increasingly violent. Regrettably, Adelia's shy nature and her childhood stuttering greatly annoyed him. If not for Thomas's increased height and size, not to mention his devoted protection, she was positive she would have suffered far worse injuries than she'd sustained.

Eventually, she had overcome the stuttering at her father's command, and it had taken only a few painful beatings for her to realize if she spoke slowly and softly, she could control the affliction. Thus, by the time she came out into society, she no longer had the speech impediment—except, to her shame, when extremely nervous or too tired to think clearly. If possible, she barely spoke at all, at least not to those outside of her very narrow acquaintance.

Unfortunately, she had never been able to alter her inconvenient shyness and dreaded most every outing. The only good part about a bruised cheek or a sore arm was being excused from social gatherings until she healed.

And then, nearly two years earlier, the earl fell ill from what seemed to be pyrosis followed by an attack of the purples. After a long, lingering decline of six months, he grabbed his chest one day and died.

The physician said he had inflammation of the heart, but she and Thomas could see the more worked up their father became, the more significant his symptoms.

"I vow the world annoyed our father to death," Thomas said after the funeral.

Thus, when her brother began spending time at Teavey's West End pugilist's club, she worried her brother might suffer similar health issues from an overabundance of bile and aggression.

"Just the opposite," he told her. "When I punch a man and he socks me back, we sweat like the devil and our muscles ache, and then we're done. We shake hands before and after, and when I leave Teavey's, I feel worry-free."

Adelia placed the invitations on the edge of her side of the table, on the intricate lace cloth.

"Business is going well?" she asked.

"It seems to be. Victor said he has a way to improve productivity. Upon speaking with Mr. Arnold, however, he informed me profits are up this quarter. Therefore, I told Victor to stay the course at present." He paused and cocked his head. "He asked after you today."

Her stomach tightened, and she stared down at her soup. "Did he?"

There was nothing wrong with their engineer except he was a man and a stranger. She didn't want her brother to think anything would come of trying to get her together with Victor Beaumont.

"He did. He wondered if you had formed any attachments this Season," Thomas added.

She pursed her lips. After a moment, she replied, "That seems rather personal, perhaps inappropriate."

"Not at all. He cares about this family. He might come to care for *you* in a particular way."

She'd been right. Thomas would be pleased if she showed some inkling toward the man who was so important to their company.

Her father, on the other hand, never would have entertained the notion since Mr. Beaumont was decidedly middle-class. But her brother adhered to newer ideas of barriers being broken down and of classes mingling.

Adelia thought it was a good thing when she considered it at all, but she didn't want her brother's radical ideas to involve her. It was bad enough she had to deter any interested noblemen, either with her fake braying laughter or by ignoring them completely by studying the wallpaper. Both tactics worked well, particularly the noisy laughter.

However, if she now had to also worry about dissuading all the other men of London, the bankers and engineers, the lawyers and stockbrokers, then she would have to stay indoors forever. The notion was entirely too taxing.

Men were loud, frightening creatures, apt to strike out in an instant. Her brother was an exception, and even he could be loud sometimes.

"I do not wish him to care for me in any way at all," she said as reasonably as she could.

"Dilly," he began, "I know you are a timid mouse, but you were meant to marry and have children. Don't you think it's against God and nature for you to do neither?"

She sighed. "I would prefer to remain living here with you. And I would appreciate your permission not to carry on with any more social events this Season. That is, unless I wish to attend."

Thomas frowned.

She didn't find it at all galling to ask his permission, despite him being younger. He had always taken care of her, and he was now the head of the family. What he said would be the law. Thus, she held her breath.

"For your own good, I cannot agree to that. Not yet. What if you stay home and miss the man who was meant to be your husband?"

Adelia dropped her hands into her lap and clenched her napkin.

"I don't want a husband," she insisted.

"You don't know what you're saying. What about love and babies?"

"Love?" she exclaimed, staring at her brother, wondering how he could be so idealistic. "Do you truly believe I shall find my heart's desire in a ballroom, dancing with a man who haphazardly scrawled his name upon my card? The chances are as slim as my happening upon a gold sovereign in the street." She shook her head. "How has it worked for you?"

To her surprise, his cheeks reddened slightly.

Oh! "Have you found someone, Thomas?"

After a hesitation, he said, "No. In truth, there was a lady in whom I might have been interested." He shrugged. "But before I could have a first dance with her, it became impossible."

"I don't understand. Why impossible? Did she become engaged to another?"

He shook his head, his brown hair lifting and falling as he did. "She died."

Adelia gasped. Very few deaths had occurred amongst the *ton* this year. Lady Sarah Cantor had been struck by a carriage in the darkness after a ball the month prior, but she had already been engaged. And, luckily, there had been no severe outbreaks of cholera or influenza. That left only . . .

"Lady Sophia Burnley?"

Thomas nodded, making an expression of regret. "I barely had a chance to speak to her, and thought, next time, I would engage her in a longer discussion. But there shall be no next time. Terrible shame!" He shrugged. "At any rate, while I cannot be certain, dear sister, either one of us may find our heart engaged and at any time, too. It could happen for you at a ball. However, it unquestionably will not happen if you stay inside this house."

He gestured at the pile on the table. "Let's see what invitations and new opportunities have arrived for the lovely and charming Lady Adelia Smythe, shall we?"

CHAPTER TWO

O wen slammed his hand down upon the detective's desk, making everything on it rattle. "Not good enough!"

The policeman rose from his chair. Detective Sergeant William Garrard looked as if he was ready to throw the viscount out of his office, no matter the consequences.

"I will thank you to calm yourself, Lord Burnley, and to take a seat. Questioning people in the area of your sister's death—"

"Her murder!"

The man stared a moment. "Questioning people to determine if anyone saw anything is the best way to go about this."

"It does not seem to be efficient or particularly expeditious. I think your bobbies are stumbling around in the dark, hoping naively for someone to hand the answer to them on a silver platter. And the more days that pass since the crime, the less likely the murderer remains in the area or that anyone will recall anything useful."

The detective paused. "Sadly, my lord, we do have a number of murders to deal with besides your sister's.

Stabbings and poisonings and other nefarious dealings happen almost daily."

Owen felt the blood drain from his face. "Are you saying my sister is merely one of many victims to whom you are too incompetent to provide justice?"

"I am saying we are working on it, my lord. And, I assure you there is no more carefully selected and trained, well-conducted and efficient body of men than the Metropolitan and City of London Police forces."

Owen could have put his fist through the wall so great was his frustration, but he restrained himself.

"My sister was not one of the East End whores, whom I assume are the usual victims of such sickening violence. She is . . . *was* a lady. An earl's daughter. Doesn't that warrant some special treatment?"

"All victims were special to someone," Garrard said. "Or nearly all, anyway. Be that as it may, in answer to your question, my lord, yes, the murder of Lady Sophia does, in fact, warrant special attention. For one, it has been kept from the newspapers. Secondly, I have two uniformed constables on the case. But there is no evidence left by the killer except for the rope, and it's a rather ordinary one, to be sure. It was used, perhaps, so the murderer didn't have to touch your sister. She probably couldn't get close enough to scratch him even if she had taken off her gloves."

"Which she had not!" Owen asserted, feeling as if, even after her death, he must defend her reputation.

He could not understand why Sophia had been in such a low and mean place to begin with and dressed in a regular day gown for visiting with friends or shopping. Indeed, that was how her day had started. But it was late when they found her, already dark, with a nasty damp in the air for which her lightweight mantle was insufficient if she'd intended to be out at night. Obviously, she hadn't.

His friend, George Whitely, on his way to the Carlton Club, happened to stop by Burnley's parents' house on Berkeley Square. Owen's habit of taking his Friday midday meal with his mother, father, and sister was well-known to his friends. Thus, George had hoped, if Owen had finished dining, they could go together to the club on Pall Mall.

In the street, however, Whitely had encountered the Burnley driver in a distraught state. The man had dropped Lady Sophia off at the Burlington Arcade in Piccadilly, watching her enter prior to driving away. She'd instructed him to meet her there in two hours.

"I went back and waited another hour more, my lord," the driver had explained once he'd been brought inside. "Then I began to walk through the building, looking in the shops for Lady Sophia. It's a very long arcade, as you know."

Before Owen and Whitely could head out to search for her, the maid who'd accompanied her returned home. Bewildered by her young mistress having dashed out of a shop, disappearing so quickly she couldn't catch up, Abigail had searched each shop on the main floor and knocked on some of the doors on the second, although they weren't all open to the public. As time passed, she'd become terrified she would be blamed for losing her mistress. Finally, the girl had made her way home on foot.

Owen's father, the Earl of Bromshire, had headed straight to the police station to declare his daughter missing so the detectives could lend a hand in searching for her. Meanwhile, Owen and Whitely took the maid with them so she could show them precisely where Sophia had vanished—right outside a small shop selling perfumes from abroad along with cheaper toilet water and lavender oil made in England.

Recalling a conversation with his sister about her specific perfume just days earlier, Owen pushed the door open and went inside.

He'd caught her holding a bottle up to the light.
"I'm nearly out of it, brother dear," Sophia had said.

"*Shall I pick you up a replacement when I'm out? If you write the name down, I shall do so.*"

But she had shaken her head. "I wandered into M. Lubin's perfume house when I was living in Paris. And my favorite scent, La Rose d'Amour, is only available in one shop in London that I've found so far. While everyone else is going to Floris in Jermyn Street, buying the same spicy musk, I go to Piccadilly. And I will go, myself. It's fun to sniff the other fragrances."

"*Even if you end up buying the same one,*" *he had teased her.*

"*Even so,*" *she'd agreed.*

With the shopgirl's help, Owen had recalled the correct name of the French perfume, and he and Whitely were taken to the appropriate counter. Very quickly, the assistant recalled the young, fair-haired lady who wanted that particular perfume a few hours earlier. Owen sniffed it to make certain it smelled like Sophia.

"She bought it, my lords," the shopgirl said, smoothing her apron, "and was about to leave the counter when a boy approached her. Scruffy young'un. He handed her a note."

"Did she appear to know the lad?" Owen had asked, and that was when he'd felt the first prickle of foreboding.

"No, my lord. I don't believe so. She read the note and frowned," the girl recalled. "Then she set it down in order to put the perfume bottle in her reticule. While she was doing so, the boy ran off, and your Lady Sophia hurried after him."

"This tells us nothing," George had muttered.

"You said she put the note down. I don't suppose she left it?" At the time, Owen remembered being convinced the answer would be a resounding no.

He had been wrong. The shopgirl said his sister had, in fact, left it. To his utter amazement, she bent down and retrieved it from the rubbish bin behind the counter.

He'd snatched the small scrap from her outstretched hand. An address and the command to "Come!" were written in a tidy scrawl.

He and Whitely had gone to the unsavory pub on Whitechapel Road immediately. They had been too late.

Now, Owen withdrew the note from his pocket. "I don't believe I ever showed this to you, detective." And he handed the piece of paper to the man, yet still somewhat loath to release it, knowing Sophia had touched it last and that her eyes had gazed upon it.

But it had led to her murder.

"You may keep it," Owen told him. He had studied the writing until he could reproduce it himself if necessary, for all the good it would do.

Detective Sergeant Garrard nodded.

Owen paced again. "In any case, it tells us nothing. We already knew where she was murdered."

"Actually, my lord, it tells us a lot." The detective continued staring at the note. "It tells us she wasn't killed randomly. It was premeditated murder in an arranged location. It also means I don't need to focus on the riffraff of Stepping and Aldgate and Wapping any longer. I can rule out the cut-purses and common thieves, the low-life scoundrels who prey on the weak in the poorest streets leading off of Whitechapel Road."

Owen stilled and looked at him. "I don't understand."

"The paper is thick and perfectly uniform, my lord. Better than anything you'd find in the hands of an East End inhabitant. Also, there's the dark ink. Not watered down to make it last. Thus, it was written by a person of quality, perhaps even in the nobility, one who isn't worried about using up his supply and buying more."

Garrard held it up to the light coming in a four-paned window behind his desk. "A watermark—*JD* and a crown."

Owen realized he'd never thought about a note or notepaper from the point of view of class.

"If it had been written in pencil," the detective droned on, but Owen stopped listening. *A person of quality?*

That brought up the other bit of evidence he had found with his sister. Clutched in her hand was a handkerchief, very white, very clean, scarcely scented with a fragrance that definitely wasn't *La Rose d'Amour*, more like laundry soap. He hadn't recognized the lace or the pattern, an anvil in one of its corners. He'd removed it before the police had arrived to take his sister's body to the city morgue.

"Is there something else, Lord Burnley?"

The detective was smart. If he could help in some way, then Owen didn't want to hamper his efforts. He drew the handkerchief from his pocket.

"My sister had this in her hand."

Garrard's eyebrows shot up. "You should have given it to me immediately."

"Actually, I'm not giving it to you now. I'm merely showing it to you. It is more likely I will find its match when I am out and about in society, than you will happen upon it in your investigation."

The detective considered Owen's words and nodded. "Very well. Let me look at it."

Reluctantly, he handed it over. Garrard studied it thoroughly, before sitting down and grabbing a tablet and pencil. He sketched a crude drawing of the handkerchief's pattern.

"It is unusual," Owen said.

"Agreed. Not a simple monogram that might narrow down its owner."

Still, it was better than nothing, and Owen silently thanked his little sister for somehow hanging onto it. He held out his hand, and the detective gave it back.

"Is there anything else?" Garrard asked.

"I suppose the shopgirl at the arcade could give a description of the urchin who brought the note luring my sister to her death."

The detective shook his head. "I've tried that avenue already, my lord. Sounds as though he looks like every other guttersnipe of indeterminate age. Sandy hair, malnourished, grubby clothing." He shrugged. "I could more easily find a needle in a haystack."

18

Owen left feeling hopeless, except for something Whitely had said when he'd looked at the handkerchief.

"Get back into the Season," George told him. "Keep your eyes open for a similar handkerchief. I shall do the same."

His other good friend could be of no help. Lord Christopher Westing had very limited vision, shadowy shapes, at best. And he and his wife, Lady Jane, barely ventured out due to their new baby. The best thing Owen could do was go back into society and hunt for a pocket square.

Beyond that, he had one lead to follow. Leaving Scotland Yard behind, Owen directed his driver to the less fashionable area above Hyde Park. The D'Anvilles, neither well-known nor well-off, kept a London home there. When he'd been staring at the handkerchief the previous night, the hulking son of the family came to mind.

Owen pounded on the door before realizing what he was doing. Withdrawing his hand, he pressed the bell. Half a minute later, the door swung inward.

"Yes?" inquired a butler.

Owen thrust his calling card into the man's hand.

"I wish to see Lord D'Anville."

"Of course, my lord. Which one?"

"Any will do."

The butler didn't raise an eyebrow. He simply stepped back and let Owen enter.

"Please, my lord, will you wait in the front room?"

The butler led him into a small drawing room and departed to find his master. While waiting for some member of the D'Anville family, Owen surveyed the room, trying to determine anything about them. The paintings were unremarkable landscapes, and the few books on display were dusty, boring tomes of the plays of Euripides and Gibbon's *History of the Decline and Fall of the Roman Empire* in six volumes, looking as if they were only there for display.

Just when he heard footsteps, however, he spied a volume with a French title, *Julie ou La Nouvelle Héloïse* on the small table beside the sofa.

Sliding it toward him, he considered Rousseau's epistolary novel of passionate lovers and picked it up. Someone had been reading in French. A shiver ran up his spine. In fact, he thought he'd seen the very same book in his sister's hand not that long ago.

Flipping through the fictional letters between the two main characters, Owen wondered if this could be a connection.

"Good day, Lord Burnley."

He turned at the greeting, the book about a fallen woman who rehabilitates herself clutched in his hand.

The elder Lord D'Anville met his eyes. Owen couldn't find it in him to say the niceties. No day was a good day at present, which was why he could not imagine returning to London's ballrooms or dining rooms without feeling physically ill.

In the end, he nodded slightly.

"I was sorry to hear about the death of your sister," the older gentleman said directly, making Owen feel exposed. He didn't want a stranger discussing Sophia when she was no longer there to speak for herself. Yet, that was the very reason he had come.

"Did you know my sister?"

"Not at all," the man said, appearing surprised at the question.

What had Owen expected? An instant confession? It was unlikely Sophia would have had interaction with the father anyway.

"You have a son, do you not?"

"I do." D'Anville was starting to frown, probably unused to being questioned in his own home.

"I must speak with him," Owen said curtly.

"I am not positive he is at home," D'Anville responded cautiously. "May I ask what this is about?"

"His friendship with my sister." The detective had been correct about the privilege of privacy regarding the manner of her death—her gruesome murder hadn't been splashed across the papers for people's entertainment. What's more, if the D'Anvilles knew nothing except Sophia had died, with causes left unstated, then they should be entirely open and forthcoming.

The man hesitated. "I don't believe they had a friendship. I have never heard him mention her."

"Nevertheless, I wish to speak to him." Owen knew his tone had hardened, but he couldn't help it.

"Very well." D'Anville rang the bell and, when the butler appeared, ordered him to summon this son.

"It will be but a moment," he said.

"So, he is home, and you knew it," Owen surmised, causing the father's mouth to draw into a line.

"One can never be too careful," the older man said. "Would you care for a drink?"

"No," Owen snapped, unable to dredge up the barest civility to thank him.

"You may sit," his lordship offered, footsteps in the hall heralded the younger D'Anville's entrance.

Owen took his measure at once, a soft young man, overweight, pampered, not at all someone who would interest his sister romantically. Sophia had once pointed out a renowned pugilist in the newspaper, muscular and fit, and had said he was most appealing. This man was the opposite.

However, that could mean spurned attention, unrequited love, and heated emotions.

"Good day," the younger D'Anville said, sounding precisely like his father.

Again, Owen nodded in return. "Did you know my sister, Lady Sophia Burnley?"

"I did," D'Anville said, surprising Owen.

Also, surprising his father, for the elder D'Anville exclaimed, "Did you?"

"When did you see her last?" Owen fired at him.

The younger man frowned. "Why?"

"Because I have asked you." Owen was unable to keep the menace from his tone.

Young D'Anville paled. "At a ball, I suppose."

"Which ball?"

The young man swallowed, looked to his father, and shrugged. "Maybe two weeks ago."

Owen tried to recall a ball of two weeks earlier. He usually escorted Sophia.

"Which one? The Cragmores? The Pelhams? What did she wear? What did you talk about? With whom did she dance?"

D'Anville took a step back from this barrage of questions, and his father said, "Now, now. What's all this about?"

"My sister met with foul play. I am trying to determine if your son had anything to do with it."

"That's ridiculous," said the older D'Anville.

"Is it?" Owen asked. He turned to the younger man. "Parlez-vous Francais?" Possibly Sophia enjoyed this potato's company because he could converse in French with her.

"No," he said.

"Then who was reading this?" Owen spat out the words while holding Rousseau's novel in front of him, seeing young D'Anville growing flushed around his fleshy jowls.

"That belongs to my wife," the father answered. "Not that it is any of your business what any of us read in this house. I want you to leave at once."

"When I get some answers from your son. If he knew my sister, he might know something that can help me."

"I cannot help," the younger man said.

Instantly, Owen saw red. *Was D'Anville playing a game with him?*

In a flash, he had him by the throat and was pushing him backward until his head slammed into the wall.

"You can help me, and you will," Owen growled, while the elder D'Anville started to yell. Undoubtedly, he was pressing the infernal bell for help.

"I lied," the young man wheezed. The younger D'Anville was very red and having trouble speaking.

"Let him go!" came the father's voice behind him.

Suddenly, the butler was in the room, too, and laying hands on Owen's shoulders.

He shrugged the servant off, not relinquishing his tight hold on D'Anville. "What did you lie about?"

"Knowing her." The younger man reached up, gripping both of Owen's wrists, trying to pry them away. "Please! I didn't know her."

Feeling the butler tugging at his shoulder and seeing young D'Anville, red and sweaty, pleading for the chance to breathe, Owen released him and backed away.

"Get out!" the elder D'Anville yelled. "I am reporting you to the police."

Owen rolled his eyes. He couldn't think of any threat that held any weight with him. The worst had already happened to his family.

"Do you have a handkerchief?" he demanded.

Young D'Anville's eyes widened. He nodded.

"My lord," the butler said, "you must come with me."

Ignoring him, Owen kept his eyes trained on the man in front of him. "Do you have one on you?"

Again, D'Anville nodded.

"Let me see it at once."

While staring at Owen as if he were insane, the young lord pulled out a white handkerchief.

Owen snatched it from his grasp. It had no lace and a simple *D* embroidered upon one corner.

"Shouldn't it be an *A*?" Owen asked.

Silence met his question.

Ignorant people, he fumed. The *D* was nothing more than French for "of." Why would they choose a monogram

23

representing the word *of* instead of their family name of Anville?

He growled and wanted to punch the young lord simply for the stupidity of his family. If it had been an anvil on his handkerchief, Owen would have turned the younger man's face to mincemeat.

"Why did you say you knew my sister?"

"She's dead," he said. "She couldn't say I didn't."

Owen shook his head uncomprehendingly.

"I don't know many people," D'Anville mumbled. "Saying I knew your sister would elevate me."

Owen recoiled. This man would use a dead girl's status with the *ton* to better his own? *How repulsive!*

He gave in to his desire and popped the young lord squarely in the face, relishing the look of surprise as the blood began to flow from his nose. At once, the cries of outrage followed from the elder D'Anville.

Before the butler could speak again, Owen brushed past him to the door, where he dropped the offending handkerchief as he saw himself out.

CHAPTER THREE

A delia's brother was not entirely closed to the idea of her retiring from society. Neither had he given her permission to do so. At least, not immediately.

"Finish out the Season, Dilly-girl," he'd said. "Then, we'll see."

She could do it and with grace, too. Moreover, she might add a few more stories to the ones in her head. One never knew when some supposedly proper young lady was going to speak too loudly in a noisy ballroom about her tryst with her parents' groundskeeper or footman.

Thus, together, she and Thomas entered Lord and Lady Walthrops' corner mansion off Edgeware Road. As a chaperone, Thomas was an easy one. He went about his business and, based on her appallingly boring history of doing absolutely nothing, left Adelia to her own devices. As usual, she skirted the edges of the throng, kept her wrist with her dance card down in the folds of her skirt, and found herself a discreet site by the wall, away from the refreshments. Often behind the musicians was a good spot that kept her entirely isolated.

Tonight, that wasn't possible given the musicians' placement, so she settled near the French doors to the gardens. Depending on the promiscuity of the crowd, this could be a busy area, but the couples were usually so distracted trying to slip in and out as quickly as possible to avoid notice, they didn't linger, nor would they see her standing there.

She hummed to herself as the music started, and she even allowed a little toe-tapping, but she didn't look out over the dancers. That led to the possibility of making eye contact, and then, someone invariably felt they must come speak to her. Out of pity, she supposed. Offering them her profile was the best way to avoid conversation, and she could keep her undamaged ear toward the room.

Occasionally, despite this off-putting stance ended up with her having to fend off some young lord. After all, she was an earl's daughter, and not a penniless one, either. And other gentlemen, those who had no need of her dowry, probably assumed they were doing Adelia a gracious favor by paying her their special attention. Thus, she had danced with practically everyone who was anyone over the course of her past four Seasons.

Usually only once! She would emit the hideous braying laughter she had mastered, and that was enough to send them running. If not, she would trip herself or them during the dance or while walking off the floor afterward. If all else failed, she turned to the wallpaper completely and ignored their attempts at conversation.

That was actually her favorite ruse, for it was entirely passive on her part. She didn't have to look at an astonished expression or feel the awkwardness of the moment. Sometimes, her face was so close to the wallpaper, her eyes crossed.

She sighed. How many minutes had passed? How many hours to go until her brother got tired of looking for love and took her home? She settled into the story in her brain and worked on her latest novel, unbothered until she heard a roar of outrage.

Glancing toward the dance floor, she saw people dodging out of the way as if a horse and carriage were plowing across the room. When the last couple parted, Adelia could see blond, attractive Lord Owen Burnley hauling a man by his coat sleeve in his wake.

"You will answer me," Lord Burnley declared, and to Adelia's astonishment, they were coming in her direction. All eyes turned toward her little section of the room as her peace was shattered.

She didn't recognize Lord Burnley's victim, and he could only be labeled as such since the man appeared as if he'd been attacked. His jacket was in disarray, his ascot was askew, and his hair was mussed. He was a young lord in his first Season, and he made wild eye contact with Adelia as Burnley dragged him past her and out through the French doors.

Gracious! What was that all about?

In true London fashion, by morning, everyone would be discussing the strange occurrence over their eggs and bacon. Presently, however, those on the dance floor pretended to ignore the incident and went back to dancing. As to the rest of the guests, fans went up, and whispering started immediately.

Adelia frowned. No one would think of going out after the pair to see what was occurring in case they were somehow dragged into a disreputable situation. Nor would anyone get involved to offer assistance, despite Lord Burnley wearing a thunderous expression and looking as if he might do bodily harm to his captive.

Suddenly, Lord Whitely appeared. He seemed to be in a hurry, and Adelia imagined he'd been in the far corner of the room or maybe elsewhere in the building. After having heard the racket, he'd probably been told it was his friend who'd caused it.

Usually, the two viscounts were thick as thieves, towering over women and often each leading a pretty miss outside, albeit in a far gentler manner than had just been the case. They used to be part of a handsome trio, but the third of their group, Lord Westing, had been in a terrible accident a couple years earlier and rendered blind. That had not heralded the end of Lord Westing's otherwise blessed life. The marquess married a woman universally admired, Lady Jane Chatley, settled down, and started a family. The two bachelors were left to haunt the Season's events by themselves, sometimes in rakish fashion.

Adelia had observed Lord Burnley more than any other gentleman, as she thought him most appealing. Moreover, she had never seen the fine-looking viscount behave in such a strange and violent fashion.

Lord Whitely came to an uncertain stop a few yards in front of her, and their gazes met. *What else could she do?* She pointed toward the French doors beside her. Nodding, he rushed outside.

Adelia waited until all eyes eventually stopped looking in her direction. Then, with her usual inconspicuous movements, she slowly followed. *Why not?* It was infinitely more interesting than anything going on indoors.

It wasn't hard to find the three men. Lord Burnley had taken the other man out of sight behind the first of a series of hedgerows that formed a very small maze. Adelia could easily stand on the other side of the yews and overhear everything.

An appalling practice, she told herself as she froze in place, *and one which she was already in the habit of doing.* In the future, she would endeavor to stop.

"Let him go." This from Lord Whitely. "You're going to hurt him, and his father is—"

"I don't give a fig who his damned father is," Lord Burnley growled. "Farrier, here, was seen talking to Sophia recently, and a farrier uses an anvil."

Adelia tried to make sense of the conversation.

"You're mad!" This came from the aforementioned Lord Farrier, whose father was, in fact, an important member of Parliament. Even Adelia had heard of him.

"Let me see your handkerchief, dammit! If you'd shown it to me when I first asked, this would be over. Unless you're a filthy murdering swine!"

"Owen!" Lord Whitely sounded agitated.

"I told you. I don't have one on me," Lord Farrier protested.

"What kind of gentleman are you?" Lord Burnley demanded. "We all have handkerchiefs, the same way we all have shirts and pants."

"The kind who, minutes ago, gave my last one to a young lady who spilled her lemonade."

"Prove it! Take me to her and show me the handkerchief," Lord Burnley insisted.

"Will you explain yourself if I do?" Lord Farrier asked.

Ignoring the question, Lord Burnley insisted, "Take me to her, *if* said lady exists, or I shall splinter your nose and make you spit out every single tooth in your head."

Adelia silently recoiled at the violent image. But during the pause, she realized she must move, and quickly, in order to hide or retreat. They would be coming out from behind the hedge at any moment.

"If I do, will you behave civilly?" Lord Farrier asked. "And take your hands off me, or we shall end up exchanging fisticuffs, teeth and nose be damned."

Adelia darted back to the steps and turned as if she were only then coming out, exactly as the three men appeared from the maze opening. She forgot to look away, and her gaze locked with Lord Burnley's, making her gasp at the seething anger in his expression. Next, the three men brushed past her.

At the last instant, she heard herself addressed by Lord Whitely, with whom she'd played croquet a few days earlier at Lady Turbity's.

"Lady Adelia?"

She turned and nodded.

"Are you unaccompanied?" he asked.

Again, she merely nodded, knowing her voice might come out in a squeak or not at all.

"Then you had best get yourself inside or find a chaperone!" Lord Burnley declared loudly. "Ladies should not be alone in public."

She felt her mouth drop open. In essence, that was true, but to hear it stated thusly, it sounded patently absurd. After all, there was a room full of people mere yards away.

She gestured over the men's shoulders, but glancing around the garden, she realized no one else, thus far, had come outside, not even for a stolen kiss.

"You will come with us," Lord Burnley commanded in a tone that would no dispute. "And be quick about it." He fixed her with an impatient glare.

She sighed but turned and followed them. As she climbed the steps, the men parted to let her by, and Adelia spared a sympathetic glance for Lord Farrier. When Lord Whitely opened one of the doors, she preceded them inside.

As if each guest had been awaiting their return, which, of course, was the case, every head turned, each eye watched them reappear in the ballroom. It seemed as if even the music faded slightly, and the dancers hesitated in their steps.

"Where is your chaperone?" Lord Burnley asked her.

But Adelia couldn't speak. She couldn't draw breath with so many people looking in her direction. She blinked at him, feeling her cheeks heat up with mortification.

"I asked you a question, Lady . . . Adelia, is it?" he asked gruffly. "What game are you playing?"

She wished she could get to the wall and lean against it.

"I . . . ," she tried, but she still couldn't seem to get enough air into her lungs. "I . . . ," she whispered as spots appeared in front of her eyes, and a buzzing filled her ears. She had to sit down.

Too late! The ballroom dissolved into dizzying darkness.

OWEN BARELY REACHED HER in time but managed to catch Lady Adelia's lithe form as she sagged, just before she collapsed onto the parquet. Out of the corner of his eye, he saw Farrier slip away. *The devil!*

If the man believed Owen would not pursue him to the ends of the earth to look at his damned handkerchief, he was going to find himself sorely mistaken. At present, however, he literally had his hands full.

Lifting her in his arms, he took a few steps forward, looking around the room. Everyone was murmuring and whispering. He sighed. *Did she have family there? Perhaps a negligent mother seated at one of the tables?*

"Whitely," he ground out. "To whom does this lady belong?"

"She's the Earl of Dunford's daughter."

Owen frowned. "He's dead, isn't he?"

"Yes, about a year ago. I played croquet with her recently, the day I rounded out Lady Turbity's foursome in your stead." George paused, then added, "Truthfully, she wasn't much more entertaining that day than now. And she spoke almost as little."

Owen took another few steps, heading toward the refreshment alcove. Maybe he could toss some chilled lemonade on her face and revive her.

Looking down at his burden, he noted she was a pale, pretty thing, with light brown hair and eyelashes a shade darker, as were her eyebrows. He adjusted her in his arms, and she turned slightly, her cheek resting against his chest. He'd seen her at many events and was positive he'd danced with her once or twice. For the life of him, though, he was unable to recall ever speaking with her.

Of all the women he'd flirted with over the years or suddenly grown an attachment that ended a week later, why had he never had a dalliance with this one? She was certainly attractive enough, with curves to spare from what he could tell. Even then, he could peer down her décolletage and see a shapely bosom.

If he was so inclined.

Naturally, he wasn't.

"What the devil do I do with her?" he grumbled.

The beverages were not yet set out, so they crossed the width of the room, and he was about to walk the length of it with her, when she stirred.

"Mm," she murmured.

"Move," he ordered a young gentleman and lady seated on the only nearby chairs. At his tone, they jumped up.

Thereupon, he heard a man's voice nearby call out, "Dilly!"

Owen eased her onto the chair as her eyelids fluttered open. For a split second, she looked into his eyes, and he felt her green glance like a candle flame sending a sizzle right through him. *What the hell!*

He took a hurried step back as she gazed wildly around.

"Thomas," she said, too quietly for anyone but Owen to hear.

Thomas? Then it dawned on him—Lord Thomas Smythe, the current Earl of Dunford, and head of the rival, coal-mining family. He knew little of the young man and had hardly ever spoken to him. When they'd encountered one another occasionally at their pugilist's club, they focused on punching each other with hardly any conversation passing between them, as was usual.

The earl rushed forward and knelt in front of Lady Adelia, taking her hand. "Are you all right?"

She nodded, and Owen was relieved to see color returning to her cheeks, like pale roses against a creamy palette.

What drivel had filled his head?

"Your sister was wandering around unsupervised. And then, she fainted," Owen said, unable to keep the derision from his voice. "If you are her chaperone, you are doing a piss-poor job of it!"

The young lord glanced up at him, and Owen had to hand it to him. Smythe appeared calm and collected, managing to give him a look that nearly quelled him.

Except while he had been playing nursemaid to this man's worrisome sister, his quarry had gotten away!

"If you can take care of your responsibilities from now on," Owen continued, "I have more important matters to which I must attend."

With that rude statement, which he instantly regretted despite it being true, he nodded to the earl and his sister in turn, catching the full glare from the young man and the mortification of the lady's green-eyed gaze.

She tugged at her brother's hand, and he brought his ear close to her lips. Owen watched fascinated as she whispered to him. Nodding, Lord Smythe drew her to standing.

"Thank you, my lord," Smythe said stiffly, and they walked away when Owen was the one who had sought to hurry along.

He turned to find Whitely watching the entire scene play out.

"Enough dallying! Which way did Farrier go?" Owen demanded.

"MORE IMPORTANT MATTERS," THOMAS fumed when they were seated in their carriage and heading home. "The nerve of that pompous jackass!"

Adelia had been thinking the same thing, but it sounded so ungrateful she had to defend her savior.

"Lord Burnley prevented my collapse onto the floor in front of everyone."

"He could have been infinitely more gracious about it," Thomas noted. "And he didn't know if I was close by or answering nature's call down the hallway. Obviously, if I'd been right there, I would have caught you myself."

Adelia smiled to herself. Her brother had always had a rather small bladder, and thus, in all probability, had been in the gentleman's retiring room, passing water. *Only a brother and sister could discuss such things*, she thought. A moment later, she recalled the Burnleys' terrible loss. The viscount could never again have a silly conversation with his sister.

"Remember what has only recently happened to Lord Burnley's family, Thomas. That young lady you hadn't the chance to dance with, as you said, was his beloved sister. Would you feel very gracious if I had just died? I know I would be deeply in mourning if the situations were reversed."

A fleeting, mulish look crossed her brother's face. Then, his expression softened.

"You are right. Frankly, I wouldn't be out at all if something had happened to you. I think he should have stayed home as he is obviously unfit for polite society at present."

"He didn't seem to be there for the dancing. Were you in the room when he dragged Lord Farrier outside to the back garden to question him?"

"No. I was not. Question him about what?"

"A handkerchief," Adelia murmured.

Her brother frowned. "As I said, Burnley ought to stay at home behind the black crape hangings and do everyone a favor. At least for a little while. It's almost indecent!"

She nodded, but her heart went out to the viscount who'd saved her from sprawling on the floor. He seemed very angry, perhaps at the unfairness of life.

"What did Lady Sophia die from?" Adelia asked.

Thomas stared out the window. "Who knows?"

THE NEXT MORNING, ADELIA went out early, her maid, Penny, trailing behind when she alit from her carriage on Oxford Street. Her favorite stationer's shop beckoned her invitingly.

The bell tinkled above the door at Adelia's entrance.

"Good morning, Lady Adelia," said the owner's wife.

"Good morning, Mrs. Schnell." She glanced around the shop. It was otherwise empty at that hour, which was precisely how Adelia preferred it.

"Are you out of paper already?" the round-cheeked woman asked, looking astonished.

"Almost. I shall buy a new tablet for when the inevitable occurs in a day or so. And I wondered if you had any new nibs."

The shopkeeper pulled a tray out from behind the counter as the bell tinkled again. "Try out any you like, my lady."

A loud family had entered the shop, causing Adelia to try to shrink in size as noise always did. Glancing over her shoulder, her gaze took in Penny, waiting patiently by the door. Her maid gave her an encouraging smile, and she relaxed. It was only a mother and three children, asking for colored pencils and drawing pads.

Keeping her back to the shop, Adelia indulged herself a few minutes by dipping pens into the testing ink and scrawling across the top sheet of a stack of low-quality paper. She didn't really need another nib, but she loved the smooth feeling of a new one. Ultimately, she would wear out the metal tip on her Perry pen, but for now, it was akin to an old friend she couldn't bear to part with.

Feeling a little guilty for using up so much of the stationer's ink, she decided to buy another pot at the very least.

After the family had made their purchases and left, she turned to locate Mrs. Schnell just as the door opened again.

To the accompaniment of the tinkling bell, in strode Lord Owen Burnley.

CHAPTER FOUR

Adelia faltered when the tall, handsome viscount stopped in his tracks upon seeing her. His scowling face slowly softened into something resembling civility.

"Good day, Lady Adelia."

She nodded, knowing if she tried to return his greeting, it would stick in her throat. She always needed a moment to gird herself for interaction with men. And this man, even more so. His blue eyes, which had scorched her the night before, were the loveliest she'd ever seen on a man. And she greatly admired the flaxen gold of his hair, curling out from beneath his top hat, so much prettier than her own dull brown.

"I shall be right with you, my lord," Mrs. Schnell intoned to him. "Is there anything besides the tablet, my lady?"

Adelia wanted to ask for the ink, but her voice had deserted her, so she shook her head.

Lord Burnley approached and pulled something out of his pocket, slamming it atop the counter, making Adelia jump as the shopkeeper pulled out her accounts ledger.

While Mrs. Schnell recorded her purchase, which would be settled at the end of the month, Adelia couldn't help

glancing at what Lord Burnley had so violently set down—
a scrap of paper, blank except for the letters *J* and *D* and a
crown sketched in pencil. The markings were familiar.

She glanced up at him to find his intense gaze upon her.
Then, he raised an eyebrow.

"Do you come here often, Lady Adelia?"

Suddenly realizing he was quite close, not giving her the
well-mannered amount of space to conduct her business,
she took a step away from him.

What was his question? Oh, yes.

She nodded.

"Her ladyship is in here all the time," Mrs. Schnell added,
and Adelia felt her cheeks heat at the unexpected discussion
of her personal habits.

"You are a devotee of paper and pens, I take it," Lord
Burnley said. "Thus, may I assume you write a lot of
letters?"

It was none of his business, but he had her fixed with
those piercing eyes, so she nodded again.

"There you are, my lady," Mrs. Schnell said, sliding the
new tablet toward her.

Glancing down, Adelia noted the watermark, not very
noticeable but apparent when one knew of its existence.

Again, she glanced at Lord Burnley, who looked at the
tablet, too. He visibly startled, apparently seeing the mark.
Without warning, he reached out and took her tablet
precisely as she was reaching for it. She was caught in the
awkward situation of both of them holding an opposing
edge.

"I have more of those, my lord," Mrs. Schnell said into
the tense silence.

He continued to hold onto it, staring at the top sheet, so
Adelia released it. He lifted the page, held it up, and turned
toward the front windows of the shop.

Adelia could plainly see the crown and the initials of the
paper manufacturer.

"Is this very common paper?" he demanded, his back to both Adelia and the shopkeeper.

They exchanged questioning glances before Mrs. Schnell responded.

"It is popular, my lord. Produced by John Dickinson, out of their Apsley paper mill. Would you like to buy a tablet? I can also have it monogrammed if you wish."

He turned around and stared hard at Adelia, making her insides quell uncomfortably. Next, he looked at Mrs. Schnell.

"Do you keep a list of people who purchase this particular paper?"

"You mean anyone who buys Dickinson?"

"Yes. Precisely," his tone was sharp. "Any paper with this watermark."

"I keep account books in which I write down whatever is purchased."

Adelia glanced at the one open on the counter, and under "Smythe, Ly. Adelia," she could see a long list of supplies purchased, including the words "tablet, J.D." on many occasions.

"But I am not the only shop in London that sells it, my lord," Mrs. Schnell added.

He sighed, sounding extraordinarily weary, and his face looked momentarily far older than his years, which Adelia guessed to be less than thirty.

Finally, he handed the tablet back to Adelia, who tucked it under her arm.

"Nonetheless," he said to the shopkeeper, "I must learn the names of everyone who uses this paper." His hands clenched on the counter. "If you would compile a list of all your customers who've bought it in the past six months, I shall pay whatever you ask."

Mrs. Schnell's face whitened. After a few seconds of consideration, she said, "I shall charge you for two hours of work as if I were preparing something for the printer."

He nodded.

38

"Are you going to do the same at every stationery shop hereabouts?"

At first, Adelia thought he wasn't going to answer Mrs. Schnell's brazen inquiry.

"Yes," he said after a brief pause.

Adelia was dying to know why. It was extraordinarily eccentric. First, the altercation about handkerchiefs and now this! If she'd been any other female, she would let her curiosity overrule her courtesy and boldly ask about both his odd quests. Yet, she could not.

Nodding her thanks to the shopkeeper and with another nod to his lordship, she started past him.

"You seem to write a lot of letters," Lord Burnley said, making the incorrect assumption for once again.

Adelia would not have responded if he hadn't further asked, "Are there others in your home who write a lot? Your brother, perhaps?"

She halted at the door and turned back. *Stranger and stranger.*

"No. Lord Smythe is not one for letter-writing."

Lord Burnley said nothing more, although his eyes narrowed menacingly.

She hoped they were finished, but his gaze flicked over her, head to toe, and her cheeks warmed at his perusal. *How mortifying!* That she should blush over a man's cursory glance as if she were a debutante.

Having long since given up hope she would outgrow or overcome her shyness, Adelia wished she could disappear through the floorboards entirely. Given that impossibility, she turned on her heel and left. Her usually enjoyable outing had been all but ruined.

OWEN WATCHED HER GO, feeling more morose the instant she left the shop. This was a lonely, sad business, attempting to track down Sophia's murderer. And when he realized how a normal person, such as the quiet, unassuming Lady Adelia, could buy a tablet of the very paper he sought and multiplied that by the number of ladies and gentlemen in London, he understood the frustrating futility of his search.

What choice did he have?

His mother was still so distraught, she could no longer function. His father, instead of conducting either the business of mining coal or the business of Parliament, haunted City Police headquarters in Whitehall almost as much as Owen. The cremation and funeral had been private, and they were keeping Sophia's ashes until such time as they returned to the Burnley country home in southern Wales. She would be interred in the family cemetery, alongside grandparents and siblings who had not survived infancy.

It still seemed utterly impossible his sister was gone.

Suddenly, he didn't want to be alone. Nodding to the shopkeeper, who undoubtedly believed him a lunatic, Owen hurried out after Lady Adelia. She was only half a block away, a maid he hadn't previously noticed straggling behind her.

What did he intend?

Again, he was spurred by an irrational notion that it was better to be in her company than alone, so he closed the distance and called her name.

"Lady Adelia." His tone was perhaps a tad brusque, but his mood was one of bleak simmering fury nearly all the time. It was too late to try a softer voice.

The young woman turned, those lovely green eyes of hers growing wide at seeing him following her.

Out in the daylight, her hair was a pleasing caramel-colored shade of brown, reminding him of one of his favorite horse's manes. And she wore a jaunty blue velvet bonnet perched atop, giving her a pleasing appearance—far more welcoming than her actual manner.

Her maid turned, too. In fact, all those on the pavement around her also glanced at him before moving along. He wanted to bark at every one of them to mind their business.

Lady Adelia stood motionless, waiting for an explanation. He didn't have a good one. He had been spontaneous in calling her name and certainly impetuous.

"May I walk with you?" The words spilled out.

If ever he'd seen an expression of sheer horror, Lady Adelia wore one now.

"I . . . I . . . ," she trailed off, shaking her head.

No matter. It couldn't possibly be him personally she disliked. There was no reason he could think of for her to have an unfavorable sentiment toward him. They'd barely spoken, and he'd carried her out of harm's way the other night. Perhaps she was merely embarrassed, in which case, he would ease her mind. After all, he was known to have a way with females.

Too easy of a way, in fact, and then too fickle once he attracted them. His best friends, Westing and Whitely, judged him alternately too quick and then too capricious, as he dismissed one woman after another for various and sundry reasons.

In any case, he knew how to talk to the fairer sex and how to set their minds at ease. Usually, this led to an assignation in a garden bower or an empty drawing room with neither party having regrets.

As for Lady Adelia, she was positively the most reticent woman he'd ever met. A rare gem, in fact, unless one was longing for a chatty companion. At that moment, he would welcome someone to take his mind off the impossible task he'd set for himself.

Without her permission, Owen moved into position abreast of her. He gestured ahead of them, intending to get her walking again.

"Are you perfectly recovered after the other evening's fainting spell?" he asked, taking a few steps, unsure whether she would fall in next to him or refuse to move.

After a brief hesitation, in which she looked around and back at her maid, she did, in fact, begin to walk once more. However, she did not answer his question, nor did she say anything, continuing along beside him in silence.

Normally, that might be uncomfortable for two strangers, but as he sensed silence was her usual state, he took no offense. He hoped she didn't mind if he did the talking.

"I am not often in a stationer's shop," he began. Truthfully, he'd never been in one prior to that day. "I do not write letters," he admitted.

He hadn't written much of anything since school days. He considered the paper in his own townhouse. There were tablets in his desk drawer and monogrammed paper, too. He used these to pen an occasional invitation or thank-you note. He had never committed the folly of writing a love letter since the receiver could use it as evidence of a formal arrangement.

"When I do—write, I mean—paper seems to be there. I suppose my butler ensures I have adequate supplies."

She nodded at his inane talk, keeping her gaze directed in front.

"You seem to have a particular type of paper you prefer," he continued, "and it was the very same which I sought. A coincidence, don't you think?"

She barely lifted a shoulder by way of a nonchalant shrug.

He had the inexplicable desire to tell her why, to confess he wasn't randomly looking at stationery but for this particular paper, and explain the importance of one person who had owned a sheet of it.

"May I ask, Lady Adelia, where one procures a handkerchief? In this neighborhood, I mean." Truthfully, Owen meant anywhere. It was another thing he left to others. His valet maintained an ample amount, all with the letter *B* embroidered on the corner in silver thread. He considered them quite attractive and handed them out to young ladies in precisely the manner that a medieval lady would hand out ribbons to show favor to her knights.

Now that he thought about it, it was a somewhat expensive habit, and he often wished he could get some of them back. One never knew when one lady for whom he had a new fondness was going to see another lady to whom he'd previously paid court waving around his monogrammed token.

Lady Adelia didn't answer. She looked to her left at the shops they were passing as if a handkerchief shop might spring up alongside her. Eventually, her steps faltered until she stopped walking altogether.

"A draper," she said so quietly he had to lean close to catch her next words, "such as Harvey Nichols." After a pause, she added, "Or a tailor."

By this time, her words were so softy spoken, he wondered if she had a sore throat. He'd never heard the like in a female who didn't need a lozenge or, at the very least, some hot whiskey and honey.

"Are you ill?" Owen asked, again hearing an unusually irritated quality to his voice that he didn't care for but couldn't seem to stop.

She shook her head.

He sighed. He would simply ask his valet, who, if the man was worth the cost of his service, would know the whereabouts of every handkerchief seller. Nevertheless, Owen wasn't ready to release Lady Adelia. Not that he wished to torment her, but he wanted to discover why she was so intent on *not* speaking to him.

"We have danced together, have we not?"

She nodded.

"Have I offended you in some way?"

She shook her head again.

Infuriating woman! If asked, he would still be unable to tell a soul whether her voice was that of a sweet angel or a raspy old man.

"Is your driver close by?"

43

She pointed over his shoulder, and he realized a carriage was following along a few yards back.

"Good." For if she were ever in trouble, he doubted she could yell for help.

Had Sophia yelled with no one to come to her rescue? He fisted his hands at the painful question. He had best leave the lady before his temper flared, making him unfit, according to Whitely, for company.

In fact, he noticed her glance take in his clenched hands, and he purposefully relaxed them.

"I am sorry to have taken up your time. I hope to see you again at some event this Season. I bid you good day."

She offered a ghost of a smile, perhaps relieved he was finally taking his leave.

Bowing to her and receiving a nod in return, he went back the way he had come. Belatedly, it occurred to him how Lady Adelia had been in ballrooms and at dinner parties for a few years now. Why she hadn't been snapped up, pretty as she was, he could not fathom. He supposed next to the likes of his sister or any number of friendlier women, Lady Adelia had always seemed . . . well . . . exactly as he found her today—particularly disinterested and unresponsive to any overtures to engage in conversation. What's more, she was not the least flirtatious.

Off-putting to a fault.

Be that as it may, perhaps he should show her the handkerchief because she, as well as any lady, might have needed to borrow one in the past or, at the very least, know the owner of the kerchief in question. He very much doubted if Lady Adelia had ever used one for the more coquettish reason of signaling to a lover. Nonetheless, he couldn't discount her as having information.

Anyway, he needn't tell her why he had it or why he wanted to find its owner. Turning, he surveyed the crowded pavement in front of him, only to discover she had vanished. She might be quiet, but she wasn't slow.

Hailing his driver, Owen had half a mind to head to the police headquarters at Whitehall and berate the detective sergeant once again but thought better of it.

"Westing's house. Arlington Street," he added, in case his coachman took him to the Duke of Westing's townhouse on Grosvenor Square, rather than to the more modest home of his friend, the marquess, near St. James's Palace.

When his footman closed the carriage door, Owen settled back to think. Instead of any useful ideas about finding his sister's murderer, however, his mind returned to Lady Adelia Smythe.

She didn't seem weak or feeble-minded to him, yet she could barely speak above a whisper. He tried to recall anything definitive he'd ever heard about her. No broken contracts of marriage, no hint of scandal, no gossip about her at all. *How could that be?*

The only thing he recalled was what he and Whitely had discussed the other night, that her father, the Earl of Dunford, had passed away not too long ago. But Owen seemed to think her mother had died many years prior to that.

He had no knowledge of whether she'd always been a reticent person or if something in her life had caused her to behave in such a manner as to hardly fit into well-bred society at all.

When he alit from his carriage and knocked on Westings' door, he was none the wiser for his ponderings. Thus, as the butler allowed him entrance to the foyer, his mind remained elsewhere. He didn't realize at first that his other friend, Whitely, was already in the parlor until he heard the latter mention his own name.

"I don't know what we are going to do about Burnley. I've never seen him in such a state. I tell you, I fear for his health."

"He's not as bad as all that," came the tempering voice of Lord Christopher Westing, heir to the dukedom.

"Not all the time, no, but when his temper flares, it is white-hot. You must try to knock sense into his head," George insisted.

Knock sense into his head! As if anyone could knock away the memory of Sophia lying dead on the floor of a shabby upstairs room in a tavern.

"I shall go to his home at once," Chris said. "If Spencer hadn't had the touch of stomach flux, I would have been over there yesterday."

"Is the baby well now?" George asked.

Owen waited for the answer with bated breath. He'd already suffered a devastating blow. He didn't think he had it in him to witness his friend's son come to any harm.

"On the mend with Lady Jane at his side," Chris reassured Whitely. "I doubt she'll leave Spencer to go with me to visit Burnley, and that's just as well. I don't want him to have to pretend to be social at a time like this."

"I have been over there a number of times," George said, "and believe me, he is not worried about civility or being social. Although to spare Lady Jane, maybe you are right."

"Is Burnley drinking too much?"

"Strangely, no. Personally, I can imagine diving into a bottle of brandy and not coming out, but he said he refuses to muddle his mind until he's caught the killer."

"That's a good thing," Chris said. "If he was in a drunken rage, it would certainly be worse."

Blazes! To listen to his friends speak about him as if he were a reckless buffoon did nothing to help his mood.

"Shall I go with you?" George asked.

"No need," Owen told them as he strode into the room, feeling his anger surge. "I'm already here, and I will thank you two not to talk about me behind my back."

"We said nothing we wouldn't say to your face," George protested. "How are you?"

How was he? Mad as hell at his own ineffectiveness so far. Slightly offended, too, that Whitely would even ask him how he was.

"Better than my parents," he snapped. "And I'll be far better when I catch the murderer. At least I can work toward something. My mother doesn't particularly care about the killer. It won't bring Sophia back, and that would be the only thing which could lift her from her despair."

"I am terribly sorry," Chris offered. "Perhaps the helpless feeling is the hardest part."

Owen didn't think so. The hardest part was knowing he could never see Sophia again.

"The irrevocable finality of it," he muttered, his voice catching.

They were all silent a moment.

"Do you want to know why I came here uninvited?" he asked finally. In truth, he'd had no reason in particular, except wanting to be with friends.

"You don't need to explain yourself," Chris assured him. "You are always welcome. And I hope you'll take a meal with us. You're looking a little thin."

Owen shrugged before realizing Westing couldn't tell how he looked—thin or fat.

"You're shrugging, but I cannot see you," Chris pointed out.

"It seems you can." Owen almost smiled at the wonder that was his friend, a marquess who'd had everything at his feet prior to being blinded. With Lady Jane's help, he'd got it all back again and more. Naturally, he'd married her.

"Apparently, you can detect the thinness of my body by my voice, too."

Chris gave a lopsided smile.

Owen might as well ask them the question that would raise further queries from his friends. "What do you both think of Lady Adelia Smythe?"

CHAPTER FIVE

"I'll tell you what I think about Lady Adelia," George quipped. "Absolutely nothing at all—for she contributes nothing to any gathering at which I've ever encountered her, including the recent croquet match in which I filled in for you. I rounded out one of the foursomes as requested. Yet, with Lady Adelia, it seemed like a threesome."

Owen frowned. Whitely was being unkind.

"What about you, Westing? What is your impression of her?"

The marquess paused, which Owen appreciated, as he was a thoughtful man.

"On first impression, I would say Whitely is correct, but that's only because I haven't taken the time to speak with her. I have to confess to laboring under similar misconceptions about my wife. And I recall you both said she was not my type. Too stuffy or too retiring or some such drivel. But Lady Jane is, as you know, absolutely perfect for me. As soon as I took the time to know her, it became so obvious. I couldn't believe my own prior stupidity in not noticing her."

Owen considered his words. "It's very difficult to have a conversation and get to know someone who won't speak two words to me, and when Lady Adelia does, her words are so damnably quiet, I cannot tell what she's saying."

Whitely laughed loudly, then stopped abruptly. It was what everyone around Owen did since his sister's demise. No one felt they could laugh, including him. It seemed disrespectful. Perhaps it would forever be thus, even after he caught the killer.

"I ran into Lady Adelia at a stationer's shop today," Owen told them.

He paused at his friends' expressions. "Why are you looking like that? What is wrong?"

"Why were *you* at a stationer's shop?" Chris asked.

Whitely sent him a questioning look. Owen hadn't shared the killer's note with anyone but him.

"I had a note," he told Chris, "from the murderer."

"How on earth?" Chris asked, and Owen explained the circumstances.

"What do you mean *had*?" George asked.

"I gave it to the detective after he pointed out the watermark. I located the type of paper it was written on at the stationer's. In fact, Lade Adelia was buying a tablet of the very same paper. John Dickinson is the manufacturer."

Chris nodded. "My mother has always written on a J.D. watermarked paper. I don't know what my wife uses, as I cannot see it."

"I understand it is common, and probably impossible to find every person in London who has it. But it does indicate a person of quality," he said, echoing the detective.

"Indeed," Chris agreed. "Was there anything else?"

"Yes," Owen paused as his throat closed with emotion. "Sophia had a handkerchief clutched in her hand. I didn't give it to the detective, but he drew the pattern so he knows what to look for. Whitely didn't recognize it. I hoped you might."

"May I hold it?" Chris asked.

Owen handed it over and explained what his friend was feeling, "It looks like the shape of an anvil sewn into the lace."

Westing frowned.

"And before you say anything," George said, "Owen has already ascertained it does not belong to the D'Anville family by assaulting them."

"What?" Chris turned his face toward him.

Owen grimaced. "I didn't assault all of them, only the whey-faced son. Not my finest hour, I admit, and their handkerchief was not the one I sought. Nor that of Lord Farrier."

"Whom he dragged outside at a ball," George added.

"Owen," Chris warned. "You're going to find yourself locked up if you're not careful, and then you won't be any help to your parents."

Owen dismissed his friend's warning with a wave of his hand, belatedly remembering his friend could hardly see more than a blurry shadow.

"Regardless, in the past, did you ever see such a handkerchief?"

"Nothing comes to mind. We shall ask Lady Jane when she comes downstairs."

"Thank you. If you will do so on my behalf, I would greatly appreciate it. I should get going."

"Nonsense," Chris said. "You should eat. Whitely says you have skipped a few meals. I would be insulted if you didn't break bread with me, just because I am a poor blind man."

That remark did finally make all three of them chuckle. Chris was one of the most fortunate of men despite his impairment. Nevertheless, as they all knew, good fortune could change in the blink of an eye.

Tamping down his constant, seething anger at knowing the killer was freely walking the streets of London, Owen agreed to dine with his friends.

ADELIA WAS MOST UNHAPPY when the butler informed her she had a visitor. Her brother was out, and she had never considered it necessary to tell Mr. Lockley she wasn't seeing visitors, for the simple reason that she never had any.

For an instant, she imagined it might be Lord Burnley, as their paths had intersected more than once, and she couldn't get the man or his blue eyes out of her thoughts. The viscount had asked her if they had ever danced. She couldn't blame him for not being sure, despite her recalling their two dances with pleasure. Her heartbeat sped up at seeing him again, and her unfamiliar reaction intrigued her nearly as much as it frightened her.

However, when Mr. Lockley said it was Mr. Victor Beaumont, their company engineer, she felt a frisson of alarm.

"Please tell him my brother is away." Undoubtedly, it was Thomas he wanted to see.

"He asked for you, my lady."

More and more disturbing! After what her brother had told her, that their engineer had expressed an interest in her, she was even less inclined to meet with him alone.

Hailing her maid to accompany her, Adelia entered the parlor where Mr. Beaumont was standing, his back to her as he looked at the ceiling.

Behind him, she peered upward. *What was he looking at?*

Finally, she cleared her throat to alert him to her presence. He turned quickly, wearing a pleasant smile, his shrewd brown eyes staring at her from a plain but not unkind face.

"Lady Adelia, so good to see you." He took a step toward her, and she steeled herself to keep from retreating as he took hold of her hand with both of his, imprisoning it. Next, he lifted it to his mustached mouth and soundly kissed her knuckles, more than once.

Not quite properly done, she thought.

"Mr. Beaumont," she murmured, tugging to free her hand, which he released.

"Good crown molding, if I do say so."

Luckily, that statement required no response, so she merely nodded.

"May we sit?" he asked.

She hesitated. *Oh dear! Was it too late to simply leave the room and let her brother deal with the man upon his return?*

She nodded, then glanced at the far end of the room to make certain Penny was on a chair by the potted ferns before she sat. Gesturing for him to do the same on the far side of the coffee table, she waited.

If Mr. Beaumont launched into any kind of flowery speech about her attributes, she was fully prepared to get up and walk out.

"I am worried about your brother."

Of all the things he could have said, that might be the most unexpected.

"Whyever for?" she asked. She had taken breakfast with Thomas that very morning, and he had seemed perfectly fine and in good spirits for the upcoming day.

"He seemed quite overwrought about something the other day when we met to talk business, and his usually calm manner was rattled, to say the least. I wonder if you know what has him disturbed?"

She shook her head. She hadn't marked anything strange about him.

"Really?" Mr. Beaumont sounded surprised. "I suppose as he is now head of the family, he seeks to keep anything from you, which might upset you."

Upset her?

On the contrary, they usually told each other everything, as close as any brother and sister could be. Which reminded her again of Owen Burnley losing his sister Sophia. Strangely, her thoughts seemed to keep returning to the viscount.

"I see by your expression," Mr. Beaumont said, entirely mistaken, "that you are not undisturbed by the prospect of your brother getting into trouble."

"What trouble?" She was already fed up with his innuendo and intimation.

"It is not for me to say. I only urge you to stand by him, if something untoward comes to light. The company needs him at its helm."

Mr. Beaumont rose to his feet, and she did the same, feeling more confounded after their conversation than before.

"I do not un . . . understand," she confessed, aghast at the slightest faltering of her speech.

"Hopefully, you won't need to." Again, he took her hand, and once more, he kissed her knuckles.

She was hard-pressed not to wrench it from his grasp.

"I don't think you should tell him of our little talk," he advised.

Oh, she most definitely would. Adelia sighed, glad when the engineer had left.

In fact, as soon as her brother returned from his club, she cornered him.

"Are you well? Is something of import happening?"

Thomas wore his usual affable expression, however for the briefest of moments, she saw concern flash cross his features.

"Such as?" he asked.

"I'm sure I do not know."

Thomas cocked his head. "What is this all about, Dilly-girl?"

"You must ask Mr. Beaumont. He stopped by today and seemed worried about you."

At this, Thomas looked surprised. "I have no idea what that's about. Perhaps he really came to see you and to determine if you showed any interest in him."

She frowned. "Very well. We shall set it aside for now. At least he didn't declare his intent to court me."

"Would that truly be so terrible?"

"Absolutely," Adelia declared.

A‍s soon as Owen entered the Tourney's ballroom that night, trying to look amiable despite the constantly churning desire to punch someone, he searched for Lady Adelia. Not for pleasant social reasons, but on the advice of Westing's wife. Unfortunately, Lady Jane had no more knowledge of a handkerchief with an anvil than her husband.

"You must go to every social event," Lady Jane had advised him.

Owen had shaken his head. "And walk around demanding handkerchiefs? I shall find myself confined to an asylum."

"If you have a lady-friend who could help you," Lady Jane had suggested, "she would undoubtedly have better luck securing gentlemen's handkerchiefs than you. From my recollection, Owen, you have an entire battalion of ladies at your disposal."

With a sardonic grimace, he had told her, "Not an entire battalion, I promise you."

Moreover, the women whom he had wooed and left were not his friends. Each had wanted a proposal; each had wanted to become his viscountess. They all had been sorely disappointed.

Nonetheless, he might be able to enlist the aid of Lady Adelia since he had never wronged her. Unobtrusive, she would be able to sidle up to any number of gentlemen and obtain a handkerchief without drawing attention to what she was about. And since she didn't speak, much less appear to gossip, her task wouldn't spread like fire around the room.

If she was willing to help him.

To that end, he found her easily in the very place he'd always seen her, at the far end of the ballroom, against the wall, her head turned as if speaking to an invisible companion. She must have heard his footsteps, for she turned at his approach, verdant eyes widening slightly in alarm before she nodded by way of greeting.

She reminded Owen of a swan, with her long graceful neck, dipping to communicate, while all the time remaining silent, lovely, and regal.

"Good evening, Lady Adelia. I trust you will not be fainting tonight."

Her cheeks bloomed with color instantly.

What an idiotic thing to say! It was extremely ungentlemanly and impolite to refer to the spectacle of their last ballroom encounter. He almost slapped his hand to his forehead.

Why did she make him feel awkward? Probably because his usual conquests were chatty ladies who filled in the silences with inane banter, often loud and apt to make grand gestures, waving their gloved hands, swishing their fans, and jiggling the feathers in their hair, along with their cleavage directly under his gaze. They were bright and sparkly, glittering peacocks in comparison to Lady Adelia's serene swan.

She had a calm stillness about her, and that very quality would make him work harder to impress her.

He reconsidered his thoughts. *No!* He wasn't trying to impress her, merely obtain her assistance.

"Forgive me. I should not have brought that up. You look especially lovely tonight," he added. And she did, in a rich blue satin gown with cream-colored trim and pearl accents.

His flattery, no matter how genuine, did not work its usual magic. She didn't melt and flutter her eyelashes and make a moue of her lips. *Quite full and attractively shaped*, he noticed for the first time.

Nor did she shrug suggestively, causing the neckline of her gown to gape and give him a generous view down her décolletage. *More's the pity!*

Lady Adelia blinked at him and nodded again.

He leaned forward and spoke into her ear that was toward the wall, away from the crowd of dancers.

"I need to ask you a favor."

She drew back and shook her head.

"No?" He couldn't help but smile at her expression as if he'd demanded her last farthing or her firstborn. "But you don't even know what I am about to ask."

Leaning forward, she murmured, "Forgive me, my lord. Would you repeat yourself?"

And she turned her head to the wall so he could speak into her other ear.

Strange and stranger.

And all at once, he realized the utter inappropriateness of asking someone he barely knew to gather handkerchiefs from strangers. He couldn't do it. At least, not without becoming better acquainted with her and forming some modicum of friendship.

"Will you dance with me?"

She turned again, nearly knocking her nose against his. Then, she recoiled like a skittish horse.

He was going about this all wrong. Gesturing to the dance card dangling from her wrist, he asked, "May I?"

Lady Adelia slowly raised her arm, which he could see was trembling. He grasped hold of the small, white card, noticing her gaze had become fixed upon it. Owen drew a pencil out of his pocket, knowing his valet always put one in when he was attending a ball. Swiftly, he scrawled his name upon the first blank line. It wasn't hard to do since all the lines were blank, and she had no partners for any of the dances.

Frowning, he looked at her lovely face, watching while her glance rose from the card to meet his. Startled again by the rich greenness of her eyes, he was reminded of the hills of south Wales where his family kept their country home. One thing was blatantly clear. If Lady Adelia didn't insist on being a wallflower, she would have a full dance card. She was as desirable as any woman there. Moreso since she was an earl's daughter.

Regardless of both those facts, something about her was making his insides sizzle and dance.

Offering her a reassuring smile in the face of her social failure, a smile she did not return, Owen wrote his name again farther down the card. The space of an hour separating their two dances would not draw attention to their having a second one.

"I shall return to collect you when the music starts," he told her. "It should only be a few more minutes."

Still, she said nothing, acknowledging his words with another nod. He might as well be talking to the wallpaper behind her.

With a shallow bow, he left to go look for Whitely and found him easily enough, chatting up a young lady. Or rather, listening to her as she talked.

Whitely had the look Owen recognized, one of feigned interest while his friend's thoughts were obviously elsewhere, perhaps wondering if he would be able to maneuver the woman into a secluded alcove for a tryst. She couldn't possibly keep on nattering while being kissed.

"My cousin decided upon the roast beef, whereas many would have chosen the leg of lamb," the woman seemed to be saying, or maybe that was simply what Owen imagined he heard in the midst of her nonstop blather.

Without thinking, he interrupted her, "Do you have a handkerchief?"

With her mouth open, she turned her attention from Whitely, who barely seemed to notice she'd stopped speaking, to Owen. She blinked up at him, then laughed.

Owen didn't think his request was the least bit funny.

"Why, yes, my lord," the young lady said after a pause. "Are you in desperate need of blowing your nose?"

He growled with impatience. "Is that what passes for wit amongst the debutantes?"

She paled, compressing her lips, while Whitely bristled on her behalf.

"Here now, Burnley. Let's not forget we are in polite society."

It was damnably hard to think about being polite when someone in that very room might be holding the clue to the identity of his sister's murderer. He shrugged and tried again.

"If you have one about your person," Owen addressed the young woman once more, "may I see it?"

Obviously annoyed, she raised her arm to bring up her reticule, dangling from her wrist along with her dance card, which Owen noted was well-written upon. *What idiots in the ballroom would prefer this addlepated magpie to Lady Adelia?*

She opened the drawstrings of her beaded sack and withdrew a handkerchief with a flower pattern instead of plain white.

This, she held out to him.

He raised his hand in dismissal. "Never mind. I'll see you later, Whitely," he said and left his friend to the vapid little miss who started on about her tedious cousin again before Owen was out of earshot.

Snagging a glass of champagne from a passing server, he sipped it while searching the room for his next target. The men he knew, those who couldn't possibly have an anvil on their handkerchiefs, he dismissed at once. That still left a vast number of young swains, new to the social scene or not numbered among Owen's acquaintances.

Too many!

Despite Lady Jane's advice to enlist a female's assistance, he decided to continue the hunt on his own, at least for the time being. He tried a tall, scowling man, managing to get a look at his plain handkerchief before moving on to a stocky fellow with very dark eyebrows, someone who looked capable of wicked deeds.

Owen approached him, interrupting his conversation with others.

"May I borrow your handkerchief?" he asked.

The man frowned, but, after the briefest of hesitations, drew it out of his pocket. Owen saw at once it wasn't the one he sought but decided he'd best take it nonetheless. Nodding, he stuffed it in his pocket, gave a short bow, started to walk away.

"Don't you want to put your name on my dance card?" the man asked loudly, making Owen briefly halt his steps and causing some around them to chuckle.

Let it go, Owen told himself, wishing he hadn't paused at the man's rude question.

"Come along now. I can waltz with you as well as any of the ladies here," the man continued, enjoying the limelight. "Maybe better than some, and I'll even let you keep my kerchief as a token."

This sent those close enough to hear into peals of laughter.

Owen turned around. "Are you casting aspersions upon *my* masculinity or *your own*? Do you wish, indeed, to assume the lady's part in the dance?"

The man's face reddened. "How dare you?" He drew himself up to his full height, which wasn't quite past Owen's chin.

Owen shook his head, but his hands itched to punch the man in his now-florid face for no reason other than he was an annoying fool. Reaching into his pocket, he withdrew the linen square and tossed it back into its owner's face.

Regrettably, it landed more on the top of his head, hanging over his forehead and into his eyes.

"There, now we can pretend this never happened," Owen advised as the man whipped it off his head to the accompaniment of more raucous laughter.

"Shall we go outside?" came the stocky gentleman's next question.

Owen rolled his eyes. He hadn't intended to get into fisticuffs that evening. He just wanted to search for the blasted handkerchief.

"Sorry, I reserve my garden trysts for beautiful ladies," Owen said, which seemed to inflame the man further, although it was merely a joke. "Fine," Owen said, "let's take this outside. Do I need to enlist the services of a second?"

"What you'll need is your physician," his opponent advised and stalked past him to the closest French doors leading to the grounds behind the corner townhouse.

Owen followed, unable to entirely discount his own blame in this, while also admitting to a little anticipation at fighting a stranger outside of the pugilist's club. As soon as they rounded the shrubbery, barely out of sight of the ballroom, the man turned and put up his fists, which, in keeping with his build, were like compact hams.

"Are you positive you want to do this?" Owen asked him. After all, despite seeming to be about the same age, Owen had the advantage of height, long arms, and a general air of fitness.

"Shut your cakehole." The man hunched into a boxing stance.

"I think we should at least remove our jackets," Owen pointed out, beginning to shrug out of one sleeve.

His opponent took the opportunity to punch him in the gut. Hard!

"Dirty rotter," Owen muttered when he could breathe again, and he put his fists up immediately. The man threw another quick punch, which Owen dodged, then another that would have hit him uncomfortably low due to his opponent's lack of height.

Fully intending to have children someday, he didn't want this idiot to endanger such a possibility with a misplaced hit. Time to end this.

Owen punched him soundly in the stomach. Since they'd each landed a blow, he hoped his adversary would consider the matter at an end. However, the man socked him again, and once more, it was low in the stomach, which Owen tightened in time to deflect any damage.

"How'd you like that, missy?" he heard the challenger crow.

A red haze floated in front of Owen's eyes. And although he wasn't truly angry at this ridiculous chap, he could easily imagine some degenerate, one who fought dirty as this man did, taking out his spite upon Sophia.

With that, he let his fist fly directly into his opponent's ruddy face. The man's head cocked back, and his body followed. Undoubtedly no John Jackson, he was out cold.

"Christ!" Owen muttered. *Had his punch really been so hard?*

As a few surged forward, he realized others had followed them outside. *Good!* Let someone else wake up the wretch, offer a hand of truce, and tend his split lip or whatever injury he had.

It had been a most unsatisfying outlet for his anger. He hadn't got any closer to finding the handkerchief. And now his ribs hurt from the few punches the blighter had landed.

What was more lamentable, when Owen entered the ballroom, he realized the first dance had started. As many eyes turned to him, he knew word of the childish brawl had spread around the room through the hundred or so guests. It would be in the papers by morning. He didn't give a fig.

Quickly, he sought Lady Adelia, looking for her stunning blue dress. She was not on the dance floor, which was no surprise. Apparently, she hadn't made an effort to find a worthier partner. If her card still looked as it had earlier, he could easily partner her for the next dance or the one after that. All he had to do was locate her.

After a few minutes of searching, he saw her seated at a table with her brother, their heads close together, talking. Something inside him twisted with pain and envy. What he wouldn't give for another moment like that with Sophia.

As he approached, the young earl rose to his feet and waited. Owen bowed to him first, and next to Lady Adelia.

"My apologies for missing our dance, my lady. I hope I may make it up to you as your partner for the upcoming one."

Before she could respond, her brother spoke. "You assume she will dance with you after you treated her shabbily."

Owen looked from brother to sister. Lord Thomas Smythe was clearly offended by the slight, but Lady Adelia seemed more concerned with not drawing attention to their uncomfortably awkward tableau. She put a hand on her brother's sleeve.

"Sit, please, Thomas. It is no matter."

Owen felt a stab of shame. She didn't deserve to be embarrassed by the likes of him or her brother. For his part, he was a man of his word and, as far as he knew, he'd never left a promise to a lady unfulfilled, not even the pledge to dance with her.

"I would be grateful for the opportunity to make amends. May I have the next dance?" he asked again.

Lady Adelia stood, and Owen was certain, by her mild expression, she was going to acquiesce, but her brother shook his head.

"My sister is not to be trifled with. This was not the fifth or eighth dance when a man might be forgiven for mixing up his commitments. This was the *first* dance, and she was on the side of the dance floor, awaiting you. She will not do so again tonight."

Lord Smythe folded his arms. His sister pursed her lips, and Owen wondered if Lady Adelia would abide by her brother or make up her own mind.

"Thomas," she began.

"Dilly," her brother responded, his voice taking on a warning note.

She sighed and rolled her eyes, and in a flash, Owen again pictured Sophia. Anguish at the senseless way she'd been taken from his family filled him anew. She should be there, having fun, perhaps even dancing with Lord Smythe.

Lady Adelia was lucky to have the opportunity to squeeze every bit of joy from life. And curiously—wastefully—she wasn't taking advantage of the chances all around her at every gathering. She was squandering her youth.

"Let her dance with me, for God's sake," Owen bit out, feeling his fury surge. "It is not as if her card is filled or anyone else is lining up to set down his name upon it."

CHAPTER SIX

Lady Adelia gasped, and her gloved hand flew to her mouth. Her brother's face whitened as much as the previous stocky man's had reddened.

Strange, Owen thought, *how anger could alter someone's features in varying ways.* Moreover, his own rage had dissipated as quickly as it had come. These good people had nothing to do with Sophia or her murderer. He couldn't fathom why he'd caused Lady Adelia a moment's discomfort.

Belatedly, he realized how deeply he had insulted her. "What I meant to say, my lady, is how happy I am to put my name next to as many of the empty spaces as you will allow."

Her eyes widened at his second reference to the dismal state of her dance card. He was only trying to help. Instead, he was making a hash of it!

Looking distraught, Lady Adelia darted around the table and past him, presumably toward the ladies' retiring room.

Blazes! Owen expected her brother to call him out immediately. Perhaps he should set up a permanent encampment in the garden for boxing matches for the rest of the evening.

Lord Smythe shook his head, more with pity than anger. "You, my lord, are an ass. It is no wonder, at your age, you remain single and in want of a wife, despite your title and fortune."

Owen blinked. He'd never had a difficult time with the fairer sex, but he had never before encountered a woman such as Lady Adelia, one who didn't fawn all over him. Trying hard to make a good impression was a new experience.

"I apologize again for causing any consternation or distress," Owen said. "When you see your sister again, please give her my highest regards."

Smythe stared at him, his face blank. He'd mastered an effective stony-faced expression for someone his age. In fact, Owen quite liked the man. Then a notion occurred to him. Since he had already made himself a nuisance, he had nothing to lose by asking to see his handkerchief.

Smythe, however, took that instant to nod and walk away in the direction Lady Adelia had taken. Owen decided to leave them in peace. At least for the time being. He fully intended to claim his dance later in the night, recalling without doubt, it was the ninth dance. Meanwhile, he would search out Whitely and see if he'd found any clues.

ADELIA WAS EQUAL PARTS angry and mortified as she touched up her hair in the ladies' retiring room, patting water upon any wayward strands daring to stick up. She hadn't wanted to dance with anyone, and definitely not with him! Why had Lord Burnley approached her and shattered her peaceful existence if he'd only intended to humiliate her? She'd stood on the edge of the dance floor for the first dance, awaiting him, sticking out like a sore thumb, until every other female had been claimed and the dance had begun. *An absolute nightmare!*

She'd been forced to walk away, keeping her head up as though unbothered, eyes averted as usual so as not to invite conversation. As she'd made her way back to her brother's table, disappointment had warred with mortification. It had been the first time in a long time that she'd been asked for the first dance. A small part of her had actually looked forward to being in the viscount's arms.

Foolishly, she'd even wondered if her partner had come to some misfortune. Soon after, she'd learned Lord Burnley had been out in the garden engaging in pugilistic violence! And he'd had the nerve to show up and insult her again.

She looked at her reflection and sent a silent prayer that soon Thomas would allow her to stay home.

An hour later, she was back in her favorite spot—a long drape at her back, giving her a backdrop against which she could hide. For it seemed she was unseen if she stood unmoving against it, the drape effectively drawing people's eyes away from her.

The ball had not been entirely a waste of her time. She'd heard a most interesting conversation of adultery by the very perpetrators themselves and, minutes later, been the sole audience for a breakup. A young lady told a young man his yearly income would not be enough to secure her hand. Adelia considered the man fortunate to find out before the spendthrift female sent him into ruin *after* marriage.

Suddenly, Lord Burnley was in front of her again. He had the grace—and good sense—to look humble, chagrined, and apologetic. In fact, his entire handsome face had taken on the aspect of a naughty puppy.

She sighed at her own foolish imaginings. He was a man like any other who was attempting to get what he wanted. And for some reason, what he wanted was to dance with her!

"Our dance is in a very few minutes," he reminded her.

She couldn't help rolling her eyes.

"Why?" she asked.

He raised an eyebrow and reached for her dance card. She flinched but let him lift it from her wrist.

"Because I wrote my name right there." He pointed to it.

"Why?" she persisted.

"Why not?" he countered. "This is a ball, after all."

"Why me?" Adelia didn't want him to dance with her for pity's sake. He had no idea how much happier she was when not leaving her safe place by the wall. *Except she couldn't deny the tremor of excitement.* What's more, she didn't want to be disappointed a second time that night.

At her persistent questioning, he blew out an exasperated breath. "You are jesting, surely. I wouldn't think you one to fish for compliments, my lady."

She lifted her chin. Certainly, she wasn't *fishing*, as he put it.

When she said nothing, he added, "I wish to dance with you because I have already made a promise to do so."

She dismissed that with a wave of her hand. She would like to tell him what he could do with his promise. They were both being entirely impolite and breaking the rules of a ball. He should not press the issue if she didn't wish to dance with him, and she . . . well, she was supposed to either let him down easily with the whitest of lies or accept her fate and dance with him.

"And because, truly, there is no one else I have any desire to dance with," he added. "You are easily the loveliest, most interesting woman in the room."

She inclined her head at his words. *Why would he say such things?*

"You have a very calming way about you, my lady. Composed and beautiful. I confess, I am intrigued."

Her? Intriguing? Gracious, what nonsense! Inside, however, a trickle of pleasure slivered through her. Most people thought her awkward and strange. Intriguing and composed sounded better.

"More than that," he added. "I'm terribly sorry for missing our dance earlier. I hope you will accept my apology and dance with me."

"All right," she agreed.

He leaned forward. "Pardon me, did you say yes?"

Adelia nodded, and his face split briefly into a satisfied smile, making him more breath-stealingly handsome, if possible. The smile disappeared as quickly as it had arrived, replaced by a far more reserved expression befitting a man in mourning. At any rate, she allowed him to take her gloved hand and lead her toward the dance floor as the previous dance ended. Theirs was to be a waltz, which she enjoyed. At least, it was a dance she most liked watching. Fortunately, she could perform it adequately, as well.

He bowed, she curtsied, and he took her into his arms, his black mourning gloves somehow having survived fisticuffs in the garden and still looked pristine.

The moment their bodies were close and his hands were upon her, her heart began to gallop. It had happened previously when they'd danced, but she'd ignored it as merely the reaction to being close to a man. Since that time, she'd discovered it only happened when *he* was the man to whom she was close.

Nevertheless, it wouldn't do to get overly sentimental about the viscount. He was the infamous Lord Burnley, admirer of many women, some said lover of many, too. Some went so far as to call him a rake.

"We *have* danced before," he recalled as they began to turn. "I remember now."

"A quadrille."

"Not much talking during one of those," he pointed out.

"And a Lancier," she added. Adelia remembered each second of being in his arms, although, at the time, she could tell he had hardly noticed with whom he'd danced.

"That dance is also not conducive to a *tête-a-tête*. So, we have danced twice at least," he said, and then twirled her expertly around the end of the dance floor before they started up the other side.

She knew he was trying to determine why he didn't recall a flirty conversation during their dances, nor over lemonade or champagne afterward. She never lingered with a partner for either if she could help it. And her partners always seemed only too glad to get rid of her, particularly if she pretended her ugly laugh.

Without warning, a longing to converse with Lord Burnley arose in her. *Perhaps a little light banter?* If only she was confident she wouldn't stutter from sheer nervousness. Yet, she wasn't sure, and thus, she simply sent him a wistful glance from under her lashes.

He saw it, and his hand tightened upon her waist. Moreover, he leaned close and said something. Unluckily, it was toward her bad ear, and she couldn't imagine what he might have said.

She offered him a small, noncommittal smile. Whatever he'd said, he didn't seem bothered by her lack of response. Hopefully, it hadn't been about a bug in her hair or something in her teeth.

After their waltz, feeling exhilarated—ready to return to her post by the draperies and muse on how wonderful their dance had been—she almost forgot to take his arm. At the last moment, he made an awkward grab for her hand and placed it on his forearm.

"This way, Lady Adelia, to the lemonade and champagne," he offered.

She shook her head. *What if he thought she could carry on some flirtatious or seductive conversation?* She nearly tripped over her own feet with fear.

"Come now," he urged her. "On the dance floor, I asked if you would, and you didn't say no."

Because she hadn't heard him.

Since the rest of her dance card was empty, she could hardly beg off due to a prior commitment. Thus, she let Lord Burnley lead her to the refreshment table. In any case, there was only one more dance prior to the intermission, and it was a treat to get a cold drink ahead of the horde of dancers who would rush the tables.

Normally, she stayed put and out of the way during intermission, or, if her brother was not escorting a young lady, he would bring her a glass of lemonade or burnt champagne.

"Will your brother escort you downstairs for supper?" Lord Burnley asked as they sipped champagne and watched the other dancers finish out the set with a Mazurka.

After intermission, there would be four more dances before their hosts called them to a meal in the two rooms set out for dining on the lower floor.

Would Thomas be free? She had missed out on more than one meal when her brother was otherwise occupied. In such instances, she would let everyone go into the prepared supper and usually remained in the ballroom. That wasn't always as easy to do as she hoped since the hostess of the night would try to make certain any stragglers had an escort. More than once, she'd had to dodge a well-meaning gentleman sent to look for her by hiding in the ladies' retiring room.

It made for a long night, but an easy way to keep one's figure trim.

In response to Lord Burnley, Adelia took the opportunity to search the floor for Thomas. He was with a young lady whom she'd seen once or twice. She could tell by the bored look upon her brother's face, this was not the love match he was hoping for. And who knew if he would be partnered with someone for the important fourteenth dance?

It was tradition for the gentleman during the last dance directly before supper to escort the lady to the meal and sit with her.

She lifted a shoulder. It was out of her hands.

Lord Burnley frowned, then she saw the instant he realized what he needed to do.

"We have only danced once. Will you dance the fourteenth dance with me?"

She glanced at her card, knowing it was empty but wondering what the dance would be prior to dinner. A Caledonian.

She couldn't think of a reason to say no. Besides, she desperately wanted to say yes. Of course, she couldn't speak for her bubbling excitement. She would probably stutter out a long series of sounds, and he would walk away from the embarrassing spectacle.

She nodded quickly and emphatically.

At her response, Lord Burnley didn't hesitate to formalize their arrangement. "May I have the honor of escorting you to supper? I believe Lord and Lady Tourney will have something beyond the mere obligatory soup and chicken."

In four years, this was the first time a man had specifically invited her to dine, and not because she was his dance partner at the time of the supper break.

"You have a beautiful smile," Lord Burnley added, and she hadn't realized she'd been beaming at him.

"Yes," she said.

"Yes, you know you are beautiful?" he teased. "Or yes, you will dine with me?"

She felt her cheeks warm. She was practically having a flirtation.

"Yes . . . to dining, my lord."

To her delight, it worked out. Thomas had a partner for the Caledonian, and thus, she didn't have to worry with whom her brother would dine.

Having someone other than Thomas draw out her chair, Adelia felt mature and entirely feminine in a way she never had before. While she hadn't keenly felt the lack nor believed herself missing out, she now recognized a world of difference between the comfortable meal she would have had with her brother and the deliciously nerve-wracking experience she was having with the garrulous, charming, popular Lord Burnley.

Already understanding her aversion to loquacity, he more than made up for it, ensuring she had everything she needed, commenting on the various courses to make her laugh, and naughtily making sport of some around them who were not in hearing range. Most fortunately, he sat on her left, allowing her to catch everything he said.

It was the most enjoyable dance supper she'd ever attended, and she was sorry when the dessert of sponge cake with strawberries and cream arrived, signaling the meal was nearing its end.

"We have had two dances, but in many of the polite balls, couples are now allowed four."

"Are they?" The words came out unbidden without her worrying whether she would stutter.

"Oh, indeed. Thus, since we are having such a fine evening, may I claim you for two more?"

She glanced at her card. There were seven dances left, and for the first time ever, she wasn't sorry to see the remainder of the ball stretch out ahead of her.

"Yes," Adelia agreed and held her wrist out to him.

He chose another waltz and a polka. "I shall claim you on time. I promise, I will not let you down," Lord Burnley vowed. "I also cannot leave you unattended." He looked particularly discomfited at the notion of doing so.

"Absurd," she said. No man had ever worried about that, not with her. While she knew it was expected for a woman to go from one dance partner to the next before being returned to a chaperone or to her male escort for the evening, she and Thomas had done things differently. Mostly because her brother knew she would never be involved in anything remotely improper.

"Nevertheless, I have a task to do," Lord Burnley said, "and thus, I must leave you until our next dance. May I take you to your brother's table?"

"Of course."

As it turned out, Thomas showed up as they reached it.

Lord Burnley bowed over her hand, nodded to her brother, who stared with surprise, and then took his leave.

"That was unexpected," Thomas said, "as was Burnley being your dinner companion. I take it you accepted his watery apology."

"I did." She gave her brother a smile. "The viscount was truly sorry for his behavior earlier. Besides, I enjoyed his company tonight. We have another dance coming up."

She decided it best not to mention they actually had two in case her brother read too much into it.

He cocked his head. "You know Burnley isn't a schoolboy or an angel."

Apparently, he *was* already reading into it.

"I know." Everyone knew Lord Burnley had courted many women, and most of those courtships had begun and ended in the ballroom. And in rather short order, too. She'd been witness to many of them over the past few years.

Pretty, sparkly young women—all of them engaging, talkative, commanding the attention of the men around them as a nectar-filled flower drew the bees.

"Why is he suddenly paying court to you?"

She felt a wave of misery crash over her. She knew what her brother meant. Hadn't she asked Lord Burnley the very same question earlier? He'd said there was no one else he wished to dance with and that she was intriguing.

How foolish of her to listen to him! On the other hand, he hadn't behaved in an untoward fashion. It wasn't as if he'd tried to get her outside into the gardens.

Why hadn't he? She'd seen him lead any number of women into secluded situations over the years. But not her. She scanned the room. He'd said he had a task. He wasn't dancing with anyone else. He was clearly making the rounds, talking to his peers.

"I don't know," she confessed to Thomas. "I am a good dancer, and I'm not unpleasant to look at. Am I?"

"Good God, of course not! You're as pretty as any woman here. Even I can see that, and I'm your brother. I meant Burnley must know I am keeping an eye on him, and he also is undoubtedly aware of your unblemished reputation. So, if he's up to his usual tricks, he will be sadly thwarted. Unless he considers you a challenge he cannot resist. In which case, I shall end up calling him out, pistols at dawn, and all that."

She wasn't entirely certain her brother was joking.

"And if he doesn't show up on time for your next dance," he left an unspoken threat hanging.

Luckily, Lord Burnley did, and in plenty of time for Thomas to get to his dance partner, too.

"Were you worried?" Lord Burnley asked.

"No," Adelia said. "My brother was."

He laughed, and it was a smooth and sensual sound that resonated deep within her. However, he stopped far too quickly, his grin replaced with a somber face, an expression of regret, maybe shame.

She thought she knew why. He considered laughing to be inappropriate after his sister's death. Many would condemn him for being out and for dancing, and assuredly for laughing.

All at once, Adelia realized she hadn't seen him on the dance floor since reading about Lady Sophia's passing in the papers. She'd encountered him now twice at balls, vastly altered from the Lord Burnley of a month ago. He had not appeared relaxed or especially cordial, neither escorting young ladies inside nor out into the gardens. And he most definitely hadn't been dancing.

Except with her. Again, why her?

She took the opportunity to look into his vivid blue eyes, like cobalt marble, polished to a glistening sheen.

"Yes, my lady?

She shrugged.

"Tell me," Lord Burnley demanded, his hand on the small of her back, guiding her expertly around the parquet floor.

"I cannot imagine why you are here," she said carefully, meticulously getting each word out.

He drew back. But instead of looking confused, he nodded.

"Indeed," the viscount agreed but told her no more.

"Why?" she persisted.

This time, he sighed. "Another place and time, perhaps," he said, and Adelia took that to mean he wished to confide in her but not there.

They finished the dance in silence, although not grimly. Her happiness at the success of the evening so far, kept her feet floating across the floor. And despite his earlier subdued demeanor, he offered her a satisfied nod when he escorted her back to her table.

In another half hour or so, he would claim her for their last dance, and after that, her best ball, perhaps her best night ever, would be over.

"One to go," she murmured, not thinking how that might sound.

"Is this all so painful, Lady Adelia?" he asked without losing his good nature.

She shook her head, feeling her cheeks warm. He would think her ungrateful and spoiled if she didn't appreciate the good fortune of a gathering such as tonight's. The music, food, and especially her dance partner had all been sublime.

"Not at all," she assured him.

At the table, there was no sign of Thomas.

"I cannot leave you here alone."

"I am not a child," she said.

"That's the problem," he quipped solemnly. "You are a beautiful young woman, ripe prey for some despicable scoundrel."

She shook her head. Glancing around, there were people close by, chatting, laughing, drinking, and dancing. No one looked the least bit threatening.

"Go," she urged, for he didn't have too long until their last dance.

He scowled and remained standing by her chair, searching the room, probably for Thomas.

If Lord Burnley had wanted to sit with her and be sociable, she would almost have welcomed it. She would have tilted her good ear toward him and tried to converse without making a nuisance of herself. Yet, seeing how he wanted to escape but felt compelled to stay with her, she grew irritated.

"Go," Adelia repeated more forcefully. "It's my fourth Season!"

Having to remind him how long in the tooth she was and how firmly she was set upon the shelf ruined her mood. She was an old maid, and no one was about to swoop over and compromise her. She had made sure of that with her behavior over the past years.

He blinked at her. "Yes, I suppose it is. A mystery I might have to put my mind to solving someday soon."

What on earth did he mean by that? She almost believed he was interested in her.

After another moment's hesitation, the viscount said, "Very well. You are not a debutante, after all, yet I do feel terribly unchivalrous leaving you unattended. It's simply that I have—"

"A task," she supplied. It was the first time she'd interrupted anyone in years. It felt . . . rather good.

"Yes," he agreed. Taking her hand, he bowed over it and said, "I shall return in time."

She nodded. When he leaned over her, she caught a whiff of his cologne as she had when they'd danced. Something woodsy, she would say if asked to describe it. It made her want to sniff his neck.

Surprised by her own yearning, she watched his tall form walk away. For her, their next dance could not come soon enough.

And then, he ruined it all by not showing up. Again. The last waltz began, and Lord Burnley was nowhere to be seen.

CHAPTER SEVEN

Luckily, Thomas had returned and was showing signs of ennui. Not telling her brother about Lord Burnley's second egregious outrage, Adelia crumpled her sparse dance card and shoved it into her reticule!

"Ready?" she asked. "To depart, I mean?"

"Yes." Her brother sounded older than his years. "By all means, let's go."

Without a backward glance, Adelia left the Tourney's ballroom and descended the great staircase to await their carriage.

Despite the disappointing ending, she had experienced how fabulous a ball could be with the right partner. Perhaps that's how all those other young ladies had felt, too, during the week or so Lord Burnley had graced them with his attention.

Adelia hadn't been able to hold onto the viscount's regard for even an entire evening. Perhaps it was her own fault. She shouldn't have reminded him how many Seasons she'd had. It truly was shameful. In the morning, she would press her brother again to let her retire before she needed a cane upon the dance floor.

However, the next day, her brother was gone when she went down to breakfast. Mr. Lockley said Lord Smythe would be out most of the day and reminded her she had a boating party to attend in the early afternoon.

Wrinkling her nose, Adelia immediately considered sending word of a sudden headache. After all, Thomas wasn't there to push her to go. Albeit, if a megrim were to seem genuine, she wouldn't be able to send word until the last minute, which gave her hours to worry over whether she should engage in such subterfuge.

To take her mind off the potential embarrassment of boating, forced to join one of many small parties in which everyone else chatted away while she sat silently, Adelia turned to her writing. She had plenty to write about, including her own exciting, new sensations from the previous night to flavor her stories.

The doorbell rang at one minute past eleven o'clock. When Mr. Lockley entered, she was prepared for him to say Mr. Beaumont was there again.

"Lord Burnley wishes to know if you are receiving visitors, my lady."

Lord Burnley?

She glanced down to remind herself what gown Penny had laid out that morning. Not a bad choice for her first outfit of the day, a pale green dress with gray trim. Certainly not a ballgown, but good enough for receiving visitors and going out to the shops.

Good enough for meeting with a man who'd left her without a dance partner. Twice!

"Show him in and bring tea, please."

"Yes, my lady. Shall I send in Penny?"

She hadn't considered a chaperone, but Lord Burnley, for all his scowls, terseness, and clenched fists, didn't alarm her the way other men did.

"No. I'll ring if I need her."

Mr. Lockley raised an eyebrow but said nothing. A few seconds later, he showed in Lord Burnley, who was dressed impeccably in dark gray.

The viscount did not approach too closely, nor take her hand. Instead, he bowed deeply, and she returned the gesture with a curtsey.

Wishing she could launch into a pleasant welcome and tell him how unexpected his visit was, in lieu of such grace, she cleared her throat. No words came, so she waited for him to speak.

Clasping his hands behind his back, he stared at the floor by her feet.

"Frankly, I'm surprised you agreed to see me after last night," he began.

She shrugged, which made him raise his gaze to hers and shake his head.

"You are not like other women."

She almost gasped. *What an awful thing to say! How could he know——?*

"You are kind and forgiving. I can only imagine the tongue-lashing I would receive if I'd behaved thusly toward any other female member of the *ton*."

Adelia realized he was complimenting her and not referring to her shyness or her stuttering.

"You had a reason," she suggested softly, carefully, slowly.

His eyes lit up, and he nodded. "I did, in fact. Thank you for understanding."

Thereupon, the kitchen maid brought in the tea tray.

"Tea?" Adelia offered.

Lord Burnley hesitated before replying, "Thank you. I will." He gestured for her to sit so he could as well.

As she poured, Adelia hoped he would enlighten her on his reason for not making it to their final dance. He didn't. Instead, he watched her with scrutinizing eyes, nearly making her hand shake as she passed him a cup and saucer.

OWEN THOUGHT HER THE sweetest of females, while having a strength about her, too. He was grateful she hadn't forced him to discuss his ridiculous quest of the previous night, which had taken him upstairs into their host's private apartments. He'd unforgivably ransacked Lord Tourney's wardrobe, looking for handkerchiefs. When the notion took hold of him, it was like a fevered madness.

By the time he'd returned to the ballroom, Lady Adelia had left.

As she raised her cup to her lips, he made a decision.

"May I escort you *somewhere*?" he asked rashly, his tongue getting ahead of him.

She frowned at his cryptic query.

"That is to say, I wish to take you to the theatre. Tomorrow night," he amended as a plan formed. "Do you enjoy Shakespeare?"

She nodded.

They were back to barely speaking, it seemed.

"You do, or yes, you will go with me?"

She hesitated a long while, and he feared he was about to be shot down like a pheasant on the first day of October.

"Yes, I like Shakespeare," she agreed and added, "We have a box."

"No matter. My family has a box at the Theatre Royal. One of Shakespeare's gloomy history plays is there at present. One of the *Richards* or the *Henrys*."

Slowly, she said, "Perhaps it is *you*, my lord, who does not enjoy Shakespeare."

While her words were proffered with no hint of a jesting tone, she was plainly teasing him, a good sign, suggesting a burgeoning relationship at the very least. He wanted that.

He wanted her! The notion struck him out of the blue, and he couldn't gainsay it, despite knowing it was a dreadful time to form an attachment. He was mourning Sophia and desperate to find her killer. Nevertheless, some feelings couldn't be tamped down. His body was already attuned to Adelia's from dancing with her. He knew her citrusy perfume, her generous curves, her warmth. And he wanted all the rest of her that he hadn't yet seen.

"May I fetch you tomorrow night and escort you to the theatre?"

Despite having asked her once already, this direct question caused her to jiggle the cup she was lifting to her pretty lips. Whether with alarm or happy anticipation, Owen couldn't fathom, but drops of tea spilled over the skirt of her day gown.

"Drats!" she exclaimed, perhaps the loudest word he'd heard from her.

After sending him a tremulous smile as if he might be offended, she yanked a handkerchief from her sleeve.

His attention instantly focused on that small square of linen as she dabbed at her skirt.

Open it, he silently ordered, for he couldn't clearly see anything more than its whiteness and that there might be an edge of lace.

After wiping at the tea spots, which had almost disappeared into the green of her gown, she was about to tuck it back into her sleeve. Rising from the sofa cushion, he lurched forward across the low table to snatch it from her hand.

"Oh!" she said, surprised, her lovely eyes staring at him.

"Um . . ." He had no explanation, so he flicked it open. It had no anvil, of course. *How stupid of him!* He looked at her. "May I assist you?"

Her expression was clear. If he leaned over to touch her, she would undoubtedly shriek. He glanced toward the inevitable potted fern at one end of the room, the domain of the housemaid predictably brought in to protect her mistress. Strangely, the chair beside the plant was empty. It was his turn to be surprised.

"My apology," he said, handing back her handkerchief. "I overstepped."

She nodded, tucking her kerchief back into the cuff of her sleeve.

Owen decided to depart before he behaved incorrigibly once again. Setting down his saucer, he stood.

"I shall be here at eight o'clock," he promised, although she hadn't exactly said yes.

"Will you?" she asked, rising to her feet. Again, she was teasing him.

"If I'm not, you may send your brother out to blister my hide."

Her smile fell. Perhaps the reference was too violent for her.

"I will be here," he promised.

As he rounded the table between them and took her hand, he hoped she wasn't skittish. She wore no gloves, having been—he spied the tablet and pen—writing letters and apparently not preparing to go out. It was a blissful experience to touch her bare skin, brushing across her knuckles with his thumb. Slightly inappropriate, he did so anyway.

She blinked up at him, and he could see the pulse beating wildly in the hollow of her throat. The knowledge he'd caused this reaction sent a jagged spear of desire racing through him.

Unexpected. Unwanted. Unstoppable. Owen released her hand.

"Tomorrow evening, then, Lady Adelia?"

She still hadn't said yes, but this time, she nodded in acquiescence, silently glancing at her knuckles.

In a minute, he was back in his carriage, half-astonished at having made an arrangement to see the strangely captivating Lady Adelia. He would not tell his friends or his family. It was too soon to be going out for any purpose other than to hunt down the murderer, even if that hunt took him to balls and dinner parties.

However, there could be no reason for going to the theatre with a lovely, eligible lady except for his own pleasure. And as he sat back against the comfortable squabs, he realized he had no right to any such indulgence, not until he'd seen justice done for Sophia.

What a terrible brother he was! Yet he could hardly go back on his word, or Lady Adelia would think him a heel of the lowest order. He would escort her to the theatre, but he would not invite her out again until the murder was solved.

ADELIA COULD THINK OF nothing else. She was unable to write her novel, and she even forgot to claim a pounding headache to escape the afternoon's dreaded gathering on the banks of the Thames. Instead, she drifted on a cloud of anticipation to the boating venue, not minding when she was put in the last rowboat and ignored by the rest of the group.

She was going to the theatre with Lord Owen Burnley! *Gracious!*

Over dinner, she mentioned it to her brother, whose utter astonishment mirrored her own.

"What is he up to?"

"Whatever can you mean, Thomas? He wants to see a Shakespearean play, and he wants to take me." She had no idea why but didn't care. "I thought you wanted me to remain out in society."

"Yes, I do," he agreed. "All the same, I doubt there is much to be gained by your being with Burnley. Hardly the steady suitor type. I don't imagine he's got marriage in mind, either. Who will accompany you?"

She tilted her head and sent him an imploring smile.

"Are *you* free tomorrow night?" As she asked, she realized having her brother as a chaperone was not ideal. The two men had got off to a bad start.

"No, I'm sorry to say. I'm not available."

"Very well," Adelia said with a prickling of relief. "I shall take Penny along."

After he questioned her on the particular theatre she and Lord Burnley were attending, Thomas added, "As it turns out, Dilly-girl, I'm busy tonight, too."

"Are you?" Adelia asked him. "I don't recall anything to which either of us was invited."

"No, nothing with the *ton*," he said, shooting her his boyish grin. "I'm meeting up with a friend."

"Who? Where?"

He raised a brow. "You do sound like a prying older sister."

"I *am* your older sister. And I simply want to know where you will be. What if I need you? What if something happens?"

He blinked at her. "I won't be available for a few hours. I shall see you in the morning, and I urge you not to wait up."

With that, he took his leave.

How curious! It was unusual behavior for her brother. Nor had he asked how the boating had gone, and she had the feeling he wouldn't have noticed if she hadn't attended. That gave her food for thought indeed. If he remained distracted, she could probably get away with eschewing any number of frightful outings.

"Do hurry, Penny. Lord Burnley will be here any minute."

Despite years of preparing for dinner parties and dances, that night, Adelia keenly felt butterflies in her stomach. Being picked up at her home was an entirely new experience, making her heartbeat gallop. Moreover, she had never dressed to please a man. One didn't need to look alluring when one was trying to be invisible.

She didn't know exactly what she wanted to be that night. She only knew she did *not* want to disappoint, neither Lord Burnley, nor herself. This might be her one night out before she retired from society—and with a man as handsome as Adonis! She couldn't deny she was massively attracted to him. *How many men had she danced with over the past four Seasons?* Actually, not that many given her off-putting ways. In any case, not a one had struck her as memorable until now.

She remembered each of the dances she'd had with Lord Burnley, both times amazed he'd asked her. The first time was during her first Season. He had nearly tripped over her and, thus, wrote his name on her card out of politeness since they were standing five inches from one another.

The second time, at the beginning of her third Season, one of the matrons had sent him in her direction. She'd watched it happen, seen his face fall when directed toward her. But he had squared his shoulders and done his duty, and she'd escaped his presence quickly afterward, doing him a kindness by leaving him to chase the more desirable ladies.

As Penny chose the perfect floor-length, emerald-green mantle to match Adelia's gown, she heard his carriage draw up and ran to the window.

The Burnley clarence was directly outside with two prancing horses tossing their heads. The coachman opened the carriage door, and out stepped the viscount. This was truly happening. Adelia had half-expected him not to come.

"I guess it's time," she said, mostly to herself. Penny nodded and opened the bedchamber door as they heard Mr. Lockley in the foyer downstairs greeting Lord Burnley.

"You look very smartly dressed," Adelia told her maid, who wore a dove-gray gown, perfectly starched.

Nevertheless, when Adelia descended, Lord Burnley's approving gaze was fixed on her alone, and she almost bolted back up the stairs.

He removed his hat and gloves and bowed to her, and as she came closer, he took her gloved hand while she curtsied to him.

"I am glad you agreed to go out tonight," he said.

She nodded her agreement. *Very glad indeed!*

He popped his top hat back upon his head and snugged his black gloves onto his large hands, and then, she let him lead her outside. After helping her into his luxurious carriage, she saw him turn, possibly to assist Penny inside as well. However, with a cloak clasped around her, the maid scampered up onto the spare seat next to the viscount's driver.

After a pause, Lord Burnley climbed in and sat facing her.

"You are a most unusual female," he said into the silence.

Adelia didn't know to what he referred, so she said nothing.

"I would think you would want your maid *in* the carriage with us," Lord Burnley added, taking her measure.

She flinched. *Did he think ill of her?* No one had ever questioned her virtue, so she'd thought nothing of being alone with him. Since Adelia was normally with Thomas, her lady's maid had always been given a choice to sit inside or outside. Tonight, with the weather being warm, her maid had chosen to sit up top. Next to the coachman, Penny had the freedom to look around and to converse as she wished.

In the future, Adelia would instruct her maid to sit with her, despite how the girl would have to remain silent by custom.

"I trust you," Adelia explained to him after a pause. And she did. There was something innately decent about Lord Burnley. She'd never felt the least threatened or intimidated by him, even when he was storming across the ballroom chasing or dragging some poor soul.

He chuckled at her statement. "Most ladies who instruct their maid to sit atop the coach *want* me to make an overture toward them. They aren't worrying over my trustworthiness, I assure you. They are hoping I will, in fact, compromise them and thus feel obliged to offer for them. Therefore, you see, my lady, it is I who trusts you. Normally, I insist on the chaperone sitting within the carriage so I cannot be accused of anything."

That had never occurred to her. *How manipulative her fellow females could be!*

Before she could consider a response—or an excuse for the fairer sex—he said, "You look extremely beautiful tonight. The gown brings out the color of your eyes."

His compliment brought her first blush of the evening. Adelia could feel her cheeks grow warm. Glancing down, she noticed her mantle had parted to reveal her gown. She'd worn the green silk for the very reason he mentioned, and she'd added a single diamond pendant that sparkled as it swung on the short gold chain at her throat.

Penny had suggested emerald jewelry, especially ear bobs, but Adelia had feared they would compete.

When she said nothing, he said, "I hope you enjoy the theatre tonight."

She hadn't been to any theatre for over a year, and this was the first time without her brother or father. A smile tugged at her lips.

"You have a lovely smile," Lord Burnley said, "and dimples to better it."

Indubitably, her cheeks flamed and, infused with happiness, she could do nothing but continue smiling. *Or maybe, she was permitted to reciprocate.*

Taking a deep breath and speaking carefully, she managed, "I like the dark plum of your waistcoat."

His eyes widened, and she hoped she hadn't made a mistake in commenting.

"Dear lady, I appreciate that. I have felt out of sorts lately and have not wanted to put in an effort. Tonight, for you, I did hope to look satisfactory."

"You succeeded," she said, causing him to smile.

Then, all at once, he sobered as his gaze caressed her from head to foot.

Wondering what had caused the change, she leaned forward, about to ask him, when unexpectedly, he also advanced, captured her face with his large, gloved hands, and kissed her.

CHAPTER EIGHT

Adelia gasped against his lips, but the kiss didn't stop. Rather, Lord Burnley deepened it—if such was the right word for how their mouths fit together so perfectly when he tilted his head slightly.

She remembered to breathe through her nose. He smelled divinely of sandalwood and Pears soap. For a moment, as the new sensations coursed through her, she forgot she was in a carriage, settled on the comfy leather squabs. She might have been anywhere, even floating in the air, as nothing else seemed to exist, only his hands cradling her cheeks and his mouth kissing hers, tenderly and firmly.

Her hands remained in her lap until she suddenly realized she was reaching toward him and touching his pantlegs, specifically resting her palms upon his thighs.

An instant later, he broke away, releasing her. Only then did Adelia open her eyes, which she hadn't realized she'd closed. Opposite her, Lord Burnley wore a look of shock and consternation.

"I apologize," he offered at once. "Do you wish for me to turn the carriage around?"

Was she supposed to be affronted by his kiss? She wasn't. She was thrilled. Her body still hummed with pleasure, and her lips felt oddly plump and warm.

"No." She touched her gloved hand to her mouth while he watched.

"I don't know what came over me," he confessed. "It was sheer impulse. I didn't think before I . . . That is, you look so ravishing, which is no excuse, of course. And you're very calm and inviting, and I don't know what I'm saying."

Unexpectedly, a giggle rose in her throat. After all, he was an experienced man, and that was her first kiss, which had been beyond any expectation. Yet, *he* was the one babbling and discomfited.

Adelia had many thoughts, but one clear one—she wanted him to kiss her again. However, socially inexperienced as she was, even she knew it would be improper for her to ask. If he believed she might want to return home after such a delicious intimacy, he would think her entirely unsuitable to keep company with if she boldly requested another kiss.

After managing to stifle her desire to laugh, giddy with the delight flowing through her, she said, "I am looking forward to the evening ahead."

He shook his head, looking confounded. "I supposed that's what happens when you let your chaperone sit on top."

She shrugged.

"Very well. From here on out, I shall be on my best behavior," Lord Burnley promised.

That was a little disappointing, but Adelia assumed another impulsive kiss might be forthcoming in any case. Unless . . .

"Did *you* enjoy it?" she asked.

His eyes widened briefly. "The kiss?"

She nodded. If he said no, she might want him to turn the carriage around after all. For it would be mortifying to have a man take such a liberty and not appreciate it.

"Yes!" he assured her. "Very much. It's just, I've never been asked."

"Truly?" She couldn't imagine not wanting to know.

"I think most women assume the man enjoys kissing them," he mused.

"And do you?"

He frowned. "I do not believe this is a proper course of discussion."

"Isn't it?" Adelia asked, wondering why not.

"I think I know why you stay quiet most of the time."

She drew back, feeling rebuked. Strangely, he had seemed the sort of man to whom she could say anything.

"No, please," Lord Burnley begged at once, leaning forward again and taking both her hands in his. "Do not go all sullen and silent on me. I spoke in jest. For years, I haven't heard a word from you, and now every other phrase out of your mouth seems provocative. You are the most refreshing female with whom I've ever conversed. I am repeating myself when I say you are not like most women."

"We are all individuals, are we not?" She certainly didn't find men to be similar creatures at all. Her father had been brutish, and her brother was like a knight, but most men frightened or bored her. Then, there was Owen Burnley.

"Yes," he agreed, "but many, if not most, on the marriage mart are more similar than not. Let me think about your questions." He cocked his head. "No female has ever asked me about a kiss because I believe they don't really care whether I've enjoyed it or not. They want me to kiss them to display some sign I shall propose marriage in the near future. Inevitably, they are disappointed when I kiss and walk away."

He hesitated and, still holding her hands, smiled at her. "Honestly, that was one of the most satisfying kisses I've ever had."

"For me, as well," she could say truthfully.

His smile grew, and she didn't think he knew it was her very first kiss.

"I am glad you asked me whether I liked it," he confessed.

"I wouldn't mind doing it again," she told him, feeling less shy about speaking her mind. "Sometime. If you wish."

Again, he wore an expression of utter surprise, perhaps even shock. She drew her hands from his and sat back, seeking to reassure him.

"I am emphatically *not* hoping for a marriage proposal."

He hesitated. "With me? Or with anyone?"

"Oh, with anyone," Adelia clarified. The words were flowing off her tongue as water from a fountain. Never had she been able to converse so easily with anyone but Thomas. *How could she be so on edge with excitement around Lord Burnley and so comfortable at the same time?*

The viscount shook his head. "What do you hope for your future, my lady?"

The carriage rocked to a halt before she could make any further blunders, such as confessing her desire to remain a spinster. Nor would she disclose her hopes for the success of her silly scribblings, which she sometimes fancied good enough for publication.

In fact, she would dearly love to have someone smart and well-read look over her finished stories, but she doubted Lord Burnley would have the same taste in fiction as she.

"As to the immediate future, I intend to savor tonight's performance, no matter how gloomy the play. Any Shakespeare is better than none."

"In that case, I hope you shall not be too disappointed," he said and helped her down from the carriage.

She looked up at the theatre to find they were not at the Theatre Royal in Drury Lane but at Her Majesty's on Haymarket.

"As you see, I took the liberty of changing the venue," he confessed. "I was not up to bodies all over the stage in a typical Shakespearean tragedy."

And no wonder, not with death so recently touching his family.

"Perfectly fine," Adelia told him, waiting while the coachman assisted Penny down. Now it made sense how they could have arrived so quickly. If not for the venue change, they would have had much more time for conversing and, perhaps, another spontaneous kiss.

Soon, they were in the Burnleys' private box on the third level on the left side of the theatre. Although she tried to maneuver into a better position, Adelia ended up on his lordship's right side with the stage forward and to her left. This would not do, for she would have to look away from him all night to bring her left ear forward in order to catch what the actors were saying. Lord Burnley would have to suffer through a view of the back of her head for hours.

While her maid settled two rows behind, closest to the box's privacy curtain, Adelia fretted. However, as Lord Burnley leaned over and spoke into her left ear, she realized it was better to hear him and to pretend to hear the play.

"I would like to do it again, too," he whispered.

She froze at the words she wouldn't have heard properly if he'd been on her other side—exceedingly glad not to have missed them. Her entire body was infused with warmth as if they were already kissing once more.

Smiling at him, she relaxed and took time to look around the theatre. It was quite full. Some in nearby boxes were craning their necks to look around and, strangely, seemed to be focusing on her.

At first, Adelia wasn't positive. However, after a few minutes, she knew without a doubt that people from the other side of the theatre as well as in neighboring boxes were staring at her. Heads leaned together, fans were raised to cover mouths or to gesture toward their box.

What on earth?

"Lord Burnley, I fear something is amiss."

He leaned close to her, following the path of her gaze. Then, he sat up straight.

"The boxes are sharing a few cups of gossip-water, I'd wager, and you, Lady Adelia, are the tea leaf of choice."

94

"What? Me? Whyever for?"

She heard his rueful chuckle.

"Because you are out with me, of course. You are obviously my latest conquest."

"I beg your pardon!" That should not thrill her, but it did, right down to her toes.

"And they are flabbergasted, especially the ladies with whom I've been linked in the past, and their pushy mummies, too. I would wager my last farthing they never saw you as a threat."

Slandered and insulted, she thought. She ought to resent being considered anyone's conquest. And yet, she was the one seated with Lord Burnley, at least for one night, and she was utterly content.

On the other hand, it was galling to think the other females didn't view her as significant enough to be competition, not that she could blame them.

"Don't let it worry you, my lady. Others have survived being linked to me with the same lurid rumors."

His words deflated her. He was all but telling her how inconsequential she was, merely one in a long line. Adelia considered his words, recalling the many women she'd personally seen him escort outside onto a terrace, probably to go deeper into the garden for a tryst.

How many of them had also sat in the very seat she was in, thinking they had captured the heart, or at least the hand, of Owen Burnley? The luster went off the evening a little.

Just prior to the gas lamps dimmed and the curtain drew back, she glanced over to her own family's box, expecting it to be empty.

It wasn't. There was her brother with a woman she'd never seen before.

More curious still!

AS IT TURNED OUT, Adelia gave Lord Burnley a view of the back of her head out of fascination with what unfolded upon the stage. In lieu of a work by Shakespeare, it was a gripping abolitionist play from America. She had never read the book *Uncle Tom's Cabin* but found the play fascinating and heart-wrenching.

During the intermission, Lord Burnley told her of a Scottish weaver, William Thomson, who'd traveled through the southern states and came home to publish an account in 1842, insisting the American slaves had better lives than the laboring poor in England and particularly in Scotland.

"Of course, while our class was secretly thrilled to learn of America's misfortune and the challenge to its so-called liberty for all," Lord Burnley explained, "I don't recall any lords, especially members of Parliament, my father included, being nearly so pleased to have the conditions of our own poor tossed in our faces."

"I admit to being woefully uninformed," Adelia confessed. They were sipping wine in a luxurious lobby, and she felt ignorant, not to mention spoiled.

"Better uninformed than to be a hypocrite," Lord Burnley remarked, looking about at his fellow theatergoers. "My family, for one, has always ensured our miners work in safe and sanitary conditions, no matter the cost to our profits."

Adelia frowned. She would have to ask Thomas, whom she now knew was attending the play, whether the conditions of their own mines were acceptable. Thinking of him, she looked to see if her brother had come out into the lobby.

"Are you seeking someone in particular?" Lord Burnley asked.

"My brother," she started to answer when two ladies and a gentleman walked by, not bothering to disguise their blatant interest in Adelia. Clearly, she overheard the phrase "boring mouse."

Recoiling under their scrutiny, she turned her back, finding herself facing a pillar.

"Idiots," Lord Burnley bit out harshly. The next instant, his hand was upon her arm, gently trying to get her attention. Unfortunately, he also leaned down and said something into her bad ear. *Worse and worse!*

Turning to him, her cheeks hot, she wished only for the darkness of the theatre's interior.

"Do you agree?" he asked, standing close, his back to the lobby, shielding her from sight with his tall body and broad shoulders.

Having no idea what he'd asked, she shrugged evasively and sipped her wine.

"Chin up," he said. "You have no reason to lurk in the shadows."

Despite his kind words, Adelia wanted to draw the attention away from herself. "Do you read many novels?"

And to her happiness, he said he did. She questioned him further, listening with interest to him tell of his favorite authors, many she knew and had read. Maybe it would be possible to share something of her own writing with him, anonymously, of course.

Soon, the dimming of the gas lamps signaled the end of the intermission, and they all streamed back into the theatre. If the Burnleys' box hadn't been around the other side from her own family's, she would have stopped in to meet Thomas's lady-friend.

In any case, when they returned to their seats, she glanced over to see the Smythe box was empty. Perchance the play had not been to their liking.

THE EVENING HAD TURNED chilly by the time they left Her Majesty's Theatre. Adelia insisted Penny sit inside the coach, despite it precluding another kiss with Lord Burnley, if one had been forthcoming.

With her maid slumped in the corner, apparently happy to close her eyes and nap, they sat in silence for what would have been a short ride home if not for the snarl of theatre traffic.

"My brother was there," she mentioned after a few minutes.

"I like it when you speak without being asked," Lord Burnley confessed in a low timbre.

Shivers traveled down Adelia's spine. When she said nothing more, Lord Burnley stretched his legs out, his right one touching hers, and he responded to her words.

"Odd your brother didn't come over to say hello. Perhaps he doesn't approve of your being out with me."

Adelia doubted that was the case. "Thomas might not have noticed us. I didn't see him during intermission, nor after. Besides, he had a woman with him. Perhaps he wanted to keep her to himself."

"Did you recognize her?"

"Not at all," Adelia confessed, "and I believed I'd seen everyone this Season and the last. And the ones before that," she added belatedly realizing that didn't reflect well upon her. She clamped her mouth closed.

Normally, speaking so infrequently, her words rarely got her into trouble. Around Lord Burnley, however, she seemed to be almost a chatterbox.

He ignored anything untoward she had said about her many Seasons, instead asking, "Light or dark hair?"

"Dark," she said, realizing they were having their own cup of gossip-water. It was a considerably amusing pastime, although she would never say anything ill of her brother. "A pretty woman, from what I could see."

"Naturally," Lord Burnley said as he spread his arms along the back of the seat. "Your brother is a good-looking young man and an earl. That aside, unless this mystery woman had something unusual about her, a horn growing out of her forehead, for instance, or a pair of elephant ears, there are certainly too many dark-haired females running around London to help provide an identification."

She grinned at the images he invoked. "I suppose I shall simply ask him. We don't normally keep secrets."

She watched Lord Burnley's face fall and knew he was thinking of his deceased sister.

"How are your parents?" she asked.

His gaze flickered up to catch hers. "Not good," he confessed.

"I am very sorry. When my mother died, it was a blow to our family."

"And your father's passing, too, I imagine, made quite an impact since it left you and your brother alone."

Blissfully alone, she thought. Nonetheless, she hated to contradict Lord Burnley or speak ill of the dead, so she nodded.

"Probably harder for a parent to lose a child," he considered, losing himself in his private musings.

"Undoubtedly so," she said, wishing their conversation had not turned so morose. "Only time will heal Lord and Lady Bromshire's hearts." How inadequate her words, but she didn't know what else to say.

"Yes," he agreed.

Oh dear. How could she bring him out of his gloom?

"Will you escort me somewhere else again soon?" The words were out of her mouth before she knew what she was saying.

Instantly, he glanced up at her again, looking as stunned as she felt. *How forward of her!* He had every right to be affronted at her assumption he would not only wish to see her once more but to do it soon. However, his attractive face relaxed, and he did appear less sad.

"I would like that," Lord Burnley answered after only the slightest hesitation. "You know it will not take too many outings until the *ton* decides we are a couple," he pointed out.

The very notion thrilled her. Not only that, he wanted to escort her again!

"Of course, they will jump to conclusions whether we go out again or not," Lord Burnley surmised. "The very next time we are at a ball or party, if we so much as glance at one another, they will think they know the truth."

Adelia wondered what that truth could be.

"Do you enjoy the ballet, perhaps, or a concert?" he asked.

"The ballet," she said without hesitation, fearing she would miss too many notes of an orchestra. "I've always wished to see one."

He sat forward. "Are you saying you have never been to the ballet?"

Oh dear! Yet another circumstance that would mark her as odd. But she saw no reason to lie.

"I have not."

"How is it possible when you can hardly walk into a theatre without being assaulted by limber young women tossing themselves hither and yon across the stage in diaphanous costumes?"

She laughed at his characterization.

"It is possible because my father hated the ballet, and my brother is not any fonder of it. I could not go alone, and I have no . . . that is, I . . ." She gave up. Wallflowers didn't go anywhere with anyone. He may as well learn that now.

"In that case, I am honored to be the first with whom you will attend the ballet."

"That's kind of you, but if you find them tedious," she began, watching him shake his head to halt her.

"I don't, and even if I did, I would not, were I to watch with you."

If it weren't dark in the carriage, he would see her cheeks glowing bright pink again. She glanced at Penny, practically forgotten, snoozing in the corner, and back at Lord Burnley.

Clearly, something about her maid curled up like a dormouse struck them both as funny, and they grinned at each other and lapsed into silence once more. Adelia could scarcely comprehend how her existence had changed so much in a week. Ever since fainting, it was as if she'd awakened into another woman's life.

And she rather liked it! More so when Lord Burnley took up one of her hands and held it. Ever so slowly, he drew her forward, putting a finger to his lips as he did. In truth, she needed no warning to stay quiet, not with Penny inches from her side.

Her heart galloping, she waited impatiently for him to lean in and kiss her. He did not disappoint. Softly, almost reverently, he claimed her mouth once more. Closing her eyes, she let the tingling overwhelm her body. He tilted his head sideways, and their mouths sealed perfectly.

Startlingly, the longer his lips were against hers, the more reactions she had. Her breasts felt heavier and her nipples . . . *gracious!* . . . they stiffened against her shift. Low between her hips grew heated and somehow achy, and unmistakably, a pleasant throbbing began in her—

She nearly pulled back, but curiosity as to whether he would do more kept her motionless. His tongue touched the seam of her lips—*his tongue!*—and instinctively, she opened them. He slid inside and explored her mouth while she sat stunned, wanting to melt back against the seat, feeling her body becoming liquid.

What magic was happening to her?

If he hadn't been holding her forward with his hands grasping hers, she would, indeed, have leaned back and probably slid to the floor of the carriage.

Ever so carefully, she touched his tongue with hers. He froze, then astonishingly, sucked the end of it. *Good Lord!*

It was exquisite, and she wanted more. But what more could they do in the confines of the carriage with Penny beside her? Apparently, nothing. For at last, Lord Burnley broke away and stared into her eyes for a long moment, although it was too dark to read his expression.

Finally, he released her hands.

The carriage came to a halt, and the best evening of her life was at an end.

CHAPTER NINE

Owen plowed his gloved fist into the man in front of him, picturing Sophia's murderer.

"Easy on, chap," his opponent urged, backing away. "I'm here for exercise, not to get my ribs broken."

"Sorry," Owen muttered. He wanted to purge the guilt he felt for enjoying himself so thoroughly in Lady Adelia's company the previous night. He had definitely not intended to go out with her again until after he'd found his sister's murderer, but she had easily enticed him.

No woman had ever invited him in such a straightforward way. Invitations were usually a slightly raised skirt to display a slender ankle or a handkerchief drawn across rouged lips to indicate a meeting or a fan carried in the lady's right hand and held in front of her face, demanding he follow her to a private place. All those signals, he'd received and responded to.

And still, nothing was quite so exciting as having Lady Adelia plainly ask him to escort her somewhere again.

He threw another punch.

"That's all," said the man with whom he'd been sparring for the past ten minutes at Teavey's. "I have had enough."

Owen stood up straight and nodded. Next, they touched their boxing gloves together in a pugilist's handshake, and he looked around for his next challenger. Whitely entered the club and hailed him.

"Shall we go get a drink?" George asked.

Owen rolled his eyes. "I cannot. I need to do something useful."

Whitely stared at him. "Such as bludgeoning people with your hands?"

Owen frowned. "If I find the right person, yes, that is precisely what I want to do. Anyway, get changed and strap on some gloves."

"Why?"

"So we can spar, of course. Isn't that why you came?"

Whitely looked at Owen's previous opponent, rubbing his gut.

"I want to keep the contents of my stomach where they are, thank you. And what if you were to miss wildly as I cower and direct a flyer at my beak. I'm exceedingly fond of my face. Anyway, I came to find you and wondered if I can help in any way. Except for offering my body to your fists."

Owen considered. "We could go to Parliament to search for the anvil handkerchief." He had been thinking of doing so, but it made more sense to go with Whitely. "You can pretend to have a nosebleed through that precious beak of yours, and I'll hurriedly ask the MPs for an extra handkerchief."

Whitely shrugged. "It seems as good a plan as any. Just promise me you won't start pummeling any of our peers."

"Only one when I find him." Owen hoped that day came sooner rather than later.

As they were leaving, he spied Lord Thomas Smythe entering with a man Owen didn't recognize. Giving him a friendly nod, Owen wondered if Adelia's brother had any reservations about his sister keeping company with him, knowing he had a bit of a rakish reputation.

However, Smythe acknowledged him with a benign nod in return, at the same time, drawing the other man's attention. The stranger's face markedly altered as if they were acquainted, despite Owen not recognizing him. Before he could think more of it, the two men disappeared inside Teavey's club.

ADELIA FELT A LITTLE let down when no invitation came by courier the next day. She and Lord Burnley—Owen, as she now thought of him—had ended the night on such a pleasant exchange and with the promise of another evening together. On the other hand, she had no idea how these things worked. Perhaps there was an acceptable length of time between outings, some etiquette of which no one had ever made her aware.

Meanwhile, over her morning tea and coddled eggs, she sorted through the Season's recent invitations and tried to quell her excitement about the next ball. *What a wonderful new emotion—excitement!*

"What are you doing, Dilly-girl?" Thomas asked her when he came to breakfast, helping himself to a plate of eggs, fried mushrooms, sausages, and thick bacon from the covered dishes on the sideboard.

Another night had passed, and he'd been away from home all the prior day and out late. It was the first time she'd seen him since the theatre.

"Reading the invitations," she confessed, having put to one side the ball she was most hopeful Owen would attend, as well as a dinner party. In another pile, she had the endlessly tedious picnics, boating outings, cricket matches, and croquet tournaments.

"And you want to toss the lot of them into the fire grate, is that right?" he asked, drawing one of the morning newspapers closer to his plate and glancing at it while he stirred his tea.

"Not necessarily," she said, eying the few invitations in which she was truly interested. She knew in her heart it was folly to pin her happiness on the appearance of one man at a ball. Nevertheless, she couldn't seem to help herself from doing precisely that.

And what of her brother? He had less and less interest in the Season's schedule, which caused her to believe he'd found a love match already.

"Are you going to tell me about the dark-haired woman?" Adelia was unable to contain her curiosity any longer.

Her brother dropped the toast he was slathering with gooseberry jam but said nothing. A moment later, he stabbed a sausage with his fork and picked up the newspaper with his other hand, trying to hold it between them.

"What woman?" he eventually asked, his voice sounding flat and his gaze remaining fixed on the news of the day.

"The woman in our box at the theatre, of course."

After a few seconds, he sighed and lowered the paper.

"You said you were going to see Shakespeare," Thomas pointed out as if her being there were the issue, "at the Theatre Royal. Despite nineteen theatres in London, you and I end up at the very same one!"

She tilted her head. "So, you did see me?"

"Perhaps."

"And you left because *I* was there?" *How could that be?*

"Why are you peppering me with questions?" He rattled the newspaper, then dropped it and crammed the sausage into his mouth.

"Why are you being secretive?" Adelia demanded, waiting while he chewed and nearly choked.

Finally, he answered, "Can there not be an aspect of my life I wish to keep private?"

"Of course, but if everyone else is seeing you out in public with a young lady, why not me?"

He sighed. "Because you are the only one I have to face over breakfast."

She snapped her mouth closed. That was true. Nor she was not letting him eat in peace.

"Very well. I shall let the matter drop. For now," she added, trying to use her best older-sister voice. "All the same, I would appreciate being the first to be told if and when there is anything to know."

Thomas smiled and looked like his old self. "Of course, Dilly. I promise. And since we're being so reasonable and grown up with each other, consider yourself free of any social obligations you do not wish to attend."

She smiled at him and picked up the larger pile. Standing, she did as he'd suggested and tossed the lot of cream-colored and pale blue stationery into the fireplace to be burned with the late-afternoon fire.

He looked at the few remaining on the table and raised an eyebrow.

She shrugged. If he could keep secrets, so could she.

OWEN HAD DELAYED SENDING Adelia a missive with the formal invitation to the ballet. After all, he had to keep his head clear to find the killer, and something about the charming lady fogged his mind, making it hard to think of anything except her.

He and Whitely had spent a fruitless few hours hounding the halls of Westminster Palace, switching off which of them was pretending to have a nosebleed, until they'd collected two pocketfuls of handkerchiefs. None of them had an anvil sewn upon them.

By week's end, Owen found himself looking forward to the next large social gathering of the Season. Undoubtedly, *she* would attend, and he considered himself allowed to enjoy Adelia's company as long as he was still on the hunt for the handkerchief.

After deciding to follow Lady Jane Westing's advice and seek the help of a female—Adelia in particular—Owen arrived early at Lord and Lady Marechal's splendid mansion and kept his eyes on the door to the ballroom. He seemed to have caught the eye and the notice of every blasted female in the place, but no sign of—

Suddenly, Adelia entered. He wondered at his own previous blindness. Undoubtedly, she outshone every other lady. *How had he not noticed before?* It must have been some trickery she used to remain unseen.

Now, he couldn't take his gaze from her. It wasn't simply the perfect fall of her burgundy silk gown, as it hugged her full bosom and flared over her curvy hips. Nor was it the way her light brown hair shone while cascading over one of her creamy-soft shoulders, nor even her willowy neck set off by sparkling jewels.

It was something unfathomable about her—the way she held herself, so removed from the flighty, silly creatures around her. Owen felt as if she were another species altogether from both the malicious *ton* and the giggling gaggle of young ladies.

Her brother entered a step behind, took her arm, and led her to a table.

A table always seemed to open up for earls no matter how late they arrived, Owen thought wryly. About to make his way over, he watched Lady Adelia say something to her brother prior to leaving the safety of his company.

Frowning, Owen watched her journey to the far end of the room, looking at no one, not stopping to converse, and all the while clutching her dance card in her palm rather than letting it dangle like bait on a fishhook. And now he knew how she kept her card empty.

She tucked herself into an area at the far end of the room, a tall plant beside her, its palm leaves practically covering her. And seemingly content, she glanced out over the ballroom to watch the proceedings.

"Not tonight, my lady," Owen muttered, for his plan depended on Adelia dancing.

Snagging two glasses of champagne, he approached her. She obviously saw him coming, despite the way her head was angled. Inclining her head in greeting, she offered him a warm, welcoming smile.

That surprised him. No other woman of his acquaintance would greet him pleasantly after he had neglected her for almost a week. And he was well-aware, after how they'd finished their night at the theatre, she must have awaited his invitation to the ballet.

"You look ravishing," he offered, surprised by his own choice of words but meaning what he said. Her smile grew, and her face, already beautiful, became breathtaking. Again, he could not believe how he had failed to notice this gem right under his own nose.

"I brought you a glass of champagne."

She took it and murmured her thanks.

There was no point in delaying. Lady Jane said a female could gather more handkerchiefs than a man, and Owen was determined to see if that were true. To avoid anyone overhearing, he leaned toward the wall and whispered in her ear.

"Would it be possible for you to do me a kindness?"

She looked miserable and shook her head. *How unexpected!* Last time, at the previous ball, he had decided against asking her, but now, he thought they had a friendship, slight as it was.

She turned toward the wall as she had before.

"Please repeat yourself," she whispered, looking for all the world as if she were speaking directly to the wallpaper.

Again, he whispered, now with his lips were against her other ear. "I hope you will hear me out. The favor is a little odd, that's true, but important, nonetheless."

"What is it?" she asked, and it seemed she'd had a change of heart about helping him.

"I need to collect gentlemen's handkerchiefs. Actually, I need you to do so for me."

She turned to him, and he had to step back for their faces were mere inches apart. Glancing around, he realized they appeared to be having an intimate *tête-a-tête*.

A perplexed expression slid across her pretty face, quickly replaced by one of amusement.

"How?" was her one-word response.

Owen didn't want to put her in any danger, nor did he want her to ask for the kerchiefs outside the safety of the ballroom. More especially, he didn't want her to inquire for the particular pattern in case she alerted the murderer, who might have realized by now he was missing at least one.

"I am hoping you will ask each gentleman with whom you dance tonight for his handkerchief and collect them . . . somehow. I'm afraid I don't know how. I would have to leave that up to you."

A ghost of a smile haunted her pink lips.

"I don't usually," she said softly.

He leaned forward to catch her words.

She cleared her throat. "Dance with many, I mean."

"But you do dance when asked. I know that."

She nodded.

"In fact, you are an excellent dancer," he added.

She rolled her eyes.

Simply not a good conversationalist, he amended silently.

"Will you help me without asking why?" He waited for her answer.

She paused. Her green gaze held his, seeming to penetrate deeply into his thoughts, seeking his motives. Whatever she saw, she accepted.

Almost imperceptibly, she nodded again.

"Thank you," he told her. "I shall speak with you again later," he said, feeling a surge of excitement and hope. He was ready to dash away to play his part in the plan. Then he looked back. "Please don't leave tonight without saying goodbye."

Otherwise, how would he get the handkerchiefs?

Her brows drew together in consternation, but he merely bowed toward her and backed away. He hadn't much time. Dance cards were filling up. He must direct as many men toward Adelia as possible. To that end, he began circulating through the throng.

"Lady Adelia Smythe, where is she?" he asked each one as if he was searching for her. "Superb dancer and massive dowry. How can one go wrong?"

Many a man raised his head, seeking the lady before hurrying in her direction. It was as if she'd been invisible, and no one had noticed her presence until he spoke of her. As though he had lifted a veil, they could see Adelia standing by the back wall, clear as day, looking so becoming.

She was truly beautiful, he realized, sending another eager partner hurrying her way. This was too easy. He clapped another man on the shoulder.

"Lady Adelia, have you seen her?"

Her brother turned around with a concerned look upon his face.

Realizing who was asking, Lord Smythe frowned slightly. "Why? Are you hoping she'll faint and need rescuing again?" He paused and crossed his arms. "I didn't get a chance to thank you before."

Owen shrugged. He didn't think the Earl of Dunford owed him thanks, especially after his own ungentlemanly kisses with Adelia in his carriage.

"But you were being too much of an ass," Smythe finished abruptly, "berating me and telling my sister how more important matters awaited you." Her brother's mouth curled with irritation. "Of course, you redeemed yourself since that time by asking my sister to dance. Oh wait, then you left her humiliated on the edge of the dance floor."

Owen was shocked down to his toes. That this young buck—even if he was an earl—would take him to task in public was entirely beyond the pale. While Owen had acted appallingly at the last ball, to make mention of it was terribly rude.

Besides, Owen had escorted her to the theatre and made amends.

"Your sister has accepted my apology."

"She was too easy on you," the earl pointed out. He was probably correct.

"You are a member of the same pugilist's club as I frequent," Owen said. "In the West End."

"I am," Smythe agreed.

"I shall see you there tomorrow, perhaps," Owen offered. Let the young man take his anger out on him in an appropriate setting. Not that he was going to allow Smythe to beat him black and blue. A friendly, cleansing punch or two should suffice. "About two o'clock, shall we say?"

The earl nodded, followed by a grin. "If you are still looking for my sister, it appears she is on the dance floor." Her brother appeared surprised by that fact.

Owen nodded and moved away. He was not about to interfere with Adelia at present, although by the ball's end, he hoped to get her alone. Belatedly, he realized he should have put his own name on her card. So eager for her help and surprised by her acquiescence, he hadn't been thinking clearly.

What if her dance card were entirely full when he tried?

That was precisely what happened. Having noticed she was barely ever off the parquet, Owen hoped to lure her to the refreshment table and, in that juncture, speak privately.

Thus, while she was on the arm of her latest partner, Owen approached.

"Lady Adelia, would you care for some lemonade between dances?"

She nodded and turned to the man beside her. "So warm," she commented.

With a fan appearing miraculously out of thin air the way ladies' fans always seemed to, she cooled her face.

112

Immediately, the young lord whipped a handkerchief out of his pocket and handed it to her to blot her dewy skin. Owen couldn't make out if there was a pattern on the lace.

Smiling her gratitude, Adelia took it, touched it to her temples on either side, before tucking it into the valley between her breasts.

Owen's eyes popped. *How many had she pushed down there?*

He didn't think it possible for her to stuff so many handkerchiefs into her perfectly fitted bodice. She must move each one after it had enjoyed a moment in such a blissful setting.

Seeing her dance partner's eyes widen and stare at her generous cleavage, Owen felt an abrupt flare of protectiveness, wanting to tell the man to look elsewhere, or he would be forced to poke out his eyes.

At the same time, he also realized the brilliance of her maneuver. The man could no more make reference to his handkerchief and get it back than he could fly around the room. It would be the pinnacle of impropriety to notice where his handkerchief had gone and thus admit he was looking at her bosom.

She smiled slightly, curtsied toward her partner, and had just turned to Owen when another man stepped forward.

"Time for our dance, Lady Adelia."

"I was about to take her for some lemonade," Owen protested, prepared to mention how her health came ahead of another waltz.

Only then did her newest partner, an eager young man in his first Season, hold out a glass to her. "I anticipated by this time of the evening you might be thirsty," he said, gazing intently at her. "By having it ready, my lady, I knew we wouldn't miss a second of our dance."

Lady Adelia took the offered drink, lifted her shoulder in the smallest of shrugs directed at Owen, and walked away with the man and his damned lemonade. Owen fumed. Yet, after all, what could she do?

It continued thusly for the remainder of the ball, with Owen unable to secure a place on her card or even speak with her. Why, if he'd known matchmaking was so easy, he could have made a fortune at these things, charging a fee for his assistance in procuring partners for lovelorn men and women.

Luckily, he already had a fortune. What he didn't have were the handkerchiefs!

Hours later, he watched as Lord Smythe approached Adelia. The musicians had stopped playing, and the crowd had thinned.

Now what? Owen could do nothing but watch them leave. Before disappearing, Adelia looked around, and her gaze settled upon him. She tilted her head. Obviously, she wondered why he hadn't managed to speak with her over the course of the night.

Then, she nodded, and he took it as permission for him to call on her the next day to retrieve what she had collected. This woman could say more with absolutely no words than most could with ceaseless babbling.

Owen felt encouraged for the first time in many days. He would go to the Smythe townhouse at the decent hour of eleven o'clock in the morning, and, hopefully, the handkerchief he sought would be there, along with the identity of the killer.

CHAPTER TEN

It had been an unusual evening, the busiest ball Adelia had ever attended, and she hoped never to repeat the same again. Entirely too taxing—not the dancing but the listening, trying to catch what was being said and to summon the will to respond as necessary.

And now, the following morning, instead of being able to relax and recover, she was expecting Owen at any time. She had no idea when he would show up, only that he would, indeed, come to recover his requested handkerchiefs. Thus, she sat in the parlor, unable to concentrate on anything except reading the papers. And to her amazement, her name was in the society pages at last.

Lady A was the most sought-after dance partner at the Marechals' mansion, wearing a stunning burgundy-colored gown . . .

Adelia had to hand it to herself. After the wave of unexpected partners had washed over her and she'd discovered her dance card was full, she'd given herself a stern talking to. For Lord Burnley's sake, she would either ask outright or feign the need for each and every man's kerchief. Moreover, she'd quickly discovered how to dissuade a gentleman from asking for its return.

As she switched partners, she'd pulled the handkerchief swiftly from her décolletage and stuffed it between the slit in the side of her gown and deep into her pocket. When this became full, she had gone to the ladies' retiring room and began stowing them in her drawers. It wasn't entirely comfortable but not awful either.

As soon as she'd arrived home, which, unusually for her, was in the wee hours of the morning, she'd pulled the handkerchiefs out and flattened them prior to refolding each into a small square.

Now, she yearned to know what Owen was up to.

She didn't have to wait long.

Mr. Lockley announced the viscount's arrival as soon as polite visiting hours began, at eleven, and she met him in the drawing room. In a nod to propriety, she had Penny in tow, lest her faithful servants start to gossip.

With elegance, his lordship took her hand, bowed over it, and released her.

"I appreciate your seeing me uninvited, Lady Adelia."

"I was expecting you, my lord. I've kept the kerchiefs hidden. Otherwise, my chambermaid would have had quite the wrong impression of me, receiving so many men's favors."

He hesitated, then he smiled. "That is the longest string of words I have heard you utter, my lady. Also, I believe you made a bit of a joke."

She felt her cheeks warm. He was correct. What's more, she had spoken without worrying about stuttering, without worrying at all, in fact. Each time she met and spoke with Owen, she found it easier to converse.

She gestured to the basket on the side table.

"You may have the basket," she began, thinking he would take it home with the contents intact. But he pounced upon it and lifted the lid. Swiftly, he undid all the tidying she had done, snapping open each handkerchief with a flick and examining it for the briefest time before tossing it upon the settee. As he progressed through the contents, he sighed.

When he got to the last one, he stared at it for a long moment. It had a *fleur de lis* pattern all around the border.

She watched him sink onto the seat cushion amongst the discarded handkerchiefs and close his eyes, still clutching the last one.

Worrying her lower lip with her teeth, thinking he didn't look at all pleased, at last, she asked, "Is that the one you sought?"

He shook his head. "No." His tone was flat.

"I'm sorry," she offered.

He looked up, and then, to her surprise, rather than jumping to his feet as most gentlemen would when a lady remained standing, he brushed aside some of the cloth squares and patted the sofa cushion beside him.

What could she do? She sat. Unfortunately, he was on the side of her bad ear. She had to turn and face him, so his words could reach her easily.

"I must appear to you as a lunatic," Owen began.

She shook her head.

"That's kind of you. But if you will allow me, I shall explain."

She nodded and folded her hands in her lap. If he needed to unburden himself, she would be grateful to know. Otherwise, she would have wondered for the rest of her life.

"My sister," he began, "did you know her?"

"I'm sorry to say, I did not."

He nodded slightly. "You were a debutante ahead of her, and she went away to France."

"I saw her this year," Adelia added. "She was lovely."

"Thank you. She would have been always on the dance floor as you were last night."

"You did that," she realized belatedly.

"Yes, I—"

"Don't do it again," Adelia reprimanded gently before she could stop herself.

His expression was one of surprise. "Are you not looking to make a match?"

117

"No." Her tone was soft but firm.

"Hm," he said, staring hard at her until she looked away.

He turned his attention back to the single handkerchief clutched in his large hand. "You collected so many."

"I believe you were going to tell me why you are looking for one in particular?"

"Sophia was ... she was murdered," the viscount finished at last.

Adelia gasped, her hand going to her mouth as she shook her head in disbelief. Then, she did the only thing she could think of—she reached out and placed both her hands atop one of his where it rested on his knee.

"How horrible! I am deeply sorry for your family."

He didn't look at her, and she had a feeling he was close to tears. Yet, when he raised his head and looked into her eyes, she saw fury, not sadness. It was as if an angry beast were lurking below the surface of the civilized man, and she felt his hand clench and unclench beneath hers until she drew away.

He tossed the last handkerchief back into the empty basket.

"My sister managed to grab a handkerchief at the time of her death."

Adelia did not want to imagine that moment or hear any more details, but Lord Burnley continued speaking.

"She was lured to a disreputable room in the East End, I know not why nor how, and then killed. Strangled, to be precise. Lord Whitely and I found her—too late. So, you see, if I can find the handkerchief's owner, I will have found her murderer."

"I see." She considered the cloth squares scattered across the settee. "But you didn't tell me to take note of whose was whose."

He blinked at her as realization dawned. "I'm an idiot," he said fiercely. "You might have received it, tucked it between your ... I mean, kept it safe, and given it to me today without knowing to whom it belonged. Thus, I would have had two and still not known the murderer's identity."

She nodded at the flaw in his plan.

"I didn't tell you the design to look for because I didn't want to put you in danger, although I suppose you wouldn't have asked anyone for it specifically."

"You said 'two,'" she remarked. "You have the other one?"

"I do." He reached into his pocket and drew out a white, crumpled square of fabric. Flicking it open, Lord Burnley held it out to her. She didn't want to take hold of what might have belonged to a murderer, but she looked at it—and stifled her second gasp of the brief conversation.

Narrowing her eyes, her mouth dropping open, she couldn't credit what she was seeing. Sewn into the lace on the corner was an overlay in the shape of a delicate anvil— the tool of metalworkers, including blacksmiths and coppersmiths. It was her father's vain handkerchief design, a smithy's anvil, despite their family having been in coal mining for generations.

And while presently, she had a more feminine kerchief lodged up her sleeve, one of those which Lord Burnley sought was doubtlessly in her brother's pocket at that very instant.

Her brother! If Lord Burnley discovered the owner of this handkerchief, he would jump to the wrong conclusion. For Adelia was absolutely positive of one thing—Thomas was not a murderer.

OWEN WATCHED LADY ADELIA blanch noticeably, the blood draining from her face. There was no denying it.

"You've seen it before," he asserted, feeling his heartbeat speed up. When she said nothing, he leaned forward.

"Tell me," he demanded, unable to keep the urgency from his voice. Nor had he realized his hands now gripped her upper arms until he gave her a little shake to break the silence and bring her startled gaze up to his.

"No!" she denied, recoiling but unable to break his hold on her. At the same time, he heard her maid rise to her feet in the distant corner of the room.

"My lady?" she asked, her tone worried.

Owen ignored the girl. "Why do you look so distraught?" he challenged.

Adelia hesitated, glanced at her maid, and nodded. The servant resumed her seat.

"Just the notion your poor sister held that particular handkerchief in her hand while she died," Adelia explained. "It's extremely upsetting."

He pondered her reasonable words. Of course! He had been foolish not to understand. After all, he was used to the morbidity of carrying around something that was most probably the murderer's own. For others, it would still be a shock.

She glanced pointedly down at her arms, and he slowly released her.

"So you don't know who owns this?" His hopes were dashed again, even before she answered.

She shook her head, her sparkling gaze returning to the kerchief.

He sighed. "I offer my sincere apology. I should not have raised my voice nor laid hands upon you, especially when all you've done is try to help me."

"I accept," she said in her same soft voice.

Good, he thought. He hadn't ruined their burgeoning relationship. Whatever it was, he did not want it to end.

"I am going to continue to search for the handkerchief's owner. I hope you will consider helping me."

"I . . . I try to stay home as much as possible. I do not prefer to be out in society."

"All the same, if you are at a dance or a dinner party, whether I am there or not, I would be obliged if you would continue to look for this anvil."

She nodded and stood, evidently ready for him to leave. After his brief volatile behavior, something had changed between them. He could feel it. He'd disappointed her or perhaps frightened her. Quickly, Owen got to his feet, eager to repair the customary civility of the drawing room.

"If I have not already done so, I offer you my deepest gratitude. You collected a greater number than I had anticipated."

"It may be surprising to some what a lady can keep under her skirts," Adelia remarked.

From anyone else, Owen would think this a sexual reference, a coy come-hither statement. Not from this woman. Lady Adelia was obviously witty enough for *double entendres,* but being direct was more in keeping with her manner, whether asking for another kiss or an evening together.

Nonetheless, her statement about not wanting to make a marriage match essentially waved a flag of challenge in front of him, baiting him to pursue her, particularly as he'd always enjoyed success in that regard.

Owen knew she wasn't really doing any such thing. He was deluding himself because he desperately needed something to focus on besides Sophia's murder, especially in the face of this latest failure. Lady Adelia had always seemed standoffish, although that was too strong a word as it implied action. She was more the absence of being, managing to disappear in plain sight whenever she chose. And she chose to do so often.

Why? He had never asked a wallflower why she behaved thusly, assuming she preferred to be alone. Lady Adelia was reticent, to be sure, but he believed there was something beyond shyness that kept her glued to the wall. Obviously, she was a capable dancer and could spend an entire night in the arms of various suitors.

So why did she remain unattached and apparently uninterested?

He hoped to discover her reasons, and not merely because of her splendid curves.

"The ballet, then?" he heard himself offer, unwilling to walk away without securing her agreement to see him again. "Will you—?"

She was already shaking her head, stopping him.

"We discussed it before," Owen pressed his case. "We can go to Covent Garden tomorrow night or the Albert Saloon if you prefer."

"No, thank you."

Because he hadn't asked her in a timely fashion, she was now being difficult. He sent her his most winning smile. It had charmed many a lady right out of her stockings.

She bit her lower lip, but her stockings stayed put.

"I assumed you wished to go." He had a tone akin to pleading, which he'd never needed to use with a female. It irked him to hear himself.

"You will find many a lady who will want to accompany you."

His mouth fell open. She was placating him, mollifying him. *How infuriating, yet sweet.*

"You will honor your promise to go to the ballet with me," he insisted, knowing he sounded like a stubborn bully.

"No," she said.

"Why?"

She glanced at the anvil-embellished handkerchief in his hand. Perhaps she believed he wanted to use her to hunt for the handkerchief.

"I will put aside all thoughts of tracking down my sister's killer." Even saying it felt wrong. "No, I can't make that promise," he amended.

"Nor should you." Adelia looked as miserable as he felt. *So why was she hesitating?*

"But I can, in fact, give my brain a rest for a few hours by watching the ballet with a beautiful lady who has never seen it. Please, will you allow me that respite?"

He had a twinge of guilt, for he might have been a little manipulative, but suddenly, more than nearly anything, he wanted to go out again with Lady Adelia Smythe.

She frowned, but he could tell she was close to acquiescing. He hoped so. Determined to say nothing more, he stood in front of her, admiring her ability to keep silent without awkwardness. He had to bite his tongue to do the same.

"Very well," she said at last, as if the words were wrenched from her.

"Perfect. Until tomorrow." Owen knew he had best leave before he said something to change her mind. Taking her hand, he suddenly recalled where he was going later. "I will see your brother sooner than I shall see you."

He felt her hand tense in his. *Interesting.*

"How so?" she asked, carefully withdrawing from his grasp.

"I believe he wants to clobber me for my rudeness the other night at Lord and Lady Walthrops', when you fainted, and at the Tourneys' ball, when I missed our dance."

She shook her head. "Ridiculous!"

"Nevertheless, I have behaved abominably on more than one occasion, and you are beyond gracious to still allow me access to your person. Thus, I issued an invitation to meet Lord Smythe at two o'clock at our pugilist's club."

She looked concerned.

"Do not worry, Lady Adelia. Neither one of us shall end up bleeding. It will be a civilized gentleman's match."

He bowed and took his leave of her, hoping he'd spoken the truth. Owen would hate to collect her the following night with a broken nose or a split lip.

A FEW HOURS LATER, he entered Teavey's in the West End, feeling slightly better than he had in weeks. For one thing, he knew he likely hadn't spent the evening in the same room as his sister's murderer, thanks to Lady Adelia's handkerchief retrieval. He realized belatedly he'd left them with her and wondered how she would dispose of them. Since she liked paper, she would probably send them to a stationery manufacturer to make paper pulp, commonly done with discarded fine fabric.

Stripping down to his breeches, he warmed up with one or two club members, awaiting Lord Smythe's arrival. The young earl appeared cheerful, perhaps at the idea of popping Owen in the face. That didn't bother him one bit. He found nothing soothed the angry beast within him as did some hearty physical activity. Howbeit, he hoped what he'd told Lady Adelia was correct—they were not out to injure one another.

After Smythe had a chance to settle in and undress to his breeches, they shook hands. And as Owen had predicted, it was a friendly match of fisticuffs, over before he knew it, and neither either of them did anything ungentlemanly provoking true violence. They each threw a few solid punches to the midriff, but, as they were wearing gloves, there was no fear of barbaric knuckle-gouging to the eyes. Nor did either of them do any unmanly dropping or shifting.

Finally, they left the arena to shake hands again. Owen watched Smythe carefully, as he did every man nowadays. After dressing, the young earl reached into his pocket and drew out a square of white.

Owen narrowed his eyes. Involuntarily, he took a few steps closer, watching carefully as Lady Adelia's brother dabbed at his face. He had to restrain himself from lunging closer and demanding to look at it.

After blotting his face, the earl hesitated and flicked it open, staring at the handkerchief briefly, giving Owen plenty of time to see it was utterly unadorned—no anvil, no monogram, not a hint of lace. Then, Lord Smythe scrunched it into a ball and pocketed it. This man's handkerchief was a plain, utilitarian square of cloth, and that made the earl rise a few notches in Owen's estimation.

In fact, disappointment at not finding the anvil handkerchief mixed quickly with utter relief. Lady Adelia could still be in his life. Her brother was not the killer.

When Lord Smythe left, Owen hadn't disclosed he was taking the man's sister to the ballet. That was Lady Adelia's task to do, as well as to arrange for a chaperone. If the terrible tragedy hadn't occurred, he would have brought Sophia along to alleviate the need for one.

Thinking of his sister caused the familiar surge of anger, and he glanced around the establishment for someone who could match him or who deserved a sound beating. Seeing neither, he settled on another tepid round with an old friend who kept calm in the face of Owen's unwarranted hostility.

When he left an hour later, he did the same as he had done every few days since the murder. He visited the hapless detective and, gleaning nothing, went to see his parents. With no new information from London's finest police force, Owen endured another meal with three broken people sitting in near silence, trying to comfort each other and failing miserably.

"I am giving up my seat," his father announced over the pudding course. "I am doing nothing useful in Parliament. Despite more bobbies on the streets than ever before, crime is obviously running rampant, as is poverty. Beggars are everywhere. The East End is . . . is despicable." He stopped talking abruptly.

Owen could think of no rebuttal. He could hardly contradict anything his father said. London was filthy and smoky. It often smelled bad and was rife with pickpockets and murderers, at least in some areas. He also thought it a wondrous city in which to live. Or he had, until the tragedy. *Did he still?*

"What will you do with your time?" he asked his father.

The elder statesman shrugged. "Keep a closer eye on the mining, I suppose. Will you take up the slack in Parliament?"

"I will."

Owen's friend Westing relished going to Parliament and sitting in the House of Lords, even after losing his sight. Owen had never been quite so enamored, but he would do his duty without fail. He could imagine spending the rest of his years asking random parliamentarians for their handkerchiefs until he was condemned to an asylum.

"Will you remain in London?" He glanced at his too-quiet mother.

His father shrugged uncharacteristically. "Your mother and I will stay to be near you until the Season ends. Who knows if we will return from the country next year?"

Sophia's killer had destroyed far more than her life. He'd stripped the joy from the Burnley family.

Thank goodness his parents had each other.

And what did he have?

Adelia's face came to mind. He was looking forward to their next encounter. Escorting her to the ballet was, in fact, the only thing he was looking forward to with any happiness at all.

CHAPTER ELEVEN

A delia had managed to get to her brother's room and remove all his handkerchiefs from his bureau prior to him going to the pugilist's club that afternoon. She'd even gone so far as to tell his valet she was surprising Thomas with a new set and to please only give him plain ones until such time.

"Plain ones, my lady?"

And she'd handed the man a stack she'd purchased at an emporium as soon as her driver took her there. Why, she'd raced out of the house so quickly after lord Burnley left, she was surprised her carriage hadn't overtaken his in the street.

"If Lord Smythe asks, please tell him to speak with me, but whatever you do," she'd urged the valet, "do not let my brother leave this house with an old kerchief."

Despite his eyebrows raising nearly into his hairline, he had nodded at her orders.

"As you wish, my lady."

Next, she went to have the same conversation with Mr. Lockley.

At dinner that night, Adelia was relieved to hear her brother had an uneventful time at Teavey's club.

"I saw Lord Burnley there," he remarked.

"Did you?" She was hesitant about telling him she, too, had seen Lord Burnley. *Had Thomas lied to her about knowing Lady Sophia?* She'd wracked her brain for another explanation as to why the young woman had been found clutching her brother's handkerchief.

"Lord Burnley is taking me to the ballet tomorrow night," she said, watching Thomas's face.

"Two outings in the span of a fortnight?" he asked, smiling at her.

She paused. Although she liked the viscount tremendously, she would have turned him down if he'd allowed her. It seemed the prudent course was to put as much distance as possible between herself and the man who believed the handkerchief in his possession belonged to a killer. However, Owen had been so insistent, she had finally given in.

"Why didn't Burnley mention the ballet to me at the club?" Thomas asked her.

"I guess he didn't think he needed to ask your permission since I had already agreed. In any case, there is something far more serious we must discuss."

"Serious enough I shall need brandy?" he quipped.

"Serious enough that we cannot joke about it. Actually, yes, pour us both a glass," she requested, "and I'll tell you."

Adelia had to be honest with herself—with all her brother's mysterious comings and goings, particularly the late-night disappearances, she felt . . . disturbed. Also, there was Mr. Beaumont's intimation something was wrong concerning Thomas. Obviously, he was not a murderer, but what was he up to, and why wouldn't he tell her about the dark-haired woman?

He was behaving so strangely, and due to what she'd learned from Owen, it seemed a bad time for odd behavior of any type.

Perhaps she could start with a question.

"Where were you last evening?"

He handed her a glass with a finger of brandy. His own had a good deal more.

He shook his head. "I am not going to tell you, Dilly."

"Why?" she asked, wishing her voice didn't have a pleading edge.

"I am allowed a private life, as any man."

"Only tell me if you are in any trouble," she asked, "over your mysterious late nights, this new woman, or any other reason?"

"Absolutely not. And what on earth can you mean by *trouble*? I tell you, I am not going to speak more of her. But it shouldn't concern you."

"*You* concern me. I love you, Thomas. But if you won't speak with me about matters of the heart," she paused as he rolled his eyes, "we must speak on another matter. Did you have some sort of relationship with Lady Sophia Burnley?"

He frowned. "Didn't we discuss this already the other day?"

"Not satisfactorily," she confessed. "You said you thought you might have had an interest in her."

"That lady is deceased. What is the point in thinking about what-ifs?"

"Is there some reason she might have had something of yours?" She watched him carefully, unable to believe she was having this conversation with her own brother.

"I don't know what you mean."

She sighed. It was too awful to speak of, but she must. "Why would something of yours be found with her?"

He sipped the brandy. "You're speaking nonsense. What of mine was found where?"

"Your handkerchief," Adelia said, taking a large sip and coughing.

The lines in his forehead cleared. "I've been meaning to ask you about that very topic. Do you know what has happened to all my handkerchiefs? My valet keeps providing me with these plain kerchiefs that are scratchier than my usual ones."

He didn't seem the least concerned about what she'd said. She would have to speak more plainly.

"Bluntly, Thomas, as it turns out, one of *your* handkerchiefs was found in Lady Sophia Burnley's hands *after* she was murdered."

OWEN WAS BACK AT the location of her death, stalking the area as he did many nights. He had no idea what he was hoping to find beyond spotting someone or something that didn't belong. His sister had been appallingly out of place in the seediest section of the East End. It stood to reason, therefore, that whoever killed her also didn't belong.

He wandered into a pub, taking note of the riffraff and the rest. Probably, most of them were simply honest workers, enjoying a drink before going home, but he couldn't help looking at all of them with suspicion. Notwithstanding, he couldn't draw out the handkerchief and start asking questions. That was a fool's errand and would surely get him laughed clear out of the tavern, or worse.

On the other hand, with his manner of dress, he stood out like a horse at a dog race. Maybe he could work his way through the local taverns in a mile radius with a simpler question than one about a handkerchief.

Approaching the bar, he asked the man behind it, "I don't suppose you've seen a friend of mine lately, dresses like me, was in the area a few weeks back?"

The bartender regarded him casually.

"What are you drinking?"

Ah, the price of information. Owen vowed to buy every bottle in the pub if he had to.

"Whiskey," he said, "and lime, if you've got it."

The bartender nodded and poured, adding cloudy lime juice. He slid the drink toward Owen, who set down at least double the cost in coins.

The man eyed the payment with a discerning stare before slapping a grubby hand over it and pulling it across the wooden counter toward his own side of the bar.

"I've seen a man dressed in finery like you."

"Does he come here often?" Owen asked quickly.

"Nah, he's the Prince Consort. Never come here at all."

And the barman started to laugh. Owen nodded, tossed back the whiskey, and let the rage overtake him. With a thick haze, fury clouded his vision and his judgment.

Reaching over the bar, he grabbed the bartender by the front of his apron and hauled him up and onto the counter.

"That wasn't very nice of you, was it?" Owen asked as the man's eyes bulged. He flailed, trying to free himself, but he was at a distinct disadvantage, half lying atop the bar with his feet dangling above the floor.

Owen put his face close to the barman's. "Do you have a better answer for me?"

Behind him, Owen heard the room fall silent and a few chairs scraping. He was about to get assaulted, and he was nearly angry enough to think he might relish a good beating.

Someone tapped him on the shoulder, and he released the bartender, turned, and received a fist to his jaw. Fortunately, his assailant was malnourished and short of stature, and his punch did little in the way of damage. But he had to hand it to the little guy for trying.

Behind that one, however, were numerous larger men who didn't care for their site of relaxation, nor the source of their alcohol, being disturbed by a nobleman.

That gave him an idea. Owen decided to lie through his teeth. He looked over his shoulder at the bartender.

"I saw you pour water into the whiskey." Now, that was a serious accusation. On the other hand, with so few men there drinking anything but ale, Owen had to up the stakes.

"And I'll bet you're watering the barrels of ale in the cellar. Who's with me, lads? To the cellars!"

The cry was picked up at once. "To the cellars. To the cellars."

The room cleared of almost all but a few grizzled souls too old to make it down the steep, narrow steps at the back of the room, and a few women who looked as if they had already drowned themselves in gin.

What a sad place, he thought. He wasn't getting any answers there, but he would try again elsewhere. Maybe he would find some tavern a little nicer, more for the class of an average businessman or solicitor, somewhere that could possibly be frequented by gentry and poor folks alike.

With one arm on the bartender, he held his other hand out in front of his nose, palm up, waiting. With a struggle, the man opened his hand and let the coins fall. Owen withdrew some, leaving only enough for the whiskey.

Releasing him with a shove so the man slipped back behind the bar and onto his feet, Owen headed for the door, reaching it as the bartender ran after the mob to protect his wares.

Back on the street, Owen wandered along, feeling a little cheered by the whiskey and hardly noticing the slight throbbing to his jaw. This might prove to be an interesting night. He walked a block, looking for the next likely establishment.

In any case, fruitless as this seemed, he had no reason to go home. His townhouse was spacious, luxurious, and deadly silent. Not for the first time, he imagined a wife puttering around in it, dining with him, warming his bed, and generally keeping him company. In return, he would treat her like a queen. Also, not for the first time in the past week, the woman he pictured in such a role was Lady Adelia Smythe.

HER BROTHER'S BRANDY GLASS clattered to the tablecloth, spilling everywhere.

"Murdered?" Thomas exclaimed as the footman in the room rushed forward to blot up the mess.

"Yes." Adelia wished she'd had the foresight to clear the room of servants *before* she'd started the private conversation. Their footmen and maids were all so silent and skilled at being invisible, she usually forgot they were in the room, as was their intent. After all, she'd learned everything about being the perfect wallflower from her father's own staff.

"Leave us," Thomas told their servant, and the footman departed the room.

As soon as they were alone, he demanded, "Explain yourself."

"Lady Sophia was strangled in the East End and found, by her brother, holding onto *your* handkerchief." It sounded even worse when said aloud, no matter how many times she'd pondered it in her head.

"That's not possible," he insisted.

"I saw it myself."

His mouth dropped. "What on earth do you mean?"

Adelia realized what he was imagining. "No, I don't mean I saw *her* myself. Lord Burnley showed me the handkerchief. It was undeniably yours."

Thomas frowned and began to sop up the brandy with the napkin the footman had left. "I don't understand how that could be."

"You said you hadn't danced with Lady Sophia but had noticed her enough to think you might have an interest. When was that?"

"At Lord Waverly's ball, right at the Season's beginning. You remember, the godawful warm lemonade and the off-key musicians?"

She nodded. That had been a particularly long evening.

"I was waiting for some promised cold champagne to be served when Lady Sophia came by with her brother and another woman. They were chatting about nothing as we all do at those infernal things. Then, she said something in French to the other woman, and Burnley reminded them he didn't speak a word. Lady Sophia laughed and said that was the point. The other lady laughed, too. Lady Priscilla What-Not, I can't think of her last name, but Burnley has escorted her to a few dances."

Adelia nodded, recalling seeing them together.

"So, based on Lady Sophia's rudeness to her brother and her laughter, you decided you might be interested in her?" That seemed farfetched.

"No, it wasn't that," Thomas protested. "Lady Priscilla went to the retiring room, and Sophia said two things, one was to Burnley. She apologized and told him she was merely trying to determine if Lady Priscilla was good enough for him and, thus, befriending her."

"That was a sweet sisterly thing to do," Adelia said.

"I thought so," he agreed. "She seemed kind and reminded me of you, frankly."

"And the other thing she said?"

Thomas looked down at the table. "After Burnley led Lady Priscilla to the dance floor, Lady Sophia glanced directly at me as if she'd known I was there the whole time and told me it was impolite and sometimes dangerous to eavesdrop. She quite put me in my place, and I liked the cut of her jib, so to speak."

He shrugged. "Next I heard, she was dead. A sad thing, no doubt."

"And you didn't happen to give her your handkerchief, perhaps *after* she drank some champagne?" Adelia asked hopefully.

"Absolutely not."

"Then how did she come to have it in her hand? It makes you look guilty. Indeed, Lord Burnley is madly seeking its owner as fervently as ever Perrault's Prince Charming sought the wearer of the glass slipper, but for a far more ruthless reason."

"Is that why all my handkerchiefs have disappeared?" her brother asked.

"I didn't know what else to do," she confessed.

"Do you not think buying new ones will also make me look guilty if discovered?"

Adelia hung her head. "I suppose."

"I should go speak with Burnley at once."

"No!" Adelia protested, recalling his behavior with Farrier. "Lord Burnley will not be rational, nor will he believe in your innocence."

"What do you suggest, as my older, wiser sister?" Thomas asked.

"That you do nothing, I suppose. I burned all your handkerchiefs—"

"You what?" he asked, his tone incredulous.

"Every last one."

"They were from Belgium," he protested, "and far superior to the scratchy ones you replaced them with."

"I was scared, Thomas. For you."

He reached across the table. "You believe me, don't you, Dilly?"

His green eyes, so similar to her own and their mother's, gazed at her, unwavering. This was the same man who, at his own peril, when far younger, protected her from their father. He'd taken his share, and hers, of slaps and cuffs round the head to keep her safe. Without a shadow of doubt, he was not a murderer.

"Of course I do! You must continue about your normal life and not tell anyone that Lady Sophia was murdered. The family has managed to keep it from the papers. Apart from that, we must hope Lord Burnley never learns you are the true owner of that cursed handkerchief. We may never know how Lady Sophia ended up with it."

Jumping up, she grabbed the brandy bottle so she could pour her brother another glass. Feeling ill inside, she wondered how she would look Owen in the eyes the following night. It went utterly against her nature to be involved in this terrible deception, especially knowing how obsessed the viscount was with finding the answer to his sister's murder.

Unfortunately, the answer was quite plainly incorrect.

"You don't look settled," Thomas said.

She bit her lower lip. "As I said, Lord Burnley is escorting me to the ballet. And I rather enjoy his company. But this," she gestured at nothing and everything with a wave of her hand, "this makes me feel . . . oh, dear. Perhaps I shouldn't see him after all."

"Nonsense. There must be some reasonable explanation, but even if we never find it, you mustn't let this deter you from seeing Burnley. That is, if he makes you happy."

Made her happy? Adelia had, for so long, simply wanted to withdraw from society and not be bothered with facing people anymore. Yet, against all her prior inclinations, she now looked forward to going out with a man.

"Lord Burnley does make me happy," she admitted. *So, how could she lie to him in return?*

She supposed she could continue to help him solve the murder, except not by gathering handkerchiefs, which was now a pointless task, and certainly not by turning over her brother.

"I intend to go with Lord Burnley tomorrow night," she decided. "I don't suppose you are free to chaperone."

"I am afraid not." He sipped his brandy and didn't enlighten her on his plans.

She sighed. Her brother's secrets unsettled her. Then, she remembered the play.

"Are we treating our miners fairly?" she asked, changing the subject abruptly. She'd been meaning to ask him for days.

He started. "Strange you should ask that. I met with Victor on the very subject recently. He is urging a few measures I'm not positive are right."

"You trust Mr. Beaumont, don't you?" Adelia asked.

"Father did, so, yes, I do. But he sees things differently, from an expediency point of view, I suppose. He wants the mines to work like clockwork, but people—miners, in particular—are not cogs in a clock."

She nodded, wishing she knew something about the business so she could help. Suddenly, it occurred to her.

"Perhaps you could speak with one of the Burnleys, senior or junior. The Viscount Burnley said they maintain safe mines and happy workers, or words to those effect, in spite of the cost. And his father, the earl, is known to be very smart and fair."

Her brother nodded. "The Earl of Bromshire may not be receiving visitors."

Thomas was right to be hesitant. Lady Sophia's father might not wish to talk about mining when his daughter had so recently passed away, especially now she knew it was due to murder most foul.

Besides, Thomas ought to stay away from the Burnleys for the time being. She stared into the amber liquid in the bottom of her glass and hoped Owen never discovered her duplicity.

CHAPTER TWELVE

O wen awaited the hour before it was time to pick up Adelia with a mixture of anticipation and guilt. Again, he was going out while his sister's killer roamed free. Moreover, he was going out for the pure pleasure of being with the delightfully beguiling, utterly unassuming lady, who made him feel less as if he was going to punch a wall at any moment. Something about her demanded his civility.

Something else about her commanded his body's attention, too. He still could not believe she had stood unnoticed through the past four Seasons with her lovely face, her intelligence which he had discovered with each conversation, and her shapely figure like a goddess. He was half-desperate to cup her breasts, which were as plump peaches, and rub his thumbs over her nipples to watch them pearl.

And as he'd told everyone at the previous ball to lure them to her dance card, Lady Adelia had a favorably large dowry. It meant nothing to him, but Owen couldn't fathom why others weren't lined up to pluck this low-hanging fruit.

He arrived at her home a little early, rolling his eyes at his own eagerness. As previously, she came downstairs looking astonishingly beautiful in a silver gown with black trim. This time, however, the maid took a seat alongside her mistress in his carriage. Naturally, their talk on the way to the theatre was confined to the banalities, and kissing was impossible. He didn't even lean forward or allow his leg to touch hers.

Nevertheless, watching Adelia fizz with excitement during the first half of the ballet was an absolute joy Owen would always recall. She was well-nigh glowing as they strode into the lobby for the intermission. But soon, he was reminded of one of the reasons she hadn't been scooped up and married—the woman could make herself practically invisible.

Leaving Adelia and her maid at a small high table with beverages, he excused himself to the men's retiring room. When he returned to the lobby, he could not, at first, find either one of them. He walked the lobby's length, reaching the doors to the theatre before turning around. Frowning, he scanned the throng.

Out of the corner of his eye, he caught a movement and turned. Adelia waved her graceful, gloved hand. He had walked right past where she stood against the wall, next to a potted plant practically as tall as she was. What's more, she was turned sideways in that blasted, awkward-looking position she always chose. Thank goodness for her full breasts and a generous-sized bustle, or she would have disappeared entirely in profile.

"There you are!" he proclaimed as if she'd been hiding.

Still holding a glass of champagne, Adelia had a beatific smile upon her face. It warmed him to know he was partly the cause by bringing her to the ballet. However, she was alone, and that irked him.

"Where is your maid?" he demanded, trying not to sound annoyed although he was.

"Retiring room," she responded in her succinct way.

Well, he couldn't fault the girl for that. Relaxing, he took in Adelia's happy radiance.

"You are enjoying the ballet, I take it."

"Oh, yes!" she said. "Very much."

"What do you like best about it, if I may ask?"

"The story is so much easier to follow than a play."

"Really?" Owen considered that. "Truthfully, my lady, I prefer actors to dancers. I have no idea what any of that flitting about on stage is supposed to mean."

Her little-used laughter came out, enchanting him. That was the only word for it, for he felt utterly enchanted by her every minute he was with her. *Was this how Westing first felt with Lady Jane?* If so, he considered something special might be happening between them.

They had already shared not one but two perfect kisses brought about entirely on impulse. One moment, he'd been admiring her dimples and smile, and then suddenly, her very essence took hold of him and drew him to kiss her. He'd been overcome with wanting to taste her, to experience their first kiss. And their second.

Now, he wanted to do it again. In fact, he'd wanted to since the last one. Unfortunately, he had to deal with the maid on the way home. Perhaps he could slip the girl a few farthings to brave the night air and sit on top as she had done once before.

With that to look forward to, Owen was positively eager for the intermission to end and the next act of the seemingly eternal ballet to begin. Tonight, it had already been more diverting than any ballet performance he'd ever attended—watching how Adelia leaned forward, lips parted slightly in wonder, her eyes sparkling as she followed the movements. Moreover, she had a child-like, charming way of clapping emphatically, loudly, and a little too long.

Hopefully, she wouldn't become jaded, ignoring what was on the stage for the mean-spirited sport of watching who was there with whom. He feared it was inevitable. Women, in his experience, ended up focused on the latest scandal in the *ton* or wondering how best to manipulate the next man they met.

When had he become so damn cynical? Probably from spending so many pointless evenings with vapid females, each and every one plainly hoping he would pluck her from the marriage market when all he'd wanted—to be honest— was to satiate a physical need. While their sole purpose seemed to be to get a husband, he could not say his had been of a higher moral purpose. Occasionally, he'd been a rascal, but not nearly as often as people assumed.

Thinking of cynicism and rascals, Owen spied Whitely, who raised a hand from across the room. As his friend strode over, however, he realized the female accompanying Whitely was one he, himself, had been linked with the prior Season for about five minutes. Owen had a prickling feeling this could become uncomfortable.

Miss Lucille Spencer, a distant cousin of the Althorp Spencers, came to a stop a mere few feet away, dropping into a curtsey before him. Immediately, Lady Adelia tensed. He could sense it as much as he saw it. Her face tilted ever more subtly toward the wall, and her expression became blank, her smile chased away by their approach.

Owen bowed in return. Then, to his amazement, Miss Spencer started speaking to him as if Adelia wasn't there. She neither curtsied to her nor greeted her. To be fair, Adelia didn't do so either and seemed to be backing farther into the leafy arms of the plant behind her. Regardless, it was Miss Spencer's place to curtsey first, befitting Adelia's station as the daughter of an earl.

Owen looked at the dark-haired woman in front of him, and a thought came to mind—*Lucille Spencer had been a horrendous mistake.* He'd taken her to a play, if he recalled correctly. It didn't matter which because she'd not listened to a word of it, spending her time making sure everyone knew with whom she sat. He'd felt like the prize pig at a fair.

At intermission, he'd barely been able to keep up as she'd dashed from his box to the lobby to find her friends so they could whisper behind their fans about everyone they saw. After a few minutes, he'd knocked back his champagne and the glass he'd held for her. When she'd finally looked up at him, her cunning gaze glittered with conceit.

"I do hope everyone is noticing *we* are together, my lord." Miss Spencer had made a point of laughing loudly and twirling in front of him as if he had requested she do so, in order to admire her.

In fact, she'd reminded him of a circus tent with a performing pony underneath.

Despite feeling a measure of disdain, *occasional* rogue that he was, he'd savored more heated kisses with Miss Spencer that night in a dark alcove a step from her front door, *after* she'd dismissed her chaperone. She'd boldly encouraged him to touch her under her skirts as if a soft thigh and a surprising lack of drawers would tempt him to offer her his name.

Shocked but willing, he'd never believed she would let him do what they did against the brick wall. Nonetheless, he hadn't invited her out or ever scrawled his name on her dance card again.

Adelia didn't seem bothered about grabbing his attention every moment. Nevertheless, she had it entirely. And she didn't seem to want to attract anyone else's notice, either. He considered her above such pomp and vanity, a woman of a different caliber, such as Westing's Lady Jane.

Lost in his realization of how much he admired Adelia, Owen all but missed Miss Spencer's first words.

"I did not think you cared for the ballet, my lord. You never wanted to bring me to one. Lord Whitely was perfectly happy to escort me."

Miss Spencer gestured to her side where she expected Whitely to be. For his part, after shaking hands with Owen, Whitely skirted around the back of Miss Spencer's bustle and bowed deeply to Adelia, restoring civility to the situation.

"How are you faring, my lady?" George asked.

Owen was certain he saw Adelia sigh with resignation. Unhurriedly, she turned to Whitely, and Owen ignored the insipid Miss Spencer to focus on whether Adelia would respond.

After a hesitation that was slightly longer than normal, causing Whitely's gaze to flash to Owen's in alarm, Adelia finally dipped ever so slightly in greeting and simply nodded.

Owen hoped his friend would accept that to mean she fared well and leave her alone. However, George asked, "Are you a ballet devotee?"

Adelia paled, her fear plain upon her face. Owen wanted to strike him down for causing her even a twinkling of consternation. He watched her draw a long, steadying breath.

"I love it," she said slowly, annunciating each word.

Owen was silently cheering her on, knowing—without understanding why—that interacting was difficult for her, almost painful, it seemed. He saw the instant she nearly turned to the wall again but stopped herself.

Bravo!

Miss Spencer's face twisted into a superior smirk, perhaps because talking was a skill at which she excelled.

Owen glanced between the two women. "Lady Adelia, may I introduce you to Miss . . . *uh* . . . Caroline, isn't it?" he asked with an exaggerated frown, feigning a memory lapse as to her identity.

Before he could stop himself, Whitely chuckled at the veiled insult, which probably cost him any chance of partaking in a tryst against the young woman's favorite brick wall.

Miss Spencer reddened, finally sparing a curtsey for Adelia–not quite deep enough for Owen's liking.

Adelia bobbed her head in return.

"I don't mind the ballet," George said. "The ladies on stage have pretty figures, to be sure."

By her frown, Miss Spencer didn't care for that remark, either.

Adelia appeared to consider his statement, shallow as it was. In response, she said, "The dancers seem to . . . to

143

embody the music and p . . . p . . . perfectly interpret it at the same time."

Owen realized his mouth had opened slightly as she spoke. *The dancers literally embodied the music*—he'd never thought of it that way. When he glanced at his friend, who'd been firmly of the opinion Adelia contributed nothing, he saw Whitely nodding in agreement.

"I understand what you mean," Owen said. "While the ballet is *not* my favorite entertainment, I can appreciate the skill of the dancers representing the orchestra's notes as if telling a story. Without the music, the ballet would be infinitely diminished and vice versa."

Adelia nodded her head. Then, to his surprise, she added, "Indeed. The . . . the blend of the graceful dancers with the skill of the musicians is s . . . sublime."

Miss Spencer looked as if she were about to launch into her own opinion of the ballet. Luckily, the gas lamps dimmed, and with a quick exchange of goodbyes, they parted.

"I am so very glad you are enjoying yourself," Owen said, taking her arm.

Without hesitation or stuttering, she replied, "And I am sorry to learn you do not truly like the ballet."

"That is not actually the case," he said. "I did not take Miss Spencer to the ballet because of Miss Spencer, not the ballet."

He was glad to elicit a smile from Adelia, despite how she fell silent again and said little else for the rest of the night.

Surprising himself, Owen thought the performance came to an end too soon. Lady Adelia's company had been as entertaining as anything on stage. After securing her mantle from the coat check, they strolled toward his carriage, which had drawn up out front. Behind them was her vigilant maid.

After helping Lady Adelia inside, he turned to the girl, and as he'd been planning, he placed a coin in her hand.

"Will you sit up top?" he asked.

The maid hesitated, which he admired. Then, she handed the coin back to him with a sad shake of her head, moving past him to get in beside her mistress.

His admiration soured at once. Nevertheless, he was not one to give up easily. Swiftly barring the entrance with his arm, he stuck his head inside the carriage.

"Your servant is quite happy to sit up top," he told Adelia, "if you'll allow her to. It's a warm evening." Not balmy by any means, but not sleeting or snowing either.

Adelia frowned, looking past him to try to see her maid, who stuck her head under his arm, awaiting her mistress's response. He'd never had to work so hard to get a lady alone.

Holding his breath, wondering what Adelia would say, he tried to keep his expression innocent and nonchalant.

"Penny," Adelia said finally, "do you mind sitting up top?"

Owen released his breath and believed he heard angels singing.

For her part, the maid was quick to say, "No, my lady." Turning to him, she stuck out her hand like a true woman of business. He doubled the coinage for her loyalty to her mistress and assisted her onto the dickey before climbing in next to Adelia.

Owen was more than ready to sweep her into his arms and claim her luscious mouth. However, as soon as they were underway, seated side-by-side for a change, Adelia snared him with a concerned glance.

"Did you wish to speak with me privately, my lord? Have you found out something about the handkerchief?"

CHAPTER THIRTEEN

Adelia shivered slightly with trepidation. *Had Owen discovered something about Thomas?* Unlikely, since he would probably have brought it up at once. And by the look on his face, which instantly changed from happy to distressed, she wished she hadn't mentioned the handkerchief at all.

Naturally, it had been uppermost in her mind ever since he'd shown her the cursed linen square. He leaned back against the squabs and shook his head.

"I am no closer to solving that mystery."

Feeling the need to comfort him, she reached up and patted his shoulder. "I am terribly sorry, my lord." If it were regarding anyone but Thomas, she would gladly give Owen the information she'd gleaned.

He looked straight ahead, his own black-gloved hands clenched. *Poor man!*

Boldly, Adelia took hold of one of his fists and straightened it out, soothing the tension from him. Then, she did the same with his other hand.

He allowed her to do so in silence. Normally, she never bothered to break a good, long spell of quiet, but she felt she had to distract him from his difficult thoughts.

"Thank you for taking me to the ballet. I cannot remember a night I enjoyed so much."

Flipping his hands over suddenly, he cradled hers atop his palms. Startled by the intimate gesture, she moved to sit back and draw her hands away. Suddenly, he closed his fingers, effectively capturing her.

"What about our previous night out?" he asked. "Was this better than that one?"

She shrugged, entirely addled by his closeness, the way he lowered the timbre of his voice, the way his thumbs brushed the backs of her thin gloves.

"I do not know." Truly, any moment with him seemed delightful. Especially when he was kissing her.

"Will you let me take you out again?" he asked.

She lifted her gaze from staring at their joined hands to his eyes. "Why?"

"Why?" He cocked his head. "Do you mean, why do I wish to go out with you again?"

"Yes."

"You are not coyly asking for compliments. This, I know." His blue gaze remained locked with hers. "My answer is easy. I like your company. I like you. I wish to get to know you better."

Warmth suffused her, although she didn't know how to express it adequately.

"I see."

He squeezed her hands at the same time as he expelled an amused breath.

"Do you? That is a short, most unexpected response," he said.

Her cheeks felt as if they were flaming. She was an awkward ninny. She should tell him how much she liked him, too.

"I'm sorry," he said before she could get the courage to form such unfamiliar, sentimental words. "I have embarrassed you unintentionally. In fact, I welcome your short, no-nonsense answers."

SYDNEY JANE BAILY

Good, for that was usually what he would get.

"I was most impressed by your critique of your first ballet," he added.

She groaned slightly, recalling how she'd stuttered through her statements and nearly given up entirely. She lowered her gaze.

"Why are you moaning? My lady, please look at me."

She raised her eyes to his again.

"What is amiss?" he asked.

"I apologize," she said, and her father's presence filled the carriage. If she'd stuttered in front of him and other people as she had done tonight, he would have been furious. And violent.

"Whatever for?"

She didn't want to draw his attention back to her obvious failing, so she merely shrugged.

Suddenly, he leaned toward her.

When there was a mere fingerbreadth between them, he asked, "May I kiss you again?"

She realized then why he'd asked if Penny could sit up with the driver. It wasn't to talk about the handkerchiefs at all. *How naïve of her!*

Adelia nodded as a thrill of anticipation raced through her. Suddenly, his lips were upon hers, warm and firm. He released her hands, yanked off his gloves, and threaded his fingers through her hair. Holding her head steady, his tongue traced the seam of her closed mouth.

Parting her lips, she allowed his tongue's easy passage. As previously, instead of it feeling invasive and scary, it was pleasurable and exciting.

"Mm," she murmured unwittingly, and, since he'd released her hands, she was free to lace her fingers behind his neck and hold onto him.

Before she could acknowledge what was happening, Owen's tongue stroked hers and proceeded to explore her mouth. His hands moved from her hair to her back, coming to rest upon her ribcage. As he kissed her more ardently, he

148

stroked the sides of her breasts with his broad palms, his thumbs creating an arc across the front of each, caressing her through the silk fabric or her gown.

Her body tingled and sizzled. This time, she was not unprepared for the delicious sensations as his thumbs made their wicked sweep across each of her nipples.

It was entirely too warm in the closed carriage. She wished she could remove a few layers, at least her mantle. Outrageously, she imagined removing her gown, for she longed to feel his touch upon her prickling skin.

Sadly, she was encased in medieval armor, or so it felt.

At last, Owen drew back, but not until his mouth latched onto her lower lip, tugging gently as he released her. That slight tug seemed to send a whip of pure fire directly to her most intimate parts, causing her body to soften and—*dear God*—grow damp between her legs.

Her eyes widened, and her surprised gaze shot to his once more.

Owen must have recognized what she was feeling, and perhaps felt something similar, for he sat back against the seat, breathing heavily, his glance locked with hers.

All too soon, the carriage came to a halt, and the footman was at the door.

"It was over far too quickly, my lady," Owen protested. "The ballet, I mean."

With her heart still thumping, she bit her lip, knowing he didn't mean that at all.

"Where are we going next time?" she asked, which made him pause. "And when?"

Disappointingly, he gave her a sad smile.

"I shall send word." He got out and offered Adelia his hand.

As she brushed against him, he whispered something in her ear. She knew this by the warm breath against her lobe. Unfortunately, she couldn't make out what he said.

Should she let it go unheard? How could she? Adelia would never sleep that night if she didn't know what he'd said.

Sighing at her own affliction, she turned her good ear toward him and asked, "I beg your pardon, my lord?"

He paused and frowned slightly but bent his head low again and whispered against the shell of her ear, "I think you are marvelous."

Oh my! She was glad she'd asked him to repeat himself. Beaming up at him, not minding that Penny stood close by as did the coachman, she softly said, "I think you . . . you are, too."

Blast her nerves, causing her to stutter, but it had been the smallest of hiccups. And his lordship looked genuinely pleased. She let him walk her to the door.

Her brother was assuredly out as he'd said he would be. Where or with whom, she didn't know. All the same, the door opened, and their capable butler surveyed the scene on the doorstep. Penny curtsied to Owen and slipped indoors to give her mistress a moment alone.

"I shall surprise you with my next invitation," he said.

She watched as he took her left hand, drew off her glove, and raised it to his lips for a kiss. It was silly and gallant and wonderful, not at all as when Mr. Beaumont had done similarly.

Especially as Owen winked rakishly but endearingly before turning away.

Adelia sighed. *How could this be happening to her?*

She watched his carriage depart and practically floated up the stairs to let Penny help her undress. Adelia wanted to do nothing more than lie upon her cool sheets and recall every second of the evening.

And where did she want Lord Owen Burnley to take her next?

The most shocking notion popped into her head. *Why, to his bed, of course!*

OWEN COULD NOT GO home. Something exhilarating was coursing through his veins, something new and hopeful. And despite deciding to go directly to the East End and spend more hours on his probably fruitless task, his mind wandered to the alluring Lady Adelia. Everything about her was enticing, from her opinions to her soft-spoken manner, to the way she blossomed under his touch.

In the carriage, he had wanted her in a visceral, carnal way, and all because of the look in her eyes and the expression on her face after he kissed her. She was desire personified. It radiated from her like sunbeams. If they'd been somewhere private, he had no doubt she would have let him do much more than caress her through her clothing.

And the strange thing was, she did not seem to be husband hunting. Certainly, not trying to trap him. Nor would he consider her a woman of loose virtue, not by any means. She wasn't coy, yet neither was she frigid. She seemed to be refreshingly straightforward and honest, the kind of woman he had searched for his first two Seasons until he'd grown tired of the desperate title hunters. He'd decided to play their game for whatever he could get from them, and thus, he'd spent the past two years sporting with the fairer sex.

If they fawned over him, he let them. If they allowed him to take liberties with their person, he took them. If any of them ever started to cry, he gave them his bored look, seeing how quickly their crocodile tears became anger and frustration. If any threatened to have a brother or father call him out, he would bow low and say he welcomed the challenge before flexing his muscles and making fists of his large hands.

Usually, they changed their minds about endangering a loved one to obtain an unwilling husband.

Like most of his friends, Owen usually went to an experienced whore to indulge in satisfying sexual activity, the kind he found himself wanting with Adelia. He favored one harlot in particular and paid her well, as did her other clients. She was clean, discerning, and always insisted he wore a sheath to protect them both—the finest, thinnest kind from France.

Nonetheless, he'd grown bored and even a little ashamed, perhaps ever since his good friend Westing displayed such joy in matrimony and the deep bond he'd forged with Lady Jane. Now, in the face of Sophia's murder, Owen would welcome a return to that previous boredom. He longed for the dull existence he'd known until some monster had taken his sister.

Despite that, he didn't yearn for his life before Adelia entered it. Everything had seemed colorless and mundane until she had brought her spark.

Looking out the window into the darkness, he was getting closer to the wretchedness of the East End. *How could he ever subject a wife to the turmoil of rage and confusion swirling inside him?*

In any case, he could hardly do such a blissfully mundane thing as marrying, nothing so civil and polite, until *after* he'd brought the killer to justice. Owen couldn't disrespect his sister by having a lighthearted day at a church, despite social expectations having no strict rules for a brother grieving a sister. Also, he had his parents to consider.

They would love Adelia. The thought popped into his head. Or they would once their grief subsided a little. If it ever did. He glanced down at his black gloves on the seat, the outward sign of his mourning along with his dark suit, and he yanked them back on, almost tearing them.

Still, he wanted Adelia. And not only naked in his bed! He wanted her forever.

Good God! He was well and truly smitten.

Sighing, he realized his driver had brought him to Whitechapel Road. So quickly. He ran a hand over his face and scruffed up his hair. He was tired. No, beyond that, he was exhausted.

Regardless, he would do his duty as a brother. He should have been there to protect Sophia, and he might never get over his failing her. Now, he had a long list of people who used J. Dickinson paper, too long to be useful even if he enlisted Adelia's assistance in asking each and every household on the list whether he could see their handkerchiefs. He rolled his eyes. It was madness.

Tomorrow, he would think of a different strategy.

Meanwhile, his valet had begun asking every tailor and also the many dressmakers of London about anyone who might have ordered handkerchiefs with an anvil sewn upon them. So far, nothing.

Owen departed the comfort of his carriage, where the faintest aroma of Adelia's light floral perfume lingered. Within an hour, he had punched a man in one pub on the corner of Church Lane and turned over a table in another, shattering glassware and a few chairs.

Another hour and three taverns later, he was no closer to finding the murderer but had worked his way through three more glasses of whiskey. Lastly, he entered a nicer establishment on the corner of Osborn Street, where gentrification was battling desperately to take hold. The pub was surprisingly well lit and didn't smell of piss and ale.

From the doorway, Owen scanned the room. There, seated at the far end, was Lord Smythe and a dark-haired miss.

Although the room seemed overly warm and his vision felt a little blurry—undoubtedly from fatigue and whiskey—he considered how nice it would be to sit with friendly people, even Adelia's brother, and have another drink. Perhaps he would explain his mission.

When he raised a hand in greeting, however, instead of receiving one in return, Smythe stood, grabbed the woman by the hand, and strode for the back door. Knowing they could end up in an alley possibly full of cutthroats, Owen called after them.

Was he slurring his speech?

The young earl, dressed oddly in decidedly middle-class clothing, seemed to move more swiftly, and in the space of a few seconds, the pair had disappeared.

Owen sat down heavily at a table, wondering if he'd truly seen Adelia's brother at all or simply someone who looked like him. After all, why would an earl and his lady-friend be in a place such as this, dressed in that manner?

For that matter, Owen wondered why in the hell he was there when he could be home in his townhouse. He had accomplished nothing.

After a few moments, another man rose from a nearby table and left the same way, out the back door. *What in blazes?*

Owen would bet the man was following them, perhaps a constable on a case. Tomorrow, he would ask the detective if he knew anything about it despite Garrard being practically ready to bar Owen from his office.

Stumbling outside, he hoped to hell his driver would find him.

CHAPTER FOURTEEN

Owen left Detective Sergeant Garrard's office no wiser and having received a word of warning that he'd best stop haunting the East End. Tavern owners were starting to complain.

"To hell with them," Owen said and slammed out of the police station.

Today, he was going to Westing's for some of his good counsel. He also wanted to pen an invitation to Adelia if he could think of where to take her next. Perhaps the Westings would have a suitable idea. He would probably see Whitely later at the Carlton Club. And that night, he would be back searching amongst the lowliest of London's low. Neither the tavern owners nor the police could stop him.

He yawned broadly as his carriage drew up outside the Westings' home on Arlington Street. Wearily, he climbed down and rang the bell. After waiting a few minutes in the drawing room, Owen was greeted by Lady Jane.

She entered the room, held out her hands to him, and smiled as he grasped them. They'd had a bit of a rocky start when Owen questioned her motives for attaching herself to a blind marquess, but she had proven herself to be the best thing to ever happen to his friend.

"I'm so sorry, Owen, but Chris isn't here. He went to Parliament today. Something about a new bill regarding the poor of England and Wales, as well as coal duties. I thought he said he was meeting you there."

"Blazes!" Owen exclaimed, quickly apologizing for the oath a second later. "I am a dunce. You're correct. I told him I'd see him at Westminster. I jumped in the carriage and—" he covered his mouth as he yawned again, "—forgot all about that."

She shrugged. "Would you like a cup of tea? I have a little time prior to going out. Perhaps it will refresh you."

He hated to be rude, but coal duties were being discussed that would directly impact his family's business.

"No, thank you, I had best head to Parliament. I'm taking over my father's seat soon."

Lady Jane nodded. "I'll walk you out. I am inspecting an orphanage today. Once you raise money for one and get it up and running, you have to make sure nefarious people don't undo all your good work."

"Of course," Owen said. Lady Jane was known as a good Samaritan, who had raised a great deal for the orphans of London. "Where is the orphanage?"

"Spitalfields," she responded, already tugging on the gloves her butler gave her.

Owen felt a surge of alarm.

"Does Chris know where you're going?"

She donned a mantle and smiled her thanks at the servant. "I believe so. Almost all the orphanages are in that area or farther south, toward St. Katherine's and Wapping."

"You'll have to travel through Whitechapel," he said. *Did she know where his sister died?*

"It's not nearly as bad as one thinks," she said, seemingly unperturbed and oblivious to his growing apprehension. "At least, the Whitechapel High Street or Whitechapel Road aren't. It's the warrens of small side streets leading off those main thoroughfares, hardly more than alleyways, where the most poverty and despair are to be found. I'll be in my carriage, and I have a trusted driver."

"Anyone else?"

She looked up at him sharply. "I don't need a nanny, Owen. I can take care of myself."

Sophia believed the same thing when she went traipsing off to a far safer area to buy perfume. And yet, after heading into the East End, she'd never returned.

"I shall go with you," he decided. "In fact, I'll take you in my carriage. You can tell me all about orphans on the way."

She hesitated, but Owen didn't care what she said or did. He would not take no for an answer, and he would refuse to let her leave. He owed his friend Chris such a kindness, and he would take it up with him later. The marquess was being remiss in letting his pretty wife, the mother of his child, traipse off to God-knew-where as if the world were a safe place.

Thus, despite her protests and at the cost of missing hearing about new coal tariffs and possibly fighting them, Owen found himself with the Marchioness Westing on his way to Spitalfields.

It was an enlightening journey, not only hearing her speak about the good work her sponsored orphanages were doing, but also actually seeing one. Foundling homes, he learned, had been around for a century, at least. The luckiest orphans were the newborns, who were often quickly adopted to replace babies who'd died in infancy, even in the homes of the wealthiest members of society. The other children usually got a modest education and stayed in an orphanage until they received employment situations.

"The boys get apprenticeships at fourteen," Lady Jane said, "if no one adopts them sooner. And the girls at sixteen."

That sounded like a good system to him, but she looked sad. When asked why, she told him, "It's rare to keep them that long. Sometimes they run away and end up in unfavorable conditions, which they can rarely get out of. Or worse happens."

Worse happens. He didn't have to ask.

The streets leading up to the orphanage looked very different from what Owen saw at night, when only drunkards, whores, and cutthroats were out. In the daylight, he saw crowds of children, many shoeless, wearing rags, whose parents, if they had any, were working for pittance either at the docks or in one of the smoke-spewing factories by the river where enormous coal stacks lined the horizon.

The children looked so industrious Owen couldn't help watching out of the carriage window. Some were sweeping hopelessly filthy sidewalks in front of shops. He assumed they were doing so for pay or for food. Some were doing laundry in tubs, some held baskets, although he couldn't imagine what they were selling. And some were sitting on the sidewalk, holding a tabby cat or a mangy dog, and he felt a lump in his throat at the comfort they were giving or receiving in such a squalid life. He turned to look at Lady Jane, who nodded to him, as if to say, *I've seen it all.*

Thankfully, the orphanage turned out to be large and clean, run by ladies in white aprons. Unfortunately, it was also overcrowded with children of all ages and, thus, very noisy.

While not exactly filled with laughter and cheer, it was not anywhere near as miserable as a workhouse in which the mortality rate for children was still abominably high. Nor was it as dangerous as the gutters from which many of the children had been rescued. If they were lucky enough to secure bed and board at an orphanage, especially one of Lady Jane's, they would have a clean, safe place to sleep and hearty food at the very least, and possibly a future.

Westing's wife managed to surprise the director, a tall, gangly man with a large mustache and sideburns that almost hid his face entirely. But when faced with two aristocrats entering his office and one of them being the capable marchioness demanding to inspect the facility from cellar to attic, the director had an unperturbed air. This reassured Owen as to the man's trustworthiness.

Moreover, when they toured the building from floor to floor, the director was often greeted by the children, obviously without fear. *All the better.*

Owen took the opportunity to look at each and every sandy-haired boy he could see. Detective Sergeant Garrard was right about the number of them. Just as Owen decided to ask one if he'd ever delivered a note to Piccadilly, another popped up, and another. He didn't want to upset anyone's applecart, especially Lady Jane's, but he did sidle up to one boy.

"Do you perform odd jobs, like being a courier?" Owen asked.

"What's that, guvnor?"

Owen hid a smile over the term of address. "I mean to say, would you carry a message for someone?"

The boy shook his head. "We're not allowed to do those sorts of jobs, in case we get in with a bad lot. We have to wait for the director to give us work. I'm going to be a cobbler, I think."

Owen nodded. "Good choice."

"Lord Burnley, we are going into the yard," came Lady Jane's voice, and he left the young boy with a nod.

At the end of the tour, Lady Jane seemed very pleased, and only suggested they get the children outside as much as possible in good weather and add an extra pudding course on Sundays if possible.

The director smiled and said he would endeavor to do so, or at least to add more fruit, which the children saw as a delicacy and loved nearly as much as biscuits.

"I shall send a few bushels of apples over tomorrow," Owen promised as they reentered his carriage. As it started moving, he stared at his friend's wife, noticing she had tears in her eyes.

"Lady Jane, are you all right?"

"I always want to bring them all home," she confessed.

He nodded. "I can understand that. More than one young chap or miss caught my eye as if hoping we were there to adopt."

She looked down at her lap for a long time and gathered her emotions. "They will love the apples. Now, tell me, Owen, how are you faring?"

ADELIA DISCOVERED HER BROTHER and Victor Beaumont in a heated discussion in the library. However, since they'd left the door ajar and it was her home, she paused in the hallway. She had become too good at eavesdropping as a wallflower, and it was truly a nasty practice.

"You must not discuss the business of our company with strangers." Mr. Beaumont's voice was strident and agitated.

"Victor, I am merely seeking some good advice from those more experienced—" her brother responded, but the engineer interrupted him.

"You need only talk to me. I have a great deal more experience than you. I feel as if you are questioning my abilities at every turn."

"Of course not. My father trusted you, and I appreciate your service to the company."

"Very well," Mr. Beaumont said, apparently mollified. "I may have jumped to the wrong conclusions."

And then, Adelia heard chairs moving, and she backed away to hide in the dining room until she was certain Mr. Beaumont had departed.

When she wandered down the hall again, she entered the library to find her brother lost in thought.

"Is everything all right?"

"Yes, fine." He looked up. "Did you enjoy the ballet?"

"I did, very much. It was—"

Thomas interrupted her, obviously his mind still on Smythe Coal. "If it weren't for the ridiculous handkerchief, I would request a meeting with the Earl of Bromshire."

She wished she'd never mentioned the possibility. It was clear Thomas should stay as far from the Burnleys as possible until the murder had been satisfactorily solved.

"The viscount says his father is deeply grieving in any case. It wouldn't have been possible for you to speak with him presently." There must be someone else with whom he could consult. "I saw Mr. Beaumont leaving. Is there a problem?"

"I am uneasy about a few matters, and I think Victor continues to see me as a child. In essence, he pats my head and doesn't give me all the information I'm seeking."

Adelia sighed. Basically, Victor Beaumont was treating Thomas the way most men treated women. But she didn't think it prudent to say as such.

"You don't doubt his integrity, do you?" she asked.

Thomas shrugged. "He is an ambitious man. I believe he wants our company to succeed because he sees the success as his own. I don't mind that, and we pay him handsomely for his abilities. Victor wants to expand. Maybe we should, but I intend to visit Mr. Arnold today and make sure things are going smoothly from his perspective. I don't want any unexpected dips in revenue or massive expenses that could jeopardize us."

Adelia wished she could be of more use, but she'd never had a head for numbers or business—only for making up stories.

"I have something for you," Thomas said unexpectedly. "Wait a moment, I think you'll like it."

When he returned, he held out a fluted glass bottle. She read the label. It was French perfume.

"Whyever for?" she asked. But she could read her brother like a Jane Austen novel. "Let me guess, your lady-friend did not care for it."

Thomas's cheeks turned scarlet. "If I had a lady-friend, which I'm not saying I do, this would not suit her."

Adelia unstopped it and sniffed. She couldn't imagine any woman whom it wouldn't suit. "It's beautiful and unusual. Thank you." It was also heavier than her normal floral scent, and she would keep it for special occasions. A ball was the perfect venue for showing off perfume. The warmth of the crowded room combined with her body's heat from dancing would cause the fragrance to be released from her skin. She could only hope she was in Owen's arms on the parquet at that time.

That thought was followed quickly by a stab of regret. As she wandered upstairs to put the bottle on her dressing table, the battle within her raged—between guilt and desire. She knew she ought to stay away from the viscount whilst withholding the information about her brother's handkerchief. She had disposed of them all, but if Owen ever found out, he would undoubtedly resent her. Nevertheless, the desire to be with him was a siren song she couldn't deny, no more than she could ignore the thrilling feelings he'd awakened in her.

If it all crumbled under the weight of her deception, she would deserve the very worst.

When the promised invitation came from him that day, she was surprised. Not a public outing where they could blend with a crowd of hundreds, such as a museum or park concert, he wished to escort her to an intimate dinner party for twenty.

By showing up together, Owen was proclaiming them a couple!

CHAPTER FIFTEEN

Smoothing her pale gold dress trimmed with sapphire-blue ribbon and lace, and a matching blue underskirt, Adelia took quick stock of the other guests. Around her were established couples, some married, some engaged, and with them, her and Owen.

Although Penny accompanied them in the carriage, the maid had been sent with other chaperones to the servants' quarters as soon as they arrived. Now, Adelia waited in the short receiving line in a magnificent townhouse on Cavendish Square with her insides fluttering as if inhabited by butterflies. Doing so without her father or brother was an unfamiliar experience.

Owen, perfectly at ease, introduced her to their hosts, the Earl and Countess of Cambrey, obviously well-known to him, as he'd told her in the carriage.

"You've never come to one of my soirées before, Lord Burnley," Lady Margaret Cambrey said, eyeing Adelia with interest. "So glad you chose to grace us with your presence and this lovely lady's, as well. Welcome and enjoy yourselves. There is good French wine in the drawing room."

Adelia imagined it might take an entire bottle of wine to relax her nerves. She didn't say a word to either of their hosts, only curtseying deeply to the beautiful countess and her husband, who shook Owen warmly by the hand. She couldn't risk a drawn-out stuttering humiliation, not even to tell them what a lovely home they had.

"I'm sorry," she whispered to Owen as they entered the drawing room.

"What for?" he asked, looking down at her with those piercing blue eyes that seemed to accept her for who she was.

"I could not speak properly to Lord and Lady Cambrey."

"It's no matter," he reassured her. "A lovely woman's presence is enough without needing words."

She rolled her eyes at his silly—and very welcome—flattery.

"Wine, please," she asked. Hopefully, it would loosen her tongue.

After half a glass of claret, and with Owen's reassuring presence, she managed the customary pleasantries as they greeted the other couples. He squeezed her elbow encouragingly with each couple she met, and while her heart still pounded too hard for something so banal as a dinner party, Adelia felt almost accomplished by the time they went into the dining room.

As he had done at the ball during which they'd dined together, Owen coddled her from the second he pulled out her polished rosewood chair. If someone threw out a question from across the room directed to her, he intercepted it like an experienced cricketer with a high-flying ball, adeptly protecting his wicket.

He was seated to her left, and thus, Adelia could hear everything he said. She only had one terrifying moment when the gentleman to her right leaned close to say something. He might as well have been in another room, mouthing the words. Luckily, Owen, her savior, leaned forward, nearly putting his ascot into the third course of braised mutton, and answered for her as he knew the man personally.

"Come now, Tosh. You cannot expect this lovely lady to know about such things. Leave that for the club."

She would never know what Lord Toshlin, as she discovered his name, expected her to have an opinion about, nor did he seem to particularly care. Laughing at Owen's remark, the man turned back to his own companion. After that, Adelia kept her shoulders turned toward Owen to discourage any further attempts from that quarter.

When the pudding course arrived—a massive display of desserts dispersed across the center of the long table, including a tall nougat almond cake, a macedoine of fruits with jelly, and a towering apple *à la Parisienne*, which was placed at Owen and Adelia's end alongside a tray of dessert biscuits—they eyed each other with amusement.

Owen whispered in her ear, "I would far rather nibble on your neck."

She giggled before she could stop herself. "I fancy a small piece of almond cake." Then glancing at him from under her lashes, she whispered back, "And a large kiss from you."

His eyes widened. *And why not?* It was her first real attempt at flirting, brought on by two more glasses of wine with dinner and the secure, confident feeling Owen bestowed upon her.

Following dinner, a concert would be given upstairs in a large drawing room. In such a relatively small venue, Adelia was sure to hear it properly and looked forward to the treat.

After she picked her gloves off her lap and pulled them back on, Owen pulled out her chair and escorted her up the stairs, following the other couples. Everyone was in a good mood, and Adelia considered how grand a time it was to be living in London. At that instant, with only minor skirmishes occurring in the British Empire on the other side of the world in cities she couldn't pronounce, at home, all was peaceful.

They had plenty of food, more than enough if tonight's repast was any indication. They had theatre and luxuries to spare. And she had Owen, at least for that night. She was beginning to think she might have him for a lot longer, too. Perhaps for the rest of her life.

While everyone else was shuffling around, claiming their seats in the blue-and-white wallpapered room, they lagged back, somehow having agreed upon it without words. Maybe it was the long, dimly lit hallway stretching past the drawing room door that had put notions of escaping from the concert into her head. And his—for undoubtedly, Owen had spied it as well, like a pathway to privacy.

Perchance, for a few minutes, they might slip away unnoticed. On the one hand, it was a rash notion, given there were so few couples. On the other hand, with the guests seated in casual rows, Adelia and Owen would be less likely missed than if they hadn't been seated at the dining room table.

Adelia was ready to give Owen . . . everything. If he asked her to leave the party and go . . . well, wherever people went when they went off together, she would do so. What's more, she wouldn't care a fig for the consequences.

As if he knew her thoughts, he grinned at her. His wicked smile combined with the look in his eyes did something strange to her stomach, as if she were on her childhood tree swing at their country estate, rising up and falling fast.

While they lingered in the doorway, he tilted his head behind them and raised an eyebrow. She nodded and let him draw her backward, one step, two, and they dashed around the corner and along a floral-carpeted hallway.

Another of his exquisite kisses was in store for her, and she could hardly wait.

OWEN PULLED ADELIA INTO a parlor, empty and unlit save for the moonlight streaming in through the open draperies. Closing the door firmly behind them, he reached for her. She spun to face him, a look of anticipation upon her trusting face.

Sneaking away for private time wasn't something he expected ever to do with Lady Adelia Smythe. Furthermore, he didn't really want to take advantage. He simply wanted to hold her and say emphatically how highly he admired her.

Of course, now that they were, in fact, alone, he very much did want to kiss her. His blood was singing through his veins with pure passion. Enfolding her in his arms, relishing her warm curves against him, he kissed her.

Willingly, she opened for him, tasting of sweet custard, almonds, and French wine. But something was different.

"Mm," she sighed with pleasure against his lips.

He ignored whatever was distracting him, ravaging her mouth as his hands roamed her torso. Bending to nuzzle her soft neck, a familiar scent assaulted him.

He froze, eyes closed, breathing deeply against her skin. That was the difference—she always smelled of a light, floral fragrance. Until tonight.

Moreover, he knew that scent. His mouth went dry.

How could she be wearing the same perfume his sister used to wear? His brain wouldn't, at first, accept it.

When he glanced down, Adelia's eyes opened. She looked up at him in the moonlight, her familiar green gaze looked black, unsettling him further. She offered him an unsure smile.

He sniffed her hair, then her neck, and there it was, lingering upon her skin. His stomach turned. It was indubitably, impossibly Sophia's French perfume.

"Owen?" Adelia asked. That was the first time she'd said his name. He had dreamt of her doing so, crying it out when

..c made love to her. He had imagined whispering hers against her bare skin. *Adelia*.

In the silence, she exhaled sharply.

His hands had begun to grip her too tightly. But this was Adelia who hadn't even known Sophia. Immediately, he uncurled his fingers and relaxed his hold.

"What fragrance are you wearing?" His voice was a strange, toneless husk of its normal sound.

She cocked her head. "Do . . . do you like it?"

He wished he could say he did. But the ramifications of her having it in her possession were slowly creeping upon him.

"What is it?" he repeated.

This time, she took a step back at his gruff tone.

Would she lie? Suddenly, he realized the killer must have taken it from Sophia's reticule into which the shopgirl said she'd seen his sister deposit the small bottle. It hadn't been with her after she died. For some reason, Owen hadn't thought about the perfume since the moment he'd found her lying on the floor, lifeless. Never once had he wondered what had happened to it.

"*La Rose d'Amour*," Adelia said, and the room closed in around them.

He could hardly breathe.

"Where did you get it?" he demanded.

"What's wrong? You're . . . scaring me. I won't wear it again if you don't—"

"Where did you get it?" he yelled.

The shock on her face mirrored what he felt inside. *How could this be?* Something dreadfully sinister was afoot.

"From my . . . my brother. It was for his . . . his lady, but she . . . did not . . . she didn't like it."

His hands clenched at his sides. He could imagine only one possible way Lord Thomas Smythe had come into possession of the bottle.

"Your brother killed my sister, and I will have my justice *and* my revenge."

In the moonlight, he saw her face blanch. He'd only seen her do that one other time—when they'd discussed the handkerchief, and she'd been so upset while looking at something his sister had held when she'd died.

He wondered how she felt wearing a dead girl's perfume.

"I'm taking you home," he told her, "and I will speak with your brother when we get there."

"He's not at home," she said, worry etched into her otherwise flawless features.

"How convenient," he bit out. "Where is he? We shall go to him."

She shook her head, and it infuriated him.

"Do you think this is a game?" he demanded.

"No, of course not. I have no idea where he is." She hung her head. He could see she was telling the truth.

"Did you know?"

She shook her head in dismay. "What are you asking?"

"That he killed my sister. Did you know all this time?"

He saw a flash of something cross her face. It looked very much like guilt.

He yelled loudly, not caring they were in someone else's house or that twenty other people were in a room along the hall. He paced away from her to the window, staring out briefly into the darkness where the lamplights cast their feeble glow. Even the moon had retreated behind the clouds, making everything appear darker, more sinister.

He yelled again. Adelia's betrayal was slicing at his sanity.

What if Sophia had been looking down from Heaven and seen him dancing and kissing the murderer's sister?

"Stop it," Adelia begged, her voice coming from close behind him. "Thomas did *not* kill your sister. I know this in my heart."

"In your heart?" he repeated. He wished she'd said she knew it for the truth. The heart was not a font of truthfulness, or how could his own have fallen for such a liar.

"That perfume is rare in England," he grated, "only sold in *one* shop in Piccadilly."

"That does not mean my brother killed Sophia." He heard the reason in her voice, but it was pointless. There was only one answer. Smythe had taken it from her reticule after he'd strangled her.

"She had only just purchased it. Yet it was not with her when I found her."

Adelia bit her lower lip, a gesture he normally found intensely arousing. The only thing aroused now was his absolute rage. He had been so close all this time to the killer.

Hell! He'd sparred with the bastard at Teavey's. *Had Smythe been laughing at him the entire time?*

"Let's go," he said, grabbing her by the elbow.

"Where?" Adelia was trying to pull herself free.

If she believed she could break away from him, she was sorely mistaken.

"Wherever your dear brother might be, that's where we're going."

Adelia stopped fighting him. Approaching the door—so recently shut against the rest of the world for the purpose of their false and disgusting tryst—he yanked it open savagely. He had nearly succeeded in dragging her into the hallway when she snagged the doorframe with her free hand.

"You cannot handle me thusly as we make our way through the Cambreys' house. We shall both be ruined."

Honestly, Owen didn't give a damn about ruination, not for either one of them.

"Then walk swiftly by my side, or by God, I shall carry you," he ground out between his clenched teeth, "but either way, we're going to find him."

CHAPTER SIXTEEN

This was absolute insanity! Adelia didn't know where Thomas had got the blasted perfume, but certainly not from the deceased Sophia Burnley. Taking a breath, she nodded, and they proceeded in a stately, dignified fashion back along the carpeted hallway, not pausing at the open drawing room from which the strains of the popular Mendelssohn were emanating.

Down the stairs they went in silence and into the entry foyer. While waiting for her mantle and her street shoes, she realized her hands were shaking. She did not doubt her brother for a second, but this was a frightening situation. And Owen was a formidable man who, at that moment, was not thinking clearly. Although she felt entirely safe with him, she knew he might attack Thomas before giving him the chance to defend himself.

She had to calm him down. Utterly against propriety, she let him assist her into his carriage without any chaperone either inside or on top with his driver, who set a lit lamp in the holder and closed the door. They'd abandoned Penny entirely, and the poor girl wouldn't know it for hours. When it was discovered they'd left without her maid, tongues would wag indeed.

Frankly, she didn't care what the *ton* thought. She was *of* them but not included among them, and it shouldn't bother her what they said or believed.

It never had in the past. Except recently, as Owen's companion, she'd started to feel she belonged. She'd started to care how people viewed her. Tonight, at dinner, the people had been welcoming, and their hosts, the Cambreys, were Owen's peers. *Did they see her as worthy of the dashing viscount who could have any woman at whom he crooked his finger?*

That evening, she'd been included by the cream of society until it had all fallen apart. They remained silent in his clarence, seated on opposite sides.

Finally, she asked, "Where did you tell your driver to go?"

"We'll start with your home, in case Smythe is there," Owen said, staring out the window.

Relieved they were not going willy-nilly into the night, she leaned back upon the squabs. *Could she get through to this furious Owen Burnley?* He'd always listened to her words so carefully. She had to try.

"I must tell you about my brother, and you will understand the folly of your accusation."

"While you reek of my dead sister's perfume, do not attempt to convince me of your brother's innocence," he said, his tone scathing, while he still did not do her the courtesy of looking at her.

Gracious! The hostility frightened her, but Owen, himself, did not. She must make him understand this was a mistake before they encountered Thomas.

"My father was not a kind and patient man," she began.

Owen held up his hand. "If you are going to tell me how difficult was your brother's childhood, thereby excusing violence toward others, save your breath."

"On the contrary, he is not violent at all. Despite having occasionally fought with our father, Thomas is a gentle soul."

"Smythe likes to box. I've experienced it at our pugilist's club."

"So do you," she reminded him. "That doesn't make you a violent man."

At those words, he finally turned to look at her. "Oh, but I am. At this very instant, I could gladly wrap my fingers around your brother's throat and squeeze the life out of him."

Adelia's mouth snapped shut, and she looked away from the fury burning in Owen's eyes. It was exceedingly difficult to be in close quarters with such hostility, especially directed at her kin.

"For my sake, will you please let him answer questions? If you immediately start pummeling each other, you will not get your answers."

"For your sake?" His usually kind tone had become a cynical sneer. "You mean for the sake of our *feelings* for one another?"

The way he said it made her shudder. He was deliberately mocking her and belittling what they were starting to mean to one another. If her brother were the killer, she supposed she could understand his sudden change. But Thomas was not. *So how were they to fix this?*

"We could help you find all the users of the paper with the John Dickinson watermark," she offered.

His mouth twisted into a grimace. "Oh, yes, the second bit of evidence. Why should I look any further when I already know you keep the paper in your home? Your brother undoubtedly had easy access to it. I will be sure to tell the detective."

Adelia decided to keep quiet in case Owen brought up the handkerchief next. If he questioned her about it, he would see the guilt plainly upon her face. She groaned. This was impossible, unthinkable. It simply could not be happening.

"You groan with dismay for your brother. Only think how many groans of anguish I have made over Sophia."

She fisted her hands in her lap. "You are wrong about Thomas. You will see."

All she could do was remain calm and pray for a miracle.

When they arrived at her family's townhouse, it seemed her prayers were answered. According to their butler, her brother was out, and Mr. Lockley had no knowledge where. For once, Adelia didn't mind.

"We can wait," Owen proposed. "Or I could go fetch Detective Sergeant Garrard. Or we could go looking for your brother." He stood in the foyer of her home, arms folded, dominating the tiled space.

Adelia considered all those options. "Or you could go home, and when I see my brother in the morning, I shall tell him you wish to speak with him."

Owen shook his head. "I think not. Next time I hear of him, he will have vanished to the Continent without a trace."

"He would not do that," she insisted. "He would never leave me here."

"Maybe you will flee with him."

How outrageous! "We have nothing to flee from."

"Then let's go find him, shall we? If he were going to the theatre, he probably would have told you. We can stop off at a few of the clubs, I suppose. Does he frequent Whites?"

She nodded, though more often he would be at the Reform Club, but she wasn't going to tell the viscount.

Owen fired his next question. "Does he gamble?"

"No." Adelia didn't see how that mattered anyway.

"Does he have a mistress he visits or keeps somewhere?"

She recalled the dark-haired woman.

"No," she repeated.

"Your face says yes," he insisted.

She shook her head. "To my knowledge, no, but I did see him with a woman the night of the play. I told you that."

His eyes widened. "I think I saw them together. I'd all but forgotten. Too much whiskey," he muttered.

"Where did you see my brother? When?"

"A few nights back, maybe a week," he clarified. "I was hunting in the East End for the murderer, thinking he might be someone who didn't belong, just as my sister hadn't." He shook his head. "Lo and behold, I saw *your* brother! Moreover, he was dressed in the clothing of a tradesman. When I called out to him, he ran out the back door with that woman."

Odd! she thought. *Yet Thomas did take his privacy surrounding his new lady-friend quite seriously.*

"Somehow, I doubt he would go back after I spotted him so close to the scene of the crime," Owen pondered.

She rolled her eyes. "I tell you, he is innocent."

"Lockley, did he take his carriage and driver?" Owen asked.

The butler looked to her first prior to answering personal questions about his master. She nodded for him to respond.

"His lordship takes a hackney most evenings when he goes out."

Adelia hadn't been aware of that. She supposed with traffic and lack of parking, it was easier.

"The night we saw him at the theatre," Owen persisted, looking at her, "it was last Wednesday, wasn't it?"

"Yes." *How could she ever forget one of the few wonderful nights of her life?*

To the butler, Owen demanded, "I wish to speak with the earl's driver."

Again, the butler looked to her. "You may fetch him," she agreed.

Not looking too happy, he did as directed, and in a few minutes came back from the servants' quarters with Henry, her brother's driver, who, by the looks of him, had quickly donned his uniform, which hung slightly askew.

"You took the earl last Wednesday night to pick up a young woman. Where did you go?"

Henry looked from Owen to Adelia, who nodded for him to answer.

"To the East End, my lord."

Adelia gasped softly, drawing Owen's smug attention. "Precisely where, man?" he growled impatiently.

"Corner of Whitechapel High Street and Osborn Street, my lord. The young miss was waiting there."

"Very close," Owen muttered, and she knew he meant to where Sophia had been strangled.

"That will be all, Henry," she said. The driver disappeared the way he had come.

"I suppose we could go now," Adelia offered. For if Owen were hunting Thomas that night, she had to go, too, to protect her brother if at all possible.

"I cannot take you there. It is beyond low. To that, I can attest."

"In *your* company," she said, appealing to his pride as a strong male, "I would be well protected."

"If anything were to happen to you . . . ," he began but trailed off.

Would it bother him? she wondered. Owen seemed to be painting her with the same brush of guilt as he was her brother. Hopefully, when calmer, he would see reason.

"All right," he conceded. "We shall go to Whitechapel High Street and visit the last place I saw him. You will stay next to me," he ordered. "I don't need to remind you to keep your mouth closed. The less your finely accented tone is heard, the safer you will be. Frankly, you are the only woman I know who can stay quiet unbidden. I suggest you wear a thick black cloak and sturdy walking shoes."

She glanced down at her expensive gown. If she asked to change, she feared he would go without her. Mr. Lockley was already grabbing the necessary outerwear from the downstairs closet, and she sat on the tufted chair in the foyer to remove her lightweight shoes, which she set next to her dancing slippers. After donning her favorite ankle boots, she glanced up in time to see Owen staring at her legs.

He visibly swallowed, and his gaze locked with hers. Apparently, the sight of her stockinged feet had reminded him he fancied her, as he'd once said. *Good.* She was not ready to lose this man over what could only be a severe misunderstanding of the facts.

"Ready?" Owen asked, offering her his arm.

"Yes."

"Where is Penny, my lady?" This from Mr. Lockley, who was usually careful not to lose his staff.

Adelia exhaled in frustration. "Please send Henry back to Cavendish Square. I am sorry to say, we left her behind."

Mr. Lockley scowled magnificently. "We shall recover her at once, my lady. Will you take Meg or—?"

"She'll take no one," Owen interrupted. "It's bad enough I have to look after her. I cannot worry about two females."

"My lady," the butler protested, overstepping his position out of sheer loyalty to her family.

"Lord Burnley and I are going to look for Lord Smythe, Mr. Lockley. And there is a driver and a footman along as well. I shall be perfectly safe."

And with Owen blisteringly angry at her and doubting her every word, she supposed her person was safer with him than ever before. Kisses were not in the foreseeable future.

In moments, they were back in his comfortable clarence, and she supposed if they found Thomas, she would return home with her brother.

As they traveled through Mayfair, she tried to piece together everything she now knew. "You found your sister because of a note that she left behind?"

"Yes."

"And a young boy brought her the note to the shop in Piccadilly, which means she was being observed. Has anyone tried to discover his identity?"

"About as impossible to find one particular sandy-haired urchin as to find a specific grain of sand on Brighton beach. The detective thinks that path leads nowhere."

"Maybe, but one could begin to search the workhouses in the East End or the orphanages at the very least."

"As a matter of fact, I went to one orphanage not long ago, but the sheer number of boys is overwhelming. Also, there is no guarantee he was an orphan."

Sighing with exasperation, she understood Owen grasping onto the first solid evidence—the perfume. Were she in his shoes, she would do the same. *If only it didn't point to Thomas!*

Soon, they alit from the carriage in a neighborhood to which she had never been. No gas lamps with glass fixtures were creating any reassuring hazy glow. Instead, the occasional open pipe flamed straight up. The light was garish and looked downright dangerous.

She found herself staring at everything around her as if she were not a Londoner born and bred. People on the street were not dressed properly for the night air, especially the women. Adelia was no prude, but she had never seen the like, nor the amount of uncovered skin in public. And everywhere, men were openly chatting with the women.

"I have never been down the Whitechapel Road," Adelia confessed. "In fact, except for wanting to walk across London Bridge and see the Tower, I've never been much easterly past Cheapside."

"There are not a half-dozen people in my circle of acquaintance," Owen remarked, "who have come as far east as we are tonight. Have you heard of Poplar, Limehouse, or Rotherhithe?"

"I think so, but I am not entirely certain where they are."

"Farther east. No man's land."

He steered her past a coffeehouse as she peeked through the open door at men playing draughts and dominoes. Raucous piano and fiddle music came from the next two places, and soon, they entered a tavern.

"This is a slightly nicer one than those I've been searching in," he said, perhaps feeling compelled to tell her.

Thank goodness he did, or she would have assumed he'd brought her to the worst possible pub in order to frighten her back into the protection of the carriage. Men at tables were playing dice and card games, and women were either seated with them or hanging around the backs of their chairs.

"We shall start here," Owen said. "The odds that we find your brother are infinitesimally small, don't you think?"

"Yes," she agreed, her voice barely above a whisper.

Yet, that was precisely what happened in the very next establishment.

OWEN DIDN'T ORDER A drink. He calmly searched the tables in the first tavern before taking Lady Adelia by the hand and going a block farther, knowing their carriage was following along closely. They entered another pub with about the same shabbiness as the first.

As soon as his eyes adjusted to the lighting, he saw the young earl, seated in the back corner, the same dark-haired woman by his side.

Odds bodkins!

He knew the instant Adelia saw her brother. She stiffened under his hand. Owen wasn't going to alert Smythe to his presence this time by hailing him, nor was he going to allow the earl's sister to do so. Pulling her quickly along behind him, they headed toward the far end of the room where the couple talked in earnest, oblivious to their surroundings.

The young woman stopped midsentence as they approached the table. She blinked up at them without recognition. Smythe, however, slowly rose to his feet, his face darkening with anger.

"What can you be thinking by bringing my sister here?"

Not exactly the words Owen was expecting. *Why would he bring his lady-friend there if it was inappropriate for his sister?* He couldn't imagine what woman would accept being treated in such a manner. Unless she was a trollop.

Owen glanced at the woman again. While she was dressed plainly, she wasn't clothed scandalously, nor did she appear to be a lightskirt.

As for the earl, he was also dressed more befitting a middle-class shopkeeper than a titled member of the nobility, in a shapeless, brown sack coat and a starched bow tie. His outfit was crowned with a wool cap. *What was he playing at?*

"Isn't this where all the fine aristocrats are spending their evenings?" Owen asked.

"Are you mad?" Smythe seethed.

"Constantly," Owen said. "Would you care to introduce us to your latest victim?"

"I beg your pardon?" her brother asked and turned to Adelia. "Why did you come here?"

Owen watched her stricken mien. He doubted she would say anything, but her expression softened.

"We came to ask you some questions. It's important."

"This couldn't wait until morning?" he demanded.

"No," Owen answered. "We can either talk here or at the police station."

He watched the earl's gaze shoot to Adelia, and something passed between them. They were hiding something. *Had she known her brother was the murderer?* He could not bear the thought. By the end of the night, he intended to know everything.

"Will you introduce us, Thomas?" This from Adelia, still looking with curiosity at the pretty woman who'd remained silent and watchful during the entire exchange.

Smythe sighed. "Miss Moore, this is my sister of whom I've made mention. Dilly, this is Miss Constance Moore."

The aforementioned Miss Moore's eyes widened, and she immediately stood and offered Adelia a deep curtsey.

"Ever so pleased," she commented in an accent that betrayed her heritage as being from the country, possibly northern Yorkshire.

Adelia nodded and murmured something Owen couldn't hear. Nor did he care about this inane chatter.

"And this odious creature is Lord Burnley," Smythe said, his tone dripping with annoyance.

Again, the brown-haired miss curtsied and gave her evidently standard greeting, "Ever so pleased."

Owen nodded to her, the politest thing he could do under the circumstances when he wanted to grab the earl by his ridiculous coat and bash him into the wall behind.

"Enough of this chit-chat, Smythe," Owen growled. "Why are you hiding out in the East End?"

"I do not owe you any explanation on that account," The earl protested.

"I think you do, but let us get to the heart of the matter, shall we? The perfume you gave Lady Adelia belonged to my sister."

He watched Smythe for signs of guilt and treachery. Instead, he saw surprise. Then the earl frowned and shook his head. Finally, he said, "I believe you are mistaken."

"We should not discuss this here," Adelia insisted, grasping at Owen's coat sleeve.

He glanced around at the interested faces blatantly staring. Clearly, they were providing entertainment. Moreover, Smythe had introduced them, giving their names out loud. Someone might have overheard who shouldn't have, although Owen doubted those who wrote for London's society pages would be loitering in such a hole.

Nevertheless, it was possible their names could be sold to the newspaper, and it would be a whopping scandal, no doubt.

"I do not trust your brother to follow us home. For all I know, he will head for the coast."

"That's absurd." Both Adelia and her brother spoke at once.

"We could go to my flat," Miss Moore offered.

"Constance, no," Smythe began, but she interrupted him.

"None of *my* neighbors will mind. It is only yours we must be wary of."

"Very well," the earl agreed after a pause, and he looked at Owen. "We shall go to Miss Moore's home to speak further. It is around the corner. Do you agree?"

"Lead the way," Owen said.

To his surprise, Smythe and his lady headed for the back door. Thus, for the first time in his life, and undoubtedly in Adelia's as well, he stood in a fetid and filthy alley off of Whitechapel Road. Traversing it swiftly, trying not to breathe in the odor from the piles of detritus and mysterious greasy puddles, they came out at the corner and turned left.

True to the earl's word, the flat was just around the corner on Osborn Street, within spitting distance of where Sophia died. Through a door with a broken pane, up one flight, the earl used a key to unlock the apartment door.

Owen glanced at Adelia, and she looked back at him, eyebrows raised. Apparently, this was entirely unknown to her. Smythe stood back and gestured for them to follow Miss Moore inside.

It was as Owen expected, cramped and with the absolute absence of anything remotely resembling luxury, but it was clean. At least, there weren't piles of soiled clothing or leftover plates of food. In fact, it was nearly as tidy as his bachelor townhouse, and he had servants to keep it so.

Furthermore, she seemed to have the flat to herself. He knew from his discussion with Lady Jane how many of these small lodgings had one or even two families in them, up to ten people sharing two rooms.

Fresh flowers in a jar added a dash of color, and as Miss Moore lit the lamps, the place took on a rosy glow. *Almost comfortable,* Owen thought. Regardless, he had no intention of sitting on the threadbare sofa. They weren't there on a social call, after all.

As if they were, Miss Moore offered to put the kettle on the small stove that created the entirety of her kitchen equipment along one wall. Owen shuddered at the idea, not wanting to offend her but also not wishing to look into a cracked, chipped, stained cup or be offered curdled milk with whatever dust passed for tea leaves.

"No, thank you," Adelia answered swiftly. "Thomas, about the perfume, where did you get it?"

"You won't believe it," he offered.

"Probably not," Owen agreed.

The young earl sent him a withering look before responding. "I found it."

"Where?" Adelia asked.

Smythe shrugged. "That's the strange thing. I found it in my pocket."

Owen would have laughed if he weren't beginning to feel infuriated with Smythe's ridiculous tale.

"Which pocket?" Adelia persisted as if that mattered.

"One of my regular coats."

Owen stared at him. "I would wager you are not referring to that monstrosity you're currently wearing."

Smythe glared back. "A mulberry-red wool one to be precise."

"And you simply put your hand in your pocket and drew out the bottle?" Owen sneered. "I suppose a fairy creature slipped it inside whilst you weren't looking."

"He's telling the truth," Miss Moore spoke up. "Thomas offered it to me, but I can't be wearing the likes of that. Lavender water is what I use."

Owen glanced at Adelia. She was taking all this in with her usual aplomb, despite learning her brother had presented her a gift of perfume he'd already tried to give his mistress.

"That proves nothing," Owen pointed out, taking a step toward Smythe. "Only that you somehow have my sister's perfume. As for the truth, I don't believe we've got to that yet. Now that Miss Moore is safely home, I insist you come with me to the police station."

"The police!" Miss Moore exclaimed while Adelia moved closer to her brother.

"I am sure if we think this through," she began, "we can figure out how it got into my brother's pocket."

"In any case, I am not going to the police station," Smythe insisted. "I am taking my sister home."

Owen shook his head. "No. You will not go to the comfort of Hyde Park Street and enjoy another night of freedom while Sophia's spirit goes unavenged."

"Lord Burnley, please," Adelia began. "We can deal with this in the morning, can't we?"

He had to steel himself against her entreaties. Owen had grown fond enough of her that her distress, visible upon her lovely face, caused him distress of his own. Nevertheless, he could not let that deter him from justice.

"Will you come easily?" Owen demanded.

"No," Smythe answered, his face set in a mulish mien.

"Very well." Without warning, for Owen was in no mood for a drawn-out round of fisticuffs, he raised his arm and punched the younger man in the face. Both the women shrieked, and Smythe toppled back.

The earl was not knocked unconscious as that had not been Owen's intent, but Smythe was stunned by the surprise attack. In a flash, Owen dragged him upright and was resolved to get him outside and into the clarence without having to punch him again.

"Lady Adelia," Owen said as he reached the door, "you will come quietly. All three of us will go in my carriage."

"He's bleeding," she pointed out, her eyes sending daggers of disappointment at Owen, which he had no choice but to ignore.

Suddenly, Miss Moore stepped forward and withdrew a handkerchief from her sleeve.

"You brute," she admonished Owen with a flash of white linen.

He knew before he even saw it. Naturally, the damning evidence would appear now. *Fate had turned in his favor at last!* As the young woman dabbed at the blood trickling from Smythe's nose, Owen spotted the anvil pattern on the handkerchief's lace.

CHAPTER SEVENTEEN

Owen looked hurriedly around. If both women fought him, as well as Smythe, who was shaking off the unexpected blow, he would have a devil of a time getting him all the way down the stairs and along the street to his carriage.

"Where did you get that handkerchief?" he asked the earl's lover, his tone wooden, since he knew the answer.

While keeping Miss Moore talking, Owen spied a curtain sash. *Perfect!*

"It's Thomas's, of course," she snapped. "Whose else would I have? You *are* a madman! Whatever you think of me, I am not a strumpet."

Owen could not care less if the attractive Miss Moore slept with every man in the East End and then some. He took two steps across the small bedsit and wrenched the curtain sash free. In another minute, he had the murderous earl's hands firmly tied behind his back.

"Let's go," he urged, pushing Smythe in front of him. At that point, the young man began to struggle. Too late, with his hands bound, he had no choice but to go where Owen directed him.

Miss Moore protested again, but Adelia remained strangely silent, ever since the handkerchief had appeared.

Owen walked past Smythe's lover, snatching the bloodied kerchief from her hand and shoving it into his pocket. He had the blackguard—and all the evidence. He now knew where Miss Moore lived, and she could corroborate, albeit unwillingly, that Smythe owned the handkerchief and had possessed the perfume. He also knew Adelia would not bear witness to either. She'd known all along whom that blasted handkerchief had belonged to, and that knowledge turned Owen's heart to stone.

It was easier than he'd thought to herd Adelia and her brother toward his carriage. As they walked swiftly along, he realized why the multitude of hackneys were going up and down the dark street. Like Smythe, many of London's gentlemen frequented the area. When they did, they didn't want their own carriages parked in the dangerous area. They were free to revel in a few hours of gratification with an East End lover before heading home to the prim and proper side of London.

It took a little pushing to get the earl into the carriage, but with the driver's help, Owen accomplished it. He turned to Adelia; her gaze refused to meet his as he helped her in.

When seated opposite brother and sister, Owen stared at Adelia's ashen face. She didn't even ask for Smythe to be unbound despite her brother leaning awkwardly forward, trying to keep his head up, unvanquished.

Owen watched her put her hand on the earl's shoulder, then smooth his hair back from his forehead, waiting stoically for their arrival at the police station. She kept her eyes firmly averted from Owen's side of the carriage.

However, presented with her perfidy, he could not keep silent. "All this time, you knew the handkerchief was your brother's. Yet you led me on a merry dance, didn't you?"

She shook her head.

"An anvil," Owen murmured, drawing the bloody kerchief from his pocket.

"For a smith," the earl bit out.

"And the handkerchief I saw you use at Teavey's?" Owen demanded.

Smythe shrugged. "A new one."

Was the man about to confess? He seemed to be giving up all his secrets.

"You destroyed your others when you learned I was looking for the one my sister clutched when *you* killed her."

"No!" Adelia answered for him as the young lord shook his head.

Owen stared at her. "I told you, and unsurprisingly, you told him. Isn't that right?" he persisted.

"I did tell him," Adelia said slowly, "but he didn't destroy his handkerchiefs. I did. I burned them."

"Because you knew he was guilty." Owen's rage nearly overwhelmed him. He pounded his fist on the leather seat beside him. He genuinely admired this woman—more than that! And she had played him for a fool. All his burgeoning affection toward her was for nothing.

"Because I knew he was innocent," she corrected him in her usual soft voice.

Wasted time, wasted emotions, he seethed. She was a liar, and she'd accompanied him hither and yon with her meek, quiet ways to throw him off the track of her horror of a brother.

His hands fisted on his lap. *How dare she continue to defend the man!* In the face of all this evidence, and while still reeking of Sophia's perfume.

"If your sister were not present, Smythe, I would beat you to a pulp, and you would never live to see the police station."

Adelia gasped, but the young earl shrugged again. "Who knew Lord Burnley was such a coward. First to punch me without gentlemanly warning, and next to offer to kill me while my hands are tied."

Owen reached forward slowly to grab the man by his silly bow tie and pull him half off the squabs.

"You truly do not appreciate your good fortune in having Lady Adelia here to prevent your punishment. I cannot believe I had you under my fists at Teavey's and didn't know what a monster you were."

For her part, she was tugging on Owen's arms to get him to release her brother.

Owen gave the man a rough shake for good measure, then let him go, hoping he'd slither down onto the carriage floor, but he didn't. Instead, Smythe relaxed again onto the seat, fixing him with an irritated glare.

"This is precisely why I destroyed the handkerchiefs," Adelia said. "I knew you would react like this. Like a tyrant, as judge and executioner."

She had tried to help her brother the same way as Owen was trying to . . . well, not help Sophia, for it was too late for that. All the same, he could and would follow this obvious path through to the conclusion that would see Smythe hanged. He didn't think it prudent to mention that fact in Adelia's company.

He fought the slight swizzle of guilt that wound around his gut. While there could never be anything between Adelia and him now, he'd determined the culpability of her brother and felt sorry she would have this stain upon her name.

He felt even sorrier he would never again make her laugh, a rare treat, or kiss her lips and hold her in his arms. Briefly closing his eyes against the ugliness of what was happening, he could not allow himself to have feelings for this woman an instant longer. And they would be pointless. If she ever had any regard for him, she couldn't still, not after this.

Seemingly sooner than he believed possible, they were at Whitehall and the police station, next to Scotland Yard.

Close to midnight, Owen was not under any delusion Detective Sergeant Garrard would be in his office so late, but surely, someone would rouse him from his bed wherever the man resided. Or, at the very least, they would hold Smythe until the detective came into work the next morning.

To that end, Owen shoved Smythe into the station. He saw no policeman he recognized but let it be known he had apprehended the murderer of his sister.

Adelia chose that moment to cease being the quiet woman he had grown accustomed to.

"Lord Burnley is mistaken." Her voice rang out loudly and clearly.

Owen rolled his eyes. "The evidence is indisputable."

Luckily for Owen, the constable was not young and impressionable, nor swayed when he asked Smythe his name and learned he was not only a member of nobility, but an earl.

In fact, taking in Smythe's shabby appearance, the officer looked doubtful.

"He is who he says he is, despite his disguise," Owen said. "However, I have evidence of his guilt, and I will not let you release him. I demand you send for Detective Sergeant Garrard."

The policeman led the three of them to a small room with a table and four chairs.

"Please, my lords, my lady, wait here."

This was going to become awkwardly uncomfortable, and Owen didn't give a tinker's damn. Strangely, it was Adelia who spoke first.

"Why were you hiding your acquaintance with Miss Moore?" she asked her brother.

Smythe glanced at Owen first, then at his sister seated next to him.

"Isn't that obvious, Dilly-girl?"

Dilly-girl?

Adelia shook her head, and her brother fell silent.

Owen decided to enlighten her. "Because his mistress is from the wrong side of town, about as wrong as you can get without being from France."

Adelia's eyes widened, and she stared at her brother, who shrugged.

"As usual, your viscount is jumping to the wrong conclusions."

Her viscount? Owen's gaze went to Adelia's at the same time as she looked at him. He watched her cheeks turn a sweet shade of pink. She lowered her eyes as her brother continued.

"Miss Moore is to become my wife."

ADELIA HOPED HER SURPRISE didn't appear on her face, and she managed to shut her mouth after saying simply, "Oh!"

But Lord Burnley's shock was evident, and he offered a disparaging laugh.

"Is that so? You intend to make Miss Moore your *countess?*"

Smythe ignored him.

"I would like to see that," Owen continued unkindly in a taunting voice.

Adelia could hardly imagine the scandal. The newspapers would be brutal. The *ton* would shun Miss Moore. Absolutely no one would accept her into their homes. Thomas and his new wife would have to endure utter isolation unless they could create a salon in their home on Hyde Park Street that drew visitors to them.

But Owen spoke again, "It's no matter. Where you're going, you will not be needing a wife."

Adelia felt a frisson of terror dance along her spine. Owen intended to send her brother to jail, and she had to admit, the evidence was damning.

"He didn't murder anyone," she insisted, knowing she would be repeating that until proof arrived of his innocence. *But what if it never came?*

Suddenly, it occurred to her what she must do. Worrying about the scandal sheets' reaction to her brother's intent to marry beneath him was decidedly premature. First, she ought to be worried they might catch wind of this ridiculous accusation and ruin his reputation forever. Moreover, she must defend him as he had always done for her.

She looked at her brother, with the blood now crusted under his nose and his hair mussed, his silly bow tie sideways, and her heart ached for him. As soon as they were released from this nightmare, she intended to prove his innocence. If she could just figure out how.

Meanwhile, she began to work on the tight knots of the fabric binding her brother's hands.

"What are you doing?" Owen demanded.

"Untying him. We are in a police station. You cannot possibly think he will overpower every officer here, as well as you, and escape."

Owen glared, and she thought he would forbid her, but he remained silent. He also didn't help, and it took her many minutes until she'd freed Thomas. He rubbed his wrists and sat back in his chair, crossing his arms, and keeping a steady gaze on Lord Burnley.

She had to admire her brother for his aplomb in the face of the night's proceedings.

None of them wished to talk further. They waited silently until she heard footsteps, and the door opened. A slightly haggard man entered, already frowning at those awaiting him.

"What is the meaning of this?" The stranger, a detective by his manner of dress, directed his question to the viscount. "Taking justice into your own hands again, Lord Burnley?"

Slowly, Owen stood. "I have brought you my sister's killer."

Adelia cringed at the words, but he continued. "Lord Thomas Smythe is the owner of the handkerchief, and he has the same watermarked paper in his home as that which the note to my sister was written upon. Lastly, he had in his possession the very perfume she bought the day she was killed."

Her brother rose to his feet under the weight of this damning evidence, and Adelia stood beside him, putting a trembling hand on his arm.

"Well, well," said the stranger, his glance going between her and Thomas, taking their measure. After running a hand over the stubble on his chin and through his hair, which in truth looked as if he'd come straight from his bed, the man finally introduced himself.

"I am Detective Sergeant Garrard of the Metropolitan Police." When his gaze flicked toward her again, she swallowed with nervousness.

"Who might you be, miss?" he asked.

"She is my sister," Thomas spoke for her as he often did. "She has nothing to do with any of this," he insisted.

"And why is she here?" The detective's keen gaze was holding her own.

"Lady Adelia was wearing the perfume her brother gave her," Owen pointed out as if that warranted her appearance at the station. "My sister's!"

She glanced at his harsh expression. She supposed at any instant, he might turn her in for burning the handkerchiefs.

The detective sighed. "Lord Smythe—oh, *smith* and *anvil*, I see—what do you say to these charges?"

"I am innocent. I didn't know Lord Burnley's sister, and I had no reason to kill her. Even Lord Burnley must acknowledge that."

Adelia watched Owen carefully. He frowned.

Detective Garrard asked him, "Did your sister ever make mention of Lord Smythe?"

"No," Owen said, "but she did not make mention of any man who might be ready to kill her. That signifies nothing."

"True," the detective agreed, and Adelia's heart sank. "But there is always a motive, especially in a case with premeditation such as this one."

"Excuse me, detective," she said, drawing his attention to her, "but could . . . could you explain what . . . what you mean?"

Blazes! She was so upset she could hardly speak.

"It means Lady Sophia's murderer wasn't unknown to her. He sent her a message, probably intending to kill her if she responded. And she did."

Owen whirled away from them, apparently trying to pace, but the room was too small. He fisted his hands and took a step, then another, before turning back, his face flushed with anger. She ached for him, too. *Poor man!*

"In other words, this wasn't a crime of strangers," the detective continued. "It wasn't a result of thievery or a moment's passionate violence, if you'll excuse my using such language."

He paused and looked at her brother again. "On the other hand, I suppose the note could have been intended to invite her for a romantic assignation, which she refused. And thus, the murderer might have killed her, either intentionally or unintentionally."

Owen made a sound of frustrated fury. "How could he kill her unintentionally with a rope around her neck?"

Adelia winced at his harsh words.

The detective hesitated, then said, "We shouldn't discuss it in front of the lady, but there are people"—he coughed—"who engage in rough relations, including with ropes and whips."

"Enough," Owen bit out, although she had no idea why this angered him, nor did she understand what the detective was talking about.

"I did not kill her," Thomas insisted as fervently as ever.

"Nevertheless, Lord Smythe, you shall have to be detained due to the evidence, which sounds substantial." The detective spoke to Owen. "Please turn over everything you have. It will be needed in court."

"Court!" Adelia hadn't realized she'd said the word aloud. *How was this possible?*

"Don't you want to ask my brother where he was on the day and at the time of Lady Sophia's death? You can ask him questions now and discern his innocence."

Owen had begun to empty his pockets—two handkerchiefs, one stained with Thomas's blood, and the bottle of perfume.

"You already have the infernal note," he said to the detective, who nodded.

"I am sorry, my lady. With such tangible evidence, I must keep your brother in custody, regardless of what he tells me tonight. Of course, he will be questioned, and he will be allowed to retain his own counsel for the trial. Perhaps you can go to one of the Inns of Court later today, after the sun comes up, and find him a lawyer who works with a criminal barrister in good standing. Take care to avoid the pettifoggers. There are plenty of sublime rascals, I assure you."

Her mouth had dropped open as the detective spoke. Snapping it closed, she glanced at Thomas, feeling terror as she observed his grim face. *Dear God!* The outcome of the trial might depend upon the quality of the counsel she hired.

The small room suddenly seemed airless. If she didn't keep breathing deeply, she thought she might faint. She looked at Owen, whose hooded gaze showed no affection or pity—no longer her friend, decidedly her foe.

If she swooned again, she had a feeling he would not catch her as he had once done.

"Very well," she spoke directly to Thomas. "I promise, I'll find you good counsel. I shall return later and tell you how I fared." She put her arms around him.

"You won't find your brother here when you return," the detective said. "He'll be lodged at Newgate until he sees the magistrate."

"Newgate!" Thomas exclaimed, and she could see by his face, he hadn't expected that.

Filled with fear at the notion of him residing in such a despicable place, Adelia began to shake.

"It's all right," he said to comfort her, patting her back before drawing away to give her upper arms a reassuring squeeze. "I shall be fine."

"He will be," the detective confirmed, then spoke to Thomas. "Unlike most, you've got the coin to pay your way. Your sister will have to fetch you that, and swiftly. The jailers don't go by account. It's not pleasant, but you won't be in the worst of it, and Newgate has held noblemen in the past."

Detective Sergeant Garrard spoke to her again. "It's late—or rather, it's early. A couple of my men will take your brother over, and you can visit him there by afternoon."

She thanked the detective who was being extremely kind to her, especially considering he probably assumed Thomas guilty.

Owen had remained silent during the exchange, watching as if he were removed from what was happening instead of being the cause. Wavering between terror for her brother and frustration at her own inability to alter the situation, she rounded on him.

"He is innocent," she spat out.

The viscount's expression, while somber, was also content, satisfied. After all, he believed he'd caught his sister's murderer.

"One day, I will remind you I told you so," she added, watching his eyes widen slightly. "And you will be sorry!"

He nodded, seemingly accepting her condemnation.

Turning to her brother, she kissed his cheek. It would only be a few hours, and she would return with help. Heading toward the door, Adelia was eager for the sun to rise so she could begin her task.

"Despite being an area full of policemen and courts," she heard the detective remark behind her, "it isn't safe for her ladyship to wander outside alone, especially if she's looking for a hackney at this hour."

Glancing back, she realized he was speaking to Owen.

"I will see her safely home," he said to her brother.

No! She would not let him appease his conscience by escorting her home after he'd torn a hole in her life. Quickening her footsteps, she was nearly at the station's entrance when he caught her.

"Adelia," he began, using her name aloud for the first time.

"No!" she bit out. "Leave me alone."

A policeman opened the door for her, and she stepped out into the thick, chilly pre-dawn fog. Clutching her cloak around her, she looked up and down the street, seeing nothing but Owen's carriage and a few stray passersby. One man halted and stared at her, making the hair on the back of her neck stand up. She turned away from him and began to walk.

"Lady Adelia," Owen tried again. He wasn't behind her, but beside her, keeping pace.

She tried to walk faster but, of course, his long legs kept up easily.

"We can walk all the way back to 78 Hyde Park Street, or we can ride in the comfort of my clarence, but either way, we are traveling together. I will not let you out of my sight until we reach your door, and I see you safely inside."

She walked another block, realizing she had no idea if she was going in the right direction. Abruptly, she stopped. Her brother was back there, his nose possibly broken, undoubtedly afraid of what he faced both at Newgate jail and in court.

Thomas, her protector. Her younger brother.

Unexpectedly, tears sprung to her eyes and began to trickle down her cheeks before she could get her emotions under control. Dashing at them with her gloved fingers, she suddenly felt Owen's hand upon her shoulder.

That he would comfort her after the hell he was putting her brother through! *How dare he!*

Jerking away from his touch, she started forward again.

"Adelia, stop!" he commanded.

Feeling utterly defeated, after a few more rebellious steps, she did. Turning, she watched him approach. *What did he think to do—take her in his arms?*

Launching herself at him, she pummeled his chest with her fists, and he let her. Hands at his sides, Owen remained motionless under her assault. She continued until she heard a strange sound and realized it was herself, sobbing and moaning.

The sound of the frightened child she'd once been under her father's torment stayed her fists. Paralyzed, she could barely breathe while tears coursed down her cheeks, and her hands, still balled, rested upon Owen's broad chest.

As he drew her close, she pressed her face against his coat. He was warm, his heart beating strongly beneath her cheek, and he smelled familiar. He smelled like the man with whom she had been falling in love.

Feeling him gesturing with one arm, probably to summon his coachman, he embraced her again. She heard his carriage drawing close, and wordlessly, he turned her toward it.

Not acknowledging what she was doing, keeping her head down, Adelia let Owen help her into the safety of his clarence. He sat close on the same side, his thigh touching hers and his arm draped around her, as if he could stave off all the evils of the world and all the pain she would ever face. Yet, he was the one who'd caused the worst of it.

"I will never forgive you," she whispered, leaning her head upon him.

"I know," he said.

CHAPTER EIGHTEEN

Adelia was unable to rest despite being bone-weary. She hadn't slept a wink since Owen deposited her in her front hallway. She'd closed the door firmly on his parting words, not listening, nor did she return Mr. Lockley's greeting. Standing at the bottom of the staircase, she sensed how hollow and vacant her home was, knowing her brother wasn't there.

Nor would he be—not ever again—unless she did something about it.

Trying to rest for an hour, she lay down upon her counterpane fully dressed in her beautiful gold and blue gown from the Cambreys' dinner, now all rumpled. She doubted she would ever wear it again.

However, sleep would not come. She considered who she could enlist as an ally. Obviously, she would have to send word to Mr. Beaumont and to Mr. Arnold in a day or so, but she could think of no one else who need know or who would care.

Keenly, she felt the lack of friends and family. She couldn't even confide in Penny, who might talk to the other servants. If the below-stairs gossips caught wind of it, word of her brother's incarceration could spread throughout Mayfair and beyond by midday. Of course, his valet might ask her when to expect the master of the house's return, and she would think of something vague to tell him.

Hours later, she rose from her bed and let Penny give her a sponge bath before selecting a respectable day gown. After her maid brushed Adelia's hair, she put it up in a plain bun—hopefully the perfect hairstyle for meeting with lawyers and then going to Newgate to visit her brother and pay off guards.

She could still hardly credit what had happened.

And through the entire morning, as she collected a sack of coins and climbed into her carriage, Adelia's thoughts kept returning to Owen. The blasted perfume had shredded the screen of duplicity she'd woven between her and the viscount. She was not particularly proud of having lied to him, but she would do it again the same way, particularly after knowing the awful outcome.

On her way to the Inns of Court, knowing the massive task ahead and how ill-equipped she was to discern a good lawyer from a bad one, in desperation, Adelia opened the window and called to her driver to alter his course. In short order, she drew up in front of the townhouse of Lord and Lady Christopher Westing.

Terror gripped her, but she could think of no one aside from this couple whom Owen had always spoken so highly. Lord Westing was his dearest friend, and Owen had stood by the marquess after he'd been blinded in a gas explosion. In any case, it was not him she had come to speak with. It was his wife.

Lady Jane was known for her good work with London's most unfortunate creatures, the orphans and beggars. Beyond that, she was considered capable and organized, not to mention kind. Adelia needed all of that.

With a trembling hand, she rang the bell, mindful of the utter impropriety of showing up uninvited to a stranger's home. At least it was nearly eleven, so not too terribly early.

When the door swung open, she tried to speak, but nothing came out. The butler waited, staring at her, although not unkindly. She cleared her throat and tried again.

"I wonder if Lady Jane is . . . that is . . . if Lady Jane is . . . ," she trailed off as her voice squeaked to a stop.

The butler frowned slightly but managed to quickly become a mask of indifference.

"Lady Jane is at home and seeing visitors. May I have your calling card?"

"My card," she murmured, and the butler stared pointedly at the thick cream-colored stock in her hand.

Ninny! she scolded herself. Yet, as she raised a still-shaking hand, she found her fingers weren't working correctly. For while the man tried to take the card from her, she had trouble letting go. In fact, she could only grip it more firmly.

After an embarrassing few seconds of him tugging and her clutching, she finally managed to work her tight fingers, releasing the card with a sigh of humiliation.

As if nothing untoward had occurred, the butler read the card, bowed his head, and said, "This way, my lady."

Stepping back, he allowed her entrance into the Westings' marble foyer. After he had closed it behind them, he led the way toward the first set of double doors to the right of the entry and opened the left one so she could step through.

"Please make yourself comfortable, my lady. I shall advise Lady Westing as to your presence."

She nodded. When he closed the door, she took great panting breaths. She must pull herself together. Lady Jane Westing was merely another human being. There was no need for this abject terror. On the other hand, Adelia's reception was far from certain. Lady Jane might also consider Owen to be her close friend.

Glancing around the room, taking in its warm disposition with sunflower-yellow walls above white wainscoting and a pretty floral brocade sofa on a cream and pale green rug, Adelia wondered if she should sit or if that would be too bold. Deciding to pace instead and practice what she would say, she had barely done one turn of the room and silently recited, "Lady Westing, I am in dire need of assistance, though I know you may not wish to—"

The drawing room door opened and in swept the marchioness. Pale brown hair in a suitably elegant chignon, Lady Jane wore a violet silk day gown. Everything fit perfectly. The only thing surprising about her was she held a baby in her arms.

"Lady Adelia, I would greet you with both hands, but you see they are full. I hope you don't mind, but my son was napping on my lap, and I decided it best to bring him with me than to keep you waiting."

Adelia's mouth opened in surprise. Quickly, she recovered. "It is beyond kind of you to . . . to see me, especially if you are short-staffed." She assumed the woman either had not secured a nanny or had one who had been taken ill.

Lady Jane smiled bemusedly. "I am not short-staffed. Oh, I see what you mean." She offered a genuine laugh. "We do have a nanny, but I tend to spend an inordinate amount of time simply holding my baby. He still seems like a miracle to me. His name is Spencer, and he recently got over a little tummy trouble."

Naturally, an unwell child would have made the marchioness keep her son even closer.

"I am glad he is on the mend," Adelia offered, realizing she was speaking too quietly when Lady Jane leaned forward slightly.

"Thank you. Will you sit?" her hostess asked. "I already requested tea. It should be here shortly." And Lady Jane lowered herself gently into a winged armchair, hardly jostling the sleeping infant.

"The last time we spoke," she continued as Adelia took a seat in another chair, separated from Lady Jane's by a small round table, "was at Lord Burton's party, following the hippopotamus exhibit at the Regent's Park zoo, I believe."

Adelia nodded, removing her gloves and placing them in her lap in anticipation of the tea tray. She had seen Lady Jane several times since, but the marchioness was correct in that they had not spoken since that party.

"What brings you to see me?"

Adelia opened her mouth, hoping she could find the right words when, after a gentle tap, the door opened and in came a maid carrying a tray.

In a very short time, the tea service was set on the table between them, within easy reach. Lady Jane continued a steady stream of polite conversation about the type of tea leaf in the pot and how their clever cook had put lemon peel in the biscuit cream, and soon, they were alone again.

"I need help," Adelia blurted. That sounded as if she were drowning at sea. In fact, she did feel as if she were drowning in troubles.

"Tell me at once," Lady Jane insisted.

"Don't you wish to know why . . . why I came to you?"

Lady Jane shook her head. "As soon as my butler gave me your card, I knew."

"You did?" Adelia was confounded.

"Yes, I know through my husband that Lord Burnley has been escorting you about Town, and everyone knows they are the best of friends. My guess is you have questions about his character."

Adelia felt sick. If only her visit were on such a benign matter, sussing out the true nature of the viscount. She already had made that determination for herself. Owen was a fine, principled man, if slightly indiscriminate about the females he escorted. He seemed gentle when not enraged, which was too often, but even then, he reserved his anger for particular individuals and had never given her cause to fear him.

"Lord Burnley is involved, yes, but I have come to ask your advice about finding a lawyer."

Lady Jane sat back, surprised. She glanced down, perhaps to ascertain if her son continued to sleep. "Go on."

"This is about Lord Burnley's sister," Adelia began, wondering briefly if Lady Jane knew the horrible truth of her death. By her pitying expression, Adelia could tell she did.

"His lordship believes my brother to have ... have ... That is, Lord Burnley is convinced my brother is the perpetrator ... in short ... the murderer."

The marchioness didn't gasp. Instead, she narrowed her eyes. "Does he?"

Adelia nodded, wondering about Lady Jane's thoughts and half expecting to be tossed out at once.

"Try the tea," Lady Jane said, "before it gets cold, and start from the beginning."

Adelia sipped the tea and sighed. Her least favorite thing, a long discussion, apparently awaited her, but she would try.

In a few minutes, having mentioned all the extraordinarily damning evidence, Adelia concluded with, "I know how it appears. Truly, I do, but I also know my brother. With every fiber of my being, I know he is innocent of this charge."

Lady Jane was silent a long moment. "Besides, there is the very real question of why? If one knew why Lady Sophia was killed, I suppose one would know instantly who had done it."

"Yes," Adelia agreed. "Even Lord Burnley has no answer as to why my brother would suddenly do such a heinous thing. There is no logical reason for it. He has gained nothing."

"I suppose Lord Burnley is quite torn between his high regard for you and his desire to gain justice for his sister. It is a terrible dilemma, isn't it?"

Adelia didn't know what to say to that. A stranger could see the horrid irony of the situation, and Lady Jane didn't yet know whether Adelia returned Owen's regard.

"My intent is not to be rude or off-putting," Lady Jane continued, "but I am slightly mystified as to why you came to me."

Adelia glanced at the teacup in her lap and lifted it back onto the table. This last part was the hardest part of her visit. She took a deep breath.

"I do not have any family or anyone I can ask for advice." She stopped short of confessing she had no friends. "To put it bluntly, I have no idea how to find a good lawyer." She took a deep breath, realizing she was speaking softly and slowly, but it helped her to get the words out smoothly.

"I am sure I can fall over an attorney if I wander the Inns of Court, but everyone has heard stories of inept bunglers. And the detective warned me about pettifoggers. *Sublime rascals*, he called them. I believe my brother's freedom depends upon this counsel."

Lady Jane nodded in agreement, which sent a shot of terror racing through Adelia.

Plunging on, she added, "I know we are not friends, hardly acquaintances, but we have long been in the same circles. I heard of and have admired your resourceful nature. The way you brought about the new orphanages and your work for your husband's mother in the art world. If anyone knows how to find a competent, trustworthy lawyer, I am convinced it would be you."

Adelia closed her mouth and waited. That had been a long speech for her, and she'd made it without stuttering once. But as Lady Jane stared at her with intelligent eyes, weighing something in her mind, Adelia began to fear she had surpassed the polite boundaries of strangers.

"Given your husband's close friendship with Lord Burnley," Adelia added, "I will understand if my request seems like betrayal, and you may send me on my way."

"Nonsense," Lady Jane said with finality. "I am not thinking that at all. I am only feeling a little sorry we did not form a closer attachment years ago. I hate to think of you feeling alone. I have, shall we say, a *forceful* mother who never let me languish a single blissful day outside of society. Solitude was not an option. Naturally, she had the best of intentions."

Adelia had used up every ounce of conversational strength she had, so remained silent, only nodding in understanding.

"Your mother died, I believe," Lady Jane continued, "when you were very young."

Again, Adelia nodded.

"And your father passed, too, leaving only you and your brother, thus I can perfectly understand the importance of your mission. As it turns out, I do know an excellent solicitor, but he deals mostly with the Court of Chancery. He set up the articles for the orphanages. We can visit him this very day, as I am convinced he will know of a successful barrister."

Adelia felt as if a weight had been lifted.

"You do not have to accompany me, Lady Jane. I know you are busy and have your new son. If you but give me the name of your solicitor, then—"

"I would like to assist you, if you will let me."

"You already have," Adelia insisted.

"I imagine you are dreading the day ahead. I can go with—" Lady Jane stopped speaking upon hearing voices in the front hall.

At once, Adelia recognized Owen's sonorous timbre. The other must belong to Lord Westing, the marquess.

All the blood drained from her face, and her stomach clenched. She felt like a naughty child, discovered somewhere she should not be, such as in the pantry with the treacle toffee tin in hand.

In seconds, the drawing room door opened, and Lord Westing entered, followed by Owen. He was in midsentence and stopped short upon seeing her, his mouth instantly snapping shut.

Lord Westing was not using a cane in his own home but wore gray-tinted glasses to shield his eyes.

"We have a visitor," he declared, looking in her direction.

How did he know? Hastily, she yanked on her gloves in preparation for departing.

"Yes," Lady Jane spoke. "Lady Adelia Smythe and I are having a chat." She turned to Adelia and explained, "My husband can see shadowy shapes. And I believe you know Lord Burnley."

Adelia rose to her feet. "Good day, Lord Westing, Lord Burnley." She knew she sounded strange because her lips felt stiff when saying his name.

While each man in turn said with a bow, "Good day," Owen's tone was decidedly frosty.

Turning to Lady Jane, who had remained seated with her son, still sound asleep on her lap, Adelia said, "Thank you for your help. If you could write down that name for me, I will be on my way."

"Are you positive you won't let me accompany you?" the marchioness asked again.

Adelia glanced at Owen to see he was listening intently to every word. She swallowed.

"That is very k . . . kind of you, but I shall manage on my own." *Drats!* Just seeing the man had caused her nerves to return.

"Very well. Perhaps another time you will come back and tell me how it went," Lady Jane asked, sounding sincerely interested.

Adelia was firmly of the belief her ladyship would be kept well-informed on any news of the Smythes' misfortune. Undoubtedly, Lord Westing had already received an earful from Owen.

"Darling one," Lady Jane addressed Lord Westing, "I have Spencer on my lap. Will you please fetch me a sheet of paper from the drawer and a pen?"

"I live to serve you, my love," he said good-naturedly, finding his way about his own drawing room with ease and presenting his wife with a sheet of paper.

Using the arm of her wingchair, the marchioness wrote upon the paper, folded it, and held it out to Adelia. "Tell him I sent you. Please let me know if I can be of further assistance or if you have need of my company."

This woman was kindness personified, and Adelia wondered if she had missed out on many such paragons by her severe reticence. If they had remained alone, she would be nearly ready to confess her desire to be a novelist and ask Lady Jane to read one of her manuscripts. Perhaps another time, she would.

"Again, I thank you, my lady." Adelia clutched the folded note in her hand. "Good day to you and Lord Westing."

Her heart was pounding as she had to pass closely by Owen.

She could hardly meet his eyes. "Good day," she muttered.

"I shall walk you out," he declared, and before she could stop him, he was at her back and shutting the drawing room door behind them. When the butler appeared, Owen waved him away.

"Just a minute or two," he ordered, and the man vanished from the foyer as quickly as he had come.

"I need my mantle," she protested. Besides, they had nothing to say.

"What were you speaking to Lady Jane about?"

"That is not your business," Adelia said, although she supposed if the marchioness told her husband, he would tell Owen. She might as well confess. "I needed help finding a lawyer."

Owen frowned as Lady Jane had done.

"I simply recalled Lady Westing as being the type of p . . . person who would either know what I should do or have a s . . . suggestion as to whom I should see."

He pursed his lips. "You have never stuttered when speaking with me."

She blinked back tears. *Did he think less of her?* Squaring her shoulders, she reminded herself their association was over.

"It saddens me," he confessed.

Adelia caught her breath. A thousand emotions whirled through her at his words and their ramifications, but there was no point in following such a twisted path.

When she said nothing more, Owen asked, "Did Lady Jane provide assistance?"

Adelia nodded and unfolded the paper to see a name written in a tidy script with the cursed *JD* watermark below. Silently, she pointed it out to the viscount so he could understand its ubiquitous presence throughout the households of London.

His eyebrows rose, but he didn't comment on it. Instead, he asked, "Are you going to the Inns of Court now?"

"Yes." She tucked the paper into the small pocket in her side seam.

He grimaced, looking uncertain. "I would offer to accompany you, but . . . ," he trailed off. "Obviously, under the circumstances, we are hoping for different outcomes."

Reminded that he wanted her brother to be found guilty of murder, Adelia gritted her teeth and looked past him for the butler. "I shall leave without my mantle," she threatened.

He called out the man's name, and once more, the butler appeared from the recesses of the hallway, holding her gray mantle over one arm.

Owen took it and draped it around her. The brush of his hands upon her shoulders dredged up the memory of how it felt to be touched by him, especially when he'd kissed her soundly. Her heart beat faster, and a part of her wished she could turn in his embrace and be comforted. If she'd told him as soon as he first showed her the handkerchief that it was her brother's, the same result would have occurred—

except she would have missed out on a few weeks of being courted by this enticing man.

Sighing, she couldn't look at him. Too easily, he would see the longing in her eyes. The Westings' butler opened the door, and she headed out to her carriage, almost wishing Owen would say her name and call her back to him.

CHAPTER NINETEEN

Owen watched Adelia leave, knowing he should be the one assisting her into her carriage, not her driver, but he had to keep his distance. Seeing her today, finding her unexpectedly at his friend's home, had brought all his conflicted emotions to the surface.

He could admit to himself unequivocally one thing—he had never wanted another woman the way he did Adelia Smythe. And yet, his denunciation of her brother made any further pursuit of her impossible. He might have tried it nonetheless, so strong was his attraction to her, but he knew she would rebuke him. Particularly when her brother might end up swinging from a rope in the public execution area next to the prison.

The previous night—actually, it was mere hours ago in the early morning—his anger at her had felt all-consuming. She had lied to him. Try as he might, now that the initial shock had worn off, however, he couldn't blame her. If she felt for him the smallest part of what he felt for her, she'd had little choice but to divide her loyalties. She'd been forced to protect her brother while allowing their relationship to blossom. In a similar situation, he would have done the same.

A relationship that was now at an end. And still, he wanted her.

Owen returned to the drawing room, wishing even then that he was by Adelia's side to protect her from whatever came next.

IT HAD BEEN DIFFICULT to see Owen and more difficult to calm her racing pulse once in her carriage. Finally, she had a sweet, intense *tendre* for a man, and wonder of wonders, he had returned the sentiment—only for him to become someone with whom she could never share a life.

Bollocks! she swore as she'd heard her brother do, and it felt woefully inadequate. Reaching into her pocket, she withdrew the paper again and unfolded it. Lady Jane had written "*Mr. Brassel, Gray's Inn.*" After instructing her driver, she sat back against the squabs and, in no time, traveled from Oxford Street to Holborn. They turned left onto Gray's Inn Lane Road and stopped.

For a few minutes, Adelia sat in her carriage, her heart continuing to pound over what she must accomplish, wondering if she could actually go in, past all the clerks and lawyers whom she could see rushing to and from the buildings. And she would have to speak with strangers.

Clamminess dampened the back of her gown, and she closed her eyes. Breathing steadily, sitting quietly, she knew her driver was used to her odd habits and would not bother her until she tapped on the roof.

For Thomas, she reminded herself. She was at the Inns of Court for him. Then she said aloud, "Good day, sir. I hope I may have a moment of your time."

After practicing that thrice, she tapped on the roof. A few seconds later, her carriage door opened, and Henry assisted her. She had no chaperone or companion since not much could be safer than a building full of lawyers.

Gray's was the smaller of the legal Inns. All the same, after passing through the wrought iron gates at the main entrance on Field Court with the badge of the griffin keeping guard, it took Adelia a few minutes to wind her way through the paths between the structures. After gathering her gumption, she approached a clerk seated at a desk in the entryway of the main building.

"Mr. Brassel, if you please," she managed to address him.

The young law clerk led her through their great hall with its soaring roof and richly colored, stained glass on their way to the solicitor's office. It was impossible not to halt as she experienced a rush of wonder in the vaulted interior where stained buttresses seemed to fly from the walls to meet overhead. And on the high-paneled walls were plaques and coats of arms of the great men who'd gone before, as well as a painting of Queen Elizabeth I, whom the clerk informed her was Gray's Inn's patron lady. A statue of Shakespeare spurred the clerk to tell her the Bard of Avon had performed in that very hall as well.

Adelia took in the solemnity of the venue and its purpose. This was serious, and if she had doubted it for an instant, the interior of Gray's Inn reminded her, with all the black-robed men going hither and yon like great, scary ravens.

Finally, the clerk knocked on a door, pushed it open, and said distinctly, "A lady to see you, sir." After pushing the door open wider, he offered her a friendly nod and departed.

Adelia entered the astoundingly tiny room, with barely enough space for a desk, a bookshelf, a chair for the lawyer, and one for a guest. Already standing, a man with wiry gray hair, a blue suit, and kind eyes reached out to shake her hand across his desk, an action which she found endearing.

"I'm Mr. Brassel," he said in a rich tone that belied his age. "To what do I owe this pleasure?"

She began what she'd practiced in her carriage. "Good . . . sir. I hope a moment of your time."

She grimaced. It had come out all wrong, but he seemed to understand.

"Yes, of course. Your name, if you please?"

She could easily answer that. "Lady Adelia Smythe, sir."

"My lady," he bowed. "You seem to be anxious. Please, take a seat and tell me how I can help you."

Thank goodness her skirts were not any fuller, or there would not have been room for her to squeeze between the desk and the chair.

As soon as she sat, she conjured Thomas from the previous night, with his astonished face when told he was going to Newgate, and, on his behalf, her words came out more smoothly.

"I apologize for coming without an appointment," she said, feeling empowered at having made it this far on her own.

He smiled at her. "I would never dissuade a visit from a lady," he said, and she didn't mind his flattery, since he had not a trace of lasciviousness, but merely a grandfatherly smile.

"Without preamble, sir, my brother, the Earl of Dunford, has been taken into custody at Newgate. He will be charged with murder."

With each statement she made, the man's expression became graver.

"You know I am not a barrister, my lady. I cannot defend your brother in court."

"I understand, but Lady Jane Westing sent me to you, believing you would know the best barrister to handle my brother's case. He is innocent."

She was relieved when he did not look instantly doubtful.

"As you will find out, my lady, many lawyers, and judges for that matter, do not care about the true guilt or innocence of the accused. The barrister's job is to put forth a reasonable, believable, and most of all persuasive defense, precisely as the prosecuting lawyer will be offering a sound prosecution. The judge will decide who is the better lawyer."

She felt sick in the pit of her stomach. "Surely, innocence means something."

He gave her another kindly look. "In the hands of a good barrister, it can mean all the difference. I believe we must get your case in front of Mr. Jaggers, Esquire."

"Thank you, Mr. Brassel. I am grateful for your counsel and your assistance."

He waved it away. "As I said, I am happy for the interruption. The days can be long and tedious, especially when I am called to the Court of Chancery, as I will be for the rest of the week."

He shuffled the papers around on his desk until he uncovered a pen. Next, he opened a drawer and withdrew a piece of stationery printed with his name printed on top.

He wrote a few lines before asking, "Your brother's name again, please."

"Lord Thomas Smythe, Earl of Dunford."

He wrote that down, then looked at her. "He is undoubtedly not enjoying the facilities at the jail. May I advise you to go there, coin in hand, and liberally spread it around to anyone who asks. He'll get better food and clean bedding if you do."

"I am going to Newgate next." Adelia had a heavy bag of coins weighing down her reticule, and frankly, she was terrified. She would take her driver inside with her.

"I have half an hour until I must head over to court. If you wish to tell me what you know rather than wait for a clerk, I'll jot down the particulars and send them along to Mr. Jaggers directly. Perhaps he will say not to worry as they may not have much of a case."

"I fear they do. There is most puzzling evidence that ties my brother to the murder." She spent the next few minutes telling him what she knew.

"Strange indeed," he muttered. "I am not a trial lawyer, but this seems too easy for the prosecution. I'm surprised the murderer did not simply write '*Lord Smythe killed me*' and pin it to the poor lady's coat."

"So, you believe my brother is innocent?" she asked.

"Would a guilty man have given you the perfume, knowing you are keeping company with the deceased's brother?"

She shook her head. "Thomas gave it to me without guile, that is certain."

"Lastly, we need to question your brother and find out where he was on the night Lady Sophia was killed. Hopefully, he was at an intimate dinner party and not a ball."

"Why, sir?"

"One can always leave a ball unnoticed, slip away for any purpose, and return. It is hardly a secure alibi."

She thought Thomas might have been with Miss Moore when Sophia was killed, but he could speak for himself on that account.

"Shall we go?" he said at last.

"*We*, sir?"

"I've decided to send my apprentice in my stead to the Court of Chancery. Nothing is set to happen on my current case for a period of . . . oh . . . five years, at the very soonest."

She couldn't help smiling slightly.

"You think I am joking. Dear lady, there are cases in Chancery that started before you were born. Probably a few before I was born, too. Our court of fairness and equity has become anything but. Luckily, you will be in a very different court." He stood. "Besides, this is far more interesting than anything else I could be doing today. I want to meet your brother and hear what he has to say."

He folded the paper upon which he'd been writing his notes, sealed it with a dab of black wax and his ring, and hastily scrawled *"Mr. Nigel Jaggers, Esquire"* upon the other side.

"We'll drop this into his slot on the way out." Then, as he put on his hat and grabbed a cane, Mr. Brassel shook his head. "That Lady Westing! She knew I would become immediately interested in your brother's situation and distracted from the tedious work I already had at hand. Bless her!"

THUS, ADELIA FOUND HERSELF in the company of Mr. Brassel on her way to Newgate jail, a mere five minutes to the east, along Holborn Street. Each was in their separate carriage, as he would go next to Lincoln's Inn Hall where the Chancery court was currently meeting.

Adelia could barely breathe when she stepped out of her carriage at the entrance to the prison. It seemed utterly incredible that Thomas should be there, and she, visiting him in such a ghastly place.

She had walked past the gloomy building a number of times in her life and never considered its inhabitants more than to think they were there for good reason. Moreover, it never once dawned on her the prisoners behind the ugly granite-block walls could possibly be people she would ever know or meet.

Studying it now, it looked no better—a squat, unadorned structure that looked as if it had dropped heavily onto the corner of Newgate and Old Bailey Streets. The barred windows far overhead, on what she assumed was a second and third story, were the only telltale sign of the building's use.

"Don't be too dismayed, Lady Adelia," Mr. Brassel said. "Hopefully, your brother will not be here long. Regular visitors can only see prisoners in the central courtyard, if at all. However, as we are going for a deposition—his reliable statement of defense—we shall be allowed to see him privately in a room."

They began their journey into the infamous facility with an ordinary knock at what Adelia found out was the door of the governor of Newgate's house. After Mr. Brassel gave a servant his card, the man allowed them entrance, and they waited for another officer who would escort them inside the actual prison.

To Adelia's right was an ordinary office, one that looked like the solicitor's at Gray's Inn except larger, with room for two clerks who did not look up from their duties. Beyond them, windows looked over the Old Bailey side of the facility.

"Would they not bring my brother out here?" Adelia asked, still hesitant to go inside the jail itself.

"Part of your task here today is to grease the palms, if you know the phrase, of all the right people who will make the earl's time here more comfortable. To that end, you must enter."

She nodded. The waiting seemed endless. Eventually, a stocky man dressed all in black with a massive set of keys arrived to escort them inside. They followed him through a door opposite to the one they'd entered from the street. In front of Adelia were death masks of two men, labeled Bishop and Williams.

When she glanced at them and back at the solicitor, Mr. Brassel only muttered, "Notorious murderers," and drew her away.

Passing through that room, they finally found themselves nearly in the prison. The Old Bailey remained on their right-hand side and, on their left, a collection of irons, which she could not take her gaze from. When she saw Thomas, he would be in chains. A sob rose to her throat, and she tamped it down. They next went through a heavy wood and iron gate, studded with nails and guarded by another man who watched them disinterestedly as their escort used a key to open the gate and allow them entrance.

Ahead of them was a narrow stone passageway, which Adelia discovered led to different yards, each guarded by further gates and gratings.

"I am becoming bewildered," she said. "It is like a rabbit warren."

"Actually, my lady," the guard spoke up, "Newgate is an orderly square, made up of wards. There are yards in between for exercise. We have a separate women's side, closer to the Session House, and the men's side, which we shall go into next. You are looking for Thomas Smythe, is that right?"

"Lord Thomas Smythe, Earl of Dunford," she said, clear as a bell. "And he is innocent."

"Of course, my lady." But the man had obviously heard that often.

Mr. Brassel patted her arm for reassurance, and she realized it accomplished nothing to plead her case to a guard.

Was he one to whom she should pay a little?

Tapping her full reticule, she looked at the solicitor and gestured her head to the back of the guard who led them.

Mr. Brassel nodded. "I'll tell you when," he said softly.

When they entered the men's side of the jail, the guard locked the last gate they'd passed through. "We'll go to the receiving room. I think Lord Smythe may still be there, as all prisoners remain in it until they've been examined by the surgeon."

"The surgeon?"

"Aye, my lady. The prison has its own. Got to make sure the prisoners aren't going to die on us before trial and execution."

As if realizing what he'd said, he started to laugh, then he doubled over, hands on his knees, and laughed harder until he began to wheeze.

It sounded as though he had more need of a physician than her brother, but she kept her mouth shut.

Unfortunately, the surgeon had been there early and had already cleared Thomas to go into the general population of Newgate. Thus, they had to go farther inside. Passing through another gate, they came into one of the men's wards, a spacious, high-ceilinged, whitewashed room, with windows overlooking an exercise yard.

It was lighter and cheerier than she'd dreaded. There was a large fireplace and, in front of it, two rectangular tables with men seated, eating a meal. While looking for Thomas, Adelia couldn't help taking in the rest of the room. Along two sides ran a shelf and below it, large hooks.

At first, she couldn't decipher what was hanging upon each, until she realized they were mats, probably for sleeping. For above each, bundled onto the shelf was a rug and blanket. The ward was not only where Thomas would eat and spend his day, but also where he would sleep upon the hard floor.

Over the huge hearth, the only decoration were scriptural texts, designed to inspire, she supposed. Little else in the room would inspire any loftier thoughts or give the inhabitants hope for a better future.

"Dilly," she heard yelled from the center of a group of men. Approaching closer to their table, she could see they were all dining on some kind of stew served in crude pewter dishes.

She spied brown bread, which unexpectedly brought tears to her eyes. Her father had always forbidden it at their table, but occasionally, she and her brother had eaten some from off the servants' platter and thickly smeared it with butter. They'd both loved the bread's tangy heartiness.

Finally, Thomas was in her arms, and her tears fell freely. It seemed as if she hadn't seen him for days instead of hours, so much had happened.

Other men started making whistling sounds and calling out lewd remarks, reminding her this was not a gathering of the *ton*.

"Shut your cakeholes," Thomas yelled over his shoulder. "This is my sister."

A general quietness ensued, impressing her. Apparently, there was a code of civility even in Newgate. She glanced at the other prisoners' faces, pasty and drawn.

How long until her brother took on the pallor and demeanor of these men broken in body and spirit?

When they pulled apart, she said, "This is Mr. Brassel, a solicitor, and he knows a good barrister. He's come to speak with you and relay the information." It seemed strange how the legal system worked, but she'd been told the public hardly ever spoke with the barristers. The solicitors were like priests, and they took the penitents' confessions to the barristers, who were considered godlike in their abilities.

Thomas shook the hand that Mr. Brassel stuck out.

The guard had stood close by, and to him, the solicitor asked, "May we go somewhere private?"

"Afraid not, sir. Most folks don't get visitors in here, as you can imagine. In the yard, the lady here would be on the other side of an iron fence."

At that, Mr. Brassel nodded to her, and she realized it was time for the first payment.

"Good sir, if we could find somewhere to speak alone with my brother," Adelia said, amazed at her own steady voice, "away from all this noise, I would appreciate it.". Boldly, knowing there was no need for discretion, she held out her hand, and he immediately cupped his own to let her drop in a few coins.

He looked at them, seemingly impressed by the amount, and said, "Come this way."

Following behind as they had before, this time, Adelia had her arm linked with Thomas's.

"They took your clothing," she said. Although he wore the plainest cotton shirt and trousers, obviously not new, they looked clean, as if they'd been boiled thoroughly.

"Aye, but if you recall, I hadn't been wearing my finest suit anyway."

She intended to ask him more about the silly costume he wore to the East End, but he continued, "Luckily, I had enough coin to buy these rags and ensure I was fed for a week. But there isn't any amount that will get me a private cell or a bed off the floor. Only the wardsmen have a bedstead," he gestured to one corner by the fireplace, where she saw a small stump bedstead.

"It doesn't seem too much of an improvement over a mat," she remarked.

Her brother shrugged. "The stew is greasy and gristly, but there's brown bread."

"I saw." She couldn't help but smile at the look on his face. Even here, Thomas looked for all the world like a young boy in her memory, and she longed to take him in her arms and protect him. "We must order cook to buy brown bread for our table when we bring you home." The last word stuck in her throat, and she blinked back tears.

Soon, they were in a small, windowless room.

"Usually for the refractory prisoners," the guard said.

Not understanding what that meant, Adelia watched him leave and close the door. When she heard him turn a key in the lock, she shivered. There were no chairs, so they stood in a circle, facing one another.

"Let's get right to the heart of the matter," Mr. Brassel said. "Did you kill Sophia Burnley?"

"No!" Thomas looked affronted. "I thought this man knew the truth," he said to Adelia.

Mr. Brassel remarked, "I know what your sister has told me. I want to hear it from you."

"There is nothing to tell because I don't know anything about the murder."

"Did you know the lady at all?" the solicitor queried.

Adelia waited while Thomas filled Mr. Brassel in on the same thing he'd told her.

"I think you'd have to be an idiot to give your sister the dead woman's perfume, my lord, and you don't strike me as an idiot."

"Thank you," Thomas said.

"The next question is your whereabouts on the day and night of the murder."

Thomas sighed. "If I wasn't at home with my sister, or at the Reform Club or Teavey's—that's my boxing club—I would have been at a dinner or a ball with Adelia."

"I'm sorry," Mr. Brassel said, "we came straight here, but we shall ask the detective for the exact date, and I assume you can look at your social schedule."

Thomas looked at her. "I usually let my sister keep our calendar."

"You keep a diary of the events you've attended?" Mr. Brassel asked her.

"I do."

"If it was not a night of a ball or dinner party, where would you have been?" he asked Thomas.

Her brother's cheeks flushed slightly.

"Tell him," she insisted.

"I have a female friend who lives off of Whitechapel High Street."

"I see. And that's close to where the murder occurred?" Mr. Brassel asked.

"As far as we know," her brother said quietly.

"Might this friend have been jealous of Lady Sophia, lured her there with the note on your behalf, and killed her?"

Thomas blanched, and Adelia gasped.

"Positively not," her brother exclaimed. "Miss Moore didn't know anything about the lady's death until Burnley interrupted our evening last night."

"In any case, the detective sergeant on the case will speak with her at some point. I shall get notes from him to give the barrister," Mr. Brassel said.

He had been scrawling upon a tablet while standing. "Be warned, however, whatever your friend says, even if she provides you with an alibi, it will be of little interest to the court. They will consider her to be your lover, and hence, biased in your favor and likely as not to lie for you under oath."

"That's unfair," Adelia said.

"That's the way of it," Mr. Brassel said.

"Then let us hope the murder was on a night of a dinner party during which everyone saw my brother, all night long," she said. "Surely, the police won't discount the word of multiple members of the *ton*."

"They would be believed," the solicitor agreed, "if they're willing to speak for him."

"Why wouldn't they?" Adelia wondered.

"You'd be surprised how people suddenly become hesitant about getting involved in anything with a whiff of scandal. And murder is far more than a whiff, my lady."

A thump at the door gave them notice, and they plainly heard the key turn before the same guard entered.

"Time's up," he declared, rattling the large ring of keys for emphasis.

"For you to give to whomever," she murmured in Thomas's ear, handing him the pouch from inside her reticule. "When I come again, let me know how much more you need, and I'll bring it."

He nodded, briefly hefting the weight of the bag, and slipped it into his pocket.

"This should see me through longer than I hope to be here and provide me all the gristly beef stew I can eat.

"I'm so sorry," she said, hugging him to her again.

As her brother's strong arms went around her, tightening briefly to indicate his own feelings, Adelia vowed silently to save him. The alternative was unthinkable.

CHAPTER TWENTY

M r. Brassel, at last and with regret, said he must go to the Court of Chancery, and "waste the rest of my day," as he told her.

Adelia decided to return to the police station since it was so close to find out the exact day of Lady Sophia's death. Everything else depended upon such.

Yawning as she was shown into Detective Sergeant Garrard's office, she rushed to cover her mouth with her gloved hand.

In the space of ten minutes, she accomplished two things. She received the date she needed in order to look in her diary, and she gave the detective information about Miss Moore.

"I know very little about her except she seemed shocked by Lord Burnley's charges. And she seems to care for my brother."

With that accomplished, she went home, not having slept since two nights earlier, nor eaten since lunchtime the previous day. With no appetite, however, she lay down on her bed with the curtains drawn against the afternoon light and fell into a deep sleep.

Upon awakening hours later, for a second, she was confused until it all came crashing back into her mind, and she wanted to weep. More than that, she wanted to turn to someone, anyone, for comfort.

How had she come to this age of her life alone and friendless? Perhaps her father had been right to try to beat the shyness out of her.

Before her nap, she'd stripped off her outer garments, considering them soiled by the environment of Newgate, and had given them to Penny to launder. Now, she rang for a bath, hoping after it, her appetite would have returned.

Later, clad in her dressing gown, her hair still damp, she sat by the fire in her bedroom instead of in the dining room, unable to face the empty seat across from hers.

She could not fail Thomas.

PREVIOUSLY, OWEN HAD BEEN conflicted about enjoying the company of Lady Adelia while mourning his sister and searching for her killer. Now, it was far worse every time he contemplated the woman he'd come to care for.

He'd brought Sophia's killer to justice, and the courts soon would hand down the earl's punishment, but Owen's life seemed extraordinarily empty, nonetheless.

On top of that, Adelia was suffering. He wondered whether she would welcome a visit from him and concluded the answer was *no*.

Perhaps she might read a note if he could think of the words to say. She could not possibly have wanted him to let her brother go free from such a heinous crime. Somewhere, deep down, she understood he'd had to put the murderer in prison.

Nevertheless, Owen needed to see her. To that end, he sat in his study and put pen to paper, with a *JD* watermark, as it turned out.

What could he say? She would not be going out into society. Of this, he had no doubt, so he could not arrange to see her at a dinner party or a dance. Perhaps she would agree to go riding with him.

Dearest Lady Adelia,

I am unhappy that circumstances in which neither you nor I intentionally played a pivotal role have derailed our burgeoning friendship. I wonder if you might be willing to ride with me in Hyde Park.

Affectionately,
Lord Owen Burnley

He did not imagine his small missive could make matters worse. However, the following day, he received an angry note in return:

Lord Burnley,

I know not what you can be thinking by contacting me thusly. You certainly and intentionally did play a pivotal role in the unjust incarceration of my brother. Given that fact, it is beyond the pale for you to believe I would wish to be in your company. Furthermore, why on earth would you invite me to go riding?

Sincerely,
Lady Adelia Smythe

He would be entirely honest with her, for he had nothing more to lose:

Dearest Adelia,
Because I miss you.
Truthfully,
Owen

Not long after his courier delivered his note, Owen received one in return:

Lord Burnley,
I shall be in Hyde Park at the Grosvenor Gate on the morrow at
eleven o'clock if the weather is fine. I intend to ride down to the
Serpentine and along Rotten Row.
Lady Adelia Smythe

He couldn't help smiling when he received her latest missive. While the thrill of anticipation colored all his thoughts and actions with a joyful glow, he could get nothing serious done until he saw her. True, she hadn't been exactly welcoming, but she hadn't dismissed him out of hand, either.

Arriving early, he waited, standing alongside his horse at Grosvenor Gate on the east side of the park by quarter to eleven. He teetered between assuredness she would arrive at any instant and fear she had only said it to taunt him and would not show up at all.

Suddenly, Owen saw her, sitting tall and straight in a navy-blue riding habit, with a mounted footman a few yards behind her gelding. He nearly clapped his gloved hands with excitement. Instead, he whipped off his right glove in preparation for taking her hand in his. However, he never got the chance as she neither stopped nor dismounted.

Adelia rode right past him, acknowledged him with a nod, and turned her horse onto the southerly diagonal path toward the Serpentine and Rotten Row.

The devil! Dragging his glove on quickly, he mounted and caught up in a few trotting paces.

"Lady Adelia, it is good to see you."

She nodded again.

Ah, this was like their early encounters. He would have to work harder to draw her voice from her lovely lips.

"The weather turned out to be fine, after all."

Turning in her saddle, she said in a clipped tone, "Not in Newgate."

It was as if she had slapped him.

"Is the weather different on that street than here?" Feeling irritated at her incivility, he couldn't help baiting her.

"One cannot tell since there are so few windows in the jail, and the exercise yard is so small, one can barely see the sky."

So, she had been there already? He winced at the idea of her in such a coarse place. Then, another thought alarmed him.

"You didn't go alone, did you?"

She continued looking straight ahead for a minute. Finally, she answered.

"I was accompanied by a capable solicitor who has confirmed we have a good case."

Hm. "If that's true, I would say he is a pettifogger out for your money since the evidence is obviously conclusive."

He could see her stiffen and wished they'd been able to simply talk about the weather.

Before he could try to steer the conversation back to a neutral subject, she asked, "Why?"

He recalled what they both knew. "Because the perfume was—"

She waved her gray-gloved hand to cut him off. "Why do *you* think Thomas did it?"

He had spent as little time as possible considering the reason because it made no sense. Even he knew that.

"I have no answer."

"Because there isn't one. He gained nothing," she insisted.

"That we know of. Unless she knew something about your brother and was threatening to expose him. In which case, he gained her silence."

She turned slightly to look at him. "Are you saying your sister was a blackmailer? Shall that come out in the court of common law, too?"

"Sophia would never—" he began, but Adelia had already turned away and was shaking her head.

"You cannot have it both ways, Lord Burnley. If she was threatening my brother, that means your sister was a shifty blackmailer. If not, we still have found no possible motive."

He could think of no response.

"I am sorry for your loss," she said, "but you cannot bring Lady Sophia back by destroying my brother's life. I will prove him innocent."

She was correct, but that was not why he'd gone after Smythe.

"I never set out to ruin your brother's life."

After a long hesitation, she admitted, "I know."

They rode on in silence for a little while.

"Does anyone know, thus far, of your brother's arrest?"

"Only the solicitor," she answered, "unless you have told people."

"You told Lady Jane," he reminded her.

"That's true. I was in such a distraught state, I'd forgotten." She sighed. "Thus, Lord Westing knows as well as your other friend, Lord Whitely, and your parents. And they shall all tell people. No matter how it turns out, I fear Thomas's reputation will be ruined regardless."

He didn't think her brother's reputation was particularly important in the face of the sentence he might incur. But Owen didn't dare mention the possibility that her brother would be publicly executed.

"My family and friends are not celebrating the fact, nor telling anyone of your brother's incarceration." Actually, Whitely might, at that very moment, be spouting off at the Carlton Club or at White's, for all Owen knew. That was hardly his concern—except in how it affected Adelia.

And that concerned him greatly. Of all the women in England, he had to desire the sister of the man who'd killed Sophia. If Smythe were found guilty and sentenced to life in prison, perhaps it was possible Owen could convince Adelia they had a life together.

But if her brother was hanged!

For the first time, he considered whether he could save his relationship with Adelia by asking the judge to spare Smythe's life and let him spend the rest of it rotting in prison. At least Adelia could visit him there, which was more than Owen could do with his sister ever again.

He didn't know if the court would allow him, as the relation of the wronged party, to request leniency. Nor did he know if that would be enough to persuade Adelia he was not an ogre.

"My lady," he said before he could stop himself, "might you ever see your way clear to let me escort you again somewhere? To the theatre, perhaps?"

He could see her slump in her saddle and feared she would say no at once. Instead, she looked to the sky, thinking private thoughts.

"It would be wicked of me," she said at last.

He was the one being wicked. Undoubtedly, he should leave her alone.

"Perhaps a lowly cricket match?" he asked, feeling slightly heartened that she had not turned him down immediately.

Glancing at him, she rolled her eyes. "If this were a game of cricket, we would be on opposing teams," she reminded him. and her face became grim. "Unfortunately, this is *not* a game."

"Definitely not," he agreed. "Howbeit, we are more like spectators in the match than players, aren't we? Should we not spend any time together because our teams are at odds?"

She considered his words, and he let her do so in silence as they finally rounded the edge of the Serpentine onto the King's Road.

"*Rotten Row* is an ugly term for this lovely path, isn't it?" she asked, ignoring their earlier conversation and his question. They were together right then, so he decided to let the matter rest.

"It is," he agreed.

After another minute of silence, she asked, "Do you ever inspect your family's mines?"

A strange change of subject. "Yes, periodically, although we have a manager."

"As do we," she said. "And your father, does he still run your company?"

"He does. In fact, he's determined to give Burnley Mining more of his time and leave his seat in Parliament to me."

She sighed.

"Why do you ask?" he persisted.

"After the American play, Thomas and I spoke about mining conditions in general and the state of our mines in particular. He didn't know as much as he believed he should. Also, our engineer wants to increase profits in ways my brother isn't sure about."

"What does your general manager say?" Owen asked.

"He is also our engineer."

"That's unusual," he told her. "A manager doesn't usually have the skills of an engineer, and vice versa."

"I do not know of such things. Coincidentally, Thomas had decided he was going to ask you or your father for some advice."

Owen shook his head. *How odd and disturbing!* The young man who killed his sister was going to ask her family for business advice. He could not credit such gall. If it were anyone but Adelia saying it, he would tell her so.

"If this . . . this situation with my brother continues for any length of time, I suppose I shall have to meet with Mr. Beaumont myself. I believe Thomas does so at least weekly."

"Mr. Beaumont?" he asked.

"Our engineer and manager."

The name tickled some memory, but he couldn't quite grasp it. Perhaps he'd heard of him before.

"I would offer to help, but . . . ," Owen trailed off and shrugged. It was beyond awkward.

Her smile was brittle. "But we are on opposing teams."

Worse than that, if Owen met with the Smythe manager and gave any advice, and subsequently, the company's profits decreased, it would appear as if he were trying to take down a rival mining business. Best he keep his distance. *So, why were the next words out of his mouth an offer to help?*

"If you get into the thick of it and need to speak with someone who is objective about anything to do with your coal mines, I will be happy to help you."

"Thank you," she said softly, looking him directly in the eyes for the first time during their ride.

"Just know if your brother ever found out, he would be livid."

She shrugged. "If my brother found out many of the things I am going to do, he would be livid."

Frowning, Owen dared to ask, "Such as?"

Tilting her head a little, she declared, "Finding the evidence to prove him innocent."

CHAPTER TWENTY-ONE

Adelia returned home from her ride in Hyde Park with the man who had sent her brother to prison. She felt guilty to her toes.

What kind of sister was she?

Yet, staying away from Owen Burnley at this juncture was like closing the stable doors after every horse had already run away. It simply did no good now. If she had never applied that blasted perfume, or if she'd stayed away from the viscount as soon as she saw the cursed handkerchief . . .

Her thoughts went in futile circles. It had taken all her strength to tell him repeatedly she would not allow him to escort her to a concert, despite him asking her a dozen times. And still, in her heart, she wanted to see the viscount again. *Wicked, wicked woman!*

She was exceedingly glad when she received a missive from Mr. Brassel, telling her when he would be in his office at Gray's Inn and inviting her to come see him again.

Upon entering his cramped quarters, Adelia was welcomed by the solicitor who stood and again thrust out his hand, which she shook.

"What news, Mr. Brassel?" she asked upon taking a seat.

"Mr. Jaggers says he wishes to meet with you."

By the look upon the solicitor's face, Adelia understood this was a rarity.

"Why, do you suppose?" she asked, and why did she suddenly feel less afraid at meeting a stranger. She'd met and spoken to so many recently, it was becoming almost routine.

Mr. Brassel shrugged. "Your brother's case is an unusual one."

"If it will help Thomas, of course I shall meet with the barrister. When?"

"We can go at once, if you want. He has an office across the courtyard."

They went once more through the great hall and out a doorway on the opposite side. Up a staircase, into a lighter, airier section of Gray's Inn, she heard men's voices booming from all sides.

"Barristers practicing," Mr. Brassel informed her. "It is like a theatre production to present a case to the bench. They practice their speeches for the greatest effect. In here, please, my lady."

Mr. Nigel Jaggers, Esquire, was quite different from the solicitor, in age, form, and demeanor. When they entered his antechamber, staffed by a clerk who announced them to the barrister, Mr. Jaggers quickly appeared in his doorway, filling it and instantly commanding all the attention in the room.

A tall man, he was barrel-chested, or so it seemed beneath his robes, which he flung to his sides as he moved from his office into the outer room, his head barely clearing the door frame due to his height.

At least a decade younger than Mr. Brassel, he had a thick crop of hair, which reminded Adelia of raven feathers, both for its blackness and its glossy appearance. His pale gray eyes locked onto her as if she were a painting he was admiring or a text he was studying with all due intensity.

"Come in, come in," he boomed, gesturing with his arms, making his sleeves flap like wings.

Adelia and Mr. Brassel followed him into his spacious office, and the door was closed by the clerk behind them.

"Salutations," he said, sticking out a hand to Mr. Brassel while keeping his gaze fixed on Adelia.

"Greetings, Jaggers. This is the young lady whose case I wrote to you about. Well, not hers exactly, but her brother's. This is Lady Adelia Smythe."

"Lady Adelia," the words came out of the barrister's mouth like rich, melted toffee. He took her hand and bowed over it. But instead of saying anything flattering about meeting her, he looked her in the eyes and said, "Tell me about this excellent case."

Her gaze darted to Mr. Brassel, who gave his usual shrug and gestured for her to begin. As she started to speak, Mr. Jaggers released her hand and walked around his office, circumventing chairs and tables, swishing his robes as if it were an unintentional habit. She found it most distracting.

"Marvelous," Mr. Jaggers remarked at intervals during her recital of the facts, which irked her for the term implied something of a wondrous nature, not the horrid situation Thomas was in.

When she finished, he shook his head in amazement. "It's akin to a tale appearing in a penny-dreadful."

Personally, she'd always hated those sordid little magazines of sensational stories. They were nothing like the novels she read. "Sadly, this is real life," she said.

"And your brother maintains his innocence?" Mr. Jaggers asked.

"Yes, of course," Adelia said, "because he is."

"And yet all evidence points otherwise. Wonderful!"

She was beginning to feel annoyed, but a look at Mr. Brassel, who shook his head upon seeing her irritation, quelled her.

Calming what might have come out as a rebuke, she said, "I fail to see anything wonderful about my brother residing in Newgate. It is dismal, filthy, and filled with desperation."

"True. Moreover, it contains the innocent along with the guilty," Mr. Jaggers reminded her, stopping his movements to finally stand again in front of her. "And the distinction often doesn't come to light until too late, or never."

Never! She shuddered. "Can you help my brother?"

He grinned, a wolfish smile showing excellent teeth. "I intend to. In fact, I am fairly salivating to approach the bar and address the bench on this case. When prosecution presents its evidence, I will whittle it away to nothing."

"But how?" Adelia hoped he was not so full of bravado that he overreached his abilities.

"My lady, I apprenticed to the great barrister William Blackstone."

Mr. Brassel burst out laughing, and Adelia didn't know why. When quelled by a look from Mr. Jaggers, the solicitor stifled it, and the barrister continued.

"I studied Roman law and practiced Common law. I shall use my wits and my knowledge. *'Integra Lex Aequi Custos Rectique Magistra Non Habet Affectus Sed Causas Gubernat.'*" He looked to Mr. Brassel, his eyebrows raised.

"In translation," Mr. Brassel offered, "'Impartial justice, guardian of equity, mistress of the law, without fear or favor rules men's causes aright.' That is what it says on the wall here at Gray's Inn. Our motto, if you will."

"Precisely," Mr. Jaggers agreed. "And that is what I always strive for. It will be an honor to speak to the bench on your brother's behalf."

"That is kind of you to say," Adelia began.

He frowned. "No, dear lady. I mean it will be an honor for your brother to have me representing him."

"Oh, I see." She glanced at Mr. Brassel again, who gave her another encouraging nod, and she turned back to Mr. Jaggers. "And I profusely thank you," she added.

"Very good. You must be off," he said, flapping his arms, "and I must return to the case in which I am currently involved—and winning. We shall discuss my fee next time."

He looked to his cohort. "Brassel, send me whatever statement the earl gave. If he has an alibi, *et cetera,* that would be helpful. Meanwhile, I shall prepare the defense with all due haste."

He grabbed her hand again, bowed over it, and pushed her gently toward the door, followed by the solicitor.

Glancing behind her as it closed, she watched Mr. Jaggers disappear with a flap of his robes.

"Well!" she said. She had just met a force of nature, and that was without doubt.

As they strolled along "the Walks," as the paths were called, toward her carriage, past ox-eye daisies, hollyhocks, and an impressive hornbeam hedge, she asked, "Why did you laugh when Mr. Jaggers offered me his credentials?"

"Oh dear! I shouldn't have, should I? Only he said he'd apprenticed to Blackstone, who was, unquestionably, an inspiring lawyer, but he died last century, about 1780 or so."

Puzzled, she had to ask, "Then, why would he say it?"

Mr. Brassel shrugged good-naturedly. "Because he could get away with it, knowing you would not know while sounding impressive all the same. More likely, he trained with Lord Brougham."

"The former Lord High Chancellor?"

"The same. At least, I have heard that. Thus, I don't mind him saying his fanciful tales when the truth is even more remarkable."

"He said he was going to start working on the defense *before* receiving your notes on my brother's statement."

They had reached her carriage, and Mr. Brassel patted the closest horse to him.

"That is how barristers work," he said. "Jaggers will start the flowery part, as I call it, probably over a glass of port. And he'll fill his speech in with the particulars when he receives them, painting your brother as a paragon of virtue. Still, an alibi would help."

Distracted by the meeting with the barrister, she'd almost forgotten to tell Mr. Brassel what she'd learned.

"Unfortunately, the night of the murder, we were not attending a scheduled gathering. I was home writing . . . letters and such, and my brother was out. Sadly, that's all I know. Perhaps if I go back to Thomas and give him the day and date, he will remember where he was."

"Indeed. Or perhaps that female friend of your brothers can provide clarity. I have not received anything from the detective indicating he has spoken with her as yet."

"I shall go see her at once."

He gave his familiar shrug. "Remember what I told your brother. If they were . . . *ahem* . . . secluded in her flat, it will be of no use. They need to have been out in public where the earl's presence can be corroborated. Elsewise, the court tends to frown upon taking the word of what they would consider a woman of loose morals. If she is free with her person, they will consider her free with the truth as well, and it might make his character appear somewhat shady by association."

"Understood, Mr. Brassel. I shall get on my way and see what I can discover."

"You'll end up a detective yourself if you keep this up."

Both laughing at the absurdity of a female employed by the Metropolitan Police, he helped her into the carriage.

OWEN COULD SCARCELY BELIEVE Adelia had allowed him to ride alongside her. He was practically humming with glee. Even with all that had happened, he had no wish to stop seeing her, which was a singular occurrence. In the past, he pursued a lady who sparked his interest, and usually, within a week, sometimes two, he couldn't care less if he ever spoke with her again.

At first, he blamed the females, and then, if he considered his own capriciousness, he joked with his friends about his severe personal failing, namely his fickle nature. *Red wine or white, stilton or cheddar cheese, Elizabeth or Helen?* The number of women to whom his name had been linked in recent years had got him soundly branded as a rake.

With Adelia, he looked forward to every encounter. It was as if his blood sang when she was near. Indubitably, his manhood welcomed her by springing to attention. But more than that—at least, he hoped it was more than that—he liked coaxing words from her. He found her thoughts interesting and valued her opinion—except as pertaining to her brother.

How would she cope with an earldom without an earl? Not to mention how she now had to run a mining company.

Anger surged through him at the way her brother had not only destroyed Sophia but had also put Adelia in a perilous position. Unscrupulous men might try to swoop in for her inheritance, offering friendship in hopes of gaining her hand. Others would try to offer spurious counsel regarding the mining business. There would be some who might offer to relieve her of its worrisome burden.

A half-hour later, he was at Teavey's feeling as if he'd been the cause of most of Adelia's worries, and was forcefully boxing with Whitely.

"Ease off, old chum," George said, "or I shall stop. My face must remain perfect as it is, and I should very much like my ribs to remain whole."

"Sorry," Owen muttered. Besides, punching his friend was doing nothing for his mood. Something was bothering him, and he couldn't put his finger on it. Perhaps it was a stray thought from a conversation he'd had or something he'd seen. It would come to him if he stopped thinking about it.

Regardless, he couldn't shake the discomfited feeling, nor that it had to do with Adelia. He went to the Carlton Club with Whitely and, after, stopped in at his parents' home merely to make sure of their continued health. He was a little worried his father would let the business slip away. Despite having promised he would devote his attention to mining, the Earl of Bromshire seemed to be devoting his attention to nothing more than sitting in his favorite chair, staring into space.

"Why would an earl kill our Sophia?" his father asked as he had done each time Owen saw him since Smythe's arrest. He asked this question only if they were alone, never speaking of the murder openly when his mother, Lady Bromshire, was within hearing, as it seemed to shatter her all over again.

"I don't know." Owen tried not to spend time thinking about it since he had no answers, and Smythe wasn't going to tell him. It could have been an *affaire de coeur* gone very wrong. However, that wouldn't reflect well on his sister, so he decided it best to leave it be.

"But it makes no sense, Owen. I need to understand why this happened," his father added.

Owen sighed. "We may never know."

The earl shook his head. "She *knew* him. That much is certain. Sophia read the note and obeyed. Why? Why did my daughter go to her death?"

For his father's sake, Owen decided he would try to discover the answers no matter how sordid. "It may come out during the trial—"

"I shall not go to that," his father broke in. "I cannot. If I did, I would take a pistol and shoot the earl myself. And that would do your mother no good."

"No, I daresay having you locked up after losing Sophia would not be advisable."

Owen knew how his father felt. Wanting to carry out the justice swiftly, even to look Smythe in the eyes while doing so, would be far more satisfying than merely watching him

241

hang. Nevertheless, that would have to suffice when the time came.

He couldn't imagine how Adelia would handle that moment except to know in his heart, it would destroy her.

And as soon as he thought of her, the nagging sensation that something he'd heard or seen related to her was important. And the only way he could rectify it was to speak with her at once before it drove him mad.

CHAPTER TWENTY-TWO

Owen found himself knocking on Adelia's door at an unreasonable hour of the evening, hoping she had finished her dinner and was in her drawing room. Their butler opened the door.

"I know you," Owen said to the man, startling him. "Do I not?"

"Indeed, my lord. I have opened this door to you previously."

"No, no," Owen said testily, striding into the front hall. "From elsewhere. It only just dawned on me. Have you been the Smythe's butler for very long?"

"Twelve years to be precise, my lord."

"Were you at Eton prior?"

The man's eyes widened. "I was, my lord. I served the former headmaster for a number of years until he retired."

Could this be what was unsettling him, a familiar face he hadn't placed before?

"And how do you like serving the Smythes?"

"My lord, that is a highly unusual question. Are you in the market for a butler? If so, I may know someone. As for myself, I am content in my position here."

Apparently, the man assumed Owen was attempting to poach him.

"That's fine, Mr. Lockley. I am not in need of staff. I'm sorry I brought it up." Considering Adelia's somewhat odd wallflower behavior and the earl dressing beneath his class in order to go to seedy pubs, Owen added, "Sometimes, things seem a little strange with the Smythes, that's all."

As soon as he said it, he bit his tongue. Owen had mused out loud to a servant, and if he could call the words back, he would. *What an ass he was!*

"My lord, another unusual thing to say."

Owen nearly smiled. It was Mr. Lockley's word for inappropriate or impertinent, but the man could not rightly reprimand a peer of the realm.

"Right, Mr. Lockley. Let's leave the matter."

He was about to ask for Lady Adelia, in spite of the house feeling empty and quieter than usual, already giving him the impression she was not at home.

Before he could inquire, Mr. Lockley suddenly added, "The earl and his sister have been graced with a far less strange environment this past year."

Ah, that would be since the death of the old earl, Owen surmised.

The butler was undoubtedly telling him—without telling him—that the Smythes were better off since their father passed. He'd heard rumors the man was a hard-headed tyrant. Indeed, Adelia had started to tell him as much when defending her brother, but Owen knew nothing of him personally.

If the Smythes' situation had improved, it had now greatly worsened again. Perhaps the young earl had learned to be a savage from his father.

"I am here to see Lady Adelia."

"Neither of the Smythes are home, my lord."

The butler said it as if the murderous earl were out at a party or a play. *Did he know where his master presently resided?* Perhaps Adelia had kept the truth from the staff.

"I am not interested in his lordship, only his sister. Do you know when she is expected home?"

The man had a pained look upon his face. "She has only recently gone out."

"That tells me little. Is she next door, on the other side of Hyde Park, or headed for Spain?"

Mr. Lockley grimaced.

"Come now, my good man," Owen urged him. "You seem inclined to tell. Why don't you get on with it?"

Flaring his nostrils with distaste at possibly breaking the sacred trust of his position, Mr. Lockley looked positively tortured.

"As a rule, my lord, I do not give out private information on the whereabouts of my mistress or master."

A prickle of alarm coursed over Owen's skin. "If Lady Adelia is in some kind of distress, perhaps she would want you to tell me."

The butler, bound by professional etiquette, raised his eyes to the ceiling, then down to the floor—obviously a man warring with himself. Owen knew the feeling well. Additionally, Mr. Lockley could lose his position if he said something he shouldn't and word of it got back to the Smythes.

"Come along," Owen urged him. "Out with it, man. Or must I threaten you with bodily harm?"

Mr. Lockley, eyes wide, took a step back.

"I am quite the pugilist," Owen added. "And people know me for my temper, which is rising as we delay. Tell me where Lady Adelia is for her own good and for yours, so I don't have to twist your brittle old arm."

"If I were not alarmed at her destination, I would let you beat me rather than disclose my mistress's whereabouts," the butler declared.

"I have taken note of your loyalty and discretion. If Lady Adelia asks me, I shall defend you."

"Very well, my lord. Her ladyship has gone to the East End. To be precise, as I heard her say to the driver, to Whitechapel and Osborn Streets."

To the home of the earl's lover!

"Surely, she didn't go alone," Owen said, heart pounding with fear and fury at her stupidity for going to such an area after dark.

"No, my lord. She took a footman and one of our maids."

That did little to quell his trepidation. He was down the step, yelling the address to his coachman, and climbing in his carriage before the butler had closed the front door.

"And hurry," he ordered out the window. His ponies lurched to a start and began at a good clip through Mayfair.

ADELIA HAD WAITED UNTIL after sunset to catch Miss Moore at home, knowing the young woman had a job by the sheer fact of her inhabiting a flat by herself.

It felt quite different to be in the East End without Owen or her brother. More than a little frightening, in fact. By the time she reached the street upon which Miss Moore lived, just off Whitechapel High Street, she had only the driver with her, as she'd allowed her two servants to visit their respective family.

Of course, she realized her folly too late. She could not take the driver with her, leaving her horse and carriage unguarded. Having Henry draw up as close to the building as possible, Adelia alit from the carriage and kept her head down, trying to look as if she knew what she was about. In a couple steps, she dashed through the doorway and up the stairs to the bedsit.

"Miss Moore," she called through the doorway, knocking at the same time. Realizing her gloved knuckles made little sound, she wrenched off her right one and wrapped on the door again.

Hoping the woman was home and that no other door opened along the passage, Adelia waited, shifting from one booted foot to the other.

"Who is there?" came Miss Moore's voice.

Relief flooded over Adelia. "It is Lady Adelia Smythe, Thomas's sister. Won't you please let me in?"

Immediately, the door opened, and Adelia was met by the surprised visage of Miss Moore.

"What on earth are you doing here?" She looked past Adelia. "And by yourself?"

With that, the young woman reached out and grabbed her by the arm, yanking her inside, making Adelia squeak with surprise.

"I am sorry to . . . to come uninvited and unannounced," she began when she regained her footing.

"That's no matter, my lady. You are very welcome, but it isn't safe for the likes of you to be roaming around the East End."

"I won't roam," Adelia promised. "I only came to speak about Thomas."

Miss Moore's face fell, and her eyes filled with tears. "What has happened? Something dire, I know. Else he would have visited or sent a note."

"He is at Newgate, under suspicion of murder."

"Newgate," the woman repeated and slumped onto her couch.

"May I?" Adelia asked, gesturing to the seat beside her.

Distraught, Miss Moore could do nothing but nod. Previously, with Owen storming about the room and punching Thomas, Adelia had been unable to focus on the young woman, but now she had time to take her measure. She had a pleasant countenance, her clothing was neat and clean, and her dark hair was up in a tidy bun. They were probably close to the same age, and Miss Moore might even be a few years younger. *This was her brother's ladylove!*

"I am hoping you can help me to clear his name," Adelia said, but her brother's woman put her head in her hands and moaned.

"My poor Thomas," she murmured.

Adelia's stomach lurched to hear her pain. Obviously, she loved him.

"I have secured a barrister," Adelia told her. "And I have visited him in jail."

Miss Moore lifted her head. "Can I go visit him, do you think? Would they let me?"

"I don't know." Truly, Adelia had no idea if they let people who were not related by marriage or family into the prison. "I don't see why they wouldn't."

"In any case, he might be angry if I went."

"Why?" Adelia couldn't imagine the answer.

A laugh that was partly a sob escaped the young woman's lips. "Because, quite frankly, my lady, I am not a member of your class."

Adelia shrugged, reminding herself of Mr. Brassel.

"It seems that doesn't bother Thomas. Do you think he is ashamed of you?"

"No," Miss Moore shot back fiercely. "He is worried the *ton* would tear *me* apart, not *him*. So, he comes here where he can more easily fit in than I could in your world."

That sounded like her brother. Yet, she already knew he didn't intend to continue this secretive arrangement forever. *Had he already asked the woman to marry him?*

"Do you know his intentions?"

Miss Moore produced a smile, turning her entire face radiant. "He intends for us to marry."

Adelia sighed. *What a difficult path that would take them upon!* If they truly loved one another, though, it would be worth it.

"When?" she asked.

"*After* you have secured a husband, of course." Miss Moore said it entirely without malice, but Adelia shrunk back onto the sofa cushion.

"Oh, don't be alarmed, my lady. It's only because he doesn't want a scandal over him and me to put any kind of stain on you, nor ruin your chances to make a good match."

Then the woman's face crumpled. "But now I shall never marry him. Newgate! What if he's hanged for murder?"

Putting her face in her hands, she ended on a wailing note, making gooseflesh rise on Adelia's arms. She patted Miss Moore gently on the shoulder. If only she could assure her everything was going to be all right.

After a few more sniffles, the young woman raised her head.

"It's hard not to feel defeated," Miss Moore continued, "not only about Thomas, but about life in general when one is a working woman with a good education. We know what to expect and what we cannot expect. I've heard the vicar give sermons about hope." She raised her head and looked around. "When I see the beginning and ending of every day as it is, begun in poverty, sometimes despair, and finishing the same at bedtime, how can I have hope?"

She looked Adelia straight in the eyes with an intelligent brown gaze. "And then I ran into your brother. And because I was out of my element—meaning not behind a shop counter—and in his world, since I was in Mayfair, we could meet as . . . well, *equals* is too strong a word. I would never say that, my lady. But I had on my Sunday best, what I wore to my dad's funeral and my sister's wedding."

Adelia nodded encouragingly. "Do you have family close by?"

"My mum and sis live in Romford to the northeast, so not too far."

Adelia had no idea where Romford was or what Miss Moore meant about being out of her element. This type of gabbing was foreign to her, but it was not entirely awful. If not for the dire circumstances at hand, it would be, in fact, pleasant, especially since Miss Moore was happy to do most of the talking.

"It's all mills and cows there," she continued. "And that dratted failed canal. I wanted more to my life, so I came to London. Seven months, I've been here, and it's an easy train ride home when I need to go back."

The young woman nodded to herself deep in some private thought, until with a faraway look, tears returned to her eyes. Adelia knew she was thinking again of Thomas.

"How did you meet my brother exactly?" Adelia asked the question that had burned in her since first encountering Miss Moore.

She blushed and raised her chin slightly. Adelia hoped Miss Moore didn't think she disapproved.

"I was looking for a new bonnet, good enough for my new life in London. I went to New Bond Street, as I'd heard it was the place. Dear Lord, I had no idea!" She shook her head and added, "I could not believe the cost. I was in a lovely milliner's shop across from a store full of sparkling baubles."

"Asprey's jewelry store," Adelia supplied.

"I believe so. Anyway, Thomas had a woman's bonnet in his hand, and when he asked my opinion, I told him it was ugly. He said he'd never heard someone so honest before, and he said it in his beautifully clear voice. Don't you think it has a nice quality about it?"

Adelia had never considered the quality of her brother's voice, so she simply nodded and let Miss Moore continue.

"Thomas said most folks would preface such a frank judgment by trying to discover the other person's opinion of the bonnet first. And even so, they would cage their own in niceties and blandness until it was worth almost nothing. Moreover, most would think any bonnet that expensive must be lovely, but it wasn't." She grimaced.

"Honestly, Lady Adelia, you would have hated that bonnet. When he finished talking, I half loved him already. But he was buying for a woman, so I said to myself, this is *not* a man to look twice at."

Miss Moore sighed and added, "Then he said he was trying to buy something nice for his sister's birthday, and I said to myself, what a prince."

"He did give me a bonnet for my birthday," Adelia recalled.

"I helped him pick it out," the young woman confirmed.

"He seemed especially happy about giving me that present," Adelia mused. "Why didn't he tell me about you?"

"Because I told him where I lived, and when he came to collect me for our first outing, he realized I was not lying about my situation."

Covering her mouth as she yawned, she said, "Excuse me, my lady. As I told you, it has been a long week, and it is not over yet. I have two jobs. I work at a bookseller's four days a week and for a printer the other two days, both on Pall Mall. I brought home a piping hot pork pie, which will now be cold."

She puffed out her cheeks, looking sad. "I shall try to visit Thomas on Sunday morning when I have a free day."

"I hope they let you—" Adelia was interrupted by a pounding on the door, making her jump nearly out of her skin and causing Miss Moore to rise to her feet. Adelia stood more slowly, fear rising into her throat, and the two women stared at one another.

"I'm not expecting anyone," Thomas's lady-friend said, "but I wasn't expecting you, and here you are."

With that, Miss Moore approached her door, just as whoever was on the other side, banged on it again. Adelia flinched, her mouth suddenly dry.

"Where is Lady Adelia?" boomed a loud voice.

Owen!

"It's Lord Burnley," Adelia said.

Miss Moore's eyes widened. "The one who accused my Thomas?"

She nodded.

Miss Moore's face hardened in a mask of anger, and she yanked the door open, surprising the viscount, whose hand was raised to bang again.

Without a greeting, he looked past her to see Adelia. "Are you all right?"

"Of course. Why are you here?"

His eyes narrowed. "Why are *you* here?"

Impossible man! "I am gathering evidence."

"That is for the detectives to do."

"Well, *you* did it," she pointed out. "And you got it all wrong." With a huff, she crossed her arms and took her seat again on the sofa.

"You will come away with me at once," he ordered.

"I will not. I will scream if you try to make me leave."

He shook his head wryly. "Miss Moore, what would happen if her ladyship screams?"

The young woman, looking chagrinned, said, "Nothing much, I'm afraid. Perhaps some blokes will come from downstairs to see if you've been assaulted with hopes you've been knocked unconscious so they can rob you."

Adelia shivered and stood up again.

"Where is your maid and your footman?" Owen demanded. "I understood you had both with you."

Mr. Lockley had been none too pleased about her expedition, and plainly, he had been speaking out of turn.

"I brought Penny so she could visit with her sister, who works at a tavern down the street. I will pick her up again on my way home. And my footman, Ned, is with his father. I dropped him on Butcher Row as we passed through."

Owen threw his hands up at her words. "Your driver has to defend your carriage and you? By himself?"

"I am fine," she reiterated.

"And you shall stay fine by coming with me at once."

"I shall not. Miss Moore and I are discussing personal issues."

He banged on the doorframe. "You will come."

"Or what?" she demanded.

"Or I shall toss you over my shoulder and carry you," he threatened, and she could see by the look on his handsome face, now contorted with frustration, that he meant it.

She looked to Miss Moore.

"Please, is it possible for you to recall if my brother was with you on a Friday evening, the last one in June?"

Owen swore rudely. "Ridiculous! Naturally, she will say he was with her. Besides, how is she to recall a particular night?" His tone was insulting, and Miss Moore bristled.

"I'm not a simpleton, Lord Burnley. Many of us live here because we cannot get out. The high cost of the nicer parts of the city keeps us, even those of us who work hard, stuck in the back slum of London. For all that, we live the best lives we can, and we are not all dishonest."

He had the grace to look chagrined.

"We saw each other most Fridays, to be sure, since I go to work later on a Saturday, unless he was escorting you to a ball or dinner party," Miss Moore confirmed.

"Enough of this gossip-water!" Owen ground out. "It signifies nothing."

"What about the night of—" Adelia broke off to glance at Owen "—of Lady Sophia's death?"

"Her murder," he ground out, jaw clenched.

Miss Moore glanced at Owen, then back at Adelia. "Sadly, his lordship is correct. Off the top of my head, I cannot say for certain as to that particular night."

Adelia felt deflated.

"But his lordship is correct on *both* counts," Miss Moore added defiantly, putting her hands on her hips. "I will say Thomas was with me nonetheless."

Owen swore again. "You would protect my sister's murderer with a lie?"

"I would protect the man I love, who I know is *not* a murderer."

"As would I," Adelia murmured.

Owen roared with fury. Adelia approached him, uncowed by his anger. "It is you who must leave, Lord

SYDNEY JANE BAILY

Burnley. I will make my way home perfectly safely without your interference."

Unexpectedly, he reached out and took hold of her upper arm. With their gazes locked, she could not imagine his intent as he slowly, calmly drew her closer. Lowering his head, he whispered something into her deaf ear.

Shaking her head, she started to turn the other way, when Miss Moore spoke up.

"Lady Adelia cannot hear you on that side."

CHAPTER TWENTY-THREE

S hocked that this woman knew something so personal about her, Adelia froze, staring up at Owen. At the same time, she felt his grip tighten.

"Why?" he asked, his face the very picture of concern. And pity, which she abhorred.

She pressed her lips together and heard Miss Moore's response from behind her.

"Because her father was a brute, just like you!"

Owen's gaze locked with Adelia's again before she glanced at his hand on her arm. He released her instantly.

"I assure you what I said in your ear was not brutish in any way," he protested, but he did not repeat it. "How did . . . that is . . . ?"

Staring at the floor, wishing she were home, Adelia said, "My father liked to punctuate his anger by a solid cuff to one's head. There is nothing more to be said. He is dead, and I am not in any way bothered by my affliction, except when people point it out."

She glanced at Miss Moore, who blushed. "Or when someone feels sorry for me," she added, turning away from

Owen, who had looked as though he was going to say something of the sort.

"Back to the matter at hand," Adelia continued, speaking to Miss Moore. "If you do not recall—and why would you recall an ordinary Friday—perhaps, if you and Thomas went somewhere, others might remember the two of you. You were at a play once. That was on a different night. I saw you there."

She looked at Owen again. *On a wonderful night with Owen when he kissed her, awakening every sensual particle in her body.* "Maybe you have a pamphlet or a theatre ticket from the night in question."

Miss Moore shook her head. "That play was the only time we ventured to a public place outside of the East End. Thomas thought it too risky, more so after you saw us. Usually, we eat at a local pub, or we . . . we stay here." She blushed again at the implication of hours spent in the privacy of her flat.

With each word, however, Adelia's hopes fell. Miss Moore could lie for Thomas, but without someone to back up her statements, no magistrate would believe her.

"I saw the two of you another time," Owen's surprising words cut through the silence.

"I remember," Miss Moore said. "We left as soon as Thomas saw you."

"Another man followed you out the door that night," Owen said.

She cocked her head. "What do you mean?"

"He stood up not long after you left, and he went out through the same door into the back."

"I cannot think who that could be," Miss Moore said, then stifled a yawn.

"I am sorry," Adelia said. "Undoubtedly, you've had a long day at work, and I have stopped you from enjoying your supper."

"I haven't enjoyed anything since Thomas disappeared. Now that I know he is in jail, there isn't anything that can bring me happiness nor peace of mind." The young woman glared at Owen, who shifted from one foot to the next but said nothing.

Five minutes later, Adelia was back on the street. Her driver appeared to be on edge with an iron bar clasped in his hand, standing alert by the side of the carriage until he saw his mistress approaching on Owen's arm.

"You have to stop twice, at this hour, to reclaim your servants?" The viscount's tone was irritated and scolding.

"Yes," she practically hissed since it was not his concern.

"I shall follow behind in my carriage and guarantee nothing goes amiss," he insisted.

Adelia rolled her eyes, but as a gang of ne'er-do-wells strolled by, she was grateful Owen was nearby. Letting him assist her into her carriage, she suddenly remembered a question.

Leaning out, she asked, "What did you whisper to me at Miss Moore's?"

He hesitated but replied, "I said I could not let anything happen to you."

She wondered if that was truly what he'd said.

Then he added, "No matter how angry you became, I could not leave you there."

"Oh," she replied. They stared at one another.

"Just as I cannot let you ride off without making sure you come to no harm by stopping at a tavern and a blasted butcher's shop. Who is going to tell your maid you are ready to leave?"

"My driver, of course."

"Leaving you outside and unprotected in the carriage of an obviously wealthy person?"

She bit her lip. "I guess I could go inside the pub and find Penny."

Owen shook his head. "Let's stop this foolishness and get underway. I shall fetch your maid and footman."

Closing the door firmly, he told her driver he would accompany them, and he disappeared from her sight, returning to his own carriage.

Although Adelia could no longer see him, she felt his protection like a warm blanket and knew she would be safe.

WHEN MR. BEAUMONT SHOWED up the next day, Adelia felt not the least bit intimidated. After all, she'd had an expedition to the East End—almost by herself. True, she hadn't discovered the alibi she'd hoped, but she wasn't finished searching. She had half a mind to write to Miss Moore and ask if she would accompany Adelia to the local pubs where she and Thomas spent usually went. Perhaps some barkeeper or a serving girl would remember them and have a reason to recall that particular night.

It was unlikely, but, for the moment, Adelia was out of ideas. When Mr. Lockley announced the company's engineer, she felt something akin to relief at being interrupted from her torturous thoughts. Moreover, this time he was not uninvited. She'd sent him a missive to come.

He strode in, and as he had previously done, he grasped her hand and had it to his mouth before she could withdraw it.

"I was concerned to receive your invitation. You wrote it was a matter of some consequence."

"Please sit down," Adelia invited him without stuttering or hesitation. "You may have noticed my brother has been unavailable to meet with you to discuss business."

"Not really," the man said. "We often go one or two weeks without meeting."

"Oh." Perhaps she should have waited until Mr. Beaumont sent a letter to the house addressed to Thomas. Still, it was inevitable. "My brother has been charged with a crime he did not commit and is currently at Newgate prison, awaiting trial."

Shock transformed the man's amiable face. "I don't understand. How can this be?"

"I am working to secure his release, or at the very least, his acquittal."

Leaning forward, he asked, "Have you enlisted the services of a solicitor? I may know someone—"

She held up her hand. "I have already done so. Thank you."

He sat back, shaking his head. "Frankly, I am astonished. But I do have contacts at the Inns of Court," he added. "If you wish to tell me the name, perhaps I know him or, at least, his reputation."

"Of course. His name is Mr. Brassel, and he came highly recommended."

Mr. Beaumont nodded noncommittally, and Adelia couldn't tell whether he knew of him or not.

"Until such time as my brother can again take up the reins of our family's company, I think it best if you and Mr. Arnold handle whatever may arise. You, of course, will continue to manage the day-to-day activities," she hesitated, as she didn't really know what he did, "and Mr. Arnold can handle the financial affairs. I assume he is the one who receives and makes payments."

Mr. Beaumont looked aghast. "We cannot have the accountant who is in sole charge of interpreting the ledgers also be the one to handle the accounts payable and receivable. Most improper. He could far too easily write himself a large note of withdrawal."

Adelia considered the notion of such larceny. "You don't trust our accountant?"

Mr. Beaumont looked slightly uncomfortable. "I didn't mean to imply such a thing. Unquestionably, he is an honest man, but it is simply not done. As your general manager, I usually oversee anything to do with operations *and* finances, too. Our office clerk is our bookkeeper, meaning he enters all the figures into the ledgers, and he writes bank checks when instructed by me or your brother. Quarterly, the ledgers go to Mr. Arnold to discern our company's health, so to speak. And I bring to your brother whatever he needs to sign or make decisions upon. Perhaps you wish to make those decisions in his stead."

She shook her head. "I don't think I should."

After a pause, he stroked his chin. "I suppose I could do it," he offered. "I could meet with you as I previously did with Lord Smythe, and with your approval, I can run the company until his lordship returns."

She liked his suggestion, especially as he seemed to think Thomas would return. As long as Mr. Beaumont didn't show any interest in her personally, she didn't mind meeting with him.

"Very well, I believe that arrangement will work, and I can only hope my brother will be set free soon."

Mr. Beaumont stood up and bowed low. "I shall keep him in my prayers, Lady Adelia. A charge of murder is serious, but not insurmountable to the truly innocent. If I can be a witness to his character or help in any way, please let me know."

"Thank you. I am—" The sound of Mr. Lockley giving entrance to another visitor interrupted her. Cocking her good ear toward the door, she heard Owen's distinctive tenor.

Her pulse began to race. *How could this man who put her brother in jail continue to cause this strong reaction in her?* She ought to hate him, but she most certainly did not.

"I bid you good day, Lady Adelia," Mr. Beaumont said, reclaiming her attention.

She nodded and watched him leave, knowing her butler would show him out and show Owen in.

A moment after Mr. Beaumont disappeared from her sight, Owen filled the open doorway. He glanced over his shoulder as if studying the engineer.

"Hm," he said, turning back to her. "I have seen him somewhere before. Who is he?"

Owen behaved as if he had every right to question her visitors. It was outrageous, and she didn't answer directly at first.

"Perhaps you have met him wherever you mining company owners congregate."

His head tilted with amusement, and he smiled at her. "Like a pack of wild dogs?'

She lifted her shoulder. "I know not of such things."

"So, he also owns a mine?" Owen asked.

"No, that is Mr. Beaumont, our manager and engineer. I believe I mentioned him to you. He worked for my father, as well."

"Hm," he said again. "Now I am intrigued. His name sparks some memory I cannot quite recall. And now, his face seems familiar, too." He came closer, took her hand, and held it, looking into her eyes. "I feared he was a rival suitor."

Rival? "That implies you still wish to court me."

"Would you allow me if I did?" Owen asked.

While Thomas was in Newgate! "It is entirely inappropriate for me to be out gallivanting with you. My brother languishes in jail because *you* think him a murderer! Besides, why would you wish to be associated with me?"

He shook his head slightly, as if he didn't understand it himself. They were equally confounded. She could scarcely believe Owen had dragged Thomas to the police station and turned him in. What's more, she ought not to want to keep company with the man. It was a conundrum.

Owen released her hand, and she sighed. *How had he got over her lying about the handkerchief? And why?*

In the next instant, Adelia had her answer. The viscount drew her into his arms—*his familiar, delectable embrace*—making her heart gallop like a horse on a racetrack. She said nothing, relishing the rightness of being held by Owen. As she melted against him, she watched his expression change from questioning and waiting for permission to one of satisfaction. When he looked down at her, she saw only . . . tenderness before he kissed her.

As their lips touched, her body ignited, beginning to tingle from her swiftly hardening nipples to the soft place between her legs, which now throbbed with heat. All rational thoughts fled. While his tongue ravaged her mouth, she snaked her arms up and locked her fingers behind his neck.

He groaned, or she did. Adelia couldn't tell. He moved his leg so his thigh pressed against her most sensitive area, and she rubbed the cotton bodice of her gown against his chest.

His hands skimmed the back of her until they rested on her rear, which he grasped with both hands, drawing her up his leg at the same time as he nibbled on her lower lip. Feeling his fingers squeeze her soft flesh, Adelia moaned. Her skin was on fire. Indeed, lightning seemed to dance through her.

The passage of time stopped. Carelessly, feeling positively fierce, she sunk her fingers into his hair and drew his mouth back until it fully covered hers. When his tongue reentered her mouth, she gave in to impulse and sucked it, causing him to groan again. At the same time, she could feel his manhood pressing against her stomach, thrilling her with the possibilities.

When she released his hair and he lifted his head again, she looked into his eyes to discover they had gone nearly black, so large were his pupils. She shivered. He didn't resemble the civilized viscount she knew. He appeared like a predatory warrior, and she wondered if, in some way, she looked similar.

Indeed, she wanted to drag him to the sofa and pull him down on top of her. She desperately wanted to experience the weight of his muscular body and feel his manly part pressing against her feminine one.

Lowering his head again, he pressed his firm lips to her neck. "Adelia," he murmured, his mouth against her skin. Arching her neck, she shivered again.

How far could they go in her drawing room?

There was no one to stop her taking him to her bedchamber. *Not the fictional, priggish Mrs. Gundy they all made fun of!* She ought to have the strength of character to stop him herself.

When Owen's hand cupped her breast through her gown, Adelia ignored the moral voice in her head, savoring the sensation of his thumb stroking her nipple. *Dear God!*

"Yes," she said, wanting his touch on her bare skin.

He froze.

"Yes?"

"Yes," she repeated. *Anything. Whatever, as long as he would touch her again and more thoroughly.*

She gasped as the room tilted. When she opened her eyes, he had lifted her in his arms and was striding to the very sofa she'd been thinking of seconds earlier.

"The door," she said. He laid her upon the cushions and rushed away to lock it.

"And the other," she reminded him, watching him look wildly around to spy the other entryway, usually used by servants, almost hidden between two ferns. Again, he dashed away to the far side of the long drawing room. She sat up, regaining some sense.

What was she doing? She wanted Owen Burnley in the most intimate way despite knowing it was utterly wrong in every sense.

Suddenly, he was back. Instead of throwing himself atop her, he sat down on the edge of the sofa, and she scooted back to give him room.

"Probably a good thing your room is so big and the door so far away," he pointed out.

True. It had given her time to think, to allow the passion to give way somewhat to calm reason. *Blast it all!* She nodded.

"I want to take you to my home," he confessed, running a hand through his hair.

"Why?" she asked.

"Why?" he echoed. "Because I could have you all to myself, with no threat of your butler or maid intruding and later gossiping about what they saw. I suppose at my townhouse, if someone saw you entering or exiting, your reputation would be just as ruined."

She considered his words and asked, "Your own servants would say nothing?"

"Precisely. Once you were inside, you would be invisible as air."

"And then what?" she asked, staring at his strong neck where she'd knocked his ascot askew.

He swallowed, and she watched his *pomum Adami*, or Adam's apple as she'd heard it called, rise and fall. Oddly, she longed to put her mouth there, to kiss his throat as he had hers. Her pulse started to race again.

"I would carry you upstairs to my room and lay you upon my bed as I have here."

She coughed, her mouth suddenly dry.

"And I would begin to strip off your clothing," he continued, leaning forward to place a heated, open-mouthed kiss on the upper swell of her breast.

"Oh," she breathed.

"I would draw your skirts up your legs, like so." He reached down and began to do that very thing, raising her skirts past her knees until she lay exposed up to her thighs, where her silk stockings met her drawers.

"I thought you were going to undress me so I wouldn't have skirts on," she pointed out, watching the dark passion on his handsome face, as he stared at her legs.

Ignoring her logic, he said, "I would proceed to touch you where I know you're hot and ready for me." His fingers brushed up through the opening in her drawers, grazing her curls and then—*dear God*—the soft petals of her flesh.

As his fingers touched her core, caressing her aroused bud, Adelia arched against his hand. Eyes closed, trembling, she let him stroke her, hardly able to breathe. It was so . . .

Abruptly recalling where she was—*and who she was*—she opened her eyes and scooted away from him to the end of the sofa, yanking down her skirts.

Breathing hard, her body feeling as if it could explode with the tension coiled low between her hips, she shook her head.

Watching him, he lifted his hand to his face and touched his fingers to his nose and lips.

Her eyes widened. Owen was sniffing her scent as if she were fine perfume. Apparently, there was an entire world of intimacy she knew nothing about, but which she longed to discover with this man.

"I guess it is best I am not at your house, my lord."

"I, for one, think it's a damnable pity," he shot back.

"It would undoubtedly end with me giving you my virtue. And then, where would we be?"

He lifted his gaze to hers.

"Where indeed?" Cocking his head, he stretched his arm out so he could trail his finger down her bare arm, leaving gooseflesh behind. "Would you regret it?"

"I don't . . . I don't think so." She could hardly imagine, as an unwed lady, having a man between her legs, experiencing the ecstasy that belonged to the lawful marriage bed. It went against her upbringing for certain. But merely thinking of herself utterly unclothed with him, her insides seemed to liquify.

"I can guarantee you would not," he promised. "You would give me your virtue and give it again and again before morning. Each time willingly."

Trying to diffuse the heavy sensuality of the moment, she pointed out, "I believe I can only give my innocence once."

His face split into a wicked grin. "Truly, but there are ways to make each encounter feel new. In any case, each time we made love, you would experience this great release that is exciting and relaxing at the same time. It is as if your soul is being nourished."

Was he saying that only to get her to give him her virginity? It sounded too delightful to be real. But he had never lied to her. And in the brief time, he had touched her, it had been heavenly. If they had been secluded in his townhouse, she would willingly have given him her body that very instant.

Hadn't others felt the same way about the charming Lord Burnley? She had witnessed ladies at balls who either angrily shunned him or followed him around, hoping for his attention after having been linked with him. Without doubt, he had wooed and courted many young women, some of whom he must have taken to his bed. *Once he had deflowered her, then what?*

"And afterward?" she asked.

His face darkened, and he stood abruptly. "I have honor, despite many thinking I am all but a rake."

"I never said that." Although she could not state honestly that she'd never thought it. Or heard it, for that matter, among the *ton.*

Scrambling to her feet and smoothing her skirts as she did, her cheeks warmed at the recollection of how his hand had been upon her most private parts.

"Why did you come here?"

Again, with his telltale mannerism of tension, Owen ran his hand savagely through his hair, which had been perfect when he'd arrived. With her own fingers ransacking it and now his own, the viscount's valet would need to restore him to perfection prior to him going out for the evening.

"I needed to see you," he confessed. "Presently, you are the only light in my life."

CHAPTER TWENTY-FOUR

Adelia took a step back, having never expected such a vulnerable confession.

Jenny! In truth, Owen held precisely the same position for her. In her otherwise lonely world, he filled it with companionship—and kisses!

Nevertheless, she believed it inappropriate to tell him such. At the moment, he was as a plank to a drowning woman, but she would be forced to cut off all ties to him if her brother were convicted.

"I value our . . . ," she wanted to say *friendship*, but it had become so much more than that. Even so, she could see no future if Thomas were taken from her—making it more imperative she get her brother released. A charge of murder, as she'd since learned, usually ended in hanging, an outcome she refused to contemplate.

When she didn't complete her sentence, Owen offered her a wry smile. "We are in a quandary."

"Agreed. Do you wish to stay for dinner?" she asked without thinking, considering she was his bright spot, and he, hers.

ADELIA SURPRISED HIM WITH the invitation. One minute, she seemed to consider him the bane of her existence, the next, she seemed to care for him as he did her.

"It's scarcely past noon," he pointed out, and she laughed at her folly. It was a glorious sound.

"Oh dear!" she said. "I didn't realize. Doubtless, you have other things to do today anyway."

He shrugged. "I wouldn't say no to a cup of tea."

"Of course," she said, her cheeks becoming a pretty pink. "My manners! I shall ring for some at once."

"Do not fret," he told her as she went to the bell pull. "I believe I had you well and truly distracted since the time your engineer left."

Her hand still on the cord, she glanced back at him, her cheeks reddening further, and he was sorry he'd embarrassed her. She was simply so adorable. And sensual!

"From the instant I heard your voice actually." She frowned. "I was about to ask Mr. Beaumont a question before he left."

Suddenly, the door rattled, and he recalled he had locked her butler out. Her pretty eyes widened. However, holding her head high, she crossed to the door, unlocked it, and admitted Mr. Lockley.

Without acknowledging the indecorous *faux pas*, she instructed, "Tea, please, and some of that spice cake with the currants."

The butler nodded, and with the quickest of glances between Owen and the maid's empty seat by the ferns, he left.

Owen probably should insist Adelia get that same girl— *Penny, wasn't she called?*—into the room at once to protect the reputation of the lady of the house, if it wasn't entirely too late.

Adelia returned to the sofa, seemed to think better of it, and took a wing chair. He dropped into a matching one, glad he could have more time in her company and kept his mouth shut about Penny.

"There are men and women in Newgate for many and various charges, aren't there? Some are jailed for being poor."

Owen sobered. *Poor lady.* Thoughts of her brother were always close to the surface, which he could completely understand. He wished he didn't feel the slightest modicum of guilt. He shouldn't, but he did.

"Yes. For many reasons."

Adelia nodded. "Thus, I wonder why our engineer assumed Thomas was under a charge of murder."

Owen shrugged. "Why was he here?"

"To speak about running the company while my brother is . . . away."

"Rather insolent!" he said. The man might be overstepping his bounds.

"No, I invited him here to discuss that very thing, but when I mentioned where Thomas was, he said something about the seriousness of a murder charge. I was about to ask him why he assumed it was such when you arrived."

"I suppose that is presumptuous."

She lifted a shoulder delicately. "It is no matter. I will ask Mr. Beaumont when I see him again."

"You have a bookkeeper, I hope," Owen said. "Someone who can handle the payables and the receivables, to keep everything in the black. Or a professional accountant to oversee the ledgers."

She frowned again. "Mr. Beaumont said that would be improper."

"What?" Owen leaned forward in his chair. *An improper accountant? What did she mean?*

"I suggested having Mr. Arnold, our accountant, handle the finances, and Mr. Beaumont said it would be too easy for the man to steal."

Owen frowned, starting to get a bad feeling.

"No," she protested as Meg brought in the tea tray. "Please, do not look concerned. I think both men are completely honest, as they were with the company when my father was alive. Thomas has never had an inkling of worry, either."

"This man, Mr. Beaumont—where do I know that name from? At any rate, he is already your manager *and* your engineer, and now he wants to handle payments on behalf of Smythe Coal. I do not recommend it. Even the most honest individual can be tempted."

"What should I do?" she asked, pouring them both tea and handing him a slice of spice cake.

He set the teacup on the table next to him and rested the plate of cake on his lap. Only women would continue indulging in the niceties while discussing such important matters. It was endearing, but he also feared Adelia could make a misstep and take a great loss.

Absently, he put a forkful of the delicacy into his mouth while he considered his next words. It practically melted upon his tongue.

"Delicious," he declared, devouring it entirely before setting the plate next to his teacup.

"If you don't mind my saying so, and since you asked me, I would send a letter to this Mr. Beaumont and tell him you have considered it further. You think it best if you handle all the same documents and tasks your brother did, including signing checks."

"Really?" She sipped her tea.

"Why not? You are an intelligent woman."

She blushed again. Making her do so was becoming a habit he hoped would never stop. He didn't like embarrassing her, but it was amusing to bring color to her cheeks with a genuine compliment. Or better, with a wicked touch. In that regard, he hoped she never became so jaded or filled with *sang-froid* that her blush disappeared entirely.

"What if I make a mistake? What if I destroy our entire company and put all the miners out of work?"

"Hardly likely. If you have any questions," he began but hesitated. They were in that area, which was entirely inappropriate given the circumstances. "As I told you previously, you can always ask me or my father, I suppose. It might do him good to distract him."

"Perhaps," she said, looking doubtful.

"May I also suggest you send the same letter to Mr. Arnold, so there can be no confusion."

Her eyes widened. "I wouldn't have thought of that. I suppose one of these men could do something dishonest by keeping the other one in the dark as to my wishes."

"Precisely. For the time being, you should make certain both men are notified of anything you tell the other. Then neither can claim ignorance."

He sipped the tea. As with the cake, it was of the first quality.

"Thank you," she said softly, and he sucked the hot liquid right into his windpipe.

Coughing, he couldn't speak. It wasn't that her politeness and manners were unusual, but he knew how much it cost her to thank him for anything after what he'd done to her family.

"Are you all right?" she asked when his coughing subsided.

He nodded.

"I should be going." Before he admitted he was falling wildly in love with her, perhaps scaring her off forever. Besides, it was blatantly unfair. He knew she had feelings for him. They hadn't been coy with one another. Nevertheless, the massive mountain of the earl's trial and sentencing lay ahead of them, perhaps an insurmountable obstacle to overcome.

Moreover, when the day of the execution came, as it surely would, he wanted to be the one to comfort Adelia and knew he would be the very last person on earth she would allow to do so. It would be best if he held off declaring his deep feelings for her until after the unpleasantness was over. From then on, he would woo her for as long as it took.

"The invitation still stands for dinner, my lord."

He wanted to groan with the missed opportunity. "Regrettably, I am already elsewhere committed. I would be honored to dine with you another time, especially if there is more cake."

Standing, he drew her to her feet.

"I can promise you will enjoy far better than this cake," she said. And as their gazes locked, she blushed again. "I mean from our cook."

He almost chuckled at her unintentionally enticing words. If she knew how quickly his mind's eye pictured her lying unclothed upon the length of a dining room table, ready for him to lick and suckle, taste and devour, she would redden from the top of her lovely head to her sweet toes.

For his own part, he felt like a randy schoolboy at how much he desired this quiet, unassuming, absolutely marvelous woman who faced him.

"Eight o'clock?" he asked, nearly lowering his head to kiss her again. He very much wanted to. At the same time, he didn't want to give her the impression he was taking liberties at every turn.

She frowned but quickly laughed. "You said you were busy."

"What?" Owen laughed as well. "Yes, I did, and I am."

"Another time, perhaps," she said, and the *perhaps* gave him pause. He hoped she meant it. Now, he would be tormented all night thinking of her eating alone in her large, silent townhouse.

However, Adelia didn't look bothered by that. "I shall do as you say and write those letters."

Owen kissed her hand and left her to it. First, he had a meeting with the family banker, since despite his father saying he would retire from politics and focus on business, the earl was actually doing neither.

His parents had been only slightly mollified by the incarceration of the Earl of Dunford. They remained lost, entirely without purpose or the ability to experience contentment, and definitely not happiness. Thus, Owen was currently keeping an eye on business and filling his family's hereditary seat in Parliament. And he still hoped to get answers for his father. He just didn't know how. Perhaps Smythe would make a courtroom confession—or a scaffolding one—explaining his motive.

After the bank, he went to sit with his parents. Exactly as they had been over the past weeks, the drapes were drawn, both lord and lady of the house were decidedly at home, clad in black, and the servants were tiptoeing around as if terrified to make a sound.

Owen wanted to yell. What Sophia's death had done to his vibrant mother and boisterous, charming father was as if Smythe had brutalized them as well. At seeing their continued pain, fury bloomed within him. He stalked into the gloomy parlor, thumping on purpose to make noise in the mausoleum of a home. He hoped bringing his mother her favorite toffee would brighten her day even a little, and he also hoped to distract his father with news of the day.

Expectedly, his mother set the toffee tin down on the sideboard without opening it and returned to her seat. Enjoying a sweet was now beyond her grief. After a few minutes of trying to carry on a conversation with himself, Owen watched his father close his eyes and lean his head back, shutting out the world.

In keeping with his mother's current lackluster approach to anything social, she neglected to offer tea. When he suggested it, Owen was reminded of his earlier conversation with Adelia, and he wanted to tell them all about her. However, unless he kept her last name a secret, any mention of her would only cause more hurt.

At least he could ask his father about what had been bothering him. "Do you know a mining engineer by the name of Beaumont?"

His mother gasped. His father's eyes snapped open, and he reached over and patted his wife's hand.

Owen frowned. "What's wrong?"

"It pains your mother to hear the name," his father said. "It was wasted time when we could have had Sophia home, not far away in France."

Then he recalled. "Sophia stayed with the Beaumonts in Paris, didn't she?"

"Yes, but I don't recall any of them being engineers or in mining."

Perhaps only an unsettling coincidence. Owen had gone over to bring his sister home, meeting Monsieur and Madame Beaumont and their daughter, Annalise. Sophia had been sorely sad to tell them goodbye after a diverting year polishing her French vocabulary and her accent, as well as seeing much of the Continent.

"How do we know them?" Owen asked.

Surprisingly, his now always-silent mother spoke. "Madame Beaumont—Emma to me—we came out together, sharing a first Season. Her parents were neighbors of my parents. Emma met the Beaumonts during her second Season. They were only here for a few months, and she fell madly in love with the eldest son. Your father and I have visited them more than once. Her husband is an extraordinarily successful wine exporter."

Owen knew his mother's assessment of success meant her friend was very wealthy indeed.

"I met their daughter," Owen said. "Is there a son, perchance?"

"Two, in fact," his mother said. "One is in the clergy, and the other is in the family wine business."

"And they are all in France?"

"As far as we know," his father said. "Why do you ask all this?"

He didn't want to say too much. "I know of a Beaumont who works for an English mining company, and I was curious as to why the name sounded familiar. Now, I know."

"Which company?" his father asked as Owen could have practically guaranteed he would.

Luckily, before he had to say the dreaded name of Smythe, his mother made a clucking sound of annoyance.

"Enough. It is unseemly to talk of business, especially after . . . ," Lady Bromshire trailed off.

Owen sighed. Everything would always be categorized as *before* or *after* Sophia's untimely death. And he wondered if any conversation would ever be deemed seemly again.

When he left an hour later, he continued to be puzzled as to why he thought he'd seen Beaumont somewhere. He was positive he hadn't met the man in France. Suddenly, it struck him. Beaumont had been with Smythe outside Teavey's, but there was nothing sinister about the earl and his manager boxing together.

With that settled, he considered the evening ahead. He was having dinner with the Westings, and it occurred to him what a dolt he'd been not to invite Adelia to accompany him.

Still unsure what was and wasn't *unseemly*, to use his mother's word, in regards to ardently desiring the blood relation of his sister's murderer, Owen decided it was probably for the best that he hadn't.

Naturally, the first words out of Lady Jane's mouth were, "You should have brought that lovely Lady Adelia with you."

CHAPTER TWENTY-FIVE

Adelia had expected to receive a note in return from Mr. Beaumont, but she hadn't expected to be chased down the street by him when she was in her carriage, heading for Newgate.

She heard a voice call out, and her driver made a response, halting the horses a mere block from her own home. When the footman tapped upon her door, she lowered the window to see Victor Beaumont upon the pavement, breathing hard, apparently having run after her carriage.

"Lady Adelia," he said, approaching and sticking his head inside before the footman could even ask if she wished to speak with him. "I was on my way to see you."

His unexpected, uninvited appearances must come to an end. "You should have sent me a note, Mr. Beaumont. As you can see, I am otherwise occupied."

She was amazed at how much easier it now was to speak to people, particularly those who annoyed her. With Thomas's life in jeopardy, being shy was a luxury she could ill afford.

"I must speak with you at once about business matters. May I ride along with you?"

It was most improper. She had left Penny at home for the less her servants knew about Thomas's whereabouts, the better.

When she considered what usually occurred with Owen when they were alone in the carriage, she hesitated. On the other hand, her footman would be within hearing should she scream. And she ought to think like a woman of business in her brother's stead.

"Very well." With trepidation, she sat back as he yanked open the door and climbed inside.

Taking the seat opposite, he glanced about the interior, admiring the leather squabs and velvet hangings in the same manner as he'd inspected their crown moldings.

Most unusual, she thought, *and a little vulgar.* Further, the man leaned forward as if to take her hand in greeting, but she kept them firmly clasped in her lap.

After telling the footman to resume her journey, she asked, "What could not wait until another more opportune time, Mr. Beaumont?"

"I am sorry to intrude, my lady. I received your missive and was concerned about your change of heart regarding my signing documents and handling the finances."

She shrugged. "It is not for you to be concerned." She hoped that was the end of it, and he would vacate her carriage.

He opened his mouth, closed it, and opened it again. "I *am* nonetheless concerned. Have you spoken to someone else regarding our business? I must warn you, there are predators afoot, especially those who might be rivals for our company's customers. They will not think twice about trying to influence you to make poor decisions while Thomas is away, or perhaps bamboozle you so they can maneuver into a position of power."

Twice, he used the term *our*, and he should not have used her brother's given name so informally. He was entirely too forward and familiar, and it gave her an unpleasant feeling.

More than that, he seemed to have a strong notion of paranoia. *Did he know of her association with Owen?* She could see where Mr. Beaumont might not approve of her spending time with a rival mining company owner, but it was not his place to say anything.

"It is up to me to run *my* family's business until *Lord Smythe* returns," she said, recalling Owen's advice. "While I appreciate your concern, I assure you, it is unnecessary. Also, I had a note back from Mr. Arnold. He seemed to be under the impression you were running Smythe Coal entirely by yourself."

Mr. Beaumont flushed an ugly, ruddy color. "I have no idea how the accountant came to that conclusion."

"It is no matter. I have apprised him of my decision to handle everything my brother handled until his return."

"Very well." He paused. "And what if Lord Smythe doesn't return?"

She gasped. "I will not discuss such a thing."

"Of course," he said. Then his tone changed. "Lady Smythe, may I call you Adelia?"

"Positively not," she snapped.

He laughed as if she'd said something witty. "I would very much like to call upon you in the future."

She squirmed at his surprising change in topic. She could play the ninny. "Of course. You must come by and bring any documents I should see, *et cetera*."

"Yes, of course. But I was speaking of a personal visit, my lady. I was hoping I could pay my regards and escort you about Town, perhaps to a horserace."

She sensed she had best proceed with caution. A response of *certainly not* with the accompanying shudder that had welled up inside her would not be well received. Men did not like to be rebuffed. She'd learned that from her prime location as a wallflower, listening to the dramas, both large and small, play out around her.

Until recently, she had never been part of one and hadn't realized how fortunate she was. Now, it seemed, she was in the thick of one after the other.

"Why, Mr. Beaumont, that is too kind of you. However, as you must understand, while my brother is going through such tribulations, I cannot think of anything other than securing his release."

His eyes narrowed. Again, she wondered if he knew about Owen. *Had he seen her riding with him in Hyde Park?* Now, she was the one being paranoid.

In the thickening silence, she rapped quickly upon the carriage ceiling, and it halted with a rocking motion. Her footman jumped down and opened the door.

"Good day," she said, giving Mr. Beaumont no choice but to exit.

"Good day, my lady." This time, he didn't bother to try to take her still-clasped hands. He jumped down to the sidewalk and strolled away.

When she reached Newgate, she found her brother already had a visitor. This time, without benefit of a solicitor, Adelia had been forced to one of the inner yards in which the prisoners took the air and got a little exercise. Constance Moore was already pressed against an iron gate, her arms reaching through to Thomas, who had hold of her hands.

Her heart ached to see him. And in fact, he looked the worse for wear despite the bribes they'd paid. His hair was obviously unwashed and uncombed, and he had a hollowness to his cheeks.

Not wishing to break up their discussion, she hung back until Thomas noticed her.

"Dilly-girl!" His face lit up, and Miss Moore turned to greet her.

Adelia could see streaks of tears on the young woman's face, which made her own sad emotions flood to the surface. Regardless, she would not cause her brother more grief by joining in with volatile female emotions.

"How are you?" she asked him. "Eating well, I hope." She managed to keep a note of cheer in her voice.

"Well enough. Not like our cook's fare, that's for sure."

She nodded, swallowing the lump in her throat, and turned to Miss Moore. "I am ever so glad they let you visit."

The woman gave her a wobbly smile. "They didn't care who I was, actually. Anyone can wander in here."

If only one could wander out as easily!

"I brought you more money. I hope it helps." Adelia passed a small purse through the wide fence posts, which he took and pocketed.

"It does. An extra helping of bread or stew, a warmer blanket. That type of thing. But seeing the both of you does better for my health than anything. It's been a busy day already."

"What do you mean?" she asked.

"I also had a visit from Victor Beaumont."

"Really! That's odd."

"Why?" Thomas asked. "He still works for me." He sounded as if his pride were wounded.

"Of course he does. Yet, I only just spoke with him prior to coming here, and he didn't mention it."

"That is odd, especially considering his visit was all about you."

She had a sinking feeling in her stomach. "He wants to court me, doesn't he?"

Thomas frowned. "Maybe, but that's not what I meant. He was concerned—"

"About Smythe Coal!" Adelia shook her head at the man's gall.

"Yes. To be frank, he believed you were confused and needed guidance, and he was convinced you were going to Burnley for advice."

"Even if I was, that's no cause for Mr. Beaumont to say anything." So, their crafty engineer did know about Owen.

Thomas stared at her. "You're not talking to Burnley, are you? After what he's done?"

She considered how to answer his question. Owen had not tried to interfere with Smythe Coal in any way. He had only tried to help her.

Thomas jumped into the silence. "Dilly! What can you mean by speaking with him?"

"You intended to ask the elder Burnley, the Earl of Bromshire, for counsel, did you not?"

"That was before—this!" Her brother gestured at his surroundings. "And that was the father, *not* the son. Your viscount thinks I'm a murderer!"

She didn't know what to say except to defend herself. "I haven't done anything wrong. I didn't tell any company secrets. I don't know any to tell. And I do not condone Mr. Beaumont bothering you. First, he wanted me to agree he should handle everything, including what I believe is Mr. Arnold's purview. And when I told him I had decided I should inspect documents and sign in your stead, he came running to you. Do you think that's appropriate conduct?"

"I don't think your discussing our company with Burnley is proper conduct!"

Adelia sighed. He wasn't going to get over that point to see how inappropriately overbearing Mr. Beaumont had become.

"What did you tell our esteemed manager and engineer?" she asked, prepared for her brother to have given the man permission to take over everything.

Thomas hesitated, pursing his lips in distaste. "I told him to defer to your wishes in everything."

"What?" She couldn't believe it.

"Of course. When it comes down to it, I can trust only you and Constance." He glanced at them each in turn.

"I will not let you down, Thomas," Adelia promised, and the tears she'd fought back earlier returned unbidden before she could stop them.

He rolled his eyes. "Foolish woman. I've already had enough tears from this one." He jerked a thumb at the Miss Moore, who had stood silently beside Adelia. "Don't you start. There is nothing to cry about. Your barrister will have me declared innocent when we go to trial, and we'll put this behind us."

She nodded, unconvinced but unwilling to let him see that. Perhaps when she met again with Mr. Brassel and Mr. Jaggers, which she was doing within the hour, she would feel more confident of their eventual success.

"I do think Mr. Beaumont was trying to pull the wool over my eyes, trying to convince me to let him take over all your duties."

"He only wants what's best for the company," Thomas insisted. "He is always most concerned with our continued success."

She nodded, hoping her brother was correct. Glancing at Constance, who appeared worn out, Adelia remarked, "It's your only day off. I shall leave you two to have time alone. Please, contact me if you need anything."

"That's very kind of you, my lady," Miss Moore said.

Adelia reached through the bars of the fence to hug her brother, tamping down the returning tears.

"Don't worry," she told him.

He shook his head. "I won't." But his eyes held a sheen of apprehension he couldn't hide.

Hoping to dispel it soon, she directed her driver to Gray's Inn.

"I HAVE PREPARED MY opening statement. Would you care to hear it?"

Adelia sat next to Mr. Brassel and watched as Barrister Jaggers strolled up and down his office.

"After much consideration, and in light of the strong evidence and lack of a credible alibi, I have decided to tackle the McNaughten rule."

"*Hm,*" said Mr. Brassel, glancing sideways at Adelia prior to addressing his associate. "Having met the accused, I am doubtful he will agree to such."

"It is not his place to agree or not," Mr. Jaggers said, looking affronted. "It is my job to secure his release or, at the very least, his life. In fact, I shall not even speak with him about it."

Adelia waited for one of them to explain, but when they didn't, she said, "I'm sure my brother will be pleased with whatever defense you have come up with, sir. What is this M . . . M . . . ?"

"The McNaughten rule," Mr. Jaggers finished for her, "was created after the brilliant defense of Mr. Daniel McNaughten by my own mentor, Sir Alexander Cockburn. Small man with a large head. Cockburn, that is, not McNaughten. Also, currently our Attorney General.

"Cockburn?" she asked. "Not McNaughten?"

The barrister narrowed his eyes at her, apparently considering whether she was making sport of him. Adelia decided to keep quiet if she was ever to hear the explanation for this rule he mentioned.

Mr. Jaggers cleared his throat. "In 1843, McNaughten was charged with the cold-blooded murder of Edward Drummond, the prime minister's secretary, which was entirely a mistake."

"He didn't do it?" she asked.

"Of course, he did it. People saw him," the barrister insisted. "Luckily, a constable was on hand to prevent him from doing further harm."

"How can one do more harm to someone than murder?" she asked.

"The victim didn't die on the spot. In fact, he walked back to his office, only to die days later, probably due to the terrible care of his physicians, Mr. Guthrie and Mr. Bransby

SYDNEY JANE BAILY

Cooper." Mr. Jaggers waved his arms around, making his sleeves fly. "It is they who should have been charged with murder if you ask me."

She frowned. "Are you saying because the man didn't die right away, Mr. McNaughten was acquitted?"

"That is absolutely *not* grounds for acquittal," Mr. Jaggers practically scolded her as if she were a student of law. "In any case, McNaughten meant to shoot Prime Minister Peel, thus clearly the murder was a mistake," the barrister explained.

Adelia hated to admit it, but his words were no clearer than mud. "So, this Mr. McNaughten was found innocent because he shot the wrong man?"

Both lawyers started to laugh, which she thought extremely rude. Mr. Brassel was the first to catch his breath.

"No, my lady, he was not found innocent exactly."

"But I understood we were using this *brilliant* defense to get my brother out of Newgate."

"Yes, dear lady," Jaggers proclaimed. "My mentor managed to get McNaughten acquitted, just as I shall your brother. He shall be deemed guilty but insane."

"What?" she exclaimed. "But Thomas is not insane!"

"How else can we explain or defend his strangling that young lady?" Mr. Jaggers asked, waving his arms around again.

She rose to her feet in protest. "He did not strangle her. He is innocent."

Mr. Brassel rose to his feet as well. After a long sigh, he added, "The verdict is sometimes stated as innocent by reason of insanity, so not truly guilty at all."

"But insane even so!" she protested. "And then what?"

Mr. Brassel grimaced, but it was Mr. Jaggers who answered with a tone of triumph. "Just as with McNaughten, your brother will be transferred from Newgate to the State Criminal Lunatic Asylum at Bethlem Hospital."

She felt faint and couldn't seem to take a deep breath. When the barrister's office began to spin, she sat down again quickly, leaning her head back and closing her eyes.

Immediately, Mr. Brassel took her hand and began patting it, while Mr. Jaggers waved his notepad to create a breeze upon her.

After a few minutes, she felt a little revived and more determined than ever to solve the entire matter herself.

"I knew her ladyship would not like this notion," Mr. Brassel said, his tone morose. The solicitor obviously knew the grave ramifications of being declared insane.

"No," she said. "I do not like it at all. Even if acquitted, Thomas's life shall be ruined."

"Dear lady," the barrister interjected, "at least he will have a life."

Dread raced through her. If she agreed on this course of action, not that Mr. Jaggers seemed to be asking for her approval, she knew Thomas would not accept it. If he were in the court when the barrister began such a defense, she had no doubt her brother would speak against him.

"How will you prove him insane?" Mr. Brassel wondered aloud.

"As you know, the McNaughten rule says I must clearly prove the earl was laboring under a defect of reason from a diseased mind at the time of the murder. I think any man in the court, magistrate included, will look at Lord Smythe with his title, his townhouse, his fortune, his mining company, and whatnot, and declare he must have been insane to murder the girl with no possible gain." He rubbed his hands together.

"I shall beat it home again and again. They were not lovers, as will be attested by her family, and we can uncover no blackmail, no motive for strangling her. Albeit, he was out of his head, and there is the blatant defect of reason I need to prove. At the time of the crime, he was clearly and obviously insane."

"With your advocacy skills," Mr. Brassel said, "I believe it will work."

It might, she agreed, *but at what cost?* She'd always heard barristers were extraordinary tongue-padders, and now she understood why.

CHAPTER TWENTY-SIX

Owen no longer had to haunt the seedy taverns and streets of the East End, but his thoughts returned to them, nonetheless.

Why had his sister gone there upon Smythe's summons? What did he have over her?

His father's troubling questions could only be answered by one man who denied any knowledge and who resided in Newgate. Nevertheless, perhaps some insight was to be found amongst the earl's friends. Surely, they would know if he was unstable, if he was jealous, if he had been seen with Sophia before the murder.

So far, Owen had spoken to no one about Adelia's brother, not wanting to cause her any scandal. However, for the sake of his own and his father's sanity, he'd decided to go to the earl's favorite club and start asking questions—if only he knew which club the earl frequented. Not the Carlton, as he hadn't seen him there, and Adelia said her brother didn't gamble, so not at Crocky's either.

How would he discover Smythe's club and his friends? He couldn't simply walk into the Union or Wellington's or

Garrick's and start asking. At Teavey's, though, their common ground, maybe he could find out something.

To that end, Owen jumped into his lightweight gig and went to the fighting club. He'd seen Smythe there with his engineer, Beaumont. Hopefully, he could find others who sparred with the earl and knew more of his nature.

Two hours later, while making idle conversation after each boxing match, Owen had encountered a number of young men who knew Lord Smythe, liked him, and wondered aloud where he had disappeared to. Some went so far as to mention the earl's lovely, eligible sister, and how they'd tried to converse with her only to be shunned during this Season or the last.

That gave Owen a sense of personal satisfaction. He couldn't help being glad she'd rebuffed all these eager swains who seemed to view her as little more than a wealthy prize. All the same, he wished just one of them had mentioned a dark side to Smythe, some blight upon his name, no matter how small. Instead, they were all devoted to him as a generous, good fellow.

Considering Beaumont, once again, Owen decided to meet him. If Smythe was a shady character, perhaps the man who worked for him would know something. Maybe, now that his boss was away, the engineer would be willing to offer up a few choice words about the kind of man the earl truly was.

To that end, Owen went to the four-story Coal Exchange at the corner of St. Mary-at-Hill and Thames Street, facing the Custom House offices. Inside, under the sixty-foot diameter dome, he hastened up the stairs to the office of Smythe Coal, a floor below where Burnley Mining's own manager and his team ran their daily operations.

Owen rapped sharply on the door, one of many along the gallery, all with panels of wood and rough plate-glass to let the light from the dome reach all the offices.

"Enter," came a voice.

Pushing it open, he encountered a single room, with no clerk or secretary, only Beaumont at a polished desk reading a newspaper.

The man glanced at him and had the oddest reaction. His eyes widened, his mouth dropped, and his face paled until he jumped to his feet, his expression one of alarm.

Strange, Owen thought, unsure what to make of it. Perhaps he was unused to dealing with nobility, or he was insecure around a rival mining owner.

"Good day," Owen said, despite courtesy demanding the engineer greet him first. "Mr. Beaumont, isn't it?"

Finally, the man came out of his stupor and visibly relaxed. Perhaps it was the pleasant tone of Owen's voice.

"Good day," he returned at last.

Entering farther into the room, Owen asked, "May I have a few minutes of your time?"

Beaumont's eyebrows shot up, but he nodded. "Of course, my lord."

"You know who I am?"

The engineer hesitated but nodded again. "Yes, Lord Burnley."

"May I ask how that is so?"

"First, would you care to sit?" Beaumont asked, gesturing to one of the other chairs dotting the room at empty desks.

They all looked uncomfortable, but Owen snagged one from what was undoubtedly a clerk's desk, with its telltale signs of dried green wax from sealing documents. He set the chair down in front of Beaumont's desk and tried to lean back in it. If he was going to get answers out of the engineer, he had best appear friendly.

"I make it my business to know the other mining companies and their owners," Mr. Beaumont explained. "Plus, I recall Lord Smythe pointed you out at Teavey's"

Good, he had brought up Smythe on his own.

"I am aware of the earl's downturn in circumstances," Owen said, watching the man carefully.

Instead of looking surprised, Beaumont nodded. "I suppose it is inevitable word will spread. I only hope it doesn't affect our business. Coal is coal, and people need it, regardless of whether the owner is a murderer."

It was Owen's turn to look shocked. He had assumed the man would defend his employer, not sound as if he already knew the earl to be guilty. Moreover, the thread of rage that seemed to have permanently wound its way around his heart tightened at the engineer's blithe reference to Sophia's death. One thing was apparent.

"You do not know who he killed, do you?"

"No, my lord."

Owen was close to snapping out the answer but refrained. The fewer people who knew, the better. Still, it was difficult to hear casual mention of her murder.

With anger bubbling through his veins, he found it difficult to keep his seat. Best he talk swiftly and bluntly and leave before his temper boiled over.

"Why do you think Smythe did it?" Owen asked.

"My lord?" Beaumont queried, looking ruffled.

"Come now, you know him to some degree, and I understand you knew his father, too. Some say the old earl was a violent man. Have you witnessed Smythe's aberrant behavior? Or did he mention an enemy or perhaps . . . ," he could hardly say it, "a lover?"

Beaumont didn't speak immediately. He appeared thoughtful for a few moments.

"Do you need an engineer or manager, my lord?" he asked at last.

Owen shook his head. "No. Why do you ask?"

"Unless I have no worries over my position and my livelihood, I would be a fool to speak ill of my employer, would I not?"

The man was expressing loyalty in his way, but seemingly far more mercenary than Mr. Lockley, the Smythe's butler.

"Are you saying you would accept a position at, for example, Burnley Mining and that, if you did, you might have information on your current employer's guilt?"

Beaumont hesitated, and Owen wished he knew the man's true thoughts during that brief hesitation.

Finally, he said, "No, my lord. I am doing very well here and expect to do better. Moreover, I have no information on Lord Smythe. He has always been upstanding and treated me fairly, as did his father." Abruptly, he stood up. "I am afraid I have a great deal to do today, what with Lord Smythe being *temporarily* indisposed."

The fact he'd been reading a daily paper belied his words, but Owen stood, as well. This was getting him nowhere, and it seemed the man was tossing him out as gently as one could get rid of a nobleman without causing offense.

Nonetheless, his remark about doing better made Owen wonder. "I shall confess to you I am friends with Lady Adelia Smythe. While I shall not in any way interfere with her family's mining company, I would not take it kindly should anyone else seek to increase his personal gain by taking advantage of her lack of knowledge in this area."

Beaumont looked affronted.

"Understood and unnecessary, my lord. I want only what's best for Smythe Coal."

Owen left unsatisfied and wondering where to turn next find answers to his father's questions.

It wasn't until many minutes later, while settling down to a meal with Whitely at Dolly's Chop House off Paternoster Row, that Owen finally recalled something which struck him as odd.

He sipped his ale, watching Whitely shovel in a forkful of his jacket potato slathered with butter. "I say, I've only just realized where I previously saw that Beaumont fellow."

"At Teavey's," George said around the large mouthful.

"Yes, but after that. I think he was the man trailing Smythe and his female friend when I saw them the first time in a tavern."

"Are you certain? I remember you were pretty far in your cups, or so you said."

Owen nodded. "I am nearly positive. Why would the man have been following his employer?"

Whitely shrugged and took a bite of his chop. He rolled his eyes with satisfaction. "This is even better than the food at Crocky's club, don't you think, even with their French chef?"

Owen didn't answer. *Should he pay Beaumont another visit and ask the man outright?* Perhaps the engineer had suspected Smythe of his heinous activities and was trying to ascertain the extent. Or maybe he'd hoped to find proof and blackmail Smythe for monetary gain.

That seemed more likely. And Owen had stepped in and had Smythe arrested before Beaumont could drain the company coffers with threats. Perhaps that meant Beaumont had proof of other crimes, maybe another murder. If it were a sickness with Smythe, at least he could take that answer to his father. Perhaps it had been nothing really to do with Sophia, and she had been a random victim.

Except there was the damning note, luring her there. Owen gave an exasperated curse at so many missing pieces to the puzzle, fury surging through him once again.

"Easy," George warned, looking around. "That was a little loud, old chum. What are you thinking?"

"I miss Sophia," he confessed. "And no matter what I do, I cannot protect her any longer, nor can I help my parents. I feel useless."

"That's absurd. You've caught the killer." Whitely lifted his ale with a nod to Owen. "That's more than the bobbies could do."

Owen shrugged. He wanted to tell Whitely how much he also missed Adelia, but it seemed inappropriate.

"I think I shall ask Detective Sergeant Garrard if there are other similar unsolved murders in that area. He probably would have told me. Yet, if there is a possibility Smythe was off his chump and had killed before, that would ease my father's mind. It would be an answer of some sort."

ADELIA NEEDED HELP AND could think of only one place to turn. She made her way to Whitehall and the office of the detective who had been handling Lady Sophia's murder.

When Detective Sergeant Garrard offered her a seat, she wanted to collapse into it and blubber like a child. She didn't. With composure, she sat and turned her weary eyes to his.

"Have you any other suspects regarding Lady Sophia's murder?"

"I'm afraid not, my lady."

Taking a deep breath, she asked, "Do *you* think my brother killed her?"

The man ran a hand over his forehead, then pinched his nose. "My apologies. Today, I have a headache. Like most days," he muttered. But he directed a kind gaze upon her. "It is not for me to say. There was ruinous evidence, to be sure. And still . . ."

"Yes?"

"I've never known a criminal who seemed so normal and yet could be so stupid, almost an imbecile, really."

She'd heard this already from Mr. Brassel.

"Only someone not thinking rationally would leave those clues," she said, echoing the solicitor's words.

Maybe the detective believed her brother as insane as Mr. Jaggers seemed to.

"The handkerchief is one thing that troubles me," Detective Sergeant Garrard continued. "If Lord Smythe went to the bother of taking the perfume, meaning, according to Lord Burnley, your brother emptied the victim's reticule, how could he fail to notice the handkerchief, too? And even if he didn't see it, why would he give you the perfume, knowing you were keeping company with Lord Burnley?"

She felt her cheeks grow warm at the mention of her association with Owen.

"And why did he leave the reticule?" the detective persisted. "Perhaps he could have given it to his ladylove since he was freely handing out the dead woman's things."

Adelia could hear the frustration in his voice, and it was mirrored in her own brain, as those same questions had gone around and around in her head for days.

"Have you spoken with Miss Moore?" she asked.

He nodded. "She said nothing helpful, I'm sorry. But back to the reticule, why not take it and make it look like robbery, for who would suspect a wealthy earl of that?"

"I shall wait," came a familiar voice drifting in from the outer chamber, stopping any reply she might make. *Owen!* Adelia rose to her feet and turned as he came into view.

Their gazes locked across the few yards separating them, and a sizzle raced through her. *That would never change*, she feared.

Owen frowned, and instead of waiting as he had just indicated he would, he barged into the detective's office as if he owned it.

"What are you doing here?" he demanded of her.

Before she could answer, Detective Sergeant Garrard, who'd also risen to his feet, spoke up, "The lady may come see me whenever she wishes, as regards her brother or any other matter. Please wait in the next room."

"That's all right," she said with Owen seething beside her. It was plain the detective was annoyed with the viscount. His bluster and brusqueness probably rubbed the hard-working policeman the wrong way. "I believe we have concluded our discussion, detective. I am sorry to have taken up your time. I hope your headache improves."

"Thank you, my lady."

She turned to Owen, nodded, and tried to pass by him.

"You may stay if you wish," he offered. "After all, anything to do with the murder involves your brother and hence you, too, I suppose."

It was her turn to seethe. "I do not believe anything to do with the murder involves my brother at all. Nevertheless, since he is already locked up, what more do you need from the detective?"

Owen took a breath. "I want to know if there were other murders in that same area."

The detective gestured for them both to sit and sank again into his chair. "Do you mean *after* Lord Smythe was taken into custody? Are you trying now to clear his name?"

Owen glanced between Adelia and the detective. "No, in fact, I meant prior to his incarceration. I wonder if he killed anyone else."

"What?" Adelia surged to her feet, and both men stood again. "Why would you think such an outrageous thing?"

"I'm sorry, Lady Adelia. My father needs to know why this happened. I wondered if perhaps my sister was one in a pattern of heinous behavior."

Adelia pursed her lips. She was angry but couldn't blame Owen. On the other hand, she wouldn't sit again while this vile line of questioning continued.

"Answer his lordship, please," she instructed the detective.

"There were no other similar killings," the detective said firmly. "We have more stabbings than stranglings, to be honest. Occasionally a drowning or a knock to the head. But none of those this year had anything to do with the aristocracy, nor did they occur in that establishment. I see no connection."

Owen sighed, which also annoyed her. *As if more dead women would help his family.*

"Is that all?" the detective asked.

"Actually," Owen said, keeping his gaze upon her, "there was one other thing. I paid a visit to Mr. Beaumont—"

"What?" Adelia exclaimed again. *The gall of this man!*

Owen addressed her this time. "To determine if he had heard anything about your brother and my sister."

"And had he?" asked the detective.

Owen shrugged. "I believe you should question him."

"Surely, he didn't have anything bad to say about Thomas," she insisted.

"No, he didn't," Owen admitted, "but I saw Beaumont one night in the East End, and strangely enough, he seemed to be following your brother and Miss Moore."

"Why didn't you tell me this before?" Detective Sergeant Garrard asked.

"I am ashamed to say I'd had a bit too much to drink that night." He gave Adelia a sheepish look. "Only when I met with Beaumont again did it come to me he was the one I saw that night."

The detective nodded. "Very well. I shall speak with him."

"This is all madness," Adelia said, feeling defeated, then she recalled the barrister's defense. She wouldn't tell Owen about that as he might try to figure out a way to stop Mr. Jaggers. And, at that moment, she was beginning to think having Thomas declared insane was his only chance not to hang.

In any case, she intended to ask Mr. Beaumont why he had been following her brother. If he had a reason, maybe he'd done it more than once and could provide Thomas with an alibi on the night of the murder.

Keeping her plan to herself, she walked out of the police station with Owen at her side.

CHAPTER TWENTY-SEVEN

It seemed preposterous to have such strong feelings for Lord Burnley—indeed, to be ardently in love with him, if Adelia were honest—while being firmly opposed to his actions and his conclusions. Moreover, despite feeling sympathy for his family's horrific tragedy, she had to tamp down flashes of anger toward him at his faulty reasoning.

If one looked at the evidence in the way the detective and Mr. Brassel did, it seemed ridiculously sloppy, as if Thomas wanted to be caught.

Or as if someone wanted him to be blamed! The notion came to her for the first time. She hadn't considered such malice in the world. *And for what purpose?*

Crimes of passion were not foreign to her. She'd heard a few tales of such while eavesdropping over the years and had duly written some into her stories. The most obvious reason would be someone else vying for the attention of Miss Moore.

"You are very thoughtful today, my lady," Owen said, recalling her to the present.

Without thinking, she said, "I wonder if someone else is in love with Miss Moore."

They were nearly back at her carriage where her driver awaited.

"Why are you wondering such a thing?" Owen asked.

She was not about to tell him her latest theory, that someone might have wanted to make Thomas look guilty. Undoubtedly, he would dismiss it anyway.

She lifted a shoulder. "She is pleasant, educated, and employed."

"And pretty," he added.

Frowning, feeling a little deflated, she said, "True." She wished he hadn't noticed, but, of course, the Lord Burnley she had come to love was a renowned flirt and admirer of women.

"Why are we discussing Miss Moore?" he asked. "I suppose you feel responsible for her and intend to look after her the rest of her days."

She was taken aback. In truth, his notion was not beyond the pale. If Thomas had intended to marry Constance Moore, it might be Adelia's duty to look after her, at least until Thomas could do so again. Certainly, that would be something Lady Jane would do.

Adelia nodded to her driver, who opened the carriage door.

"We are *not* discussing Miss Moore. At least, no longer," she said, her tone clipped and off-putting. *What she really wanted was to throw herself into his arms.* "Is there anything else you wish to tell me?"

Owen looked at her with his crystalline-blue eyes, and her stomach flipped.

"Truthfully, yes, but not here and not yet."

She was surprised by the seriousness in his voice. It was almost as if he might declare himself to her.

"When?" she asked.

Owen shook his head, glancing back at the police station. "I wish I knew."

Hope fled like a rabbit from a fox.

"Good day," she said, and let her driver help her into her carriage. Through her carriage window, she watched Owen standing there as she drove away, and she wondered if she would ever get to hear him express what she'd seen in his gaze.

ADELIA WENT DIRECTLY TO the family's company office at the Coal Exchange. After her father passed, Thomas had taken her to see the impressive building built of cast iron and stone. She passed through the entranceway, a Roman temple of Doric columns under a tall circular tower seeming to stretch to heaven.

Inside, the building's main hall was crowned by a lofty rotunda, a dome rising far overhead and lined with paintings of flowers and fossil plants found in the areas producing coal. The glass cupola far overhead let in natural light, and all of it rested airily on eight piers.

Under her booted feet were four thousand pieces of inlaid wood, as Thomas had pointed out, representing the face of a mariner's compass. She hardly paused to look at it. Instead, she made her way up a flight of stairs, past paintings of Percy Pit, Wallsend Colliery, Regent's Pit, and other celebrated collieries from which coal was shipped. It was exciting to think her family played a part in this tremendous undertaking of heating the British people's homes and providing their cooking fuel.

A middle-aged clerk admitted her to the modest Smythe Coal office on the second floor. She had met the man when Thomas had brought her previously. Before that, she'd never seen the grand structure or had reason ever to be in that part of the city, between London and Tower Bridges. Her father hadn't considered it a suitable place for women.

Mr. Beaumont was not in, although he was expected back momentarily, which suited her. It gave her a chance to

SYDNEY JANE BAILY

prepare how best to broach the subject of her brother's female friend and potential rivals, and anything he might know that could be helpful.

When she assured the clerk he could go about his business and that she needed nothing from him, he left the door open for her comfort and returned to copying documents and addressing envelopes to post. Roaming the office, eventually, Adelia came to stand by Mr. Beaumont's desk, noticing an envelope on the top of a stack which the clerk had recently finished. It was addressed to someone in Romford. The name tickled her memory.

Someone had recently mentioned the very same town to her. *Miss Moore!*

At that precise instant, Mr. Beaumont strolled through the open door, looking pleased with himself until he saw her. His expression changed to concern.

"Lady Adelia, I had no idea you were coming. How can I help you?"

A hundred thoughts flashed through her brain, chief among them was why Mr. Beaumont had an envelope addressed to the same town where Constance Moore's sister and mother resided. *Coincidence?*

An entirely different question came out of her mouth. "Were you following my brother and his female friend one night a few weeks back?"

He opened his mouth to say something but seemed to think better of it.

"How do you know?"

This admission sent a thrill shivering along her spine. *Should she be frightened of Mr. Beaumont?*

"Lord Burnley saw you," she replied calmly.

"I see." He looked over at the clerk. "Mr. Bunning, please take the mail you've prepared to the post office."

"Yes, sir." The clerk removed the apron that protected his clothing from all the ink he used, before donning his coat and hat. Efficiently, he gathered up a small pile of envelopes from his desk, and as he passed Mr. Beaumont's, scooped up his stack as well.

When the door closed behind him, Adelia realized the precariousness of her situation, alone with a man in a confined office. As she had been going only to the police station, she hadn't brought Penny.

Casually looking around the room in the silence, she began to stroll as if toward the window, overlooking Thames Street. She glanced outside as calmly as possible, then she began to pace toward the door.

Mr. Beaumont beat her to it. Her heart racing, she held her breath when he reached for the handle. *Was he going to lock her in with him?*

A second later, he yanked it open. "Mr. Bunning should have known better, my lady. I apologize."

Her heart still thumping wildly, she sank into the nearest chair.

"Are you all right, Lady Adelia?"

"Yes, Mr. Beaumont. Thank you. You were going to tell me why you followed my brother."

"Of course. Naturally, I didn't want to speak in front of the clerk. He's been with us a couple years now, but one never knows to whom he might tell tales."

"Naturally," she echoed.

"I mentioned to you once that I was concerned over your brother. Lord Burnley came to see me recently, questioning me about Lord Smythe. It seemed he wanted me to report something unsavory. Unsurprisingly, I told him my employer had never acted in an untoward fashion."

"Thank you," she said, wishing Owen would leave her family and their employees alone.

"You're welcome." He paused. "However, I lied."

"I don't understand," she said, alarm returning. "In what way?"

"Lord Burnley was correct. I was watching your brother that night, but only because I had seen him on other occasions with another woman, one whom I believed might mean trouble for our business."

She ignored the familiar way in which he again seemed to claim ownership of Smythe Coal. For she could think only of one woman to whom he might be referring.

"Who?" she asked, dreading the awful answer.

"Lady Sophia Burnley."

Her tone flat, Adelia said, "That's impossible."

"Nevertheless, it's the truth. I saw him with her, closeted together in his carriage one day in the Knightsbridge area. When I saw the earl's crest, I went over to say hello," he added, staring over her head as if recalling the day. "As I approached, the door opened, and he jumped out. After looking both ways along the pavement, he helped her down."

She frowned. "He didn't see you?"

"No, my lady. Not wishing to embarrass the young lady, I ducked into a doorway. I intended to say hello after they parted company. I didn't know who she was at the time, but I saw her another day here in this very building with Lord Burnley and realized, by their familial resemblance, who she was. Burnley Mining is upstairs, you know."

She nodded. She did, in fact, know. *Why had Thomas denied knowing Lady Sophia?* "Is that everything?"

"Another time, your brother came by and asked me to have Mr. Bunning copy out two of our contracts, as he had an investor to whom he wished to show our business. Peculiar a thing, as we currently don't need any outside capital."

Adelia hoped he didn't go into great detail, as she was already thinking about returning immediately to Newgate to question Thomas.

"Of course, I did as his lordship asked, and he went downstairs where a clarence drew up with the Burnley crest as plain as day. I saw him hand the documents to someone inside."

"How do you know that was Lady Sophia?" Her head was beginning to pound.

"As the carriage drew away, she leaned out and waved goodbye to him. After that, I decided to follow him on any number of nights. As manager, it was within my purview to ask him if he was planning on merging with Burnley Mining or selling the business entirely. I never saw him with Lady Sophia again, and next thing, you told me he was in Newgate."

Adelia stood at once. She couldn't breathe in the office another second. She had to leave. And quickly!

"Naturally, I didn't tell Lord Burnley when he asked me. He was probably in on the plan with his sister. All the same, if an officer of the law asks me . . . ," he trailed off.

She felt the blood drain from her face.

"Unless you ask me not to say anything, my lady. Which I am more than happy to do to protect not only our company but also your brother." Mr. Beaumont paused, then added, "Given what you're going through, I wonder if it wouldn't be for the best if you allowed me to take over Lord Smythe's duties, the ones you intended to do."

She stared at him, comprehending his demand for more power in exchange for keeping his own counsel regarding her brother and Lady Sophia. She had no words except those that would get her away from him.

"Good day, Mr. Beaumont."

He appeared surprised at her abrupt leave-taking, but she needed Penny to loosen her corset strings as soon as possible.

At the door, unable to wait for his response or to take her leave with any manner of civility, she dashed through it. She had her hand on the railing and her foot on the first tread of the staircase when she heard him call after her, "I hope I haven't upset—"

The sound of her own footsteps, clacking upon the wooden stairs as she hastily descended, drowned him out. *Thank goodness.*

Either her brother was lying to her or, as she knew in her heart, Mr. Beaumont had just recited a massive pile of rubbish. Pure drivel. Her brother was born and bred to discretion, as, no doubt, was the late Lady Sophia. And no member of the upper class would step out onto the street in Knightsbridge or anywhere else and allow a single woman to get out of his carriage unchaperoned, in broad daylight, directly after him. In a word, balderdash!

Moreover, no lady would stick her head out of a moving carriage to say goodbye to a man for fear of losing her coiffure along with her reputation. These were obviously the imaginings of a man who didn't know any better and who had fabricated a story with evil intent. Fiction from start to end. That much was clear.

Ever since the terrible misunderstanding that sent her brother to Newgate, Mr. Beaumont had been trying to wrest control of their company. She had temporarily thwarted him by taking back the power of signature and approval. Now, he was taking advantage of Thomas's incarceration and, with this perfidy, threatening to send her brother to the gallows.

One thing she knew, she would not dignify or validate his ridiculous stories by agreeing to anything he asked in exchange for his silence. At that instant, all she could think of was going home, removing her corset entirely, and considering what to do. She could trust no one. Not Owen, who wanted Thomas hanged for murder, not Mr. Beaumont, who plainly was engineering the truth *after* the fact. And it seemed not Constance Moore, either, who professed to love Thomas but might be hiding the biggest lie of all.

Once home and comfortably in her dressing gown, she penned Miss Moore a note, asking her to come to Hyde Park Street on Sunday. One way or the other, Adelia was going to get to the bottom of all this perfidy. But she certainly wasn't going to risk her life again by heading back to the East End.

CHAPTER TWENTY-EIGHT

"A Miss Moore is in the parlor, my lady. She wishes to see you. Shall I tell her you are—?"

Hurrying past Mr. Lockley, who had entered her small upstairs study, she raced down the staircase. *Miss Moore was in her home in Mayfair! At last!*

Rushing through the open doorway, Adelia found the young woman standing in the center of the room, eyes wide, mouth open, gaping at everything around her.

Had Miss Moore ever been in a London townhouse? Adelia doubted it.

"Are you all right?" she asked into the silence, studying her visitor who was clad in a plain but clean cotton dress.

Miss Moore, usually so loquacious, was tongue-tied. In fact, her pale, scared face and demeanor, as if she wished to shrink, were all woefully familiar. The young woman could be Adelia, herself, a month ago in any ballroom in London.

"Would you care for tea?" she offered, despite being eager to start questioning her.

If anything, Miss Moore's eyes grew wider. Perhaps the notion of taking tea in a nobleman's parlor frightened her. *Well, there was a first time for everything.*

"Please, have a seat," Adelia offered, going to the bell pull to request tea.

When she turned back, Miss Moore hadn't moved a muscle. Sighing, Adelia approached her, took hold of her arm, and led her to the sofa.

"It's all right, really. Tea is tea, don't you think? No matter if it is served in a mug or a porcelain cup."

Adelia had to shove her slightly to get her to sit before taking a seat in her favorite wing chair.

"How did you arrive? By hackney?"

Miss Moore nodded and said nothing further. After Meg brought in the tea tray and served, Adelia decided she'd given Thomas's so-called friend plenty of time to collect herself.

"Come now, Miss Moore, you cannot be so overtaken by a luxuriously appointed room that your intellect dwindles to the that of a hedgehog."

That got her attention. The young woman took a deep breath.

"I am sorry. You are right, my lady. But only think, Thomas wants me to live here and be mistress of such. Me!"

"Yes, only think. You!" Adelia tried to keep her tone pleasant, but she was simmering with anger. "And what will your family in Romford think about that?"

"Oh, they will be ever so pleased. Naturally, my mum would be equally happy for me with any man I found who truly loved me."

Adelia nodded. "And whom *you* love in return. With all your heart."

"Of course," Miss Moore agreed.

"And what about Mr. Beaumont? Will he be pleased?" Adelia asked, her tone sharp.

Miss Moore's enthusiasm faltered, and her expression became guarded.

For goodness sake, Adelia thought. *Do not start lying to my face.* It would be too much to bear.

The young woman's cheeks turned pink, and she said, "Mr. Beaumont can go to the devil!"

Adelia knew she heard her right, but why? "I beg your pardon."

"I know you all think the world of him, and maybe he has done well for Smythe Coal, as Thomas has said, but I don't trust him."

"And you know him, do you not? Is he related to you?"

Miss Moore's eyes widened again. "How did you know?

"I know only that he has ties to Romford, as do you," Adelia told her. "Why don't you tell me the rest?" *Before I toss you out on your money-grubbing rump!*

Miss Moore nodded. "His cousin married my sister. She's very happy, and my brother-in-law is a nice man. When I came to London to work, Mr. Beaumont paid me a visit."

Adelia poured the tea, so she had something to do. In her heart, she was dreading hearing the rest. However, after handing Miss Moore a saucer and teacup, she said, "Go on."

"Mr. Beaumont said he was only looking out for me as family does. Then he told me to go to a particular shop on Bond Street for good gloves and a bonnet. He said I would get farther in the world with both." She touched her hand to her head, where a plain but stylish bonnet was perched.

"Curious of him," Adelia said, noticing Miss Moore had neglected to remove her gloves as was customary.

"He . . . he gave me money," she confessed.

Adelia had feared as much. "To do what?" Her voice was brittle, and her throat was dry as autumn leaves.

"To buy the bonnet and gloves," Miss Moore began, staring into the cup of tea. Finally, her gaze rose to Adelia's. "And to stay in the shop until I saw your brother and spoke with him."

All the air left the room. *Poor Thomas. Duped and swindled by this woman and her brother-in-law's cousin!*

"But you told me that my brother talked to you first. Did you lie?"

Miss Moore shook her head. "When he came into the shop, I made sure to keep standing nearby. In fact, he was so handsome, I couldn't speak. I followed him around rather foolishly until he showed me the ugly bonnet."

"Giving you the perfect opening," she said, her tone thin and disappointed.

The young woman tilted her head. "Oh, Lady Adelia, do not misunderstand. I love Thomas with all my heart. I ought to thank Mr. Beaumont, for I never would have gone to Bond Street and never would have met your brother, not in a hundred years. But once we started to talk to one another, it was as if I'd always known him." She smiled. "Or as if he were meant for me, and I, for him. It is difficult to explain."

Adelia didn't need her to. She knew the feeling all too well.

"Did you ever ask Mr. Beaumont why he wanted you two to meet?"

Miss Moore set down the cup and saucer. "Yes, of course. Before ever I went to the shop, I asked him why he was doing this. He said Thomas—he called him the earl—hadn't found the woman of his dreams amongst the *ton.*"

Adelia blinked at her. Mr. Beaumont had a lot of nerve! "And he thought you—?"

"You don't have to say it," Miss Moore interrupted. "I know how strange it is. Why would anyone think the likes of me, a bookshop girl, could be anyone's dream? Let alone an earl's!"

Adelia felt ashamed. *Why not Constance Moore as well as anyone?*

The young woman continued, "Mr. Beaumont said, after what he knew of London's high society, that an educated middle-class girl might be just the ticket. Even so, he cautioned me to keep out of Mayfair when I was with Thomas and to keep him with me in the East End, which your brother was only too happy to do. For my sake."

Strange and stranger. Adelia could hardly believe Mr. Beaumont truly cared about Thomas's happiness, but he had found a woman with whom her brother had fallen in love. Perhaps she'd misjudged him. He certainly had nothing to gain by her brother's relationship with Miss Moore. And he might actually have had the best interests of the company in mind when he tried to take control. After all, his livelihood depended on Smythe Coal's continuing success.

She sighed. "Why did you say you didn't trust Mr. Beaumont?"

"Oh, Lady Adelia. I know he is my sister's kin by marriage, but I think it was unnatural for him to pay me to meet your brother. If he truly believed I was good for Thomas, why wouldn't he simply introduce us properly? And why would he swear me to secrecy over the whole thing?"

"I suppose my brother's pride might be hurt if he knew you had displayed an interest in him in return for bonnet and glove money," Adelia guessed. *Had Mr. Beaumont been protecting Thomas's feelings?* "I don't know what to think, frankly," she added.

"I never told your brother the truth. He might be angry, and I couldn't bear the possibility of losing him."

They both might lose him in any case, but Adelia deemed it unnecessary to mention that fact.

In her heart, she believed Miss Moore. "You may call me Adelia, if you wish."

"Thank you. My first name is Constance, if you recall."

Adelia nodded. She liked the woman, in spite of having been fully prepared to charge her with the worst treachery, dismiss her into the street, and tell Thomas.

"I must say, Adelia, tea may be tea, as you say, but it does taste better in a porcelain cup. And that's no lie."

Adelia laughed despite herself. "Please, try one of the biscuits, but I suggest you remove your gloves first. By the by, do you read the books you sell?"

"I love to read," Constance declared, and a little bud of affection bloomed in Adelia's heart. "What's more, I read over the type at the printer I work for. It's part of my job to ensure it's been set correctly."

"Thus, you must have a fine attention to detail." *Better and better.* If matters had gone as her brother and Constance had planned, running a household would not have been a problem for the woman, once she'd been taught a few of the social graces.

Now, they might never get the chance. Indeed, she would count them lucky if they ever reached the point where Constance fitting in as the Countess of Dunford was their main concern.

OWEN COULD NOT STAY away. He had no reason to show up on Adelia's doorstep, nor to ring the bell. But he did both.

With the usual ritual, Mr. Lockley ushered him in, took his coat and hat, and showed him into the drawing room. It was nearly more familiar than his own. It was quite possible she would refuse to see him. In fact, she should do exactly that. Nonetheless, he knew she wouldn't.

When she entered the room, she took his breath away as usual.

"How do you become more enchanting every time I see you?"

Her creamy skin turned the color of roses, even down her slender neck. *How much would her skin blush with pleasure after passionate lovemaking?* He longed to find out.

"Apparently, constant worry suits me," she said wearily. Another woman's tone would have been tart with censure and anger, but he rarely felt she directed either at him.

"I am truly sorry for the worry this situation has caused you," he said, meaning it with all his heart. "If I could relieve you of it, I would."

"Tell the police how ridiculous your accusation is," she said softly. "Or tell me why my brother did what you say he did. Give me one reason that makes any sense."

Staring at her, unable to answer, he shook his head. Finally, he said the only thing he could imagine had caused the dreadful act. "A crime of passion."

Adelia let out an exasperated sigh and walked past him. "Meaning what?"

"Meaning I could tear your brother limb-for-limb over what he did, so huge was my love for Sophia, so deep is my anger." He clenched his hands as she blinked at him with her gorgeous green eyes. But he'd had to say it as he had never lied to her.

"If, as I suspect, your brother and my sister were lovers—"

She exhaled a puff of disbelief, but he continued.

"I can only imagine that somehow, your brother thought he would lose her or that she had played him false. In the heat of the moment, he killed her."

This time, Adelia flinched at his words. "Is that how men think?"

"Not only men. Women have done terrible deeds for love or jealousy or revenge."

"Would you ever hurt me?" she wondered, blinking up at him guilelessly.

Her question caught him off guard, but his answer came swiftly, "Absolutely not."

She took a step toward him, the opposite of what a sane person might do when they were discussing such a subject.

"If the situation were as you've described, if we were . . . lovers and I played you false, then what? In your passion—and I've seen you have a great deal of it—would you unleash it upon me in rage?"

He swallowed and searched his heart. He closed the gap between them and took her in his arms.

"I could never hurt you. If you played me false, I might despise you and possibly go after the one who'd stolen you from me. Yes, I could see harming that man, but you? No. I don't have it in me, I swear it."

"Neither does my brother," she insisted.

He closed his eyes. An instant later, he leaned forward to what he now knew was her deaf ear, and he whispered against it, "I love you."

She drew back. "I cannot hear you."

He nodded. "Your father was a beast to harm you, to lay hands upon a girl, his own flesh and blood. It sickens me."

"It sickened Thomas, too, and he protected me as soon as he was old enough. After this—" she touched her ear, "my brother made sure my father never got near me again."

"And what drove your father's anger?" Owen embraced her more tightly, wishing he could erase the damage the old earl had done.

She craned her head back and looked at him.

"He had absolutely no patience for my stuttering and shyness. He considered both to be moral failings, something I could control with a stronger will. *His*, not mine."

"I am very sorry."

She shrugged lightly in his arms, and he couldn't resist kissing her for another second. Fleetingly, he hoped she didn't mind as he lowered his mouth to hers.

Evidently, she didn't, for she slid her hands up his chest and clasped them behind his neck. Feeling her fingers at his nape, tugging his hair, was astonishingly arousing.

Owen opened his mouth and slipped his tongue between her welcoming lips. He couldn't restore her hearing, but he could let her know in no uncertain terms how very much she meant to him.

A tap at the door frustrated him from going any further, and they broke apart. She smoothed the front of her gown and took a few steps away from him before saying, "Enter."

Naturally, it was Mr. Lockley, the infernal man, always hovering. On the other hand, Owen appreciated the butler's dedication.

"A missive for you, my lady." He held out a silver tray with a single sealed sheet upon it.

It had no imprinted seal, just an ungainly blob of green wax on the folded edge. She picked it up, glanced at it, and looked questioningly at her butler.

"Somewhat late in the day for the post, is it not?"

Mr. Lockley nodded. "A very young courier delivered it, my lady."

She nodded her thanks, took the sharp silver opener from the tray, and slit open the letter. Owen watched her face as she quickly scanned the contents. Except for a lifting of her right eyebrow, she gave no indication of its import.

"Is there anything I can assist you with?" Owen asked her. He sensed it was to do with her brother by her carefully neutral expression.

"No, thank you." Adelia shook her head as she folded the paper and tucked it into the pocket of her skirt's side seam.

"Will you tell me what's in that missive?" he asked outright.

"No," she said, but she smiled.

He laughed. "All right. As long as it isn't a petition from another suitor, trying to woo you away from me."

"I promise you, it is not."

"That's good, because I wish to invite you to go to dinner with me tonight at Lord and Lady Westings'. Lady Jane gave me a tongue-lashing for not bringing you last time."

Adelia colored. "She mentioned me?"

"Yes. She likes you." He stepped closer again. "*I* like you. I know it is awfully short notice, but going there tonight entirely slipped my mind until now. It's not a formal matter with them. More as though dining with family."

She sighed. "You know the day after tomorrow is the start of the trial. We meet at the Old Bailey in the main chamber first thing in the morning."

He felt a little sick. The trial could move extremely quickly. It wasn't as if there were witnesses or much of a defense for the barrister to present."

"I will take you to the courthouse if you wish that morning," he offered.

She shook her head. "I do not think that is a good idea. I will be with my solicitor, and he and I shall meet the barrister there."

"I don't want you to get your hopes up."

Instead of looking worried as he'd expected, Adelia tilted her head and offered him a hopeful smile. "I think everything will work out satisfactorily."

Dear God! How had she convinced herself of that? He might not be accompanying her, but he was glad he would be on hand to comfort her in any way he could when it was over. She didn't seem to realize the likely outcome.

"Very well. You didn't answer me about dinner tonight? I can wait for you to change, and we can go there a little early, shocking our hostess, or I can return to collect you in two hours."

"Yes," she agreed. "Come back in two hours."

Happiness flooded him, for he'd feared she would turn him down. Reaching out, he took her chin in his hand and locked his gaze with hers.

"I hope Penny will sit with the driver," he said, letting her imagination join his in picturing another sensual encounter in the confines of his carriage.

She shook her head, but her eyes let him know she expected another kiss right then. Owen quickly claimed her mouth, not one to disappoint a lady.

As soon as he left, Adelia pulled out the letter again to make certain she had read it correctly. She couldn't believe it. Her prayers had been answered. If Mr. Brassel hadn't

314

specifically told her to tell no one, she would have yelled with glee in front of Owen and told him the truth.

She didn't wait for the bell pull but hurried into the foyer to chase down Mr. Lockley, who had scarcely had a chance to see Owen out the door.

"Please have Henry ready my carriage at once."

"Yes, my lady," Mr. Lockley said and disappeared.

There would be no need for the insanity defense. Her brother was about to be entirely cleared. After she met with Mr. Brassel, she would request his consent to tell Owen and the Westings at dinner that night. Adelia didn't see how she could go to dinner elsewise. It would be impossible to sit down at their table without the good news bubbling out of her.

Mr. Lockley appeared. "Your carriage is ready and out front, my lady. Where shall I instruct Henry to take you?"

CHAPTER TWENTY-NINE

I n less than half an hour, her driver pulled up in front of Gray's Inn. It was uncommonly short notice of the solicitor, expecting her to be free, but she supposed most men assumed women did little but sit home all day, perhaps doing needlepoint. Or, in her case, writing novels. The truth was, for her class, he was mainly correct.

Because of her destination, once again, she had not brought Penny along. She found something almost reverent about the Inns of Court and Mr. Brassel. In fact, the work of those at Gray's Inn seemed as benign as the work of the Church, especially now that her solicitor had discovered an alibi for her brother.

As she stepped out of her carriage, she was hailed by Mr. Beaumont, of all people.

He approached her. "So glad you could make it, Lady Adelia," he said, bowing low.

"I don't understand. How did you know I was meeting with the solicitor?"

"I am the one who has determined an alibi for the earl," Mr. Beaumont crowed. "It came clear to me when I considered the date. And recalling you'd told me the solicitor's name, I came directly to speak with him. Mr. Brassel promised he would invite you over immediately to ease your mind at once."

"He did just that," she agreed. "Will you tell me what you told Mr. Brassel?"

"Oh, better than that, dear lady. I will *show* you. Come, this way."

He had her arm before she knew it. Half a block farther along the road, a hackney stood waiting.

"But Mr. Brassel," she said. "I believe I am to—"

"Yes, yes. He knows all about it. He will meet us there. In fact, he's already on his way. Most exciting," he added. With that, Mr. Beaumont yanked open the door and helped her inside.

Adelia knew as soon as the door of the hired hackney closed that she'd made a mistake. She sensed it by the way Mr. Beaumont drew down the cheap black shades on either side and sprawled slovenly against the squabs.

"Here we are at last," he said.

"Yes," she agreed. "I should have asked you exactly where we are going."

"Why, to the East End, of course, the scene of the murder."

Alarm skittered through her, and she banged on the roof to alert the driver to stop.

"What are you doing?" he asked, folding his hands on his lap as the carriage continued without slowing.

She banged again. "I have realized I should have taken my own carriage, so I can get home easily afterward. I have a dinner engagement. We should stop immediately and let me take my own ride."

"Oh, no," he said, his face a picture of concern, "that wouldn't be safe at all. You didn't bring anyone, it seems, no maid or other chaperone, and I couldn't let an elegant lady such as yourself go alone to the East End."

"No," she said softly. "I didn't bring anyone."

Recalling the note, she asked, "You say Mr. Brassel is meeting us there?"

"Indubitably," he said, and she felt a little better. Besides, it was not that late, although the sun was setting quickly.

"Very well." Adelia tried to quell her burgeoning anxiety at being alone with him, despite how he had made no untoward advance. Instead, he remained leaning back in a relaxed manner, observing her. His expression was vaguely and unsettlingly smug.

"Will you tell me what you discovered while we travel?" she asked, hoping to stop him from staring.

He made a face. "I would prefer to show you. All the same, you can stop worrying over your brother."

Adelia nodded. And since she could think of nothing else to say to Mr. Beaumont, she said no more.

After about five minutes, Mr. Beaumont unexpectedly spoke, "You would never consider me as a suitor, would you?"

She managed to stop herself from visibly shuddering.

"That is an in . . . inappropriate topic," she told him, "given our close . . . close confines and lack of chaperone." *Drats!* Her nervousness was on full display.

He shrugged. "After all I'm doing for our company, and knowing how I can grow it and make it prosper, especially when my hands are not shackled by your brother's control, what is your response?"

Hating feeling trapped and pressured, not to mention fearful of reprisal, Adelia suddenly realized she felt precisely the way she had in the company of her late father. She didn't think placating Mr. Beaumont would work, nor telling him how he made her skin crawl. Thus, she settled upon the truth.

"I have an understanding with someone else. My heart is already engaged."

"Your heart, eh?" Mr. Beaumont said. "But not a formal engagement as yet? Lord Burnley is dragging his feet. No doubt, he thinks it best not to ask until *after* he sees your brother hang."

She caught her breath at his crude words and the terrible image they evoked. And he knew far too much about her relationship with Owen for her liking.

Mr. Beaumont cocked his head. "Your viscount paid me a visit, practically begging me to come up with more nefarious deeds to pin upon the earl. I cannot see how you could give your heart to a man who wants to destroy your brother." His tone was gruff with disapproval.

"I suppose it is a good thing then that you have discovered a way to save him." She wondered if Mr. Beaumont was truly angry. Or mayhap, he was only hurt at being rebuffed. Recalling his previous disclosure about Thomas and Lady Sophia, she decided to let him know he wasn't dealing with a fool

"I believe you told me you saw my brother with Lady Sophia Burnley because you hoped to frighten me into letting you take control while Lord Smythe was incarcerated."

He said nothing to that, regarding her with a blank stare.

"I am grateful you didn't tell the same tale to the police or to Lord Burnley."

He nodded. "I hoped only to prove my loyalty," he said. "I suppose I went about it all wrong."

An understatement, Adelia thought, wishing she'd told someone about the engineer's lies. However, he said he'd told Mr. Brassel about an alibi.

"Now that the earl will be released," she told him, "everything will go back to normal. He'll be grateful for your assistance."

"And what about you?" Mr. Beaumont asked, leaning forward. "Will you be grateful, too?"

"Naturally," she said, feeling uneasy.

Luckily, prior to any further discussion, the hackney came to a halt. Cab drivers rarely jumped down to open the door, and thus Mr. Beaumont was quick to push it ajar and climb out, offering her his hand.

She was loath to take it but did so, thinking to snatch it back as soon as her ankle boots touched the paving stones. Unfortunately, before she could do anything except regain her balance, the engineer had tucked her arm through his, close to his body, and led her inside a tavern. She'd only had time to see its sign, The Pig and Whistle, hanging crookedly from a piece of iron.

When Owen had taken her from pub to pub looking for Thomas, he had not taken her into this one. As Adelia's eyes became accustomed to the gloomy interior, Mr. Beaumont tugged her toward the staircase on their immediate right. She dug in her heels as best she could, aided by the stickiness of the ale-spilled floorboards.

He released her, turning in surprise. No one else in the place even lifted their head from their mugs of beer and large glasses of gin.

"What is the meaning of this?" she demanded. "And where is Mr. Brassel?"

"He is upstairs, hopefully with the detective by now. Detective Sergeant Garrard, I think was his name. Is that right?" He turned from her and headed up the stairs.

She supposed if he knew Mr. Brassel and the detective, he could not be lying. Glancing again at the establishment's sad guests, thinking one of them might become animated at any point and demand her reticule at knifepoint, she followed him.

At the top of the stairs was a short hall with three doors. The one closest to her was partly open. With a prickling of alarm, Adelia had the appalling notion Lady Sophia had also been there and met her horrendous fate.

Losing her nerve, she was about to dash back down the stairs when the door at the end opened, and what could only be a harlot popped out, wearing a sheer robe, thick red lip coloring, and far too much rouge.

Adelia froze, staring at her, plainly able to see the woman's breasts and her womanly parts through the ridiculous gossamer gown. The harlot was giggling, perhaps drunk. An instant later, a man stepped out after her, still sliding his arms into his coat.

He took a few steps along the hallway and spied Adelia. A grin spread over his pocked face, showing the few teeth he had.

"Well, now. What 'ave we 'ere? A nice bit o' stuff, to be sure."

Adelia could not speak or move, trying to flatten herself against the wall between the doors so he could pass.

"I thought I'd had me fill," he said, looking back at the nearly bare woman who nodded encouragingly, then back at Adelia. "But my stick is up again at the looks of you, luv."

At that moment, Mr. Beaumont reappeared. "There you are. Come in," he urged.

Faced with the leering man and his doxy, or the relatively civilized Mr. Beaumont, she hurried past Mr. Beaumont and into the small room. The window shades were down, but one lamp was lit, showing her its furnishings, consisting of a bed and nothing else.

"Where are Mr. Brassel and Detective Sergeant Garrard?" she asked, turning to face the man who'd brought her there.

Mr. Beaumont had shut the door and was leaning against it. Slowly, he shook his head.

"I'm sorry to tell you, my lady, I have no idea."

His simple words, his calm manner, his placid expression chilled her. Obviously, those men had never been at The Pig and Whistle and were not coming.

She had made her second grievous mistake.

SOON AFTER OWEN ARRIVED at the Carlton Club, Whitely showed up. They took seats in front of the roaring fire and ordered brandy.

"The trial starts in two days," Owen told his friend.

Whitely nodded. "I'll go with you. Will you be at Westing's tonight?"

"Yes." His mood brightened. "And I am bringing Lady Adelia."

"Truly?" George asked. "How did you pull off that miracle? Only you, old chap, could send a woman's brother to Newgate and still successfully woo the lady."

In a heartbeat, Owen's disposition changed again. "If my pursuit of her is successful, this is going to hang like a pall over our marriage for the rest of our lives."

"Marriage?" George repeated, looking shocked until he shook his head ruefully. "Something is going to hang, and not merely a pall. Nevertheless, think on it. If the lady marries you *despite* what's starting in two days—and worse at the trial's end—then pall be damned! She must really love you."

"Pall be damned," Owen repeated softly.

"I guess that means we won't be going to the Westings' together," George guessed, offering a wry smile, which Owen didn't return, unable to regain his good humor.

In any case, he agreed, "That would be one too many in my carriage." He ought to be over the moon at the notion of being alone with Adelia again, but knowing the only possible sentence for the earl—how they would both have lost their only sibling—he remained subdued.

Whitely sipped his brandy. "Promise me you two won't argue about the trial over the Westings' good roast, although if you can get Lady Adelia talking freely at dinner like a normal chatterbox, I'll toast you by the time we have cigars."

"She seems far less reticent of late." *Except when she wants to be.* Owen recalled her secretive behavior upon getting the letter earlier.

Suddenly, Lockley's words came back to him clearly. *"A very young courier delivered it."* And the hair on Owen's head seemed to stand at attention.

"The devil!" he exclaimed, rising to his feet so violently, he jarred the table, spilling both their drinks.

Whitely jumped up. "What on earth, Burnley?"

"I was at Adelia's home not that long ago when she received a missive of some sort from a boy, I believe. She suddenly wanted me to leave and return later to collect her for dinner."

"What did it say?" George asked, his tone equally serious. Clearly, he, too, remembered the sandy-haired child whom the shopgirl mentioned.

"She wouldn't tell me, but now I fear it summoned her, just as Sophia's note."

"That's only conjecture, old chum, and rather a large leap from here to there, but—"

"But I'd better follow up at once," Owen interjected.

"Agreed," George said. "Shall I go with you?"

"I'm going directly to that godawful hole where we found Sophia. Would you go to Lady Adelia's—you know where, don't you, 78 Hyde Park Street?—and make sure I'm quite insane? I pray she's there, getting ready for tonight."

"Of course. I'll go there directly and see you later. Everything will be fine."

Owen didn't hear him over the thumping of his heart as he ran from the club, hailing his driver as soon as he was out the door.

CHAPTER THIRTY

Mr. Beaumont handed Adelia a handkerchief.

She stared at the unexpected article in her suddenly trembling hand. It was one of Owen's handkerchiefs—with the gorgeously embroidered, silver-threaded *B* upon a starched white cloth.

For a moment, terror that Victor Beaumont had harmed Owen and taken the kerchief from him by physical force made her heart want to leap from her chest.

"Where did you get this?" she asked, her voice barely above a whisper.

"*Ah*, that was a damn sight more difficult than getting one of your brother's, and that's no lie. But practically every servant can be bribed. If you hang around the servants' entrance long enough, eventually you shall encounter one of the lowest of the low, the laundress!"

"You are mad!" she declared. *Why else would he be stealing handkerchiefs and handing them to women he intended to . . . ? Dear God!*

"On the contrary, I am clever," he gloated. "Far too clever, in fact, to manage someone else's business, which I built with my own two hands." He raised them in front of his face and looked at them. After a few seconds, he peered at her over the top of his fingers.

"If I'd had the seed money to start my own mining company, I would be far ahead of the Smythes *and* the Burnleys. Instead, I've been making your family rich since the day your father hired me."

"You were handsomely paid," Adelia protested, having had a discussion with her brother on that very fact. Moreover, Smythe Coal had been running successfully for a generation before Victor Beaumont ever darkened its doorstep.

He shrugged. "So says you, with your Mayfair townhouse and your maid and your carriage. Let's not forget your high society gatherings that I cannot attend for lack of title or lineage."

"You want to go to a ball?" she asked.

Part of her was actually curious, with the fascination of a storyteller, to understand what was driving this man besides greed. Most of her simply hoped to keep him talking calmly until she could somehow lure him away from the door. Help might not be directly on the other side, nor downstairs in the form of those drunkards and ne'er-do-wells, but out in the street, there might be a hackney passing by. Or she could flee to Constance's home, which she knew to be close.

Her captor snickered at her question. "No, my lady. I have no burning desire to mingle with the *ton*, except for how I wish to lord it over them in every sense of the word. I want a grand home of my own, well-tailored clothes, a fine horse, and, I suppose, a loving wife. And not a middle-class wife, at that. I want a fine lady."

She noted how he equated the same fineness to a horse as to his imaginary wife.

"And I will have all that," he insisted, "when I am the sole owner of Smythe Coal. I will grow it into the premiere mining company in Britain. See if I don't."

Then, Mr. Beaumont grimaced wryly. "I suppose you won't see it, will you? You'll be quite dead."

She couldn't help a frightened gasp escaping her as she scrunched Owen's handkerchief between her hands like a talisman to ward off this evil man. Without a doubt, his overarching ambition had caused him to murder Sophia. Now her life was about to be snuffed out, too.

"You should have let me take over for your weak-willed brother. But you told Mr. Arnold I was no longer in charge." Mr. Beaumont shook his head and took a step toward her. "You, as namby-pamby as quince jelly, want to run this company in your brother's stead?"

She took a step back, wondering if she could manage to get a window open. If there had been even a single chair in the room, she would have used it as a weapon.

"Everything you told me about seeing my brother with Lady Sophia was a lie, was it not?" She tried to remain calm, refusing to believe her life would end there.

"Of course," he confessed. "I was only watching your brother to make sure he was seen in the East End. Your Lord Burnley stumbling into the pub one night and being a witness was impossibly fortunate. If he hadn't, I would have found someone else to say your brother frequented the Whitechapel taverns, maybe Constance."

"Will you tell me why you killed Lady Sophia?" If she escaped this plight, she would at least have an answer for Owen.

He cocked his head, frowning at her question, and shrugged.

"I guess there is no harm in telling you. In Paris, she overheard me speaking with a cousin about my plans to run Smythe Coal. I didn't realize they had a young woman staying with them. She probably didn't understand what she heard, but I couldn't take that chance. I made it my business to walk in on her with my other cousin, while they engaged in an indiscretion. As she was all too aware if it were disclosed, she would fall from the heights of London's social circles."

In the midst of all this deviancy, he smiled, keeping a watchful gaze on her frightened face. "Sadly, you shall be the second in a tragic case of two families battling over mining rights. You will be the *quid pro quo* of the violent Lord Burnley, exacting vengeance for his sister's brutal murder. First, he wooed you to get close to you, and naturally, he murdered you out of revenge."

Adelia shuddered. It might actually be plausible except for the ridiculous use of the handkerchief. No one would believe Owen wanted to get caught for murder. Nor was it believable that both she and Sophia had each managed to grab their respective killer's handkerchief at the last moment.

In trying so hard to leave a clue portraying Owen as the killer, Victor Beaumont was going to make it painfully clear the viscount wasn't a murderer. She supposed she ought to be grateful for that. Moreover, another similar strangling would probably free her brother from Newgate.

It seemed to her Victor Beaumont, in his deranged and prideful brain, actually wanted credit for both killings, precisely as he wanted credit for the success of her family's mining company. He was far too vainglorious to kill her quietly and dump her body in the Thames, as would be the easiest method. If Owen were truly out for bloodthirsty revenge, that's what he would do.

She thought pride might end up being Mr. Beaumont's downfall, but she wouldn't be there to see it. Unless . . .

"I suppose we could m . . . marry so you could take over the company easily without having to get the courts involved. The Chancery court takes years, I understand, to sort out such matters."

He began to laugh. He laughed so hard tears streamed down his face. The longer he did it, the more frightened Adelia became. Finally, Mr. Beaumont collected himself and sighed.

"Coincidentally, my lady, that was the original plan. It would have been so much easier, as you say, and you and I would have made a splendid couple. I still would have had to get your brother out of the way by setting him up as a murderer. I couldn't murder him directly, of course, as all eyes would have gone to me once I stepped in to run our company. This way, the law took care of him for me."

Adelia should have realized sooner, but her father had trusted the man as had Thomas. She could only hope he would relent if she kept trying.

"Instead of more blood being on your hands, Mr. Beaumont, wouldn't you rather come to an agreement with me?"

"It's too late for that," he said curtly. "Let's get this over with, shall we?"

Her mouth was so dry with fear, she couldn't swallow or speak another word. He suddenly stooped low, and she watched with horror as he pulled out a rope from under the bed.

Panting with fear, she knew she couldn't get past him in the tiny room. She could do nothing except shake her head in protest as he draped the rope around her neck, gently as if placing a shawl.

"You may get on your knees and pray, if you want, and confess any sins."

Tilting her head, she couldn't imagine why he was suggesting this.

He shrugged. "I am Catholic," he admitted. "I assume you are Protestant, but I will afford you this mercy to your soul."

Surely, *his* was the soul condemned to eternal damnation, not hers.

"Hurry," he urged, "and keep your voice down while you do it."

For the first time in her life, Adelia looked forward to breaking her silence. If it was to be her final act, then she would leave this world making as much noise as she possibly could. Licking her lips, she put forth the loudest scream she could imagine—*bloodcurdling*, if she had to describe it. She made even her good ear ring with its intensity.

Beaumont, coming out of his shock, stepped forward and backhanded her, knocking her to the floor.

OWEN ALMOST DIDN'T RECOGNIZE the voice, never having heard Adelia being loud before. It didn't matter, of course. He would have gone to the aid of any woman—or man, for that matter—who screamed with such terror.

He had raced up the tavern stairs a moment earlier, heart pounding as he headed toward the room in which Sophia had perished. On the landing, he'd heard the terrible scream.

Trying the door, it didn't budge. Heaving his shoulder against it, once, twice. After taking a few steps back to increase the power of his charge, on the third attempt, he splintered it.

Bursting into the room, Owen took in the sight that chilled his blood. Adelia was on the floor, blood dripping from her mouth, and Victor Beaumont was on top of her, strangling her with a rope.

The world tilted. Roaring with rage, he rushed Beaumont, knocking him off her and sending him sprawling a few feet away. The brute began to scrabble on all fours to escape, but Owen easily put a booted foot to his ribs and kicked him over onto his back. As Beaumont lay dazed, he pounced. Holding the stocky scoundrel by the front of his jacket, Owen punched him in the face. Again and again.

Indeed, with a red haze of anger filling his eyes, and the satisfying sensation of his fist bludgeoning Beaumont's skull, Owen couldn't imagine stopping.

Then he heard Adelia whisper his name.

Turning to her, he saw her eyes were open, watching him, her lips slightly parted, drawing breath. All notion of beating Beaumont to death dissipated instantly.

As the insane animal of rage released him, Owen dropped the unconscious man in favor of comforting the woman he loved. In a flash, he scooped Adelia off the floor as if she were no heavier than a feather and sat down on the sagging bed with her in his arms.

With her resting against his chest, he used his free hand to pull the cursed rope loose from her neck and hurl it to the floor. At the same time, Whitely rushed in with Detective Sergeant Garrard, stopping abruptly at the sight. In a flurry of commands, two constables lifted the unconscious Beaumont off the floor and, with each supporting him under one of his arms, took him from the room, his head hanging low and his feet dragging behind him.

Adelia gazed at Owen, her eyes full of life, and the tightness in his chest eased.

"You're bleeding." He tried to reach into his pocket for a handkerchief, but she was resting atop his coat.

She held up her hand and opened it. There, crumpled on her palm, was one of his own kerchiefs. His gaze flew to hers, now brimming with tears. His own eyes filled as a hundred thoughts and memories crashed through him.

Too late for Sophia, but he'd saved Adelia from the same fate. He hoped his sister was looking down upon him and giving them her blessing. Taking the square of linen, he dabbed at the corner of Adelia's mouth.

"It's just a cut," she said softly, but her other hand went to her throat. "My neck aches a bit."

The coarse rope had caused a red abrasion on her pale skin, and he brushed it with the back of his knuckle, recalling doing the same with his sister's lifeless body.

"And my throat hurts, too, a little," Adelia added.

"That may have been from screaming," he said, tears streaming unchecked down his cheeks. "Your wonderfully loud yell. Your voice saved you, you know."

"You saved me," she whispered, reaching up and touching one of his tears.

Owen could hardly see her through his watering eyes. He went to wipe them with the back of his hand, saw Beaumont's blood, and stripped off his glove, which he sent hurling after the rope. Rubbing his cheek with the back of his hand, he discovered he was trembling like he had the palsy. He'd come so close to losing her—it would have sent him over the edge into insanity.

He couldn't help himself from leaning down and kissing her.

"Ouch," she muttered, but she snaked her hands around his neck and held him close.

He tasted her blood and her tears—and probably his own tears, too. As he raised his head, her eyelids fluttered open, and he fell headlong into the emerald depths where he wanted to stay for the rest of his life.

"Will you marry me?" he asked.

He heard Whitely, entirely forgotten, cough loudly, as if to warn him from anything rash. He ignored him.

Owen watched her eyes widen, soften, and fill with tears again.

"Yes." And that was all she said.

Neither of them gushed with a flowery speech. They didn't need to.

Then he heard a throat being cleared behind him. This time, it was Detective Sergeant Garrard still standing by the shattered door.

"Yes, Detective? I assume you are trying to get my attention," Owen said, winking at Adelia.

"Lord Burnley, will you take the young lady home or to the hospital?"

"Definitely home," Owen said. "My physician will come there." He felt Adelia restlessly moving in his arms and helped her to sit up.

"I should go home," she started to protest.

He set her on her feet and wrapped his arm around her shoulders. "I cannot let you go, not tonight."

After a long pause, she nodded.

"I will need to ask you some questions, my lady," Garrard said.

"Tomorrow," Owen insisted. "I shall bring her to your office. Can you walk?" he asked her.

"Yes, of course," she insisted, raising her chin. His heart swelled with admiration for her bravery.

"Very well," the detective agreed. "Tomorrow."

"And don't forget Lord Smythe," Owen reminded Garrard while keeping his gaze locked on Adelia's. He didn't want to take his eyes off her, not ever.

"I shall go see about the earl's immediate release." The detective departed.

Adelia sagged against him. "Thank you," she murmured.

"You did it," he reminded her.

"Whitely, will you give the Westings our regrets. Lady Adelia and I will not be attending dinner."

"Of course," his friend replied. "And you're welcome," George added wryly.

"I think I had it well in hand by the time you showed up," Owen pointed out.

"True, but it's nice to have everything tidied up and a detective on hand. When I found Lady Adelia was not at home, I decided the police had best come with me. Saves doing a lot of explaining later."

"True. And I am grateful," Owen told him, sparing him a glance. "You've stood by me through all of this, and I'll never forget it."

"You can name your first son after me," George quipped before addressing Adelia. "I am very glad to see you relatively unharmed, my lady."

"Thank you," she said, but her gaze remained on Owen. She smiled at him, reached up, and cupped his cheek. "It's finally over."

For her, it was. If only his parents' hearts could be repaired so easily.

CHAPTER THIRTY-ONE

Adelia awakened in Owen's house, in a sunny guest room. Despite a slightly painful lip and bruised cheek, she'd slept better than she had in weeks. She smiled to herself as she recalled everything that had transpired.

Although she hadn't seen him yet, she knew Thomas had been freed and, undoubtedly, was awaiting her at home. Oddly, she had no ardent wish to rush back to Hyde Park Street, feeling entirely at peace right there in Owen's home.

She stretched her arms overhead.

"You're awake."

"Oh," she exclaimed, popping up from the pillow to see Owen—*her fiancé!*—sitting on a winged chair by the paned window. He was clad only in pants and a dressing gown, which was hanging open, revealing his bare chest. No socks or shirt were visible.

"Were you there all night?" she asked, unable to look elsewhere than at the expanse of male skin she'd never seen before.

He grinned. "I tried to stay away. I got you settled and went to my study for a glass of brandy. I even tried retiring to my room, but I kept worrying you would need something, maybe laudanum or water. Or that you might awaken frightened to be in a strange place."

She started to laugh, sitting up and leaning back against the down pillow. "Do I seem such a ninny to you?"

He stared at her, his gaze intense.

"No." Standing up, he approached her bedside. "Truthfully, I couldn't rest with you being so close, not unless I watched over you."

"Did you sleep at all?" she asked.

"In that chair? Are you mad, woman?"

She laughed again and watched him swallow, his jaw with its shadow of a beard tensed.

"Every time you laugh, your . . . *um* . . . that is . . ."

Adelia couldn't recall him ever stuttering before. Instead of embarrassing as her speech affliction always seemed, she thought his was endearing. Until he gestured with his chin, and she looked down.

The thin, fine lawn of her shift, which was all she currently wore, allowed the pinkish color of her nipples to show through.

"Oh!" she exclaimed again, grabbing for the sheet and yanking it up.

"*Hm,*" he murmured, sitting down on the edge of the counterpane. "I shouldn't have told you, but it was difficult to converse sensibly when I wanted only to tug down the neckline and see them uncovered entirely."

Them! She felt her cheeks warm at the notion he was referring to her breasts as if they were discussing something not of her body, like apples. But she couldn't help giggling. It rose up in her throat and burst out of her.

"I believe you've laughed more in the past five minutes than in all the time I've known you."

"I am relieved and excited and happy, all at once."

He nodded, and she could see he felt some of it, but still . . .

She groaned and slapped her hand to her forehead. "Owen, I am sorry. How inconsiderate of me!"

His dear sister remained very much gone forever. Moreover, he'd had to relive the awful discovery of Sophia's body by finding a rope around her neck.

Adelia shivered, thinking how easily it could have ended badly. She could have died. Thomas would not have gone free, and Owen might have ended up being charged with her murder.

"Please," he said, "don't come over all grim. I adore a happy Adelia."

"How did you find me?" she asked.

"Luck and more luck, I suppose. I had an inkling you would risk everything on some natter-brained plan to prove your brother innocent—"

"Which he was," she reminded him.

"Which he was and for which I will apologize to him profusely for the rest of our lives when he is my brother-in-law."

She beamed again.

"I cannot tell you the terror I felt while driving to Whitechapel. A part of me believed I would find the same as last time. Hearing your scream, knowing you were alive, was the best and worst sound in the world."

She lifted her palm to his cheek, and he turned into it, holding it there with his big, warm hand.

"If Beaumont was guilty of anything, as I suspected, I had to believe he would go back to the same place that worked so well for him previously. In the nasty underbelly of London's East End."

She nodded. "He said you would be blamed for my murder, as revenge against Thomas."

Owen shrugged. "Unlikely. Garrard said he had doubts about your brother's guilt because of the obviousness of the clues."

"I tried to tell you that."

"I know," he agreed, "but I needed to believe I had accomplished something."

"Now, you have."

"With your help, yes. May I kiss you?" he asked, abruptly changing the subject.

"Yes, please. At once."

He lowered his head to hers. As he claimed her willing lips, liquid fire ignited in her body. He tilted his head, slanting his mouth for a better fit.

"Ouch," she said into his mouth since her lip continued to sting, but she didn't let him pull away. Wrapping her arms around him, she held him tightly until he sank down onto the mattress beside her.

"I cannot believe I am here in your home."

"Frankly," he said, "neither can I."

His confession made her giggle again. "My face?" she asked after a moment.

"Bruised a little." He touched the tip of his finger to her cheek. "Are you positive you don't wish to see my doctor?"

"Very. The blood is all cleaned off?"

"Completely. You look beautiful as always, in spite of the bruising." After a brief hesitation, he asked, "You do remember saying you would marry me, don't you?"

"Of course. I wouldn't be lying in bed with you if I hadn't."

He grinned. "And you wouldn't let me do this either, I suppose." He tugged her shift off her shoulder until one of her breasts was fully exposed. "Or this." He cupped it and brushed his thumb over the nipple until it peaked. "Beautiful," he murmured.

Shocked, she couldn't speak for the wild sensations coursing through her. She hoped there was more to follow. In fact, she could assist by removing the garment if he would—

His mouth latched onto her nipple, and she sucked in a startled breath, pressing her head into the pillows and closing her eyes. As his tongue flicked over the pebbled nub, the rest of her body turned molten—intently so at the apex of her thighs.

His other hand took hold of her still-covered breast, gently squeezing it before brushing his thumb across the tip until it, too, pearled.

"Too hot," she murmured at last, realizing her hands were now in his hair, holding his mouth to her skin. She wanted to take off the covers as well as her shift. More than that, she wanted to see Owen fully unclothed.

"Can we undress?" she asked.

He made a choking sound, then lifted his head, his gaze fixing on hers.

"It will be very hard not to make you mine entirely if we do."

"Yes," she agreed. That *was* what she wanted.

"Yes?" he echoed. "Are you saying——?"

"Yes," she interrupted. "Four Seasons!" she reminded him. Each year, thinking she would never find a man who sparked her interest, nor her passion, a man whom she could imagine undressing in front of and who wanted her as much as she wanted him. Adelia didn't want to wait another second to indulge in the exciting act of making love.

Apparently, her words didn't explain her longing and frustration, for he cocked his head, raised an eyebrow, and waited.

She tried again. "I'm not eighteen." She started to kick the covers off. "My parents are gone." She reached down and found the hem, dragging it up her heated body. "My life nearly ended last night." She whipped it over her head and tossed it to the floor. "I've kept myself removed from everyone and everything for so long."

Next, she reached for his robe, pushing it down his shoulders until he took over and shrugged it off, sitting bare-chested in front of her.

"Plainly, clearly, without doubt, I want you, Owen Burnley. Right now. So, yes!"

He leaped from the bed and hurriedly removed his pants. When he climbed onto the mattress again, he did so right between her legs, kissing his way up her bare ankles, her calves, brushing his lips on first one of her knees, then the other, up her trembling thighs toward her. *Blazes!*

At last, his hands slid under her bare bottom, kneading her soft flesh and angling her hips toward him. When his masterful mouth lowered to her core, she gasped.

His tongue gently skimmed her most sensitive spot, making her writhe under him. Tension engulfed her at once, deliciously building. When his wicked mouth latched onto her bud, she arched her neck, feeling both wanton and cherished at the same time.

Unable to keep from grinding against him, in a twinkling, Adelia felt her world exploding behind her closed eyelids, muscles coiling and relaxing, her lungs filling and expanding. Finally, she drifted softly as if returning from some extraordinary journey.

"Dear God!" she muttered and opened her eyes. "Is it always so fast?"

Owen crawled up the bed and, leaning on his elbows, looked down at her, his expression smug. He waggled his eyebrows.

She desperately wanted to laugh again but wasn't sure it was appropriate. Nevertheless, she felt light as a feather and even a little sleepy again.

"Good?" he asked, though she believed he understood how very good she felt.

"Extraordinary, actually."

He grinned again, and she couldn't help brushing her fingertips over his mouth. His wonderfully warm mouth that had just been on her . . .

"Now what?" she asked.

"What do you mean? You can have a hot bath if you wish. Or eat breakfast. Or you can eat breakfast *in* the bath."

Was he being purposefully obtuse? "I mean, in lovemaking. What comes next? When do *you* become involved?"

He closed his eyes and laughed. When he opened them, he said, "I assure you, that was me." He skimmed his palm

SYDNEY JANE BAILY

down her bare stomach to the thatch of curls. "And I was very much involved."

"I know," she said, distracted again by his touch. "But you and your..." She gestured to his bare torso and pointed lower, feeling her cheeks heat. "It's your turn for such enjoyment, and you must insert... yourself... inside me."

"No," he said, now idly brushing first one of her breasts, then the other.

"No?" *What could he mean?*

"No. I will tease you, stroke you, lick, suck, and bite you," Owen stated.

"Bite me?" she repeated, imagining all sorts of sensitive places he might do so. She shivered imagining him doing so.

"But I will *not* penetrate you until our wedding night. Some things are done a certain way, and that's that. Tradition, respect, love—it all makes sense when I think of you as my virginal wife on our very first night of marriage. And in answer to your question, it is not always so fast. I doubt either of us will sleep on our wedding night."

Her eyes opened wide. It sounded marvelously exciting, but it gave her pause.

"I don't want you going elsewhere to satisfy yourself."

He sobered at once. "Absolutely not. Never again," he promised. "You have my heart and my body, so long as I live."

"It could be months until we marry," she reminded him.

"Months?" he repeated with less enthusiasm.

She giggled. "Show me how to give you the same sensations you gave me, and we will save the rest for the wedding night."

"Very well." He rolled onto his back and sighed. "Such a demanding woman. I haven't slept a wink, and now she wants me to teach her to pleasure me. *What next?* I ask."

She punched his shoulder for teasing her and turned on her side, so she had better access to his glorious nakedness. Hardly able to believe this beautiful, strong, healthy man was all hers, she drank in the sight of him—admiring his broad shoulders and muscled arms, his flat stomach, and his . . . *oh my!* It was growing as she looked at it.

"*Um.*"

"If you wrap your fingers around it," he said, his voice sounding thick, "I shall tell you what works best."

Adelia did as he said, and despite her unpracticed hands, he said very little after that. She easily got the gist of it, marveling at the feel of him so silky smooth yet firm under her touch.

When she glanced at him again, his eyes had closed, his expression intense as she intimately stroked and squeezed him. In a short time, he groaned and spent across the sheet, all the while with her watching him, fascinated.

"You can let go now," he said after a few moments, his voice sounding lazy and contented. She understood the blissful journey he'd taken. Moreover, he must be exhausted after watching her all night.

"Do you wish to sleep a little, right here beside me?" she asked.

In answer, he drew her down on the dry side of the bed, and in a very few minutes, she drifted off to sleep next to her already snoring fiancé.

OWEN AWAKENED TO THE disconcerting sound of shouting, something he never heard in his home unless he was the one doing it. Heart racing, thinking of murderers and ropes, he glanced over to see Adelia remained safely at his side but starting to stir.

"Stay here," he ordered, climbing out of bed.

"What is going on?" she asked, rubbing her eyes and sitting up, still bare and beautiful. "I wonder the time."

"Near to noon, I'd warrant," he declared, hunting for his trousers. He yanked them on, decided against the dressing gown as the shouting grew louder, and ran from the room.

As he descended the stairs, Owen realized he should have expected the sight—Adelia's brother, bathed and dressed in the fashion of an earl once more, shouting for his sister. Fortunately, Owen's butler was loyalty personified, guarding the stairs and the rest of the house from unwanted invasion.

"*Ah-ha.* There you are!" Lord Thomas Smythe yelled upon spying Owen halfway down the staircase. "Where is she?"

Proceeding down at a civilized pace, Owen explained, "Safe upstairs."

"What! And you, walking around without a shirt!" His soon-to-be brother-in-law became flushed with anger.

"At least I found my pants," Owen quipped but felt petty when he saw the young earl's face further redden with fury. He shouldn't tease the man after all he'd been through. Besides, Owen was likely to get pummeled if he wasn't cautious.

Smythe stalked back and forth across the tiled entry. "When told Adelia was at the Burnley home, I was certain the detective meant at your *parents'* house. For it is inconceivable that a gentleman would bring an innocent young lady to his own townhouse where he lives the life of a bachelor and a prurient, lecherous one at that. Absolutely inconceivable! And dastardly, despicable, and unforgivable," he fumed.

Then he raised his voice louder. "Why, in the name of all that's good in the world, after learning the truth of my innocence, would you take your revenge by ruining my sister?"

"Hello, Thomas."

Owen glanced up at the dulcet sound of her voice—her beloved, steadying, calm voice. Smythe growled in anger, and it was plain to see why. Adelia was clad in Owen's blue robe, which was too big for her, so she'd rolled up the sleeves. Yet, even with it belted as tightly as possible, the neckline gaped. Luckily, he could see she had put on her shift, too.

He wished she'd remained in bed as directed since the earl would now be assured of her utter downfall. And while Owen would make it right in the end, he didn't like to think of brother and sister having a falling out, nor Smythe thinking badly of her.

Belying her appearance, Adelia calmly said, "No one is ruined." Lifting the overly long robe, exposing her ankles and bare feet, she hurried down the stairs, right past Owen and into her brother's arms.

It was good to see how Smythe welcomed her and clasped her soundly.

"Don't be mad," she said. "Everything is fine now. Absolutely everything."

Owen paused as the familiar shard of pain sliced through him, knowing Adelia had inadvertently forgotten, in her happiness, that Sophia was not coming back. Nevertheless, he couldn't begrudge his betrothed her joy, not for an instant.

When she drew back, she announced, "Lord Burnley and I are to be married."

Smythe's expressive face showed surprise, perhaps something akin to happiness.

"Truly?" He looked at Owen, "Are you taking my spinster sister off my hands?"

Owen was ready to punch him for such an off-handedly rude statement, but Adelia laughed, so he supposed she hadn't minded.

"I am, indeed," Owen confirmed. "I cannot wait to give my hand, my name, and my future to this delightful *young* lady."

After hesitating, Smythe said, "That's beside the point!" The note of censure in his voice continued, "This was blatantly wrong." He gestured to her appearance. "She shouldn't be here, and I'm taking her home at once. I assume your staff will be discreet."

Owen nodded. Hopefully, the detective would also. "Your shouting might have awakened my neighbors. I cannot vouch none of them are peeking out their windows even now, seeing the Smythe carriage waiting outside."

The earl sighed. "I think you should go get dressed properly before we leave. Oh, Dilly, look at your poor face."

"A few bruises," she said, glancing at Owen. "I'm still beautiful, am I not?"

He couldn't help smiling at her, this confident woman—all his—becoming a saucebox, too! He would make sure she never tried to disappear into the wallpaper again. "More beautiful than ever, my love. I think that shade of purplish-blue suits you."

With a chuckle, she dashed up the stairs, his robe flying out behind her.

"If you would come into my drawing room," Owen offered, "we can discuss the marriage settlement now."

"Very well," Smythe agreed, following behind. "Since you've compromised her, how about no dowry for you, and you provide her with a generous monthly stipend, which she can spend as she likes? Usually, she just buys paper and pens, anyway."

Owen rolled his eyes. The young earl was going to do fine as a businessman. "I know it's early, but maybe we need a little brandy while we talk."

ADELIA COULD NOT LOSE the feeling she was floating. Her feet simply were not touching the floor. And it had been the same ever since awakening at Owen's home, soon to be her own. *How was it possible to be so happy?* And to think, she'd almost missed out on all of it.

Both Owen and Thomas had accompanied her to the detective's office after lunch to relay the terrifying events of the previous night. Adelia was able to explain what she'd learned about Lady Sophia having overheard something to do with Mr. Beaumont's plans to take over Smythe Coal. As for any untoward behavior on the part of Owen's sister, leaving her vulnerable to blackmail, Adelia left that unsaid. It would only cause undue hurt to the Burnleys, and the young woman had paid for her indiscretions with her life.

Thomas, who had slipped back into his regular life with ease, was now on the hunt for a new general manager.

"Promote from within," Owen had advised her brother, "if at all possible." And Thomas intended to try. To that end, he was heading to their main mine in Bolsover, near Chesterfield, to see if one of the local managers would do.

"I have other news," Thomas said to her after saying he would depart in a few days. "Miss Moore and I intend to follow you and Burnley down the aisle as soon as it is seemly to do so."

"I'm so happy for you." In truth, she considered him a little young. On the other hand, if he was firmly in love, why wait?

"Are you prepared? Is she?" Adelia asked.

Thomas nodded. They both knew the uphill battle the newlyweds would face once the *ton* caught wind of the future Countess of Dunford's lineage—or lack thereof. It could mean extreme ostracism.

She didn't voice the very real concern that some people might take it out on Thomas by canceling their coal deliveries. If there was one thing the British elite excelled at apart from snobbery, it was pettiness. And when an earl was considered to have wasted his title on someone outside his class, retribution could be swift and consistent. Her brother would have to deal with it as best he could. Come what may, any life was better than what had nearly happened to him. To both of them!

"Anything I can do to help, I shall," Adelia offered. "I suppose it would be beneficial if I had been more of a social success, like Lady Jane Westing." Then she brightened. "In fact, I am positive Owen's friends are generous of heart and spirit. If the Westings and the Burnleys welcome Miss Moore into their midst, all will go more smoothly."

"That would be appreciated," Thomas said. "While I am determined to go through with marrying her, it would be best for your wedding to take place prior to my publicly announcing our engagement."

She smiled at him. "Good. That gives Owen and me even more incentive to hurry along with a speedy wedding."

Thomas's eyebrows rose. "Don't go causing yourself problems. We don't want rumors of impropriety after you've lived such an exemplary life. Bad enough your future husband trails such a rakish reputation in his wake."

She shook her head. "He was never that bad."

"He was never that good, either."

"I am not worried." Adelia truly wasn't. Owen had been nothing but honest with her.

"Neither am I," Thomas said surprisingly. "As he ages, I will always be younger and fitter than him. Should he ever do anything to cause you pain, I shall beat him soundly."

"That isn't your way," she protested, wanting to put all thoughts of such violence behind her. Besides, thinking of Owen's muscular physique, she doubted her brother could bring the viscount down with his fists.

"Maybe I will just beat him at billiards, then."

They laughed. She hoped her brother and her husband would become good friends.

"Is Miss Moore—?"

"Constance," he reminded her.

"Is Constance anxious about stepping into high society?"

Her brother's face broke out into a beaming smile. "Yes, naturally, but she is capable and fearless, too."

Adelia was thinking how admirably strong Constance was in comparison to herself when her brother added, "She is like you, in fact."

"Oh, dear God, I hope not."

He took her hand. "Dilly, you saved me when no one else could, and you don't hesitate or stutter at all anymore. When you spoke to the detective, it was entirely without hesitation. You do realize that, don't you?"

She nodded. "I no longer need to hide behind my shyness. It served its purpose, I suppose. After coming so close to losing you, and Owen by consequence, it now seems silly to worry about people looking at me or talking to me. Life is so much better when not lived in fear."

"Plus, you captured the hand of one of the most sought-after bachelors in London, no matter that he is a rash, noodle-headed lout." Her brother shook his head. "I would still like to know how you did that, all from the safety of your position by the wallpaper."

"That's what it said in the society column the other day when Owen's and my names were linked. Something along the lines of *how did a wallflower capture the Sun God?*"

"Sun God?" Thomas rolled his eyes.

"He is rather dazzling." She sighed, instantly picturing her blond, blue-eyed fiancé.

"I'm not going to sit here while you gush over Burnley. I can't help feeling a bit of resentment each time I see him, to be honest."

Standing, Thomas shrugged at her expression of regret. "Don't worry, I'll get over it. I shall see you at dinner. And please, Dilly, if you can, put in a good word for Constance and me with the Westings, I think you're right about that going a long way to opening doors."

CHAPTER THIRTY-TWO

They were finally going to the Westings as an engaged couple. Adelia was excited by that, but more so by the seeds of an idea that had planted themselves in her brain. She was a little worried about telling Owen but decided to brave his displeasure. After all, even when upset, he was the calmest, most peaceful man she knew.

When he'd taken her to meet his parents—good people to whom something unthinkably awful had happened—the Earl and Countess of Bromshire had greeted her warmly and shown real enthusiasm for their son's betrothed and his upcoming marriage.

At dinner in their home, however, Adelia had faltered upon seeing an extra setting at the table, realizing they kept it laid for Sophia.

She hoped the execution of their daughter's killer had helped, but she feared despite having answers, they continued floundering in the emptiness of their home.

"I have an idea," Adelia said as soon as she was ensconced in Owen's carriage, absolutely throwing all propriety to the wind by not taking Penny. Engaged couples had strict rules, but since she was an orphan and he, a reformed rake, she decided they would break them and have no chaperone at all.

The wheels had barely started turning when Owen leaned forward and kissed her, a long, thorough kiss that curled her toes in her pretty satin dinner slippers.

When he finally let her breathe, he asked, "What is your wonderful idea?"

She took a deep breath. "I did not say wonderful. It may be utterly beyond the pale. You may discount it at once, and I would understand."

"Tell me."

"Lady Jane's orphans," she said. "There are so many who could use a good, clean home and the bright future which your parents could provide."

He sat back, looking stunned.

Into the silence, Adelia tilted her head. "Are you offended?"

"No, of course not," he insisted, taking hold of her hand. "Only annoyed I hadn't thought of it. Truthfully, even when I went with Jane into one of her orphanages, the idea never crossed my mind. Perhaps because Sophia's death had been too fresh. But now . . . ," he paused, looking pensive.

Encouraged by his reaction, she added, "I suggest it only because your parents are young, and the hole in their hearts may not be filled by the mining company or by friends. But if they could literally change the lives of some youngsters, hopefully come to love them, perhaps—"

"Perhaps they would heal and find purpose again," Owen agreed. "It is as if they had a goal in seeing their daughter reach her fruition, meaning a good marriage and children, even more than they did with me. And with that gone, they are at a loss as to what their lives are for. I'm simplifying, of course, but more children in the house, especially for my mother, would give her the chance to fuss over someone and guide him or her."

Adelia told him what Lady Jane had told her. "There are so many orphans between the ages of seven and fourteen

SYDNEY JANE BAILY

who do not get adopted. They have left their cute infancy and toddler years behind, and prospective parents overlook the older ones as if it is too late to make a difference. Sadly, they must wait until their childhood is over, at which time, they are sent into servitude or apprenticeship."

He ran a hand through his hair, messing up the work of his valet. "You are being so kind to my family after everything I did."

"I know you didn't act maliciously. And my brother will come to understand that and, hopefully, won't want to throttle you every time he sees you."

Owen couldn't help but chuckle. "I shall put it to my parents gently and see how they react."

"That's a good idea. Maybe Lady Jane can suggest a suitable child."

MANY HOURS LATER, WHEN they returned to his townhouse for a nightcap, Owen reached for her.

"You are an incredibly considerate woman. I am so glad you're mine. Have I told you that?"

"Am I yours?" she asked teasingly, ducking away from his touch.

With a roar, he grabbed for her, yanking her against him, making her squeal with excitement.

"I never thought I would want a strong man touching me. But your strength is all controlled and never brutal," she said.

"Are you saying that merely because you hope by placating me, I shall *not* scoop you up and toss you onto the bed?"

"Oh no, I am saying that in hopes you will, my love. There is nothing I prefer to your muscular, naked body towering over me and then practically crushing me, except you never do. You know precisely when to be gentle," she added with a sigh.

Owen took that moment to do as he'd said he would, scooping her into his arms, hurrying up the stairs and along the hall to his bedroom. Kicking the door shut, he tossed her onto the bed.

She looked to be savoring every second of the abduction. And he would make certain she adored every minute that followed, too. He thoroughly relished the intimacy they shared, despite refraining from intercourse. It was in turn, fulfilling and extraordinarily frustrating. It brought them closer while keeping a little something in reserve. They were splitting hairs by bowing to tradition and preserving the true meaning of her honor while thwarting propriety to suit themselves.

At the same time, he couldn't wait for their upcoming wedding day. And night! He wanted everyone to know how elated he was to make her his wife, how grateful he felt that she was his. And he was chomping at the bit to show her everything else making love entailed. He was also looking forward to becoming a father. In fact, Owen was ready and eager for a life with Adelia, something he'd previously decided he would never—could never—embrace again after the terrible wrongdoing that had befallen his family.

He was well aware of the nasty moniker of *Lord Wrath* bantered about behind his back and also within his hearing. Moreover, he wished he'd never been forced to take up the mantle of vengeance, for all the good he'd done.

He had a feeling Sophia would approve of his newfound happiness. And more importantly, how he'd released the intense anger that had gripped him and colored his world for so long. Despite having gone to hear Beaumont's sentence, Owen hadn't attended the vermin's hanging. Moreover, he'd decided he wouldn't give the murderer an ounce of power over him by ever sparing him another thought. Justice had finally been served.

AFTER A RESPECTABLE TIME as an engaged couple, perhaps a month or two shorter than some in the *ton* would find completely acceptable, Adelia stood beside Owen and said her vows. She wore white like the queen had done a decade earlier, with yards of satin and lace, an entirely frivolous gown with an equally frivolous overskirt, which she would probably never wear again.

Whereupon Adelia had the idea of putting the entire outfit away and, perhaps, drawing it out for her daughter, if she were so blessed, to wear on her wedding day.

"Gently," she said to Owen, who was removing the dress from her hours after the wedding feast. "Don't tear anything," she added as he fiddled with the last of her buttons and tugged the bodice off her shoulders.

He held her hand so she could step out of the mountain of cloth around her feet, before scooping up her gown and sending it sailing through the air onto the divan in the corner of his room—*their* room, as it would now always be.

She yelped with excitement at his abrupt actions. When he gazed at her with passion turning his blue eyes dark, he completely took her breath away.

"Do you see what you are doing to me, Lady Burnley?" He stood naked facing her, parts of him jutting out quite impressively. "It is a wonder I didn't shred the dress entirely. Now, off with your—" he groaned, "—hundreds of other layers."

She giggled and helped him remove her petticoats and underskirts and her corset, shift, and drawers with a great deal of untying, unfastening, pulling, and loud sighing on his part.

Once more, he held her hand while she stepped out of her finery, and, somewhat less gentlemanly, kicked it all to the side of the room.

"That is an obscene amount of fabric," he muttered.

Adelia couldn't speak, not while standing in front of him, clad in only her garters and stockings. She wanted to get into the bed and under the covers. When she reached down to unfasten the first garter, he stayed her hand.

"Let me, my lady wife." Dropping to his knees, he unhooked the first garter, fastened just above her knee. While placing soft kisses on her skin, he slid the silky fabric down her leg. When he did the same for her other stocking, she bit her lower lip with pure pleasure dancing through her.

"You're trembling," Owen said, and wickedly placed his mouth on her thigh, gently kissing her again.

Her gaze fixed on his mouth so close to her intimate parts. Knowing what would come next in the marriage bed for the first time as she lost her innocence, she couldn't stop the nervous shivering.

"Not with fear," she said. *Perhaps a little.*

He glanced up at her. "I will never hurt you."

"Nor I, you."

He nodded, kissing her other thigh while his hands skimmed up the backs of her legs until they cradled her bottom. Shockingly, he drew her woman's core to his mouth, almost making her tumble forward but for her grip upon his shoulders.

As he'd done during their very first intimate encounter, he teased her with his mouth and his skilled tongue until she shook so badly, she feared she would fall over. But he didn't let her reach her peak. He seemed to be teasing her as he never had before.

"Let me lie down," she whispered. "I cannot . . . I . . ."

"You will," he said. "We will together, I hope." Standing, he wrapped his arms around her and drew her back onto the bed. They fell together, and it took a few seconds to sort themselves out and scramble up higher onto the mattress.

"Sorry," he muttered when they both were finally at the head of the bed, him on his side, raised on one elbow, looking down at her. "I thought that would go more smoothly than it did."

Another anxious laugh escaped her.

"I think we should get on with the . . . the main occurrence of the marriage night" she said, "so I can lose my nervousness along with my virginity and enjoy the rest of it."

His eyes widened as she spoke until, at last, he grinned.

"All right, *let's get on with it*," he quipped, "despite your making it sound comparable to an odious chore, like slopping the pigs or mucking the stables."

"Owen, please!"

His face came over serious. "Yes, my lady." He skimmed his hand down the front of her to her thatch of curls and dipped his finger inside her folds. "Still damp and ready, despite my bumbling."

Finally, as she had imagined a hundred times since knowing him, finally, he settled his hips between her thighs. He bent his head to claim her lips with a tender yet passionate kiss, and she relaxed, her body seeming to melt onto the sheet.

"I love you," he said.

"I love you," she replied as he fit his manhood to her entrance.

Continuing to feather exquisite kisses down her neck and across her breasts, he began to enter her. As he did, she put her hands on either side of his face and made him look at her.

"I want to see your eyes," she said.

His brilliant blue eyes—the first thing that had captivated her about him—now looked directly into hers, filled with love and desire.

And at last, her new husband made her entirely, irrevocably his, inch by glorious inch. When Owen had sheathed himself deep within her willing body, he paused.

"Are you in any discomfort?"

She nearly laughed. If he only knew how desperately ready she'd been for this moment. Now, with him finally filling her, stretching her, she was eager to continue.

"Please," she said, "what comes next?"

"First, I will draw out a little," and he did. "And then," he added, his voice thick, "I will enter you again as slowly as I can."

Rising up on his elbows, slightly changing the angle, he moved his hips against hers, and sure enough, his manhood filled her once more, seeming to stroke her throbbing bud as it did.

Arching her neck, Adelia closed her eyes. *"Mm,"* she moaned. "Then what?"

"I do it again."

"Yes," she hissed as his body began a rhythm that put her into a frenzy. "Owen, please," she begged after a few minutes of this torment. "I can't . . . I need . . ."

His mouth latched onto one of her nipples and sucked. Adelia would have sworn the sensation went directly to the aching place between her legs. Tension coiled low in her hips, and she felt light-headed.

He continued to stroke her insides, switching his ministrations to her other breast.

"Yes," she said again and felt the impending climax start to wend its way through her feverish body. "Faster," she commanded.

He began to thrust in earnest, and her wave of release crested, rolling between her hips. Raking his back with her nails, Adelia cried out her passion, loudly and clearly, his name like a vow of love upon her lips.

"Owen!"

As she peaked, she felt his own climax overtake him. He groaned loudly, a guttural, savage sound that thrilled her. His body stiffened beneath her fingers, except for his hips pumping rapidly, until at last, entirely spent, he stilled.

It was even better than she'd imagined. While he withdrew and settled himself beside her, taking her in his embrace, she marveled at the notion they could do this whenever they wanted to from that day on. And make babies while doing it.

What a wonderful world they lived in!

"I love you," she said against his chest, a few hairs tickling her nose.

"I love you," he replied, "with all my heart."

Adelia rested her head over that fast-beating heart with a feeling of bliss and a sense of drowsiness enveloping her. Owen had promised they wouldn't sleep on their wedding night, but she intended to doze while she could. And when, a short time later, she felt her new husband's hand begin to stroke down her spine and caress her backside, she smiled, ready to love him again.

EPILOGUE

Her soon-to-be sister-in-law, Constance, could not have joined Adelia's family at a better time. After Owen, Constance, and Thomas read her stories, Adelia was confident they were good enough to be published.

Although Thomas's fiancée had now quit both her jobs, preparing for her role as Countess of Dunford, she would help Adelia through the publishing process and have the books printed at her old place of employment. Thus, Adelia's publisher was to be Samuel Beeton, who she learned with strange and wondrous coincidence had been the first British publisher of *Uncle Tom's Cabin* that very year.

"That's why your brother and I went to that particular play," Constance told her. "My employer was very excited by its success, as it spurred book sales tremendously. Perhaps one of your novels will be made a play."

The idea! To have her story published was beyond thrilling, and Adelia was happily penning her latest one when Owen came into the study.

She sat back with a sigh of pleasure and smiled up at her handsome man.

"What are you grinning about, wife?"

She shrugged. "Life is so good, and we have so much to look forward to."

"Such as?"

"Such as children," she reminded him. Notwithstanding, she had not been at all bothered each month when her courses came on schedule, for she was thoroughly enjoying every day as Viscountess Burnley.

"Speaking of children," Owen said, "my parents went with Lady Jane and have decided to adopt two sisters, five and seven years old."

She nodded at the off-handed way he'd told her, rather subdued. Privately, she believed it to be marvelous, but his expression kept her from a grand display of excitement. "How do you feel?"

He raised his brows but nodded at her understanding. "I thank you for your consideration, my love. I am truly pleased for my parents and for those girls whose lives will be transformed. I shall be a dutiful brother to them, more like an uncle, at this point." He paused, and when he spoke again, his tone sounded thick with emotion. "But I must confess, in my heart, without Sophia, I won't feel as if I truly have a sibling. That sounds unkind, I suppose."

She shook her head. "I do understand. You may no longer have your sister, but you do have Lord Whitely and Lord Westing, and Lady Jane and my brother, too. And soon, Miss Moore. We shall be as one big family."

He nodded. "And someday, we'll start our own."

Bending low, Owen kissed her prior to taking a seat at his own desk on the other side of the room. Sharing his study was one of her greatest delights, and he never seemed to mind listening when she read aloud a particularly sticky passage with which she was struggling.

Glancing down at her work, she rifled through the pages, going back to the beginning, and picked up her pen. Across the top of the first page, she wrote:

Dedicated to Lady Sophia Burnley, without whom this writer's life would not have changed for the better. She brought me the greatest love of my life, and she touched the hearts of many.

Adelia decided she wouldn't show it to Owen until the book was published. It was the simple truth—his sister's life had not been in vain nor wasted. Lord Wrath had been banished along with a silly wallflower who'd been avoiding her tomorrows as she had wasted her yesterdays, too fearful of what other people thought, people who didn't truly matter.

"Lord Burnley," she said.

Raising his head, he gave her a questioning look. "Yes, Lady Burnley?"

And she opened her mouth to tell him how much she loved him again, just because she could.

ABOUT THE AUTHOR

USA Today bestselling author Sydney Jane Baily writes historical romance set in Victorian England, late 19th-century America, the Middle Ages, the Georgian era, and the Regency period. She believes in happily-ever-after stories for an already-challenging world with engaging characters and attention to period detail.

Born and raised in California, she has traveled the world, spending a lot of exceedingly happy time in the U.K. where her extended family resides, eating fish and chips, drinking shandies, and snacking on Maltesers and Cadbury bars. Sydney currently lives in New England with her family—human, canine, and feline.

You can learn more about her books and contact her via her website at SydneyJaneBaily.com.

Made in the USA
Monee, IL
05 October 2021

79425660R00215